Cathy hated to be so rudely awakened from dreaming about being in the arms of the man she loved. She was in a man's arms right now but it wasn't her dream rescuer—it was Drew Sloan, the captain of the ship. "What are you doing!" she protested.

"I am saving a most silly woman from sunstroke!" Drew retorted. "Am I too late? Has the sun already ruined your brain?"

Cathy thought he was rude and repugnant. Still, she couldn't shut out the warmth of his embrace, the beat of his heart, the strength of his broad chest against her body. Good Lord! Why did this man have to stir such powerful feelings in her? A decent girl, even an old maid like herself, should not go mad over a few male muscles.

Drew barged into her cabin, almost angry enough to dump her there. Then he noticed her pink pouting lips, her satin smooth skin, her ripe round curves, and he knew his stay would be anything but brief.

He gently laid her on the bed, leaned in to kiss her, and before she knew what was happening, was skillfully divesting her of her clothes and covering her flesh with his own!

Sea-Spun Ecstasy

ALLISON KNIGHT

ZEBRA BOOKS
KENSINGTON PUBLISHING CORP.

Other books by Allison Knight

Willow Embrace
Satin Seduction
Captive Innocent

ZEBRA BOOKS

are published by

Kensington Publishing Corp.
475 Park Avenue South
New York, NY 10016

First printing: June, 1990

Printed in the United States of America

Chapter One

June, 1830

Catherine Pentworth stared up at her tall, grim-faced companion. Two scarlet blotches marred her creamy satin cheeks as she cried, "No!" The brilliant mosaic of swirling ballgowns dulled to an inconsequential gray. The tinkling glasses and the sweet melody of the soft violins faded into a dissonant buzz. "I made that wager in good faith, and now—now, you tell me you are not going to honor your word?" Cathy's rich, husky tones sang with disbelief. "If I wagered with my brothers, or even my father, and they lost, they most certainly would have honored their word."

Guy Forsythe glanced down and just for a second, he let his disgust show, "Catherine, why are you making such a fuss? Your father and your brothers have spoiled you beyond thought. If your father truly loved you, as you claim, he would have taught you better manners."

For a fraction of a second, Cathy's shoulders slumped in dejection and her chin trembled, then she straightened and tried to ignore the moisture forming in her eyes. "For your information, my father loves me." The tone of her voice made her statement a lie.

Guy made a disbelieving noise, "Harrumph! Well, in less than an hour, this man who loves you so much will announce to this august assembly that you are to be my wife. Before that happens, I want some things clear in your mind. First, I have no intention of paying you a farthing for this afternoon's wager on that American's horse. Besides, I believe a lady should never gamble, especially not with a man. In fact, I do not want you to gamble at all. When we are married, I will see that you have no money or time for wagering on anything." His voice was harsh.

Catherine's round blue-gray eyes clouded with anger. "If you were a man, I'd call you out for this."

Guy's lips curled up into a sneer. "You are not a man, even if you've had the freedom of one. You've been allowed to do as you damn well please, but after tonight, my dear rebel, you will do as *I* say. From this moment on, you are going to act your age and your station."

Cathy stood scowling at the man who had begged so anxiously for her hand. She didn't bother to waste the time wondering why she had agreed to his suit. She glanced down at the glass of punch she held, then at the table. She gazed at the fluted crystal bowl of claret and fruit juices that would soon be filled to overflowing to accommodate the toasts to her happiness. An idea came to mind and she smiled innocently. "Please," she murmured and handed her glass to her intended to hold along with his. In one fluid motion, she spun around, grabbed the bowl and swiftly poured the contents on his head.

8

She tried hard not to giggle as the flood of claret colored his neat blond curls, his pristine white stock, and the shiny floor between them. She tried to still the laughter that bubbled up into her throat as one wayward drop of wine slid down his long, skinny nose. She brushed her open palms together and silently declared, "This relationship is dissolved." She turned to him and in her softest voice, she purred, "No man, not even you, Guy Forsythe, will tell me what to do."

The words were barely out of her mouth when three of the servants appeared out of nowhere and clustered around them. Cathy chanced a look at the stunned crowd of guests. Some of the men were smirking but most faces registered shock at her latest antics. From the corner of the room she saw her father coming toward Guy, his face a frozen caricature of rage. His bushy gray brows were drawn across his forehead in a straight line and his pointed chin was trembling. That motion was from anger, anger at her and she pushed against the servants until they yielded. When they were between her and Guy, she sighed with relief. Her father would have to deal with Guy before he dealt with her.

Closing her ears to the soothing words her father murmured, she watched as he led the furious young man from the room. She listened to the cadence of Guy's angry words, "No, I won't. I don't care what she inherits from her mother, I won't. No, I won't." Cathy struggled to keep her chuckles to herself.

Well, that takes care of another suitor, she thought, and she mentally listed the numerous men who sought to win her hand and her estates. For a second she tried to count the number of men who came before Guy. Was it twelve or thirteen? There was no time to count at the moment, and she turned to the people her father had invited to the betrothal ball. She smiled at the assemblage. "I'm sorry there will be no announcement tonight, but, please, don't let that dampen the party. We are also celebrating an excellent racing season," she said as she looked at some of her aunts and cousins. Their expressions were censorious and Cathy wondered if she was in for a time worse than usual.

She found Amelia Pentworth's earnest face in the crowd and Amelia's eyes were bright with alarm. "I've done it this time, for sure," Cathy mumbled as she started for Amelia. As her companion, her friend, but also her first cousin, Amelia would know how much harm this adventure would cost her.

Her maneuver through the crowd was thwarted by one of the servants. "Your father wants to see you, miss, in the library."

Cathy looked from Amelia to the servant. "Please tell my father I will not apologize to Guy. In fact, I won't talk to him at all. He said he won't marry me and I certainly won't marry him."

The color on the servant's face turned from white to a bright scarlet. "Miss, I can't tell him that."

Cathy smiled sweetly. "Then tell him I said that when Guy leaves, I'll talk to him." She dismissed the servant and walked toward Amelia.

At first glance, she saw a short, stocky man standing next to Amelia grinning in amusement. His crop of bright orange-red curls gave her pause and Cathy wondered if his American blood was saturated with the blood of the Irish. She'd met him, what, an hour ago? He was a friend of her half brother, Charles, a classmate, it seemed. Her father said something about Dr. James Rupert and

10

Charles attending school together for a time. In fact, that was why her father invited the two men in the first place, but he almost had a seizure when he realized that they were Americans.

Two men! Cathy glanced around, remembering that she had yet to meet the friend of this stocky red-headed doctor. She was looking forward to it. It was his horse that won the race, the one on which she gambled that very afternoon—the wager that Guy refused to honor. She frowned.

She was still frowning as she approached Amelia and their American guest. She said to the young doctor, "I'm sorry, sir, that you had to watch that unfortunate display."

From somewhere behind her, a warm, deep voice said, "And it was an unfortunate display. Was the young man taking liberties?"

Cathy gasped. No gentleman would ask such a question and she glanced about. She didn't have to strain to see who was responsible, because the man stepped up next to James and stood laughing at his words. She stared at the man before her. He was tall, inches above her father, and he was big. His shoulders were wide, twice as broad as Guy's and his long face had crinkled into an expansive grin. Even his perfect white teeth were huge, Cathy thought, as his lips curved to show each pearly tooth. His curly hair looked like bronze and flickered with bits of gold and copper in the light of the candelabra. A square face and a solid jaw gave the impression of strength. His amused hazel eyes were set wide under arched brown brows and there was no question, they were laughing at her.

She drew herself up to her respectable five feet, five

11

inches and glared up at him. "For your information, sir, you were the cause of that scene."

The man next to James Rupert didn't look the least bit contrite. "Oh, I can't believe that, and m'lady, my name is Andrew, Andrew Michael Sloan. My friends call me Drew."

"Mr. Sloan," she said, her husky voice full of scorn—she wasn't going to call him what his friends called him for he was no friend of hers—"You are at fault here, even if you are unaware of the problem. I usually don't explain myself, but since you can't know, unless I tell you, this once, I will choose to tell you." Catherine paused, then smiled her brightest smile. "My former fiancé refused to pay a wager on your horse. I won the bet, but he refused to pay. He seems to think that ladies shouldn't gamble." She gazed at Amelia, intending for Andrew Sloan to know that she was no longer interested in discussing the situation.

Drew laughed out loud at her dismissal, but he ignored it. This whole affair smacked of something ridiculous and he intended to have the whole story. "Ah, yes, my horse. Do you mean the horse that I raced today?" She looked back, her expression clearly telling him the conversation had ended. Drew ignored that as well. "Could it be that you misunderstood? I really believe that no man, no matter what his station, could object to a lady betting on a horse, not even his wife. Ah, but there must have been something else," he goaded her. "Perhaps a childish—"

Cathy interrupted him, "I am no child." She scowled at the gentleman, raised her nose in the air, and started to move away.

Drew was enchanted. No, she was certainly no child, from her full figure which was displayed beautifully by

12

her silver ballgown. His grin widened and he asked, "Would a lady who acts like a child care to take part in an adult dance?" He grabbed her over James's halfhearted protest, and moved her toward the dance floor.

Cathy had intended to wrench her arm from his and deliver the most scathing remark she could imagine, but at the touch of his arm around her waist, the air for words left her body. Drew placed her hand in his and Cathy felt the jolt from her fingertips down to the toes of her satin slippers. This man held some kind of magic. She gazed up at him, her ability to speak gone. She couldn't explain what had happened.

For a moment they paused and then Drew moved her in concert with the strings of the violin. Suddenly, her feet no longer touched the floor and she was moving on a cloud. Her breathing was shallow, and she wondered about the man who held her in his strong arms, and of what was he capable. She closed her eyes for a second, concerned that perhaps she had conjured up the man so that she could forget her immediate problems. With a snap, she opened her eyes and looked up. The man was still holding her. She gazed at him and his eyes danced with laughter, almost as if he could read her mind.

Before she could think of something that would stop his amusement, their forward motion came to an abrupt halt. William Pentworth laid a hand on Drew's arm and with a scolding voice, he declared, "Sir, unhand my daughter. Catherine, I will speak to you, now!"

Cathy looked at her father and at Andrew Sloan. I'm in trouble, she thought as she pulled free of Andrew's arms and gazed up at her father. She suddenly wished she could ignore the storm in her father's eyes. Her blood cooled and she knew that this time she had pushed

William Pentworth past endurance. She trembled, positive that once again she had disgraced her sire. Without a word, she curtsied to Andrew and allowed her father to take her arm and start for the arched doorway leading to the center hall.

They took several steps before Cathy turned to her father and whispered, "You are hurting me." She nodded toward the arm William held much too tightly.

William glanced down at her. "Oh, come now, daughter, you deserve much worse," he muttered as he prodded her from the room and back to the vacant library. They were through the door and Cathy thrown toward one of the chairs, before William slammed the door shut with a kick. He paced back and forth for long minutes, obviously trying to calm his temper.

Finally, he turned to his daughter. "Catherine Elizabeth, never in my life have I seen such a display. If you didn't want to marry the man, you could have come to me quietly and said as much. But to douse the man with punch, before the very group that have joined to honor your union . . . I can't begin to guess what was in your mind. I had to pay that popinjay twenty pounds to avoid a suit. I'm sure his barrister will be here in the morning trying to press more from me. And, when I come to get you, you're in the arms of a barbarian."

For a moment Cathy looked contrite. "Father, the American dragged me out onto the ballroom floor, and I'm sorry about Guy. I got so angry I lost control."

At the mention of Guy Forsythe, William bristled, and Cathy could tell that, for the moment, her father had forgotten about their unwanted guests. "My Lord, Cathy, what did Guy say? All I could get out of him was gibberish, something about a horse race. If he proposed

14

something immoral . . ." William paused and gazed down at his last child. She was beautiful, this daughter of his beloved second wife. She had his precious Marie Ann's oval face, and the small, straight nose. Her brows were shaped like her mother, round, high, and dark. Her eyes were different, a blue-gray, more like his own eyes and his sons' eyes. But her skin, with its touch of gold, and the dark brown curls that hung in profusion down her back and refused to stay in a neat coiffure were like her mother's.

Her eyes, and, of course, the dark mole that rested on her jaw an inch from her shell-like ear were his gifts to her. He almost forgot the farce of the moment, thinking about how she disliked that mole that was in exactly the same place on her face as his skin-toned wart was on his. He gazed at the womanly form she carried with such grace. That, too, was like her mother's. He sighed as he remembered. Marie Ann's figure would have stirred Venus to jealousy. He forced himself back to the moment, and remembered the frantic scene his butler described. He turned his attentions back to his daughter. At the moment, she looked embarrassed and contrite. He felt his anger melt and he said quietly, "Tell me what happened."

Cathy hesitated. She would have dearly loved to confide in her father, but ever since her mother's death, William seemed a world apart. Guy's words of an hour before rushed at her and she wondered how he had guessed that her father had no love left for her. Oh, her father saw to all of her needs, and insisted that she tell him about some of the things that were happening. But, deep in her heart she knew that he only tolerated her and her antics.

15

In an effort to explain, she told her father what Guy said and what she'd done, not sparing a single detail. As she spoke, she noticed a dark red stain creeping up William's neck. A little voice murmured in her head, Your father is angry and getting angrier.

"You threw wine on the man because he told you that as his wife he expected you to obey him? My God, girl! Didn't I teach you anything? A wife is subject to her husband. Every wife is expected to obey the man she weds. And, if memory serves me right, you picked Guy Forsythe, not I. He was never my idea. I never did like the man. Now, you are telling me that this whole stunt is because he said you would obey him?"

Cathy watched her father. She wasn't surprised at his remarks. She hadn't expected him to agree with her, but to conclude that Guy's ideas were the right ones left her cold. No, she couldn't believe that he would support— what had he called Guy?—a popinjay. Cathy shivered. She had never seen her parent as upset as he was at the moment.

He turned to her, his pointed chin quivering. "Well, my girl, you better go out and enjoy this ball, for it's your last for a time. By the end of the week, you will be on your way to Barbados. I've already written to Phillip and Charles and told them about your penchant for broken engagements. I wrote that if this latest attempt at marriage ended in disaster you would be joining them. They can find you a husband. And, I also told them, if it came to that, that I don't want to see you again until you are wed."

Cathy stared at her father, tears gathering in her eyes. Surely he couldn't be serious. She blinked her eyes and gazed into his face. There was no question in her mind.

16

When he got that tired, "I've had enough," look it was over for her. But what a tragic end. What kind of a man could Phillip or Charles produce on that island of theirs? She stilled a tremor and wondered if she were doomed to a loveless marriage. Panic surged over her and she staggered to the door. Barbados. Dear Lord, that was at the ends of the earth! Her father must truly hate her.

She started back to the ballroom in a daze. She had to find Amelia and tell her what had happened. At least Amelia wouldn't gloat with an "I told you so." She stepped through the arch of the ballroom but before she could spot Amelia, a masculine arm grabbed her and a huge hand turned her around. He pulled her up against his tall frame and Cathy felt her whole body tingle with his touch. She looked up, and for a second she was petrified that he was going to kiss her. Did she want that? Her breath caught in her throat and she struggled with her thoughts, her confusion showing. What did this man possess to turn her world upside down? Andrew Sloan grinned down at her. "You look flushed, my dear. Let us take some air." He steered her toward the French doors that led to the garden.

The air, laden with the heavy scent of a hundred blooms, beckoned to Cathy. Why wasn't she darting back to the lighted ballroom and her guests? I've lost all will, she decided, because of my father's news. She let Andrew Sloan guide her toward a stone bench in a corner of the garden. She sat down before she realized that on this bench they couldn't be seen from the house.

She glanced from her escort to the house and back. Something about Andrew's gaze gave her pause. He was going to try to kiss her here in the garden, she knew it. Did she want him to kiss her? No, she didn't think so. She shot up from the bench as if the stone gained the heat of an iron skillet. "I must go back," she muttered.

"No, m'lady. Please stay for just a moment. Let me drink in your beauty, here among the little blossoms that are God's touch of elegance." Drew gently drew her into his arms.

Cathy smiled at his words. He could wax poetic with the best. She turned her face up to deny him and at that moment his lips gently touched hers. That touch belied the scorching impact of pleasure that hit Cathy. She stood in his arms unable to voice her surprise, her ability to form her words gone in a second of bliss. She leaned into him, wanting something solid for support.

He lowered his head once again, and she felt his warm breath against her lips, teasing, melting, seeking that same delight of a second before. Again, she felt his lips, the texture strange and wonderful against her own. Heat invaded her body, changing her blood to a cascade of lava. She could not think, or breathe, or pull away. She would not deny herself this joy.

Drew was the one to pull away, and Cathy stared at the knowing look of conquest on the face of the man before her. She lowered her arms that had somehow found their way around his neck, her embarrassment swirling around in her head. Drew said, "Now, m'lady, I believe you still owe me a dance."

Something in Cathy snapped, and she stared at him, as if he were the devil incarnate. Obviously, her kisses meant nothing to him. She could not stand such mortification. "Sir, I wouldn't dance with you if you were the only man on the face of the earth." Cathy warmed to her subject. "You are nothing but a savage, just like the savages for which your country is known.

You don't even have the decency to respect a lady. Before you dragged me out here, my father took exception to my gambling on your horse, and my conversation with you. Now, I have been banished from my home. Get out of my sight, damn you." That wasn't quite William's reasoning, but Cathy was so angry she would have told the man before her any story to make him leave.

For an instant, Cathy's words cut Drew deeply. Patricia Gamble, Andrew's last love in Savannah, called him a savage and said that he had no respect for ladies. Of course, as far as Drew was concerned, Patricia was no lady, and he grinned at the thought. He turned his attention back to Cathy and her anger. "Ah, yes. So the punishment for the day is banishment. But I'm sure that all you will have to do is bat your pretty blue eyes and your pater will relent. After all, a spoiled little girl almost always gets her way."

Cathy pushed against him with both arms. He didn't even know the color of her eyes. For a second he resisted but then he let her pass. She hurried off to the ballroom.

Drew watched her go, with thoughts of his own. She was probably going off to pout and she'd insist that the girl James spent the evening with sit and hold her hand. Drew followed Cathy back to the house and stood watching as Cathy whispered to Amelia. Yes, Drew decided, the plain girl that James had set out to conquer was going to follow the spoiled child. Any minute now James would be ready to leave this party.

Drew ambled toward the butler, requesting his evening apparel. James was only minutes behind. "You ready?" Drew asked. James nodded, his face wrinkled in displeasure. "Well, you can always make arrangements to meet later," Drew offered as he signaled their

19

borrowed carriage.

He swung into the carriage, suddenly angry about the evening. He wasn't certain why he was angry, but he was. Catherine, who was nothing but a spoiled child, was a good part of his anger. Something about her irritated him, pushed at him, as nothing ever had before. Maybe irritated wasn't the proper word, but something about the girl got under his skin and he wasn't behaving as he usually did. Usually, he tried to see the humor in any situation, but with her, nothing seemed funny.

In fact, he had seen little humor in the last several days. Why, it was on the first day of this past week when things began going poorly. He let his thoughts drift back over the month to the beginning of his visit. He had arrived in England in May. That first week he sold his cargo of cotton, made arrangements with his agent for several other cargos that would be arriving later in the year, and then, as he promised James, they made the grand tour of breeding farms. He was looking for likely prospects for his stable. He found two mares at the first farm they visited, but he wanted a stallion before he went home.

For two weeks they invaded the private world of the breeding farms, visiting a dozen stables. At the beginning of this week, he and James went to Berkshire to look at a three-year-old out of King Herod. He liked what he saw and when the horse was brought out to be auctioned, he bid low hoping to get the horse at a steal. It was not to be. Someone from one of the islands bid against him and before the bidding was done, Drew had spent three times what he wanted.

He chuckled as he remembered his anger at himself over the amount he spent. However, he did get the horse and, in an attempt to recoup some of the animal's cost, Drew immediately made arrangements to race him in one of the minor races on Friday.

James, through another friend of Charles Pentworth, met one of the members of the prestigious Jockey Club and Drew and James were able to take their place close to the finish line of the race in which Drew's horse ran. The horse, with his name changed to Sultan, won by a head and Drew got at least half of his cost back on that race alone. That must have been the race on which Mistress Catherine Pentworth wagered. The lady was a very lucky lady, given the words of his jockey. It was amazing that the horse had even finished, let alone won.

Billy, the young lad who rode Sultan, told Drew about the big bay that ran against the wall next to Sultan for most of the race. Billy whispered, "Couldn't see it, gov'ner, from where you was, but the jock on that bay used the quirt on Sultan every chance he got. I had the devil's own time keeping him in line."

At first Drew wondered if Billy was trying to up his fee, but when Billy showed him the marks on Sultan's flank, Drew became a believer. Billy said softly, "You got an enemy here in England. Every Englishman knows how important a horse race is. And, with yer money so tied up, if ya lost this race, could ya have kept the horse?"

Drew looked at Billy and at the horse. It was a logical conclusion. He had carried on so at the auction about the price, that if anyone other than James heard, they would have thought that he had no money left at all. Logically then, if the horse lost today, he should have been reduced to nothing. Of course, the horse did not lose and even if he had . . . Drew laughed at the situation, and thought of James's Irish grandmother and one of her favorite

21

sayings, "Don't borrow trouble, it finds its own way to yer door."

He banished the problems of the last week and straightened his shoulders. For several minutes, he watched his friend. James was nearly despondent. Drew chuckled and wondered if Dr. Rupert had fallen for that girl, that . . . Amelia. "James, what say we try our hand at a bit of faro?"

James sat up and scratched his mop of carrot red curls. "Now?"

Drew laughed. "Of course, now!" He lifted his cane, banging on the ceiling of the carriage to attract the attention of the coachman. "Take us to someplace where we can gamble," Drew shouted, his deep, rich voice carrying in the night.

Her husky voice carried through the whole house as Catherine tried to explain to Amelia what her father had said the night before. Amelia shuddered and looked at her raging friend. "When did he say we must go?"

"I didn't say 'we,'" came the quiet words from the door. William leaned against the doorjamb. "I'm sorry, Amelia, but I want you to stay here with me. As your uncle and your guardian, I've failed you a bit. It's long past time to see about some kind of life for you. Also, I want no one with Catherine who will aid or abet her ridiculous ideas. This time, she will have to deal with her situation by herself."

Cathy's eyes filled instantly with tears. "But, Father, Amelia has been my companion for ten years. You can't separate us, not now. I need her."

"I'm sorry, Catherine. When you marry, Amelia will

22

not stay with you, and it's time the girl had a chance to look for a husband of her own." Amelia was shaking her head as rapidly as Cathy was sobbing. William turned to go. "Amelia can help you pack, but this time, daughter, you go alone. If you want to come back to England, then hurry up and find yourself a mate."

The week flew by and William Pentworth remained adamant. Catherine Elizabeth was on her way to Barbados where one of her two half brothers was going to find her a husband. Often during the week, Cathy thought about the tall American with the twinkling eyes and how he'd goaded her. His words haunted her, so she refused to bat her eyes and try to reason her father out of his decision. Of course, when Andrew Sloan baited her, he failed to mention tears and Cathy shed copious amounts. However, they didn't work any better than her pleadings did.

She had a chance to explain some of her anxiety to Amelia. "It's my brothers I'm concerned about. Both of them are my very best friends, other than you, of course. Why am I trying to tell you? After all, they're your cousins, too. Do you know, I remember Mother talking about Charles and how he watched me and played with me constantly. Both Phillip and Charles loved me, and they loved my mother. Phillip told me once before they left for Barbados that he and Charles were so happy when Father married Marie Ann that they had their own little party." Amelia nodded her head, as miserable as Catherine.

Cathy thought about her half brothers and the task her father'd given them. Could she twist either one of them around her fingers and get one of them to help her keep her independent life? She shook her head, certain that as

23

much as they loved her, they would not oppose their father's decree. He had stated clearly that she could not come home until she had a husband. Once again the tears started.

Through the daylight hours that followed, Cathy grimly helped with the packing. On Friday, six days after the fateful betrothal ball, William piled Cathy's belongings in the carriage and Cathy told Amelia and the servants good-bye. Then they left for Plymouth.

When she was unpacked and safely secured in her tiny cabin, her father kissed her on the forehead and left her in the care of the captain of the ship, an acquaintance of his. Cathy watched the coast drift past and finally Land's End was gone. England was only an image in her memory when she turned away from the railing of the ship. A deep depression settled on her as she realized that her father had done what he had threatened. Unless she found a husband, her father didn't want her to come home, ever.

Chapter Two

The endless blue-gray sea and the slap of the waves against the side of the ship kept time for Cathy. The tedium of the journey wearied her. She read a bit and rearranged her clothing in the tiny cubbyhole that was her cabin. When they had time, she talked to the officers of the *Cornucopia*, the square-masted ship taking her to Charles and Phillip. In the mornings she was free to stroll the deck, the captain said, between the hours of ten and eleven o'clock. Often, though, the officers were much too busy to talk to her, and she spent her time thinking about her life to date, the last four years especially.

She remembered each one of the men who begged for her hand. In her lonely cabin, when she was trying hard to fill the time, those suitors that she accepted as her due paraded through her reverie. She thought of the first of these men who came to woo her.

Two dozen men came courting after her coming out at seventeen. Two men had impressed her and both of them asked for her hand. She agreed to wed one of the men and he courted her for two months. She smiled, remembering. At the time, she was positive that she was in love with the man. Now there was no question, she had been in love with love.

One night her intended tried to seduce her in the garden and she resisted for all she was worth. She didn't want his kisses, they were wet and sloppy and turned her stomach. She tried to push him away but her struggles did little until she spotted her riding crop. It rested against the doorjamb and without a thought, she grabbed it and hit him hard, not once, but several times. She didn't want his kisses, she told him bluntly, ever.

She broke off the engagement, saying she was too young and her father agreed completely, much to her surprise. The next man who sought her hand fell out of favor when she found out that he became a bounder when he drank too much, and he seemed to drink too much all of the time. Once again William agreed with her. When had he started to disagree? she wondered. When had she become aware that her father didn't love her?

Things changed after the Scotsman. She distinctly remembered him. And her father had liked that man. She had too, until she began to plan her summer wardrobe. Her fiancé complained bitterly about the cost, and he wasn't even buying the garments, she reminded herself. After he complained for days, he told her there would be no new gowns when she was his wife. It was a waste of money. This time when she broke the engagement, her father didn't agree and he started making little noises about spinsterhood. That had been last summer.

Since then, there had been Jeremy Fellows, Paul Plisskin, Todd Banister, and now, Guy Forsythe. Of course, from his parting comments, it was clear Guy

Forsythe was only interested in her estates. She wiped at a tear. More than one of the men who came to call snarled that her estate wasn't worth the effort to court her. And she had no one she could blame. For some reason, her father let her choose every one of her suitors. After the Scotsman, she decided that her father didn't love her enough to care who she married.

Whenever she thought of marriage, she thought of her mother. If nothing else, William Pentworth loved Marie Ann. And Cathy was not going to settle for less than they had. Charles and Phillip told her how happy Marie Ann and William were when she was a baby and she saw with her own eyes how much love they shared for each other until Marie Ann had died in childbirth.

And William's first wife, Agnes, had been well loved, too. The older servants proclaimed that William Pentworth was a lucky man for he had had two women who had loved him and whom he had loved in return. After Marie Ann died, he told his three children that he had been more than fortunate with two loving women, and he would not look for another love. Cathy'd been tempted to add that he wouldn't want to look for the love of a daughter either.

Throughout her musings, a memory of a face and a kiss kept plaguing her. She tried hard not to think of the huge, imposing form of Drew Sloan, but his face and the warmth of his lips teased at her memory a little each day. She didn't want to remember the strange effect he had had on her or the way she had breathlessly leaned against him. She refused to allow herself to dwell on those passionate seconds. Well, he had done one good deed for her, whether he realized it or not. He had bought that stallion and raced him that day in June.

Thank goodness for that ridiculous horse race. It certainly showed Guy's true nature, and for the first time since he began to court her, she got a glimpse of the real man. Never could she have been happy married to him, she admitted as she strolled around the ship on her daily walks. No, the horse race was a blessing, even if the events that followed were most unpleasant.

As Cathy sailed across the Atlantic toward her brothers, her father tried to deal with the repercussions of her behavior. William smiled grimly as he thought of Catherine and her reputation. Young women of breeding did not pour punch over the head of a prominent member of society and get away with it. His only thought was to remove his lovely daughter from the taint of censure, and while once before he had sent her to stay with his aunt for two months, this time he had to send her out of the country.

He sat quietly in his study and considered his niece Amelia. Catherine's actions had caused enough of a scandal to affect Amelia as well. Now he would have to wait the better part of a year before he could concern himself with finding a proper spouse for his ward. He sipped slowly on the glass of Scotch whiskey he held and thought about the evening after he had returned from Plymouth. He intended to relax and he went to his club. One of his business associates was talking to a group of mutual friends and he sat, unnoticed, listening to the comments.

The man's loud voice grated on William's nerves. "My friends, she has had a total of twelve serious suitors. If I didn't know for a fact that Catherine Pentworth would inherit from her mother, I would be concerned that William was trying to sell the chit. No, I have it from the best authority that she is brainless and frigid as well. Guy himself told me that his slightest attempts at affection were met with brazen disgust. The girl is passionless, without one redeeming attribute."

William could listen to no more. "Sir, if you have the courage, apologize now, or I'll see you under the oak on the morrow."

The gentleman in question blanched and mumbled a word of apology and William bolted from the place, relieved that the man had been more afraid of him than he was of the gentleman in question. There was no question, Catherine was much better off in Barbados with her brothers. His whole intent in sending her so far from England, was to spare her this latest round of gossip. It was during times like this that he questioned the goodness of the Lord. Right now, Catherine needed her mother desperately, and had needed a woman's advice for the past several years. He had tried his best, but his only daughter was nothing but fodder for the gossip mongers and she had been since the fisticuffs with the man she agreed to marry when she was only seventeen.

William thought back to that day and cringed. Catherine and the man she was pledged to had been to some affair together, William could no longer remember what it was. When the man brought Catherine home, he tried to get a little too familiar with her. And, Catherine, instead of trying to quietly dissuade the man, had hauled off and punched the scoundrel on the chin. Her riding crop was close at hand and she took it upon herself to beat the man with the crop. Her two brothers taught her early on how to defend herself and she put every bit of that knowledge to work that evening. The man in question had cried off with his eye turning black and blood dripping from his nose.

One upheaval was bad enough, but his Catherine followed the first fight with a second deplorable confrontation. Poor Basil Wallington! The boy was a lush, there was no question. William hadn't known it at first, not until Catherine tried to teach the boy a lesson. They had attended some affair and the boy had imbibed too much. On the way home, according to Catherine, he'd lunged for her and she had dragged him from the carriage, pushing him into the Queen's fountain.

That scandal lasted for several months and he had to send his daughter to his own aunt until things quieted. And after Catherine came home, that same aunt responded with a terse note. She would never again allow him to dump Catherine into her arms. She was too old and set in her ways to have the vivacious child in attendance.

For the past three years, Catherine had abandoned one suitor after another and each in a flamboyant manner that left all of London on the edge of its seat. Now this! There wasn't a man in all of England that would take his daughter to wife, he was sure. And he was just as sure that she would find something wrong with anyone who tried. With any luck, nothing of this latest abomination would travel to the islands. Charles and Phillip had to find her a mate.

He frowned as he remembered her deathbed request and his promise to Marie Ann. The doctor had left them alone, telling William that there was nothing more he could do. The woman from Spain was slipping away rapidly. She'd tried to smile and gripped his hand.

"Promise me," she whispered, "that Catherine will be allowed to choose her own mate." He had agreed; he would have promised her anything at the moment. He had tried to honor that promise. Wiping at the beads of perspiration on his brow, he thought of all of the men in his daughter's life and he groaned. "Marie Ann," he muttered, "I don't have a choice now. The boys will do right by her."

Nelson Goodspeed was thinking of the eldest Pentworth son as he sat in a corner of a London pub listening to rumors. He rubbed his hands in glee. Finally, something good was going to come from this pathetic trip. The chit being discussed here today was traveling to his island and if that wasn't enough of a boon, he counted the wife of Phillip Pentworth as one of his friends. He scowled at the man who came to clear the table. If only he had known all of this a week ago, he could have made arrangements and sailed with the girl. By now he would have seduced the little bitch and she would have been his by default. Of course, until his business was complete, he was stuck in London for at least another fortnight.

Nelson thought back over his first two weeks in London and the humiliation that he had suffered. That damned American had almost sent him back to his own plantation in the Caribbean with no remaining capital. On top of his monetary loss, he had to admit that the man was not someone he could take on alone. Drew Sloan was much larger than he. If only Nelson had known the bastard was going to bid on that stallion, he would have never placed himself in a challenging position. The fool had cried so hard to his friend about how much the horse had cost that Nelson forgot one of his cardinal rules.

He should have checked Andrew Sloan out more thoroughly. Instead, Nelson had believed every word that he heard from the man when Sloan shouted at his friend the day of that auction. As a result, he, Nelson Goodspeed, made a complete fool of himself at the race. He thought about his stupid attempt to force the horse to break stride and lose the race. After that debacle, he did some checking and what he learned made him livid. Andrew Sloan had already met Catherine Pentworth. He was a wealthy young man and his doctor friend knew the Pentworth family. It was enough to send Nelson into a frenzy. He would cause the man in question a great deal of pain before he left London, that much he knew.

If nothing else, Nelson thought himself honest, at least with himself. And one thing he knew was that he didn't like to lose, not in an auction, or on a race course, or with women. He grinned in triumph; he might have lost the horse and the race that followed, but he would be in Barbados soon enough and the girl and her estates would be his. Andrew Sloan would be nothing but an unpleasant memory.

At that moment, Drew Sloan would have been happy to be just a memory to London. James had tried for two weeks to see the girl, Amelia, and with no luck. Her uncle, her official guardian, told the good doctor that Amelia was not interested in his attentions. It took another week to find a servant willing to pass notes. James wrote and Amelia finally responded. Grimly, Drew watched his glum friend pace the floor. James was waiting for an answer to his proposal to meet, accidentally, of course, near a teahouse.

Drew glanced at his friend. "Don't pace so, James. She'll agree." James's condescending look negated Drew's attempts at encouragement.

When word finally came, by way of one of the stable boys, Drew wanted to say he told him so, but one look at the haggard face of his friend and Drew knew he must keep his comments to himself. He couldn't for the life of him imagine how one female could nearly destroy the balance of a man like James Rupert. Why, James was a medical man, a man who dealt with disease and the very essence of life. Yet a chance meeting with a plain woman, already by any set of standards an old maid, and his level-headed friend was a mass of indecision. "Good Lord," Drew mumbled at nothing in particular as he followed James to the carriage for this "chance" meeting. "I wouldn't want him treating me if I were sick, not just now, at least."

Amelia and her maid were standing on the steps of a small shop near the tearoom, when James and Drew drove up. Once again, Drew was struck with her plainness and James's infatuation. She wasn't tall, probably not more than five feet and two inches. With the exception of her brilliant green eyes, with their perfect oval lids and dark curling lashes, there was nothing about the woman to make her stand out. She was not ugly, just plain. "Must be her personality," Drew said to himself as he followed behind his lovesick friend.

James and Amelia, with her maid in tow and Drew far behind, walked the distance to the tearoom where James, Amelia, and the maid sat to enjoy a pot of potent brew. Drew stayed in the background thinking of the young woman who had accompanied Amelia the last time he saw her. According to several of the men he and James had dined and gambled with, Catherine Pentworth had disappeared.

Drew was leaning against the wooden doorjamb when a thought struck home. He was certainly doing a great deal of thinking about the feisty brunette he met at the ball. He couldn't put her out of his mind either, for circumstances seemed to be conspiring against him. Only the week before, two dinner companions of James claimed to know the girl and insisted that she was without passion, an iceberg of the first order. Drew smiled, wondering if she were truly passionless, or if, as one of the men intimated, she had been seduced and hurt by one of her suitors. He remembered the kiss he gave her in the garden. She didn't seem to be without passion then.

He shook his head and tried to justify the many minutes he had thought about Catherine Pentworth. She was an enigma and his curiosity was aroused, he told himself. To add to the mystery, no one seemed to know where she had gone. And, that, Drew decided, was why he was thinking about the girl. As James rose to take his leave of Amelia, Drew told himself that he would probably never see Miss Pentworth again.

But, once more, later that week, Andrew Sloan was reminded of the young woman who had sparked his curiosity. He and James had attended a play and gone to dinner with two fellows, both acquaintances of Charles Pentworth. Catherine's name came up in the conversation twice and the second time, Drew decided to satisfy his curiosity. He turned to the first man to mention her name. "Basil, how is it that you know so much about this particular young woman?"

Basil Wallington actually blushed and glanced down at

34

the glass of spirits held in his hand. "She, well, it was several years ago, but, you see . . ."

Dick Trophiney laughed and leaned forward to confide in Drew. "Our friend here felt the bite of the lady's sarcasm. He was her second or third betrothed in several weeks."

"Oh, really?" Drew turned toward the blushing Englishman. "Then you are just the man to answer my questions."

Over the next hour, Drew learned a great deal about Catherine. It seemed that Basil was only her second intended but he had been followed by at least a dozen more men interested in either the challenge the lady presented or her estates. And she did have estates, Drew discovered. Basil confirmed that she was cold and without affection. "Why, every time I tried to snuggle up," Basil slurred under the influence of drink, "the faster she moved away. I think I kissed her once, no, twice in the month that I courted her. I know I held her hand no more than thrice."

"Tsk, tsk," Drew sympathized. "That cold, hmm?" Basil, feeling no pain, nodded his head in agreement. Drew proposed the theory which he had heard, that the lady had been hurt grievously by her first suitor.

Basil studied the idea for several long minutes then, after a long drag on his glass of whiskey, he commented, "All the time I was trying to get to know her better," he grinned, his eyes half-closed in an arrogant leer, "I had the feeling she wasn't what she seemed. It wouldn't have surprised me to find that she cried off marriage because she's not the marrying kind, if you know what I mean." He laughed at his ribald joke. "She's probably waiting for an old man who wouldn't know a virgin from a lightskirt."

Drew watched the other man at the table. It seemed to him that Dick Trophiney was on the verge of agreeing with Basil. Well, Drew thought, it wouldn't be the first time a young woman married under a cloud of suspicion, if she ever did marry. Drew, once and for all, tried to dismiss the fascinating woman from his mind. All of his objectives were met and by the end of the week, Drew wanted very much to quit the English shores and head for home, home to his fields, his own house, and to his stables, the true love of his life.

Early next morning, Drew was on his way to the stables and then Hyde Park to exercise Sultan, with James, angry and tired, in his wake. "I never," James said with disgust, "will understand why a perfectly sane man will rise before the dawn to make a horse exercise. The horse could exercise later in the day and this impossible time is no good for anyone's health."

Drew grinned at his complaining friend. "It's not my fault you can't sleep. You know as well as I do, that if we wait much later, there will be too many people to really give the horse his head. As it is now, the poor animal will be confined for too long a period in the hold of the ship."

James pretended a shocked expression. "You mean to tell me that you are not going to let the creature have your stateroom?"

Drew's brow creased in a frown and he ignored the doctor's comments. James hadn't been himself since he met Amelia and his disposition was getting worse as he realized that the girl was not ever going to be available to him. Even the time spent in the tearoom, only days before, had not improved his friend's emotions. "Lord,"

Drew mumbled, "the trip home is going to be a nightmare."

Drew and James were nearly around the track when a second group of riders came near them. Drew identified the man sitting rigidly on his horse as the man who had tried so hard to outbid him for Sultan. He was older than both he and James, but probably not by much. He was nearly his height, Drew decided, but the man was slight of build. His face was long and thin and from the lines already carved deep into the taut skin, Drew wondered if he smiled at all. His long thin nose was almost aristocratic, but the gray eyes were small and beady, rather like a ferret, Drew thought.

The man was not pleasant, even though he had that wealthy, devil-may-care attitude that Drew had seen in many of the younger men of London. At the moment, his gray eyes were fastened on Drew. Drew glanced away and looked at the other riders. They were gentlemen that he recognized from several weeks before, men who had attended the ball at which James met Amelia. Strange, he thought, and glanced back at Nelson, wondering why he hadn't seen him at the ball. Mentally, he shrugged the evening from his mind and moved aside to let them pass.

Nelson Goodspeed had no intention of passing. He'd spent several days planning this showdown, even to knowing exactly what he would say to the American. After all, farmers were notoriously poor swordsmen. He slowed his horse and stopped several feet from Sultan. "Well, if it isn't the American. Gentlemen, you remember Mr. Sloan and his friend, Dr. Rupert, don't you?" He turned back to Drew and straightened his shoulders. "Did I tell you that Mr. Sloan had the poor taste to race his horse only days after the auction?"

Drew opened his mouth to remind the man that it was something that was usually done, then forced his lips closed and glanced in James's direction. For some reason, this man was baiting him. Drew could read the surprise in James's eyes. Drew turned back to Nelson, smiled, and asked in a friendly voice, "I'm sorry but I don't remember your name, sir, nor the names of your . . . friends."

Nelson grimaced. The slight was intended but subtle enough that he could do nothing about it yet. "Oh, I am sorry. I thought you farmers had such good memories. I'm Nelson Goodspeed."

Drew frowned. Goodspeed was deliberately trying to provoke him into an argument, but why? All of this over a horse? It certainly seemed unlikely. Drew forced Sultan to take several steps back, closer to James and to the rail. He lowered his hand to his saddle and pinched the flesh of James's horse, hard. The horse whimpered and James, understanding instinctively what was needed, jabbed the poor creature with the heel of his boot.

The horse reacted immediately, nearly throwing James from his seat before he took off at a gallop. In the confusion, the horse nipped at Nelson's mount. With a strangled slur, Goodspeed slid from the back of his rearing animal. Drew mumbled a rapid "I'm sorry," and took off after his friend. When they were both far enough away from the three men so that he was sure they couldn't hear or see him, he threw his head back and howled. James was not a terribly good horseman, but, Drew slapped his leg in appreciation, he had carried this day.

That evening, over kidney pie, James and Drew

discussed the confrontation from every angle. Drew frowned. "I still can't believe that the man was prepared to fight over a race or a horse."

James grinned and between bites commented, "You would have provoked a fight over either. Why don't you think another man wouldn't?"

Drew pulled himself up straight and glared down his classic nose at his friend. "I would not consider a duel over a horse."

James's laughter carried through the room. "Oh, no?" Then he grew more serious. "You do feel that the man was after a fight?"

"No question about it," Drew answered. "I just can't figure out why."

Nelson sank into the copper tub of hot water and cursed the tall American for the hundredth time that day. He despised Andrew Sloan. It wasn't enough that the American had bought that horse, but that he had won a race which Nelson had tried to fix, Nelson losing, therefore, a great deal of money on the race. Now he was short of cash, he hadn't gotten a stallion for his own stable, and he had damn near broken his neck trying to teach the odious man a lesson.

He pulled himself from the cooling water. Well, things would look up once he got back to the islands. Little Miss Frigid would be waiting with her pounds, and they were his for the taking. He smiled as he dried himself and pulled on his underdrawers. Even with poor seas, by now, Catherine was surely in Barbados and tomorrow he would arrange passage for himself. Soon, he promised himself, soon. He sank into the feather mattress, ignoring the pain in his bruised extremities. With confidence, he dismissed the cause of his disasters in London. Andrew Sloan had done his worst and it wasn't enough, not nearly enough. He had survived. Nelson rolled over. He struggled to ease his pain and lull himself to sleep imagining a picture of Catherine's northern estate. With that edifice firmly imprinted in his mind, he counted the pounds of income from such an estate. He didn't get to a hundred.

Chapter Three

Cathy stood at the rail and watched the indistinct shape on the horizon grow larger and larger. Then green hills became distinguishable as well as ships in the bay. Cathy's mouth dropped open in surprise as she quickly counted thirty-seven large vessels and nearly the same number of sloops and yawls drifting in the placid blue-green water. As they drew closer, she saw countless launches and longboats scuttling from one vessel to another creating a scene of antlike activity.

She let her gaze drift over the land beyond the bay and her eyes widened. The rolling hills which surrounded the town formed a near perfect frame for the picturesque village. Nothing prepared her for this kind of beauty. She watched from her vantage point as two of the longboats shoved away from the sand of the beach and moved in their direction. For a second Cathy wondered if it were her brothers. No, she told herself. It was probably an official from the island, coming to check on the ship or greet the captain.

When the longboats bumped against the wooden

planks of their vessel and a soft, lilting female voice asked to come aboard, Cathy was stunned. Another voice, a bit more harsh, but with the same musical cadence begged to also be allowed to board. Cathy glanced at the captain, and was even more surprised when the man looked as if he had been expecting the dulcet tones.

In seconds, two huge, dark-skinned women, their heads tied up in bright turbans presented their cards to the captain and in lazy tones explained the advantages of their—their inns? Cathy gazed at the crowd of sailors, the women, and the captain, speechless. These women were trying to convince the sailors of this ship to come to their establishments. Cathy's imagination supplied the kind of entertainment the women provided. She strained to hear what the women were saying and even to her the prices they were quoting seemed outrageous. Of course, she had little exposure to the cost of an evening's sleep, and whatever else the women were selling.

The night before, the captain told her that she would stay on board until her brothers came for her, so Cathy relaxed against the rail and watched the women argue with the sailors and the officers. Obviously, all the men on the ship had been there before and they were not in the least bit interested in securing rooms from the women. When one of the sellers glanced in her direction, the captain none too gently escorted both ladies to the rail, thanked them for making the trip, and waited for the two to climb down the rope ladder dangling from the deck of the ship. Cathy almost laughed at the look of disgust that darkened the face of the larger of the two women. They must have been expecting to sell their space, Cathy decided as she leaned over the rail and watched the longboats race for the golden sands of the beach.

After the women had disappeared from sight the *Cornucopia*'s longboat was lowered and several men and a couple of officers climbed down the ladder. The captain strolled up to Cathy. "I'm sending word to your father's man. His office is near the square and the government buildings. He'll send word to Phillip. I'll expect to see both of your brothers in the morning."

Cathy grinned. "Then I'd better pack. Charles might wait for me to finish packing but Phillip has always been impatient." Despite the fact that Cathy wasn't terribly excited about being there, the thrill of seeing her brothers sent her running to her cabin, her spirits high. As she worked, she hummed a nursery tune that she learned years before. With any luck, her brothers would feel sorry for her, ignore their father's orders, and after a short visit, send Cathy back—without a husband. She stopped in her packing to consider the consequences of that move. With her spirits dampened a bit, she finished her packing.

The hours slipped by quickly and by dinnertime she was ready to leave the ship. Her excitement prevented her from eating much of a meal, and after she retired for the night, she tossed and turned in her bunk. She tried to remember the last occasion she spent time with the two men coming to take her to their homes.

Phillip left England first and married Martha after a year on the island. He came back several months after his marriage, but since Martha was expecting their first child, she remained in Barbados. That had been six years ago. And that boy had a brother now.

Charles brought Roselle home to meet Catherine several months after their wedding. Cathy smiled at the memory. Roselle was Spanish, a distant relative on their grandmother's side. When Charles paid the family a visit, he met Roselle and fell in love. Cathy was delighted with the romance. In fact, both families were pleased and after the wedding, when he brought Roselle to England and Cathy was introduced, she understood. The girl was dark, a delicate flower, soft and shy, perfect for the fun-loving Charles. Although Charles never allowed them much time alone, Cathy and Roselle got along beautifully.

She grinned as she thought of Charles and the woman he married. If she could find a love like that, she would be more than satisfied to enter into the married state. No sooner did the thought pass through her head than the face of arrogant Andrew Sloan appeared through her mental fog. For a second, she was stunned and then she pushed the face back, back into oblivion. Certainly Mr. Sloan was NOT someone of whom she could approve. When she thought about it, his face had risen from her memory only because he was exactly what she didn't want.

Cathy slept late the next morning, but it didn't matter, for her brothers hadn't arrived by noon. By the afternoon tide, Cathy's fears began to mount. What if something had happened to Charles or Phillip or both of them? If something had happened, would the captain be willing to take her home? Then there was her father's edict. By the time the bell rang for the evening meal, Cathy was beside herself. Why hadn't her brothers arrived for her?

She rose at dawn, and the hours dragged. She was desperate by the time she spotted a large open landau at the dock, followed by a wagon. Suddenly, the whole area seemed to pulse with activity and Cathy hung from the rail of the ship trying to identify someone in the distant

44

group. A sixth sense told her her brothers had arrived. Before the longboat had covered half the distance from the dock to the *Cornucopia*, Cathy was waving and shouting, happy tears running down her face. Charles and Phillip both were grinning from ear to ear and waving back at her.

Cathy threw herself at Charles the minute he cleared the railing. "Where have you been? I was worried sick."

Charles turned to Phillip, as the older man climbed over the railing. "Ask your big brother."

"I'm so glad to see you," she purred as she pulled her bodice back in place and grinned at the fair Phillip. When Phillip only grinned back, Cathy jabbed her hip with her fists. "So where were you?"

Charles and Phillip dissolved into laughter, and Charles slapped his brother on the back. "What'd I tell you?" he said. Cathy stood glaring at the two, as they glanced at each other and then at their sister, the laughter booming from them. When Charles and Phillip calmed enough to answer her question, Cathy's lips were two thin pink ribbons. Finally, Phillip took her arm and dragged her to the edge of the ship. "It is my fault and I'm sorry. We got Father's first letter nearly two months ago. Martha wanted to start decorating then but I told her that you'd never come and I doubted that Father would send you, anyway. I'm afraid I teased Martha unmercifully about wanting to decorate and using you as an excuse. Martha went north to help a friend and when Father's letter came I sent for her." He started to laugh. "She didn't believe me. She thought I was joking. I had to go get her myself."

Charles stepped up behind Phillip and Cathy. "Your sister-in-law is furious, not only with Phillip, but with

45

our father. Since she's never met you, and has only heard our tales . . ." Charles and Phillip started to laugh again.

Cathy blushed. "What did you tell her? Surely you told her I was a child. Why, the two of you left years ago. I haven't done anything much—" Cathy clamped her mouth shut, suddenly concerned that her father had explained in detail the reason for this trip. One quick glance at Charles told her that her fears were well founded. She sighed and then mumbled, "What will she think of me?"

Phillip grinned over Cathy's head at Charles. "Well, I think we should put my poor wife out of her misery. Come on, little sister. Let's go meet the family."

Cathy glared at her brother, embarrassed, and a little put out. She didn't think it was that funny. On the trip to the dock, Cathy said little and once Martha took over, Cathy didn't get a chance to say anything at all. The days passed swiftly and Cathy found herself falling into the family routine, but by the time she had been on the island for ten days, she was bored beyond anything she had ever known. Even her two young nephews, William and Paul, provided no entertainment. They were in the care of their nurse and Martha didn't want their routine changed for any reason.

She tried to describe her feelings to Phillip who only laughed at her concerns. "Oh, in another week or two you'll be busy with parties and dinners. We're very social, wait and see."

Cathy let her lip curl over her teeth in disgust. Surely her big brother didn't think teas and parties would content her. She approached Charles, who chuckled, "Father was right. You do need a husband. And a house full of children."

She talked to Martha and that, she deemed, was a greater waste of time. What she got for her efforts was a lecture on wasting time and energy, learning to be a gracious hostess, a caring wife and mother, and not ever, under any circumstances, allowing the men of the world to see her anger. Cathy threw her head back and glared at Martha in defiance. She had tried to like her sister-in-law, but the plump little woman considered herself an authority on everything, especially on being a lady.

"I've had enough," Cathy growled as she headed for the stable. If they had nothing for her to do, she would find something on her own. In a matter of minutes she had the bridle and bit on a large white gelding. Ignoring a saddle, she mounted and turned the horse to the east. She was down out of the hills and racing along the white sand littered with coral rock in less than fifteen minutes. For two hours, she rode, walked the horse, played in the surf, and enjoyed her time immensely.

Her sense of direction was uncanny and she had no trouble finding the path back up the hill. She urged the horse back along the trail she'd come, back to Phillip's sugar cane plantation. By the time she could see the out-buildings, she decided that she would ride several times a week, perhaps every day. But before she reached the barn, her intuition told her something was wrong. Her brother's ashen face confirmed her suspicions. "Phillip? What on earth is wrong? Did something happen to Martha? Oh I never should have gone for a ride."

She looked at her brother, his face losing its pallor and quickly turning beet red. "Riding! You went riding? You don't know anything about this place. And, for your information, the only thing wrong with Martha is that she's worried sick over you. Young lady, you are never to try a trick like that again." He lowered her to the ground and snapped at her, "You are not to even think of taking a horse and going off like that, not ever again, do you hear?" He shook her for good measure.

Cathy shook off his hands and stood erect, announcing in a scathing voice, "Phillip, no man, not even my brother, will tell me what to do. If I want to ride, I'll ride, and if I want to swim, I'll swim, or read, or do anything else I want to do." She was shouting, her husky tones shrill with anger.

Phillip glared back. "It's time you moved to Charles's house. Maybe he can do something with you. I won't have you upsetting Martha this way."

"Well, Martha upsets me," she snapped as she flipped her skirt out in front of her and stomped off toward the house. Before she got to the door, her anger had cooled. She went looking for Martha who was in the conservatory, wringing her hands, her face as gray as her husband's had been. Contrite now, Cathy said softly, her voice husky with emotion, "I'm sorry, Martha. I didn't mean to frighten you. I rode at home when I got bored and you've made me feel so welcome here, that I just did what I had done at home."

The short, plain woman, her long, thin nose flaring in her round face scowled at her sister by marriage. "Ladies do not go riding off by themselves. Not here, not in England. I'll not have it. Why, your reputation will be in tatters."

Cathy glared back at Martha. "Phillip wants me to spend some time with Charles. I'll be leaving tomorrow."

Martha squared her round shoulders and narrowed her blue eyes. "I don't think that is a good idea. Neither Roselle nor Charles will be able to handle you. What you need is a husband, and I'm going to make it my business to find the right man for you."

Cathy panicked for a second, then whispered, "I don't want a husband."

Martha smiled, but Cathy thought that it was much more like a sneer. "Well, you are going to get one, or I'll know the reason why."

As Cathy packed, she tried to quiet her sense of foreboding. At least for the next couple of weeks she would be with Charles and Roselle. Maybe she could talk Charles into sending her home. After dinner, she tried not to listen as Martha and Phillip engaged in what was very close to an argument. Cathy wanted to cry. She had been in Barbados less than two weeks and already her oldest brother and his wife were taking sides against each other and all because of her. She frowned, a little annoyed at her thoughts. But still the idea persisted. If Charles and Phillip felt that she was a threat to their own lives, surely they would send her home before any marriage contract could be struck.

On her way to Charles's home the next afternoon, she ventured to discuss her thoughts. Charles only laughed. "Sis," he grinned, "Martha tries the patience of a saint. Phillip breaks down every once in a while and argues. You're not the cause."

But she couldn't let it go. "Charles, I really don't want to get married. I've never met anyone—"

"Oh, but you're going at all of this in the wrong way," he interrupted. "First, you pick out the individual's good points and then appraise the bad. If the good points outweigh the bad then you give serious thought to the possibility."

Cathy decided that was ludicrous. "Is that what you

49

did with Roselle?"

"W—well, no, but I'm a man."

"Charles," she said, "and I am a woman. Women are even more romantic than men. Don't you see? I won't marry until I fall in love. Father loved twice. You have the woman you love, and she loves you. I won't settle for less."

Her brother frowned and looked down at her. "But will you give it a chance?" She only nodded.

The next four weeks were a flurry of parties and dinners and balls. Often to escape the endless preparations, Cathy would sneak off and go for a ride. Charles was closer to the beach than Phillip and she would throw off her outer garments and play in the sea. She returned to the house, her hair wet, explaining to Roselle that she loved the water, she wasn't in any danger and please, don't tell Charles. She wondered if Charles knew how often she took one of his horses and went swimming.

Her answer came one day when Charles called her into his study, his dark oval face wreathed in a frown. "Cathy, one of our neighbors saw you out riding yesterday. He said your hair was wet and stringing in your eyes. How long has this been going on?"

"I ride almost every day, and sometimes, if it's hot, I go swimming," she replied, her shoulders straightening in defense of her activities. "You know how much I rode at home, how much I like the water. When we were children you took me swimming a lot of times. Don't you remember?"

"This is not England, Sis. You can't go swimming like that. If you want to ride, you must have a companion. And don't even think of asking Roselle. She doesn't like to ride."

"I don't need a companion," Cathy whispered, her voice soft, almost pleading in its tone. "If I wanted to be around people, I would have stayed here at the house."

As Charles was saying something about Martha finding out about her antics, Cathy looked about her. The study was light, with soft wood covering half of the wall. The furniture was light and tall windows allowed the bright afternoon sun into every corner. Charles's and Phillip's two-story houses were similar. The first floor was raised above the ground by almost six feet. Under that main floor were the storage rooms and rooms for the house servants. The second floor bedrooms were spacious, with wide windows and special shutters to shade the rooms from the warm sun and inclement weather.

". . . and Martha will end up with the final say." Cathy stared at her brother, knowing that she'd missed a good part of his discourse. Cathy grinned at him. "Then send me home."

Charles's frown grew darker. "You didn't hear a word I said, did you?"

Cathy tried to look contrite. "No, I didn't. Charles, please. I have to have something to do. I don't like staying indoors and Roselle is precious but I don't want to interrupt her routine." She raised her chin in defiance. "And, no matter what you, or Phillip, or even Martha says, I intend to keep right on riding." She turned toward the door, her disgust with her adored brother reaching explosive proportions. She'd have the last say. "You might as well know now, before someone else makes it a point to disclose the information. At home, there were times on the farm when I couldn't sleep. Sometimes I'd saddle a horse and ride in the moonlight. I intend to do the same here, and I have no

51

intention of waking a servant to ride with me."

Charles stood and muttered, "Not at night!" but Cathy ignored his words. Charles watched her swish from the room, his mouth hanging open in disbelief. My Lord, he thought, as he raked his hand through his hair, what was she trying to prove?

Over the next two weeks, Charles, then Phillip, and finally Martha delivered edict after edict. Cathy grinned and proceeded to break each new rule that was laid down for her. "No, I will not follow that custom." "No, I won't subject myself to that hair style." "It's too hot for several petticoats." "I will ride, and if you don't like it, then lock me in my room." Nothing worked. She was uncontrollable.

Something had to be done. Phillip and Martha met with Charles late one Sunday morning after church. The week before, Charles announced that at long last Roselle was expecting his first heir. Since Roselle was not at her best in the morning, Cathy volunteered to stay with her instead of attending the service. Charles took the opportunity to arrange a meeting with Martha and Phillip. Cathy had been in Barbados for all of two and a half months and she was driving them all to distraction.

Martha sat quietly while Phillip and Charles talked about Catherine. Finally Martha couldn't keep her opinions to herself. "You have to find her a husband. That's the only solution. When that's accomplished, it won't matter what she does. By then she will be her husband's responsibility. I pray to God that it will be someone who plans to leave the islands. Do you know that Matthew Chesley saw her out riding last week. You know how the Chesleys talk. At least if she has a husband her name will be his and she will be out of our homes."

Charles scratched his head and Phillip frowned in concern. Both brothers responded together, "Where will we find this man?"

Martha smiled. Charles mentioned a friend arriving from the States and her own candidate would soon be back on the island. "Well," she said, in command, "Bart Waverly is arriving within the week and although he's English, he plans to make his home in the United States. Maybe Cathy would like him. That would take her away from the island."

Charles smiled and lifted his hands. "And Bart's a handsome devil. It might work."

Martha smiled at him tolerantly. She had entertained Bart the last time he had visited and Cathy would never be able to stomach a man like Bart. However, Charles's friend would make her candidate appear in an even better light. She turned to her husband. "Nelson Goodspeed will be back soon. He always planned to go back to England. And don't forget, he and Cathy share a love of horses and horse races."

"Tell you what," Charles said with some excitement, "why don't I have a grand ball? I'll introduce Cathy to Bart and if your Nelson Goodspeed is back, we'll introduce him to Cathy as well."

Martha and Phillip smiled. It seemed to be the answer for which they had been searching. Introduce Cathy and wait. Phillip frowned. "What if she doesn't want either of them?"

Martha answered before Charles had a chance. "You're her oldest brother, and you already have your father's blessing. You'll have to pick for her."

Two days later, Martha received a card from Nelson Goodspeed. He had returned from England. By Wednesday Bart Waverly was stepping from the longboat, Charles clasping his hand and shaking his arm with enthusiasm. The ball, Martha declared, would be on Thursday evening of the following week and she would move in with Roselle to help with the decorations and keep Cathy in hand.

Chapter Four

That very day, Martha moved in with Charles and Roselle. In less than an hour, Martha began issuing orders and making decisions about the affair that Charles was calling "Bart's ball." The rest of the day was torture. Every time she caught Martha watching her, Cathy shuddered. *"You are going to get a husband, or I'll know the reason why"* played over and over in Cathy's head.

Cathy was no longer concerned about her brothers and their plans. Now, she only worried about Martha's schemes. In fact, Cathy was frightened. Martha wanted her married and Cathy wondered if Phillip had given his wife permission to see it done. Martha watched every move Cathy made. By the end of the third day Cathy mumbled, "She's not going to let me have a thought of my own." Cathy wanted nothing more than to escape the confines of the house, but Martha read her mind, lecturing, "There's no time for a ride. You're going to behave like a lady if I must follow you around every second."

Martha trailed Cathy, giving orders, polishing manners, issuing ultimatums, until Cathy wanted to scream. Finally, the day of the ball arrived. In spite of Martha's opinion, Cathy dressed carefully, preparing to meet the many friends of Charles and Phillip who had been invited to the ball. She would never dream of embarrassing her brothers by looking less than a perfect lady. She stood before the long mirror adjusting the bow of her exquisite dress, a seven-day creation that Roselle's dressmaker had made at Roselle's request. Something stylish, Roselle had said. Oh, it was that.

The dress, fashioned from a soft rose crepe, had the newer long line that ended in a small point at her waist. The full, puffed sleeves were trimmed in a delicate pleated ivory lace that was repeated above the hem of the full skirt. Tiny crepe rosettes swirled above the skirt lace. The dressmaker supplied four additional rosettes of the same material. Roselle's maid worked them in to the crown of curls twisted from Cathy's shimmering dark hair. Roselle even insisted that Cathy use her new lace shawl to cover the bodice of the new gown. "It's just a bit too daring for this evening," Roselle whispered as she pushed Cathy from the bedchamber.

Cathy made her way through the hall, down the steps to the large foyer, then to Charles's side. He would perform the introductions for her and for Bartholomew Waverly. Cathy stood on Charles's left side and the man Charles called Bart stood on his right. Cathy had yet to meet the gentleman, but she gave in to her curiosity and glanced over to catch a peek at the man who came to visit. He was about thirty years of age, Cathy decided, and very handsome. But, oh lord, he was tall, even taller than Phillip and thin, almost to a fault. In spite of his height, his dark velvet coat and tan cotton breeches fit him well.

While the other guests milled around the room, Cathy studied the face of Charles's American friend. It was a classic face, long, with a Roman nose that flared above a full large mouth. Dark arched brows curved above his round, soft brown eyes. His features were a study in symmetry. Even his full dark brown head of hair was combed back to lie in the same manner on both sides of his head. Neat and precise, Cathy thought, a chuckle escaping, and very boring.

Cathy raised her eyes to the roomful of guests, and for a second another face floated up from her memories. She shook her head, trying to dislodge his memory. Why on earth had she thought of him then, at that precise moment?

Phillip broke her reverie when he approached the receiving line to introduce another one of their guests. Cathy found herself gazing up into small gray eyes. For some reason, those gray eyes made her feel uncomfortable. Not only that, but there was something about this man that was so familiar, she was sure she had seen him before. She frowned slightly, and Phillip looked displeased. She tried for her brightest smile and accepted the introduction. "How do you do, Mr. Goodspeed."

Cathy tried not to stare. The man was as tall as Phillip, an inch above six feet, but he was not as tall as Mr. Waverly. There were other differences, for while Bart had a classic face, this man had aristocratic features. His nose was narrow, his face long, his eyebrows thin curves above almond-shaped eyes. He was good-looking, every bit as attractive as Bart Waverly, but for some reason, he made her uneasy.

Perhaps, Cathy thought as she moved a fraction of an inch closer to Charles, it was the way he looked at her, or the way his eyes shifted. She didn't know what there was but, at that instant, she felt an intense dislike for Nelson Goodspeed. His words interrupted her thoughts, and she knew she should have listened after the introduction. ". . . attend a horse race on the morrow. I have several excellent jumpers. When may I call for you?"

Cathy stared at the man, disgusted with herself. "Oh, I'm so sorry, but I can't attend tomorrow. I must help my brother's wife. I certainly can't leave her after tonight. She has not been well, you know."

Nelson moved away and Cathy glanced at Phillip. Her brother looked as if he wanted to clobber her, force her to attend the races with Nelson. Cathy pinched herself, not able to believe that her brother truly thought she would be interested in *that* man for a husband.

Cathy found, in the two weeks that followed the ball, that both Phillip and Martha did expect her to be interested in Nelson Goodspeed. It was equally ridiculous, but Charles and Roselle were championing Bart Waverly. Cathy tried to tell both brothers that she was not interested in their choices, but Phillip and Charles didn't want to discuss it.

"This is stupid," she told her mirror at the end of one particularly bad evening. "I cannot survive like this." She'd been required to flee to her bedchamber to discourage the two men who were now central to her life. And it wasn't the first time, either. She sat on the bed and fidgeted. She wasn't sleepy, for she had napped away most of the afternoon to avoid those men. Even though the house slumbered around her, she had to find some way to get away, to ride and forget her troubles. But Martha had given orders. Cathy rode in the afternoons but only with an escort. The escort was either Bart

Waverly or Nelson Goodspeed.

The two men had nothing to do with the fact that Cathy was locked in the house. She couldn't get out the front door if she wanted to. Charles had the key.

She chuckled to herself when she remembered the evening she found out about that key. It seemed that every night before Charles went to bed, he dropped a small basket down the stairs to hang about five feet above the floor. The basket was hidden during the day which explained to Cathy why she never saw it until the one night she had tried to sneak down the stairs to go riding. She was halfway to the bottom of the stairs, when noises from the second floor sent her scurrying back to her room. She had noticed the basket hanging at the head of the stairs, though, and she was consumed with curiosity.

At breakfast, she'd asked about the basket. Charles gave her a questioning look and then he grinned at her. "I know I told you about the slave uprising. No one wants to be done away with in their beds, so all of the plantation owners hang similar baskets down the stairwell at night. Their overseer or one of their trusted slaves locks up the house and puts the key in that basket. Pansy locks up here and I pull the basket up and grab the key until morning. Just before sunrise, I either throw the key out to the cook, or if it's late, I go down to open the house myself. That way, I'm the only one who can let anyone in or out of the house after we've retired."

So I'm locked in, Cathy thought. At the time, his explanation had effectively stopped any attempt at a late night ride. Tonight, however, she didn't care. She had been leered at by Goodspeed, bored to tears by precise Waverly, goaded by Martha, and pushed by her brothers. Tonight she was going for a ride, locked house or not.

She eased up the sash of her window and gazed at the cluster of trees at the back of the house. Two of the trees stood close and one tree in particular had branches that were similar to the maple trees at home. But, better yet, the branches were quite large and scraped against her window in a breeze. If she could just reach out . . . There, she had it! She grabbed a ribbon from her hair, tied it to the end of the branch and then to a nail in the window frame. With any luck it would hold the branch close until she needed it.

Discarding her dress, she rummaged through the pile of clothes she had thrown around the room in a fit of anger several hours before. Near the bottom she found what she was looking for, an old set of breeches and a flannel shirt she had confiscated from the stable three weeks before. In no time at all she was dressed and back at the window. She pulled down on the small branch knowing it would not hold her weight. She scratched her head.

She yanked hard on the branch and a much larger limb came into view. Cathy snickered in delight and pulled harder on her small branch. The thick stem descended enough so that Cathy could grab hold. Her success made her dizzy. In a most unladylike manner she wrapped her legs around the branch and worked her way to the main trunk. Slowly she maneuvered down the trunk. As she touched the ground, she wanted to shout, "I'm free!" Staying in the shadows, she made her way to the stable. The bright moon lit her way and promised a ride of spectacular beauty.

Cathy led a horse from the barn and threw herself up. No need for a saddle, not with her borrowed breeches hugging the sides of the beast. Against the chill of the night, she rode toward the sea, her hair trailing after her like a banner. Ah, Martha could demand and make rules, but Cathy would find a way to break them, each and every one.

By the time she reached the ocean, her thoughts were a long way from Barbados and her brothers. She gazed across the beach and the coral at the shimmering water. Somehow, she knew that her brothers were soon going to ask which of the two men she wanted for a life partner. Neither, she would have to shout at them, for she couldn't bear the thought of being tied to either man. What was she going to do?

The cool night air and the silver white ball of light hanging in a sea of indigo, offered no solutions to her problem and did nothing to soothe her tortured mind. In disgust she rode back to the house. With the stealth of a thief, she sneaked back up the tree and into her room. She grinned in satisfaction; her absence had gone undetected. She'd have another late night ride and soon.

In spite of the exercise from the ride, it was hours before she fell asleep. When she awoke, the sun was bright. The household was quiet and she wondered about the time. After she dressed she opened the door to her room and glanced at the large clock in the hall. Ten o'clock! She'd slept past the morning meal.

Cathy tiptoed through the hall. She didn't want to risk running into Martha this late in the morning. At this time of day there was an excellent chance of meeting her sister-in-law. Martha had gone home the day after the ball, but the Charles Pentworth household was not free from the observations of the oldest woman in the clan. Martha had become a daily visitor.

Cathy was nearly to the doorway at the back of the

house when Martha's angry voice stopped her. Martha shrilly said, "Cathy doesn't know her own mind. I tell you, one of you boys will have to pick out her mate. Let's be done with it."

Cathy strained to hear the answer, but Charles was speaking much too softly. Martha's next stinging syllables made Cathy's blood freeze. "Oh, yes, Nelson is older and I feel because of his age he is the better choice. He wants to return to England, so she'll not be here to be an embarrassment to any of us."

There was more conversation from Phillip, but again she couldn't make out his words. Martha's voice carried straight to Cathy's heart. "They share a love of horses, too. I don't think it will be a bad union. She'll learn to have some feelings for the man. And a December wedding would be perfect. In the spring . . ." Her words faded away and Cathy turned and as quietly as the falling salty tears on her cheek, she climbed the stairs back to her room.

For several minutes, she sat on the edge of her bed, her heart in her throat. She didn't want to marry and she especially didn't want to marry Nelson Goodspeed. She had to think of something, anything, to get her away from the house, the island, and that man. At least a dozen scatterbrained ideas floated around her head. For an instant, she wondered if she could feign illness or a mental disorder to worm her way out of such a distasteful union. No, both Charles and Phillip knew her too well. She'd have to leave. Of course, she couldn't go back to England, not right away. Instead, she'd have to travel to some other country. She could go to France. Perhaps north was a better choice. From everything Bart Waverly said, America was the kind of place where she could survive. And if nothing else, her father would not want her in America.

She jumped up from the bed and went to the jewelry box on the dresser. She hated to part with any of her mother's gems, but she had those and several gold pieces her father had given her so that she wouldn't be a burden to Phillip and Charles. Both would help her get settled once she got to America. And there was always the chance that her running away would grant a reprieve from her father. All she had to do was get to America, find a decent inn, and write to her father. She was sure that he loved her enough to rescind his orders for a loveless marriage. Time was what she needed.

She turned her thoughts to getting away from the island. It would have to be immediately. Martha was more than shrewd and the woman was getting brilliant at reading Cathy's thoughts. Given any time at all, Martha would guess what she was up to. Martha would force a promise from Cathy. And Cathy's honor would prevent her from making such a pledge and then running away. No, she had to get away in the next couple of days.

The first thing she needed was a ship to carry her away from Barbados. Bridgetown bay held a dozen vessels. She needed to talk one of the slaves into taking her to the city. And, even more importantly, she had to think of a reason to travel into town.

Grimly, she fingered one of her mother's diamond brooches and thought about securing passage. A deep frown furrowed her brow as she thought about talking to the captain of a vessel. What captain would sell her space without telling either Phillip or Charles? For a second, she considered using a fictitious name, but she knew that wouldn't work, not at all. She'd already met several ships' captains and her presence on the island was no secret. Someone might recognize her and start asking questions. To protect herself, she'd have to sneak aboard a ship like a common criminal.

She wasn't very good at sneaking, she decided, and grabbed her shawl. She made her way down the steps, trying to think of a reason to travel into town. She needn't have concerned herself, for Charles was waiting for her. "I was about to send Pansy up to wake you. Roselle wants to go into Bridgetown. I thought the trip might do you some good, too. Will you accompany her? Of course, Bart's going along but Roselle will play chaperone."

Cathy nodded her agreement and desperately tried to look less enthusiastic than she felt. She wanted so badly to chuckle at the relieved expression on Charles's face. Now she'd have a chance to find out about transportation.

The trip into Bridgetown was exactly what Cathy had foreseen, boring Bart sitting silently beside the driver and Roselle pointing out the sights. Once they got to town, Roselle ordered the carriage stopped and she pulled Cathy aside. "I wasn't honest with Charles. I insisted that I come to town, because I have an appointment to see a doctor while I'm here. I want to make sure everything is as it should be with this little one. I don't want Charles to know how concerned I am."

Cathy looked surprised. "Is everything all right? Are you ill?"

Roselle shook her head quickly. "It's just that it took so long for me to start a child. I want to make sure everything is all right. This doctor is well known. . . ." Her voice faded in embarrassment.

Cathy grinned; this was far better than she could have planned. Roselle was taken care of, now for Bart. Cathy smiled at Roselle. "I have a favor to ask of you. I want to see if an English packet is sailing soon. I want to send a letter to my father, without my brothers knowing. That means we'll have to find something for Bart to do while you see the doctor and I check on a ship."

Roselle's lips twisted into a conspiratorial smile. "All right! You keep my secret and I'll keep yours. But where are you going to send your escort?"

Cathy laughed and glanced at the man still sitting in the carriage next to the driver. "I'll say I'm going with you to the dressmaker for fittings. From there can you get to the doctor? The beach is only a hundred yards or so from the dressmaker."

After Cathy and Roselle decided on a meeting time, the women got back in the carriage and directed the driver north to a dressmaking shop. Bart helped Roselle and Cathy from the carriage for a second time and Cathy thanked him, commenting, "Mr. Waverly, this will probably take two hours. Could you come for us at, let's say, four?"

Bart reluctantly climbed back into the carriage and sent the driver on his way. As soon as he disappeared around the corner, Roselle started north and Cathy took off for the beach. She spent the better part of an hour talking to the fishermen and one sailor before she had the information she wanted. Riding at anchor, side by side, were a four-masted English ship and an American schooner. Both ships, the sailor told her, were leaving with the tide, the very next morning. She asked as many questions as she dared about both vessels. Now, if she could find out about the captains without more questions, she'd have all she needed to know.

She almost laughed out loud when the sailor started

talking about the men in charge. He claimed that he knew them both through their crews. "Ain't a better capt'n than the bloke from England. 'Course the American gent ain't a bad sort. For a colonial, he ain't bad atall. Kinda young, but fair, they say. In fact, if truth be known, both ladies run under the best."

The fishermen got into the conversation. "Got good crews, too—trustful, honest—if you can believe dat. Don't destroy our island, don't ruin our fishin'." Cathy asked about their leave-taking, and one of the fishermen supplied the necessary time. "Oh, they be gone before first light. Tide goes out about five in the morning." Cathy left the beach, glancing back twice to make sure she marked the ship's location, something to identify it from all the rest. In the dead of night there would be no identifying flags to see. She squared her shoulders, and gathered her sagging courage. Tonight was the night and the American schooner was the ship.

She hurried back to meet Roselle. Minutes later, Bart helped them into the carriage. Cathy said little and when Bart commented how quiet she was, she set the stage for the night, complaining of a bothersome headache. She added the thought, "Perhaps for once in my life, I may have taken too much sun."

That was the excuse that Roselle used when she told Charles why Catherine was to be excused from dinner. "I'm sorry, Charles," Roselle said softly to her husband. "I let her go without her bonnet and the sun was so bright today."

Charles shook his head and led his wife into the dining room. "I'm beginning to think that Phillip and Martha are right. The chit needs, no, she demands a husband. She'll be the death of us all if we don't get her married off."

Upstairs, in her room, Cathy began geting ready. Carefully, she tucked her mother's gems into handkerchiefs and tied them inside a petticoat. She packed two dresses, a nightgown, and several changes of undergarments in a small valise knowing that she could take only what she could carry and hide easily. Whatever else she needed, she would have to purchase when she arrived in America. She hid the bag in her closet.

She waited quietly for the maid that Roselle had given her. Little Storm was a sweet girl and much smarter than Cathy had expected. Days before, Storm told her she would have to choose between the two men. It grated on Cathy's nerves to have to tell Storm that she was right.

Cathy wondered just how smart Storm really was. Cathy could get away from the house and she could even get to the beach, but getting out to the American schooner was going to be a problem. She would have to trust Storm to help with her plans. Why, hadn't the little black girl hinted that she would be delighted to thwart Martha's plans?

When Storm came to help with preparations for bed, Cathy explained what she'd overheard. "I'm afraid you've been right from the start," Cathy whispered. "I'm leaving this night."

Storm looked at her mistress, her warm brown eyes wide with concern. "Ya thought about it good, have ya? It's what ya want? Ya knows how to go and where to go?" After Cathy nodded enthusiastically, Storm added, "Yer brothers ain't gonna like it none."

Cathy shrugged. "I have no choice. I'm not marrying Nelson Goodspeed or Bart Waverly. I can't abide Nelson and Bart is so boring that I'd be a lunatic in weeks if I married him." Storm clicked her tongue in sympathy. "You have to help me," Cathy said, and her husky voice quivered with emotion. "I found a schooner. It's leaving tonight, but I need help getting out to it."

Storm smiled. "I knows just the man. But, I tell ya this, missy. Ya goes, and so does I."

Cathy sat, stunned, "No, you—you can't. Why, Charles would have my head if I took one of his people. I can hide myself, but not—"

Storm interrupted, "No ways will I go with ya. My man, the man that will see ya to the ship, he's coming for me tonight. Martha bought me away from his island. Now, I go back. He's earned his freedom and he'll keep me safe. So, I ain't stayin' here. All I's askin' is when they find ya, iffin' they do, ya'll tell Charles ya ain't seen me. If I help ya, ya can do this thing fer me, sure as not?"

Cathy nodded in agreement. What else could she do? After all, Storm had a way of getting her from the beach to the ship and she needed that above all else.

Storm stood with her hands on her hips, her face wrinkling into an unpleasant frown. "Hows ya gonna get outta this room? I ain't got no key."

"I'll leave through the window, I've done it before." Cathy smiled. Storm grinned back at her, then left detailed instructions. They would meet at the stable in several hours, and Storm would have horses ready. The black girl slipped from the room and Cathy curled up under the bedcovers. Tonight she would slip from the house and leave her two unworthy suitors wondering why.

After the family dinner hour, Charles stuck his head in the door to ask how she felt. She groaned for effect and was pleased when Charles closed the door carefully. She smiled at his words to his waiting wife. "The girl is truly indisposed. I feel bad. I was certain she was only trying for our sympathy."

On the ride back from Bridgetown that afternoon, Roselle mentioned that they had nothing planned for the evening. The house was locked up early. Long before Cathy attempted her escape the occupants of the house found their beds.

Getting away from the house that night was no more difficult than the night before. She had clear access to the kitchen and stopped to pack what she hoped was enough food for at least a week. Waiting in the shadows of the stable, Storm stood holding the reins of a small burro. She laughed at Cathy's concern. "I done this afore. That ole man, John, borrows me his burro. He knows I plan to meet my man. And the burro ain't stupid. He'll find his way back to John."

With a swift mare in tow, Cathy and Storm scurried across the plantation grounds, trying to stay in the deep shadows. Far from the house, Cathy mounted the horse and Storm crawled up on the burro. The moon had started to wane, but there was more than enough light to guide them over the trail to the city. The creatures of the night called out to Cathy. She smiled in pleasure. Another adventure was beginning, and this time, it was one of her own design.

Chapter Five

Dawn was still several hours away when Cathy and Storm climbed down from their mounts and stood on the beach. Storm's man stepped from the shadows of a ring of trees. In the shimmering moonlight, Cathy saw a longboat bobbing up and down in the gentle surf. She stared out at the ships, trying to ignore the first several moments of greeting between the black girl and her lover. When the lyrical sounds of soft words told Cathy they were now talking, she turned around to listen.

Storm told the man a vague tale about Cathy's brothers not letting her go home and she hinted at a lover. Cathy watched as the tall man at Storm's side listened and seemed to mull over what she said. After several minutes, the big man turned toward the boat, and Cathy held her breath. Was he going to leave, or was he going to row her out to the ship?

While they waited, Storm turned to Cathy, her large eyes snapping in the fading moonlight. "He'll take ya out. Now, I helped ya. I know ya can take away my chance fer a life of my own, but know this. If ya turn us in, I'll cut out yer heart." Cathy looked at her former maid, stunned that Storm would question her intent.

"Storm, I won't tell. You're helping me and I'm helping you. It's a fair exchange." Cathy glanced out at the longboat. Storm's man urged them forward. In minutes they cleared the small-crested waves that pulled the boat toward the shore. As the man rowed the boat forward, Cathy stared ahead. She could only pray that she was doing the right thing. Suddenly her own desires seemed petty when she thought of all the trouble her disappearance would cause. This was the first time she could remember that she worried about what her adventures would cost others.

When the boat bumped gently against the American schooner, Cathy grabbed her valise and her cloth bag of food, and climbed the knotted rope Storm's man secured. When she stood on the deck, she leaned over and waved the longboat away. With as much stealth as she could manage, she crept toward the stern. Gazing around the American ship, Cathy suddenly realized that activity didn't exist. Nothing moved. Her heart took a dive. Had the fishermen given her wrong information? No! This vessel had to sail with the tide. She wouldn't think about any other possibility.

Keeping to the deep shadows on the silent deck, she inched toward the back of the ship. By the time she gained the hatchway, she detected movement on the forward deck. She distinctly heard one of the sailors cajoling a mate. "Come on, get a move on. Ya'll be glad ter get back ter the States. Why, iffin' we stayed here another night, ya'd be married off by morn. Time to leave the little darlin'."

The fishermen had given her the right information!

She closed her fingers against her lips to stop the involuntary sigh of relief. She wasn't safe yet. She had to stow away in the hold before she could breathe deeply or even think of a sigh. Clutching her valise and her package of food against her side, she crept over the casing to start her descent.

Pausing often to listen, she felt her way down the wooden planks that formed the steps of the vessel. One level! Two levels! She started down the third level, and from the smell and the sounds she knew she'd found her destination. The steps were slick and she felt her leather boots slip against the wood. "I've got to be careful," she told herself. As she took another step, she clung to the damp rope railing, the only means of steadying herself.

No sooner was the thought complete than her feet skidded away from the step, out into the space of the stairwell. She clutched at the rope but the coarse fibers dragged against her palm and she lost her grip. Thoughts rushed through her mind. She would be found. . . . She would have to marry Nelson. A sharp pain at the side of her head stilled her fear and she sank into a dark oblivion.

The scurrying sound of a dozen shoes invaded his restless dreams and Drew opened his eyes to the darkness of his cabin. Soon, in a matter of minutes, they would quit the shores of Barbados and head home. He sighed in contentment and crawled out of his bed. He lit the lantern beside his bed and gazed about his quarters. The cabin was plain, almost severe, except for his bed. It was the one acquisition that he refused to explain to anyone. Not even James knew why he insisted on a feather bed aboard a ship. All the other cabins had bunks with thin straw mattresses or hammocks that stretched from beam to beam.

He smiled in the soft light of the lamp, knowing that his friends would never understand. He didn't bother to explain to anyone that he was too large a man to sleep on a bunk. The only reason he insisted on that bed was for his own comfort. At times, he felt selfish, but he wasn't going to defend himself to his crew or his friends. "What the hell," he muttered. It was his ship and if he wanted a feather bed, then he should have it.

He started for the heavy ironstone bowl and pitcher, willing his large frame to shake itself free of the weariness that lately plagued him after a night of troubled dreams. Damn that girl, he thought as he shoved his leg into his pants. He thought himself immune to the charms of a vaporous female, but the taunting face of Catherine Pentworth followed him across the Atlantic. Almost every night she came, offering her lips and lush body, teasing him into a restless, aching dream state. Strange, he never suffered a thought of her until he and James were ready to leave England. Then, he remembered her, and the brief moment of ecstasy when he brushed her burning lips and felt her supple form leaning into him. Since he remembered the dance and the kisses, he hadn't been able to get her out of his mind.

The girl was ruining his mental peace. He slammed his fist against the wall and damned her face to the devil for perhaps the twentieth time. After all, she was nothing but the spoiled daughter of a rich man.

Then, he remembered his vow. While they were still in England, before the gossip mongers caught on to Catherine's disappearance, he promised himself that no woman would cause him the kind of pain that he'd seen on James's face for weeks. No, Drew told himself, no woman was going to ruin his disposition.

His thoughts turned to the reason for the doctor's long face. Poor James. At least the young doctor made his lady love promise to send messages often. Along with the messages, they made what Drew thought was an almost solemn pact to meet again before the next year was finished. In England, he had his suspicions, but now he was sure of it: James Rupert was desperately in love, and it appeared that the lady loved him too. The only thing that stood in the couple's way to a life of happiness was her guardian. A guardian of dubious ability, Drew thought, as he considered that the man could not even control his own daughter.

Drew snuffed out the lamp and stepped out into the dark corridor of his ship. First a stop in Jamaica, then one in Philadelphia, then they would head for home. Somehow, he promised himself, he'd wipe the face of Catherine Pentworth from his tired brain. And, by the time he got home to Savannah, if she wasn't gone from his thoughts, he would find someone who would help him forget the fragrant English flower.

Above him he heard the rapid paces of his crew as they raced across the planks to scale the mast and maneuver the ropes and sails that would push the *Savannah Lady* home. His drowsiness gone, he rushed up the steps to give directions.

They had been at sea for nearly an hour. In the gray light of the early morning, Drew watched as James stepped over the stair casing. Drew grinned in sympathy at the grim face and the drawn eyes. It seemed the good doctor hadn't slept well either. Drew sent the cabin boy off for a cup of coffee for James and commented on his condition. "A sea voyage is supposed to help you sleep."

James frowned. "Help me sleep? Not until I have Amelia at my side. Then a sea voyage might have some benefit."

Drew chuckled. "I told you we could kidnap the girl. You talked me out of it. I told you that you'd be unbearable without her."

"And I told you that I couldn't do that to her. She said herself that she couldn't live with that kind of disgrace. I don't want to be the cad responsible for the ruination of my own wife's reputation. Besides, she just might be able to convince her uncle that I am a worthy contender simply because I could have run off with her and didn't."

"Like as not," Drew smirked, "that man will think you're not truly interested, that you were only dallying. I still think we should have stolen her and brought her along."

James shook his head. "William Pentworth will know I'm serious. I intend to send word to her frequently. He'll see the letters. In fact, I sent two letters from Barbados. I even wrote to him, declaring my intentions once again."

With the sails to set and his charts to study, Drew strode across the deck, his words echoing through the morning stillness. "Don't blame me if she doesn't wait. Women are fickle creatures."

For the rest of the morning, Drew saw to his ship but James's attitude plagued him. Before they left London, Drew promised his friend a stop in the islands hoping to dispel some of the melancholy that crept over the doctor. Now with Barbados behind them, James was still depressed. "Damn," Drew muttered to no one. "Women!"

Morning grew old and Drew confined his thoughts

76

about women to a corner of his mind. It was nearly time for lunch when Samuel, his first mate, sought Drew out. "Ya want to have a short barrel of rum for the men this first night out?" Drew smiled at the question and nodded to Samuel. Not once in his seven years of sailing had Drew watered the rum. The crew appreciated Drew's rather unorthodox manner of sailing. Most of the men on the ropes or in the rigging had sailed with him for several years. He tried to be a good master, a good captain. He must have succeeded, in part, for time and time again they gave a little bit more than they had to to make the voyage a little shorter, a storm less bothersome, a sailing smoother.

Drew called after Samuel. "The seas are calm. Break out the keg before the sun sets. See that everybody gets a mug before dinner and another after the meal." He smiled at his words. Most captains would fear that the crew would take advantage and start the voyage dead drunk. He glanced around at his men. Everyone was sober, and already most of them carried a healthy sweat from their morning labors. They deserved a treat.

Drew rushed toward the stairs calling out to James, "Time for the noon fare." He bounded down the one flight, rubbing his hands together. Breakfast was a long time past. Plain fare deserted the table for several days after an island stop. The grouch who did the cooking lavished them all for at least a week with tropical treats for which he traded or bartered. While Drew waited for the feast to come, he poured himself a touch of rum and handed another to James. A thump on the door signaled lunch and Drew called, "Come in."

Drew didn't expect Samuel, and his presence signaled a problem. Drew's aggravation was marked. "Hate to

77

bother, sir," Samuel muttered through his dark curly beard, "but ya'll have to come."

"Where? What's the trouble?"

"In the hold," Samuel threw over his shoulder as he bounded for the stairs. "Better bring the doc."

"Damn," Drew hissed. "James, he says you better come. One of the crew has probably fallen. I hope to God it's not serious." A chill shook him and he found himself wondering if a troubled voyage threatened.

As Drew started down the last flight of steps, a cluster of his men stood in silence. Their lack of conversation and the stiff manner in which they held themselves told Drew that when they reached home, he would be visiting a sailor's family to explain the man's untimely death. The group divided as he took the last several steps. A vague thought teased at the corner of his mind. Why was James needed if the man was already dead? Samuel shouted above the noise of the sea, "Here's the doc."

High above his head, one sailor held a glowing lantern to light the path for the doctor. Drew glanced down at his feet. The slender form of a young boy—Drew's mind stopped thinking as he gazed at long dark hair spread in wild profusion about the head of the injured person. "Sir," Samuel's voice cut through the mental fog that blinded Drew, "it's a girl."

"I can see that. Is she . . . How badly is she hurt?"

James stepped forward and knelt at her side. "Hold the lantern down," James directed. With the lantern lowered, he began a quick but thorough exam. He turned once and glanced at Drew, the strangest expression on his face.

"What's wrong, what is it?" Drew asked. He'd never seen that kind of a quizzical gaze on James's face before.

That look had to mean something, some kind of difficulty. But James didn't answer, instead he barked orders to two of the sailors at his side. Then, he pushed Drew aside and started up the stairs, the body of the girl following on a makeshift stretcher. "James!" Drew bellowed.

"You'll know soon enough," came the faint reply from the second level. Drew heard the doctor once again directing the sailors up the next flight of steps, leaving him at the bottom, next to the valise that must have belonged to the girl. He grabbed it and took the steps three at a time. James was not shutting him out of this. It was entirely possible that one of his men had broken one of his company's cardinal rules. No man was ever, for any reason, to bring a woman aboard his ships, but it seemed that someone had.

Word passed from one man to the next and soon the entire ship knew of the girl, and even worse, where Samuel found her. Always the same reaction. Someone was in trouble, terrible trouble. Each man pitied the poor devil. The criminal would feel the lash a dozen times. But there was more. At the first island they passed, he would be deposited with food and water and nothing else, nothing to show for the voyage. And, from the scowl on the captain's face, there would be no reprieve.

Drew gave the order quietly. With few words, Samuel lined the men up on the forward deck. Drew straightened his shirt and vest and stepped before his men. Who? Who had been so stupid? And why? They'd been in Bridgetown for nearly a week. The men had plenty of time on the island. They had funds, every one of them. Drew knew exactly what pleasures could be purchased. Why, he'd stopped there to provide James with just such an opportunity.

Drew squared his shoulders and pulled himself up to his full six foot four inches. "Men, the rules on board are simple, the punishment known to each and every one of you. Today I found a woman in the hold. I want to know how she came to be on board. I want the name of the man who brought her here." He stood quietly, waiting.

No one made a sound. No one stepped forward. Drew's brow gathered into a frown. There wasn't a man on the ship that hadn't sailed with him before, and many of the men were making their fourth or fifth tour with him. He glared at each man. And, without exception, there wasn't a trace of guilt in any eye. Drew wondered, had the chit followed one of the men on board? There was always that possibility.

Drew gave the order, "No one move. I will get to the bottom of this yet." He pulled Samuel off to the side. "I'm going to question each man individually. Perhaps someone saw something and failed to report it."

He retired to the bow of the ship. As if they were penitents before a father confessor, each member of the crew approached Drew, said his piece, and crept back to his place in line. Finally, with the words of the cabin boy ringing in his ears, Drew knew that none of his men had attempted to bring the girl on board. The only explanation that was possible was that she followed one of his men. Then the thought occurred, had she stowed away on the wrong ship?

He had to talk to her himself, he decided. Dear God, let's hope she can settle this, he thought as he turned away from his crew. He gave instructions to Samuel and the men dispersed. They stood in small groups huddled against the fall winds, waiting for the captain to leave the deck. Drew shook his head in confusion. Well, with any luck the creature that James had taken into his cabin was alert enough to withstand some questioning. He had no intention of waiting long for some answers.

Drew stalked to his cabin and when he would have pressed his entry, James inched the door open, stepped out into the corridor and gently closed the door. "She's not regained consciousness yet," James murmured. "There's no serious injury except for her head, but, I must warn you, we can't know how bad that is for some time yet. It could be very serious."

Drew stepped up to the door. "Let me see her."

James pushed against the cabin door, wondering what Drew would do when he saw the face of the girl in his bed. For the past hour, as James sat with the young woman, he thought about the twist of fate. How he would have preferred to have another, uninjured, Pentworth in the bed.

He thought about the missing pieces in this puzzle. What had the sister of Charles and Phillip Pentworth been doing in Barbados? James thought about her two brothers. Of course, he'd never met Phillip and it had been over two years since he'd heard from Charles. Their correspondence always had been haphazard. The last letter he sent found Charles in Spain, intent on taking a Spanish flower to wife and Charles left James with the impression that if he did marry he would stay in Spain. Of course, James never discussed Charles with Amelia or her uncle. At the time, he was too set on pressing his own suit.

James followed Drew into the cabin and stood at the foot of the bed. Drew's reaction was slow in coming, for as agitated as the girl had been in the bed, her dark brown hair now covered a good part of her face. James stepped forward and took her wrist, checking for the pulse that told him she was recovering. He watched as Drew reached down to push the long mane away from the girl's features.

James heard the gasp and nodded when Drew looked up, his face drawn and pale. "It's . . . it's Catherine Pentworth. My God! How did she get here? Is she going to be all right. What is she doing on my ship?" The questions tumbled out, one over another. James was even more startled that Drew remembered the girl's full name.

"She's getting restless. Sometime in the next twenty-four hours we may have some answers. And we may not." He looked pointedly at Drew. "Let's let her rest. I'll stay here unless I'm needed elsewhere." James watched his friend. Drew was more than stunned with the presence of the girl and James had to wonder why. If appearances were any judge, Drew Sloan'd spent a lot of time thinking about this girl.

His own thoughts a plague, James scowled at the plank above his head. He never liked head injuries. The ones that looked serious sometimes turned out to be nothing and others that appeared as nothing took the life of the poor soul. No good doctor could say, even in the thirties, who could survive and who might die. Maybe someday . . . He moved to hold the door for Drew.

The day faded into night and Cathy tossed and turned in the feather bed. Drew checked on her several times, and each time he opened the door, James's stocky frame crouched over the girl in concern. Would she recover? Drew wondered. He refused to put the words into a question for James.

At midmorning the next day James sent for Drew.

When Drew arrived, James commented, "She's coming around. If everything is all right, she's going to have a king-sized headache. I expect that she'll do some vomiting as well. That's usually the pattern."

Drew got out the words, "And if she's not all right?"

James shook his head. "I'm not about to borrow trouble." Both men waited but after a quarter hour, Drew went back to the deck of the ship, his heart heavy. He might never have the answers to his questions. He told himself that explained why his heart felt sore, ached in his chest. Drew tried hard to believe his own lecture.

For another hour Drew wandered the deck and when no word came from James, he made his way into the hold to feed and brush the horses he brought from England. They seemed to be weathering the trip a great deal better than the girl in his bed. Samuel found him there. "James sent for you," his first mate confirmed. "She's come out of it, but the doctor said to tell you, no questions."

Drew bounded up the flight of stairs and nearly ran to his cabin. If James said no questions, then was the girl all right? It didn't seem likely. He stopped at the door to his cabin. Should he barge in or knock? He chose the latter, and tapped gingerly at the door, remembering that James had said she would have a headache. He had no time to follow the first tap with a second, for James pulled the door open wide.

The doctor stepped out of the room and before Drew caught a glimpse, James eased the door closed. "She's awake. It's as I said. She has a blistering headache and she did some vomiting. But, Drew, she's in trouble. She honestly doesn't know who she is or what she's doing on a ship."

"Are you sure? It could be an act if she recognized

you." Suspicion marked Drew's face.

"I took that into account. The panic on her face when she couldn't tell me her name was genuine," James whispered.

Drew looked frustrated. "What do we do now?"

James smiled at his friend. Patience was never one of Andrew Sloan's virtues. "It's probably a condition that will not last long. However, there have been cases where the memory never returns. We have to wait."

Drew screwed up his face in disbelief. "Never returns! You can't be serious."

"I said there have been cases. Do you want to see her?" James looked at Drew. "Maybe you better wait. I don't want you upsetting her."

"No, I better see her," Drew said quietly. "And I won't upset her."

James eased open the door and Drew inched his way to the bed. There was no recognition on Cathy's part. Her eyes held pain and Drew was loath to even think about questioning her. He swallowed his curiosity and told her that all of the crew wanted her to get well.

"I'm sorry. I can't think. My head . . ." Her weak voice trailed off.

"Don't worry! You are fortunate that James Rupert is sailing with us. He's a fine doctor and a good friend. He'll be your friend too." Drew wanted to say more but Cathy's eyes drifted closed. James shook his head and Drew backed away from the bed after patting her hand. He glanced at James. Did the gesture show too much concern? he wondered, and stumbled toward the door.

James followed him from the room, but this time the door remained open. "How long before we know if she'll be all right?" Drew whispered. James shook his head.

Drew wondered if that meant that James didn't know. Damn, he thought as he turned to make his way to the deck. He wanted to scream his frustrations to the setting sun. He certainly hadn't counted on this.

Drew paced the deck, and a chuckle slipped past his lips. He shook his head with the thought. He doubted that James Rupert had given Amelia Pentworth a thought in the last thirty-six hours. With Catherine to care for, James had given up his depression. "Mistress Pentworth, at least you did that," Drew mumbled to the clouds racing against the sky.

Chapter Six

Cathy lay frozen, suspended in a deathlike cocoon of numbness. Any slight movement created the vilest sensation in her head. She took a deep breath and fought the nausea that had been threatening to consume her since she'd forced her eyes open into slits.

The gigantic feather bed in which she was tucked belied the notion that beneath her the waters of the ocean capped, crested, and swelled to push her toward a foreign land. She would have named the doctor a liar if the lamp above the bed hadn't swung back and forth. Why was she on a ship? The pulsing pain in her head made any more thought an agony. She closed her eyes and let herself drift back to sleep.

It could have been hours later or only minutes when she opened her eyes again. The doctor, James Rupert, leaned over her bed. "Ah, you *are* back among the living, I see."

Cathy's eyes widened. "Did I almost die?"

James's smile looked a bit guilty, she thought, but he responded, "No! I meant that as a teasing remark.

Haven't you ever been teased?"

Cathy's eyes clouded with fear and uncertainty. "I don't know. I can't seem to remember who I am. My head hurts so. I don't want to remember anything, not right now."

"I'll bet it does," James murmured quietly. "Now, I want to make sure that when you fell you damaged nothing but your head. That's bad enough, but let's check the rest of you. You lie very still and if it hurts when I poke you, let me know. Do you understand?"

Cathy started to nod her head and she was certain at that instant that the entire human race tried to march through her skull. She groaned and squeaked, "Yes." James waited for the awful pounding to slow and then he pushed and prodded from her shoulders and arms to her feet. She couldn't help the searing red flush that heated the surface of her complexion with the placement of his fingers. Well, she thought to herself, she obviously wasn't married. A married woman would never suffer such embarrassment with the doctor performing an examination and with all of her clothes on as well.

The thought of marriage triggered a memory of a man with red wine running down his face and staining his blond curls. Somehow, she knew that she was responsible for the mess. She opened her eyes, eyes that she had squeezed shut in embarrassment and looked at the doctor. The man of her memory was not the doctor. James Rupert's hair was nearly orange, not a touch of blond. The doctor was a shorter man than the man she had seen in her mind's eye. The doctor smiled at her. "I can tell by your eyes that you remembered something."

"I saw a flash of a tall, blond-haired man with wine punch running over his face. I think I poured the punch on his head." She glanced at James to see if she was making a fool of herself. He looked genuinely surprised. Then, he laughed.

"You are remembering. Perhaps you took exception to something the man in your vision did."

"He wouldn't pay a bet!" she said, her voice clear and nearly ecstatic. Her comment brought about the return of that terrible pounding in her head and she whimpered much less enthusiastically, "I am remembering."

"It will come," James said softly. "Don't try to rush it. As the headache disappears, I'm confident your memory will return. But, for now, I want you to get more sleep. One of your ankles was twisted in your fall and your head is not nearly healed." He explained that if she moved she would probably make herself sick. She was not to try to move by herself, not for any reason.

A soft tap on the door preceded the largest man she'd ever seen. He filled the doorway completely. His face twisted in concern and Cathy wondered why he seemed familiar. James introduced the man as Drew Sloan, the captain of the ship on which they were sailing. Then, the doctor excused himself and left the cabin.

Cathy waited until Mr. Sloan stood beside the bed before she asked, "Where am I going?"

Drew chuckled, "I hoped you would tell me. This ship is traveling from Barbados to the United States."

She struggled with the name Barbados. There was something unpleasant about that place. "I'm from England," she said and her brow wrinkled into a frown. "Now, why did I say that?"

"I'd say you needed to rest," Drew admonished and he moved away from the bed. She closed her eyes. All she needed was to rest, to heal, and her memory would return. Her head had to improve so that she could understand why Dr. Rupert seemed like someone she had always known, and the captain tugged at her memory.

Cathy awoke to soft masculine voices and for a moment fear raced along her spine. She lay still, preferring for them to think that she still slept until she determined who the speakers were. She drew deep, steady breaths trying hard to distinguish the voices. One of the voices belonged to Dr. Rupert and the other voice came from the captain.

The discussion centered on this voyage and Cathy let her breathing grow shallow so that she could hear. The doctor said, "There's Isaac Peterson in Philadelphia. He could look at her! He's good and since we were going there anyway. . . ." They were discussing her.

The captain answered, "If we follow our original plan, we can go ahead and stop in Jamaica, pick up the cargo of sugar, then sail for Philadelphia. If there's no improvement, we'll sail for Savannah and I'll send word from there, but James, we're talking four to six weeks."

"I thought we agreed," James's voice sounded angry, "that we were not going to send word until she was out of the woods. I don't want to have to explain how she came to be here . . ." His voice dropped to a whisper, and Cathy wondered if she had inadvertently moved and given her consciousness away.

She heard the scraping of furniture and the voices raised in plans for the evening. Once again she felt herself drift into a soft, warm, painless place.

When she opened her eyes, she wondered if she'd dreamed the voices. Had two men really occupied the cabin and discussed what they were going to do with her? From the porthole at the side of the cabin, a bright stream of light spread across the bed. How late in the day was it and, as far as that was concerned, what day was it? The door opened and she rolled herself toward the sound. The terrible pounding no longer stopped her movement, but she still felt very sore. She lifted her hand to touch the hurt and she was startled when she found that a large part of her head was wrapped in some kind of linen.

James walked into the room followed by Drew. "Ah, my patient is well enough to wonder what I've done to her. There was a scrape along the temple and it was bleeding. I cleaned the wound and bandaged the area. I didn't want you to get an infection with the headache you have. By the way, how is the head?"

Cathy tried to lift her head and immediately knew she'd made a poor choice. The pounding returned with a vengeance. She didn't even want to try to respond to James's question. She mouthed the word, "Hurts!"

James chuckled. "I should have told you not to lift your head. In a day or two the pounding should go away and the pain will dull and then vanish. Drew," he addressed the captain, "I'd say by Friday the lady should be feeling more like herself."

With her voice hoarse with disuse, Cathy struggled to make her thoughts known. "How am I supposed to feel like myself when I don't know . . . who I am?"

Drew answered, "James says it'll come back. You need to be patient. Your poor head took quite a bump and it has to recover."

"Where did I fall?" As the words left her mouth she could feel herself falling. The question haunted her. Where had she fallen?

"It appears that you fell down the steps into the hold. We found you at the bottom of the steps."

"What was I doing in the hold?" she asked, almost afraid of the answer.

Drew looked at James and then down at her, his eyes full of concern. "We don't know. We're waiting for you to tell us."

"I'm a . . . a . . ."

"You're a stowaway, yes. But you may have mistaken this ship for a ship that you had passage on. We don't know," Drew tried to reassure her.

In a strangely tight voice, she whispered, "What's going to happen to me?"

James stepped up to the bed and tried his best bedside manner, warm and confident. "We're taking you with us. If your memory has not returned by the time we reach Philadelphia, I'll take you to see one of the city's doctors, one of the best. Then you'll go to Savannah with Captain Sloan and me. Captain Sloan," he nodded toward the man at the end of the bed, "thinks he might know your family in England. If you don't remember who you are, he'll write and find out if the family he knows has a missing daughter. If they do, then he'll make arrangements for you to go there, or for the father to come to Savannah. So, you see, you don't have a thing to worry about."

The pounding in Cathy's head had slowed to a dull thump. Cathy rested her head on the soft pillow and the doctor's words conjured up images of an angry man, tall with blue-gray eyes and thick gray brows. Cathy knew the man of the vision was her father. In that instant, she also knew that when he found out about the position in which she had found herself, he would go into a rage. Maybe it would be better for everyone if she didn't remember anything more for a while.

92

The face of the gray-haired man danced before her eyes. A sudden thought told her she'd done something else to infuriate him, something for which he'd ordered a punishment. She decided that if she did remember anything, anything at all, she'd better keep it to herself. In fact, it might be to her advantage to have no identity at all.

She looked up at the captain. "What day is today?"

Drew laughed. "This is Tuesday, and it's the twenty-first day of September."

"When do you think we'll get to Philadelphia?" she asked.

"If we have good weather, we should be there by the middle of October. We're stopping in Jamaica to pick up a cargo and then we sail to the States."

Ah, she hadn't dreamed it, Cathy thought, somehow elated that her mind was sound and probably getting better every minute, just as the doctor said it would.

James watched her closely. "What is it? Do you remember something about Philadelphia?"

Cathy tried desperately to mask her expression. The man was too much. How was she going to keep an identity to herself when the doctor seemed to be able to read her mind. She shook her head and looked up at the doctor. "Whatever it was is gone now."

After the men left, Cathy agonized over the vision she knew was her father. Could he be worried sick over her disappearance? Something about Barbados was important too. When she thought about Barbados, she grew breathless, panicky. Something unpleasant happened in Barbados. However, she was certain that she was English, and that the gray-haired man was her father. He was angry with her for doing something, but what? The

93

questions rolled around her head until she thought her scalp would split with her efforts. Enough, she screamed at herself. She closed her eyes and forced herself to relax. Sleep, then she would remember, became her litany and soon she drifted into a world of peace.

She struggled, but by the end of the third day the pieces fell into place. She was Catherine Pentworth. Her father William sent her to Barbados to stay with her brothers until they found her a husband. She stowed away on this ship to avoid their choice. At least, all things considered, she was safe for the moment. And, now that she knew who she was and why she was running away, the easy trip to Savannah was almost worth the pain in her head. For now, she had a soft bed, clean clothes, and good meals. None of those things would have been available to her if she had had to stay hidden in the hold.

She knew she'd have to pretend that her brains were still scrambled. A thought struck her. How long could she carry on such a pretense? Please, she prayed, at least until we get to Philadelphia. By then, I can get a room and send word to my father. If she was discovered before they reached America, something told her that Captain Sloan would insist, would feel obliged, to send her back to Barbados, back to Nelson Goodspeed and a wedding she didn't want. "Please, at least not until we get to Philadelphia," she muttered.

With that thought in her mind, she snuggled down into the mattress for her nap. The captain mentioned that after her rest, he had a surprise for her. She wasn't excited, for what she really wanted was to be allowed out of the bed. Her head hurt very little now, and the stiffness from which she suffered the day before, disappeared yesterday. Besides, her curiosity was nibbling away at her. She wanted to be up on deck soaking up the late summer warmth, viewing islands she'd never seen and watching the sailors work the sails. After her nap, she'd demand that she be allowed up!

She stretched in bed, the daze of sleep fading away. Awakened instinct told her someone else was in the cabin with her. She glanced around the room. Captain Sloan stood next to the bed, smiling in his confident way. Over his arm was draped a garment of dark blue velvet. He said softly, "I promised a surprise. How would you like to get up for a bit? I think you can sit in that chair over there for a while and if you get along fine, then James and I will have our dinner here with you tonight."

He held out the garment and Cathy knew that the velvet robe was a part of his own wardrobe. It was enormous and probably weighed a ton. "I can't eat dinner and wear that." She pointed at the robe.

Drew grinned. "My lady, there is more fabric here than in two of your dresses put together. It will do, let me assure you." He helped her into the robe and with a litany of things to be careful of, he pulled her to the edge of the bed. She blushed when she couldn't cover her legs fast enough. "Girl," he said sternly, "worry about getting from here to there." He pointed toward the chair.

Cathy blushed and struggled up to her feet. At his direction, she took deep breaths and the dizziness he warned her about passed. She crept from the bed to the chair. The sense of accomplishment she felt when she sat primly in the chair dumbfounded her. Drew seemed to understand. "Feels good, doesn't it?"

She nodded her head a bit too energetically and for a second she suffered a sharp pain near her right ear, but like the pounding of several days ago, it faded. "Sir," she said, intent on convincing him that she remembered little, "you can't go on calling me 'girl,' or 'my lady.' If you think you know who I am, then can't you tell me what my name is?"

Drew scowled at her. James wanted her to remember on her own, but except for that first day of consciousness, she offered nothing about herself. Perhaps what James said about a long, slow process would hold true. Giving her a name might help her. He hesitated, then suggested, "How does Catherine sound?"

"Catherine." She let the name roll from her mouth. Silently she formed the word with her lips, pretending that it seemed foreign. "No," she said quietly, "I don't think that's right. How does Victoria sound? Vicki? That feels good, right, like it might be mine. Catherine is too . . . oh, too stuffy."

"Then, how about Cathy?" he asked, trying to hide his disappointment.

"Cathy." Once again she said the word slowly as if she were tasting it. "Cathy," she repeated. It would be good to be called by her own name. Now, how could she tell him it was acceptable and leave enough doubt in his mind? She smiled. "Cathy is a beautiful name. I like that. I don't think it's mine, but I like it. I wouldn't mind if you called me Cathy."

Drew frowned. That was not the reaction for which he hoped. He thought back to his conversation with James the evening before. The doctor hadn't been encouraging. Drew remembered lashing out. "Damn it, I can hear her father. He'll blame us for everything. My God, what if she never remembers? You said it was possible. If that's the case, then you better forget all about your Amelia. The man will never let you within a continent of her. You better do whatever you can to make that girl remember. Why don't we at least tell her what her name is? That might start the ball rolling." James had stood on the deck, shaking his head.

Drew helped Cathy back to bed, his face glum. The name triggered nothing, and James would probably be angry. Well, tonight they would have dinner together and perhaps something would jar her memory then. He started for the door. "Dinner is in about two hours. You'll be fine until then."

Cathy was pleased with Drew's sour expression but she was displeased as well. He seemed so disappointed when she pretended the name meant nothing. She brushed aside her guilt. After all, she had to get to Philadelphia, or she would end up as Mrs. Nelson Goodspeed and that she could not bear. Someday, perhaps, she would be able to explain.

She buried her guilt and thought about the dinner that would be served here in the cabin. Her meals had been taken alone, but tonight Andrew Sloan was coming to dinner. For some reason her breathing grew ragged and her mind replayed the night of the ball. Her palms grew damp and her face felt flushed. She didn't like him, not really, so why was her heart beating erratically, and why was she shivering?

"This won't do," she said to herself, but she knew that she wasn't listening. Something about the man did things to her that had never happened before. "I must stay away from him," she mumbled as she scooted down into the mattress for another nap.

She was awake when James and Drew both came through the door. Dinner followed them in less than a minute. While the cabin boy bustled around the table setting places for three, Cathy struggled from the bed. James helped her to the table, and Andrew held her chair. She gave her thanks and raised her eyes to her host.

Her breath caught and she fought with herself. This man must not know how he affected her. She must never let him know that she even had an inkling of who she was. Once they docked in Philadelphia, then she could remember, but not before that. She lowered her eyes and kept them on her plate. Let him think what he wanted.

Dinner was a chore and before the men were finished, she raised her eyes. "I think I better go back to bed."

"A bit too much," James chuckled. "Well, I don't want you pushing yourself." Before James was out of his chair, Andrew had her in his arms. She couldn't help herself. As she tried to avoid his chest her whole body shivered from her head to her feet. Suddenly, she was burning up and she knew she could not breathe. Andrew's face was dark with concern. "She has overdone herself," he stated flatly.

As he laid her in the bed she protested, "No, just a little bit too much for tonight. Perhaps if I got some sun . . ." Dear God, she asked herself, what is wrong with me. After her behavior at dinner, the doctor won't let me up for another week. She glanced at James Rupert, praying that his face would not be wreathed with censure. Instead, he was grinning.

"I think I agree with that. Yes, I think Cathy needs some sun, fresh vegetables, and fruit. Tomorrow you can carry her up to the deck and I'll fix her a bed. She can soak up the sun, relax, and eat in the fresh air. I'm sure she'll be fine."

Cathy missed the relief on Drew's face. Her concern was for James's reaction. She had the strongest sensation that he knew exactly what was going on inside her head. Instinct told her that he'd guessed that she had remembered everything. Well, tomorrow she would insist that she speak to him alone. The good doctor was going to tell her what tonight was all about and why he was laughing at Andrew Sloan.

Chapter Seven

Her chance to speak to James alone never came. Early the next morning, Drew stopped at her cabin, waited until she was dressed, then carried her onto the sun-bright deck where she rested on a makeshift pallet of blankets for most of the day. James brought Samuel to meet her and Samuel introduced her formally to each member of the crew. By dinnertime she was tired, but for the first time in weeks she was happy.

She ate alone, telling herself that she was thankful the men chose to eat together and without her company. The next day was Sunday and Drew mentioned earlier that he held a brief prayer service in the morning. The rest of the day was spent by most of the sailors on personal things: their laundry, swimming, a little carving, or even a little fishing. Afraid that Drew was going to tell her that she'd be excluded, she waited for his orders to stay in her cabin. Instead, he said quietly, "I'll come for you before the service, if you want to attend, and then you can stay topside for the rest of the day."

She nodded her head, grateful that the throbbing and

pounding disappeared as James said they would. She still felt weak, dizzy sometimes, and her ankle ached nearly all of the time, but she knew she was healing. She couldn't bear to be cooped up with only four wooden walls to gaze at, even if it was the nicest cabin on the ship. She whispered in her husky voice, "Yes, I want to come."

For the next three days, Cathy sat in the sun, talked to the sailors, and helped with some mending, a thing she'd always managed to escape doing at home. She even tried her hand at cutting hair. The men talked to her easily and she relaxed a little more each day. Her husky laugh drifted over the deck so often now that the men no longer raised their heads when they heard it.

Thursday was warm, warmer than usual, and Cathy slept poorly the night before. All night, dreams of her father in his study, his eyes ringed with red and his sobs slicing into her heart, tore through her. A distant part of her knew that her father never sobbed and the only time she ever saw her father shed a tear was on the day Marie Ann was buried. He had not sobbed even on that day. The tears flowed from his eyes, but without a sound he mourned his second love. In her dreams, though, she heard him cry, a sound as heart wrenching as anything she ever imagined. Her guilt nearly consumed her. She knew she should send word, but if she did, William would send word to Phillip and Charles, then Nelson would hear. . . . No, better to leave things as they were.

Her nightmares sapped her strength, but she refused to stay in the cabin and rest. On the deck, though, in the warm sunshine, the temptation to close her eyes was more than she could stand and she gave in to her body's need. James had warned her and Samuel had warned her not to fall asleep in the sun, but she couldn't help it. Her eyes closed and she drifted into the nether world of peace. In the marvelous dream that followed, her soul mate found her, scooped her out of the sea, held her close, and carried her away to be his forever.

She struggled out of the dream and for a second, her confusion bewildered her. Oh, she was in the arms of a man, all right, but not the man of her dreams. This man was the captain of the ship. She tensed and glanced around. Andrew Sloan held her carefully as he descended the steps to the cabin she occupied. Her husky voice registered alarm. "What are you doing? Where are you taking me?"

"Silly woman! James and Samuel both warned you about going to sleep out on the deck. I was on my way down for some maps and I brought you down to get you out of the sun. Am I too late? Has the sun already ruined your brain?"

"I . . . I . . . I didn't sleep well last—" What was she doing, explaining to him? She closed her mouth and tried to ignore the warmth of his arms, the beat of his heart, the strength of his broad chest against her body. Good lord! Whyever did this man have to stir up her feelings like this? A decent girl, even an old maid like herself should not go mad over a few male muscles.

For a second she struggled, and he pulled her tighter to him. "Hold still. I'll put you down in the cabin." He wasn't going to admit, not even to himself, that holding her felt wonderful. The sweet feminine smell, like the soft spring flowers in the fields at the farm, drifted up to tantalize his nostrils. Sweet heaven, what was she doing to him? He grabbed at the door and pushed into the cabin.

For a second the temptation was too great, he couldn't release her without tasting of her again. He dipped his head, brushing against her full pink lips. But that small taste wasn't enough, might never be enough. With a gasp of surprise her lips opened and his own mouth swooped down to claim her again. For a long minute he gave in to the surge of passion that bolted through his body. She was sweet, sweeter than the tiny white flowers at home and he drank deeply. Then he set her feet on the floor, released her, and left the cabin.

Cathy sagged against the bed, her thoughts in shambles. He kissed her once before, but never like that. He had touched her heart. She lifted her fingers and brushed her tingling lips. There was no denying it! The man was capable of magic, great magic. She walked toward his shaving mirror above the washstand. She couldn't look the same, not after that, she decided. However, Catherine Pentworth, as she had always known herself, peered back from the mirror. There was no change. She didn't look any different.

She stepped away from the washstand and sank into the soft feather mattress. She let her mind drift, wondering what wonderful tingles those magical lips might create if he touched other parts of her body. In horror, she stiffened. Was he controlling her mind? That was the only explanation for her thoughts about his lips pressing against her skin. Could he direct her thoughts from a distance? She frowned—she'd have to be on her guard with him. She could never allow him into this cabin when she was alone.

For the next two days, she tried hard to convince herself that she dreamed the whole thing when she fell asleep on the deck. But why then, she asked herself, if it was a dream, did she wake up in the cabin? She could find no reason for the rapid pounding of her heart when she glimpsed the captain on his rounds. Her tortured soul kept her awake long hours each night.

She still rose shortly after dawn and on Friday, just after breakfast, the call came from the crow's nest high above the deck, "Land ho!" and Cathy stumbled to the rail to gaze at the growing dark dot on the horizon. Before her questions formed, Drew leaned against the railing beside her. She asked quietly, "Which land mass?"

Drew laughed. "That, dear girl, is Jamaica. And I have the unpleasant task of telling you that until the ship is docked, the inspection completed, and the cargo unloaded, you must stay in your cabin."

She opened her mouth in order to deny his orders. Instead, for once in her life, she chose to find out the reason behind the order. "Why?"

"Well, the inspection by the officials can be of anything and everyone. Since you cannot yet remember who you are, I feel you would be more comfortable in your cabin. And, Cathy, you don't want to be on deck when the cargo is unloaded. It's a hard, dirty job. The men will not appreciate your presence then."

Cathy couldn't fault his reason. "How long will all of this take?"

Drew laughed. "Just like a woman. Maybe four hours, maybe four days. Cathy, there are too many things to consider. I can't answer that."

She bristled. "I won't stay in that cabin for four days!"

"I'm afraid that you will. I'll give you as much time as I can, but before we drop anchor, I'll come get you and you'll go below," he said over his shoulder. She ignored him, leaning against the rail and watching the growing landscape. She would not stay in her cabin for four days. Drew Sloan could go . . . go . . . to the devil!

She ended up staying in the cabin, at least during the day, for three days. James had the unenviable task of walking her around the deck very early in the morning, and again after the sun set, but all the rest of the time she paced the floor of the cabin. To make sure that she stayed in the cabin, Drew Sloan gave the order that she was to be locked in. Her blood sizzled with his orders and she refused to say a word to him the few times she saw him.

By the time the inspector finished with the ship, and the cargo replaced, Cathy was furious enough with both James and the dear captain that if she had had a weapon, she would have used it. She already threw most of Drew's possessions at the door the last time James locked her in. "I'll get even," she yelled at James after he turned the lock. "I'll not stay locked in here another day."

When James came the next morning, she was waiting. It had been light for almost two hours when she heard the key in the lock. "Where have you been?" she snapped as she ran through the doorway. She was halfway up the stairs when she turned around and looked at James. "I'm not going back. I'll tell you that right now. I'll jump ship if you think you'll lock me back in that cabin."

James chuckled and started up the stairs after her. Drew Sloan was a coward. He refused to talk to the doctor about Cathy and the reasons for her sequestration. But, James told him last evening, he wasn't locking her in that cabin again. Last night she had almost gotten hysterical. And what appetite she had disappeared the second day of confinement. As a doctor, he knew she would soon be ill and he was not prepared to be responsible for making someone sick. However, with the inspection complete, they could leave the ship. He sighed in relief.

Cathy spent three days in Jamaica and loved every

minute of it. Late afternoon their second day, James arrived at the small inn where Drew assigned her rooms with a beautiful mare following his horse. "I thought the lady might like to go for a little ride. You do ride, don't you?"

Her face broke into an expansive grin and she started to laugh. Then she realized that she was supposed to be missing her memory. She tried for a blank expression. She tried to look surprised. "I don't know. I felt very happy when I saw the horse. Does that mean I know how to ride?"

James looked a bit perplexed and answered, "Well, let's see. If you don't fall off of the beast, we'll assume that you know how to ride."

The ride was marvelous and she got to see a bit of Jamaica. When they arrived back at the inn, Drew stepped from the porch. "Where in the hell have you been? I was waiting dinner."

The next afternoon, shortly after lunch, James was back, this time with a different mare and they rode for several hours.

After dinner, Cathy gathered her things and the two men escorted her back to the ship. "We sail at dawn," Drew told her. "You will be staying in the cabin across from mine. Samuel is giving up his cabin to you. I hope you'll remember to thank him."

"I can stay in one of the cabins for hire," she said quietly. He looked at her, concern in his eyes. "If you are worried about my paying you, I can assure you that I have money."

Drew almost laughed. "How, if you can't remember anything, do you know you have money?" The girl was beyond anything he'd ever met unless, he paused, unless

107

she knew exactly who she was. He felt his anger starting to build. She could be feigning her loss of memory. In fact, she could be like most females her age, ready to lie or twist the truth when it served a purpose. She was probably playing them all for fools, right from the beginning. He glared at her.

Cathy realized what she'd said the minute the words were out of her mouth. She glanced at Drew to determine if she could read his mind for a change. Had he figured out that she was remembering? She stared at his angry face; he'd understood her only too well. Trying to cover her mistake, she pointed out calmly, "I looked at the garments in the valise you gave me. They are quality fabric. Don't ask how I know, I just know. Stashed in the bottom of the case were a cache of gems. They looked expensive, too. So I naturally decided that I'm not a poor serving girl."

Drew looked skeptical and James turned his head away from them both. Once again, Cathy sensed that James Rupert had the whole thing figured out. When it came to reading minds, he did much better than Drew. What would she do if he decided to share his suspicions with the captain? She shivered in fear. Not Nelson, never.

At dawn the next morning, the ship set sail, and Cathy promised herself that she would be on the deck. She missed their arrival, but she was determined to view the island as they sailed away. The chilly gray morning conspired against her, though, and she soon deserted the deck. She had nothing else to do so she went back to bed. When she came back up from her cabin, the sky was lighter, but by only a few degrees. The sailors were busy, and Cathy sensed a tension that had not been present before. She caught the whispers. It seemed that someone had dropped a glass of some kind. By noon, the wind was rising and she looked for Drew. Someone needed to tell her what was going on.

Drew was preoccupied but he sent her to James. "What's happening? Are we going to have a storm?"

James was stern for once. "Cathy, there are some things you need to know. First, yes, we are going to have a storm. The glass, it's correctly called a barometer, is falling fast and far. That means a storm and a bad one. The Atlantic is famous for bad storms this time of year." Her face lost some of its color and he hastened to reassure her. "This ship is watertight and unless it's much worse than normal, and we won't know that for a while, we'll be fine. But, and this is important, you have to stay below. The seas run high and the waves slam into a ship often sending those who aren't prepared to a watery grave. It takes some knowledge and skill to stand upright on the deck of a ship in the middle of a storm. If it will make you feel any better, I'm staying below during the worst of it."

"Is there any way to tell how long it will last?"

He shook his head. "Unfortunately, no. The storm itself may blow through us in several hours, but the seas will still be bad. Remember, it's not even here yet and already the waves are getting rough." He shook his head as he stopped to look out over the water.

Suddenly, Cathy was afraid. "Maybe you should ask Drew to turn around and go back to Jamaica."

James laughed at her suggestion and when he realized that she was serious, he said softly, "Cathy, the storm is coming from that direction."

She simply said, "Oh," and moved to the stairway.

"Cathy." James stopped her with his hand on her arm. "I want you to go to the cook and get some fruit for your cabin. He'll give you a small jug of water and tell you about the bunk. Also, no lantern. We can't risk a fire, so extinguish your lantern. And don't be frightened. Someone will check on you from time to time."

Don't be frightened! That was impossible. With every one of his comments she grew more fearful. When she started for the stairs again, she asked, her voice breaking, "We'll be all right, won't we?"

James answered quietly, "The ship is a good one, the captain experienced. It's a serious storm, but with the help of the Almighty, we should be all right."

She stopped at the stairway. "How do you know it's going to be this serious?" She tried to gather some hope—after all, James wasn't a sailor!

"Cathy, the glass! It's still falling and so quickly. The lower it goes and the faster, the worse the storm."

Cathy rushed to the cook, got her supplies, and nearly ran to her cabin. She followed his direction and tied herself into her bunk. The wind growled, the sea churned, and Cathy prayed. Before the afternoon was gone Cathy noticed that the floor was rising and falling with some regularity and occasionally the craft shuddered as if in complaint. The noise was what terrified her. The wind whined and whistled, with an occasional roar that sent her head under her blanket. A dozen times she was positive the creaks and groans announced the end.

Darkness fell and Cathy crawled out of her bunk to attempt a bite to eat, but as soon as she put her feet on the floor and attempted to stand, the ship pitched forward. After another attempt and a corresponding jerk backwards, Cathy grabbed at some fruit and crawled back to the bunk. She never imagined something this bad and for a moment her thoughts turned to the captain, James, and

110

the sailors she'd met over the last weeks. She wondered if any of the men on board had already been gobbled up by the angry sea. She tried to push the thoughts away. Once more, between bites, she muttered the prayers of childhood.

She was much too frightened to sleep, she told herself as she listened to more groans and creaks. Would this ship become her coffin? She fought an overwhelming urge to open her door and crawl, if she had to, to the deck. At least on deck she had a chance for survival.

The night grew longer, the darkness deeper, and Cathy listened to the crack of wood, the screams of the wind, and the roar of the sea. Still, she prayed. At any instant she expected the ship to turn, end over end, finishing them all. As the hours crawled by, Cathy tried to squash her terror, but the louder the noise, the more frightened she became. She envisioned the worst. What if all of the men had been swept overboard and she was the only one remaining? What if only one or two men clung to ropes only to die, waiting for her to come to their aid?

Part of her terror concerned the captain's fate. For a moment she let herself honestly appraise Andrew Michael Sloan. She liked him, he was special to her, even if she could never admit it to him. Thoughts of her lack of honesty brought her brothers to mind. They would never know what happened to her. Oh, they would mourn her disappearance and so would her father, and it was her fault. Her selfishness had deemed it so. She wiped a tear from her eye and remembered some of the happy times from her past. This was it, she thought. Before you die, your past comes back to haunt you. Now she was reliving hers so it could only mean she was going to die. She sagged against her binding, her body tense, her breathing shallow, waiting, waiting. . . .

She awoke with a start. Surely, in the midst of the storm, she had not fallen asleep. The gray light shining through the porthole told her it was at least morning. What had the dawn brought? The vessel churned up and down, and once again, her body trembled in terror. Cathy glanced around and took comfort in the fact that she was alive. How long, though, were they going to be trapped in the viciousness of the storm. "Let it go away soon," she mumbled to herself.

Once again she managed to eat her fruit and take a drink of almost tepid water. Could she afford to sprinkle some on her face? Or would the storm prevent her from refilling her bottle? Of course, if the cook wasn't in the small kitchen space to help her fill it up . . . She let the thought drift away. Shudders of fear consumed her. The thought that she was all alone on this vessel came back to haunt her and she jerked around and again fled to the bunk, her hot tears scouring a path down her face. Nothing in her training prepared her emotionally to handle this kind of trauma.

"At least," she muttered, "the noises have died down a little." She crawled back against the bulkhead and closed her eyes, willing the tears to stop. A knock at her door stunned her. She wasn't alone! She swiped at her face. "Yes, I'm coming. I'm getting out of the bunk. I'll be right there." She didn't want whoever was at the door to leave. Oh, no, please God, don't let them leave.

She threw the door open to face Drew Sloan. "I wanted to make certain you were all right," he said above the howl of the wind.

"How much longer," she shouted, "will this last?"

"Another couple of hours," he yelled back. "I'll be

back to check on you when things are better. Stay in your bunk."

She nodded at the closing door. At least, she thought with a grateful smile, she wasn't alone. Just then she heard a crack, followed by a crunch, and she dove for her bunk. Once again tears flowed unchecked. "I'll never live through this," she muttered into her hands. She sank into the thin mattress and began her prayers: calm seas, or if it had to be, a swift death.

Chapter Eight

An hour or perhaps two passed and once more she crawled out of her bunk to investigate a banging at the wooden portal. This time it was James, and he came bringing fruit and a fresh jug of water. He even held a small tin of biscuits. She watched him as he stood in the doorway, his legs spread far apart, balancing himself against the door frame. "You're not sick, are you?" he said. "Sometimes a body can waste away to nothing with seasickness."

She shook her head. "I don't get sick."

James grinned. "Good. You'll be all right. Drew says the glass has started to move. This will be over soon."

"Thank goodness," she muttered and thanked James for coming. Her knees were weak with relief. It would be over soon. After she stored the extras, she sat on her bunk and ate some of the fruit and one of the biscuits. She drank her fill of water and even used a tiny amount to splash against her face. She prepared to wait for the slacking of the storm.

The minutes drew into hours and she was positive that

she had been on her bunk for at least the entire morning and a good part of the afternoon. The wind, a dark memory before James came, again howled through the cracks in the boat. The waves seemed to change directions continually and the boat now rocked from side to side while it moved up and down. There were several times when she wished James had not mentioned getting sick, for her stomach was not in the best condition. She nibbled at the biscuit, sipped her water, and was more than a trifle glad when nothing further developed with her stomach.

Slowly, it dawned on her that the weather was worse, not better and her fear turned into panic. Suddenly, it wasn't her stomach she was worried about, not with the boat swinging from side to side and the angle of the floor changing every second. This storm wasn't going to end and piece by piece, she could hear the vessel beginning to split apart. Once again she faced the idea of her death. She didn't want to die. She wanted to live to tell her father that she was sorry, and that she loved him, even if he didn't love her. And her brothers . . . She could no longer still the racking sobs that rose in her throat.

Slowly, as her sobs turned into a drizzle of tears, the room grew dark with the night and she knew that she could not live through another twenty-four hours of this storm. Her mind made up, she pulled herself out of the bunk and crawled to the door, weaving from right to left. She aimed for the exit, but twice she was thrown against her bunk. Finally, she lunged toward the wall that offered passage, but her grasping fingers missed the doorknob and she crumpled against the chest. She pulled herself up into a crouched stance and gave in to her panic. Her cry of frustration drowned out the sound of the party on the other side of the door asking for admittance.

She sobbed in relief when the door swung open and she started through the opening with only escape in mind. Drew stopped her and pushed her back into the room. "Here, what are you doing? You can't go on deck, it's not safe up there. The storm's picked up a bit and I don't want to lose you."

Cathy's teeth started to chatter and she grabbed onto his waist, holding on as if their flesh and cloth had been fused together. Her voice was strained and she begged without a thought, "Please, don't leave me. Please, don't go. You can't leave me. I don't want to die alone."

He stared down at her pale white face. "Cathy, you aren't going to die. None of us are going to die, not from this storm." He couldn't believe the flood of strange emotions that flowed over him. He wanted to protect this girl, keep her from hurt, still her fears. He had no explanation for his desires and for a second he wondered if the moon of several nights ago had produced the lunacy that some suspected it caused.

She didn't hear his words. "Please don't go, I want to die with someone. Not by myself, please, not by myself."

He shook her a bit. "No one's going to die. Not while I'm captain. Cathy, did you hear me? No one's going to die."

She looked up at him, her desire to believe him almost a living, breathing thing between them. Her lips parted but not a single sound slipped past and Drew wondered if she were in shock. Damn, he should have insisted that James stay with her when he brought her the fruit and water. He set her aside for a second and closed the door.

117

He gave her room a quick glance and decided upon his course of action. Despite the weather, he kindled a tiny lantern, one that would not burn up his ship and then he pulled her back into his arms. She was cold, so very cold, and she needed his warmth. He ran his hands briskly up and down her arms, all the time watching her face, staring into her eyes, eyes that reminded him of the frightened eyes of a small bird he'd captured as a boy. He couldn't leave her, not like this, and his hands began to trace the flesh of her arms in a warming caress.

He lost himself to the fragrance that drifted up from her hair to tease his nostrils. Wild flowers, sweet, spring flowers touched a chord of memory and he wondered if it was her soap. He nestled her against him, and strong feelings of possession grabbed at him. This girl was his. He had met her in London, been teased by her, and then when he thought she was gone from his life forever, the fates had handed her back to him. She was his, all his, for now, next month, forever.

He chuckled as a thought bounced through his head. His mother was going to be very pleased. She had wanted him attached for years. Other ideas rattled through the cobwebs of thoughts. She was to have been engaged, but rumor said that she was cold, unfeeling. How could the public judge her unfeeling when she was clinging to him in almost wanton abandonment.

Shocked, Drew realized that his tired brain had already registered her position before he consciously made the discovery. Could she be as jaded as he first thought? A spark of decency claimed that she was an innocent. She was his, she needed him, and he would warm her, love her, make her completely his. He lowered his lips. . . .

118

She relaxed against him, and when his lips touched her, she gave herself into his care. She gave no thought to her position in his arms, or what his large, warm hands were doing to her. In fact, thought wasn't possible. He was there. It was enough. She felt the cold for a second and then he wrapped a blanket around her and tucked her into the bunk. Drew was beside her. It was all right.

Drew felt her surrender and quickly he pulled the buttons from their tiny holes. Carefully, his hands eased her dress from her shoulders but through it all his lips never lost contact with hers. He grabbed the blanket from the bunk behind her and wrapped her chilled form in the warm wool. While he pressed a series of tiny breathless nibbles across her forehead, her eyelids, her nose, he lifted her into his arms and gently placed her on the bunk. With quick confidence, he stripped off his shirt and breeches and joined her.

He gathered her into his arms and with a tight rein on his escalating passion, he pressed his lips to hers again. He whispered against her mouth, "Open, sweet Cathy," and her lips parted enough so that he could taste the flavor that was Cathy. Her breath caught, but he continued his exploration, suggesting with light nips and torrid tongue play that she participate. When she brought her tongue into the game, he cringed from his craving and denied his desire. Not yet, his tired brain reasoned.

Cathy was startled when he asked her to open. She intended to ask him what he meant, but his tongue gave the answer. At first she couldn't believe the emotions that boiled down her spine. Never had she been kissed like this, and in a million years, she never could have believed that a kiss could bring about such feelings. The need to do to him the things he was doing to her rose inside her and she found herself imitating the motions of his tongue. She wanted to smile at the quick breath that jarred her breasts.

Those breasts were heavy and hot and she could feel the nipples contract against the wool of the blanket. The tiny part of her mind that could think and reason wondered what it would feel like if he touched her there. As if the thought brought the action, she felt his fingers spread the blanket and stroke the underside of her breast. Why didn't he move his fingers up to the nipple, she wanted to ask, but he heard the thought even though the words had never slipped past her mouth. Suddenly, tiny bursts of fire were traveling from the tips of her breasts to her whole body and she could not still the moan of pleasure that gushed from her.

She twisted and turned against him, dragging the blanket from around her body. The sensation of flesh touching flesh seared her soft body and she realized that no clothing covered his limbs. It didn't matter, nothing mattered, except that he stay with her.

She felt his hands graze her ribs and move across her stomach and she gloried in his touch. She wondered if she should return the touches, and she lifted her arms and let her hands slide over his shoulders, down his chest, and his waist, pulling him tighter to her.

It seemed to be some kind of signal, for he lifted himself above her, forcing her knees apart, and she whimpered, "No, don't go."

"No, sweet angel, I am not going to leave you," he

whispered back, his voice vibrant with longing.

Slowly he sank down until he surrounded her and she felt a stabbing at her secret place. In that instant, her mind cleared of the drug of passion and she heaved against him, the word of negation on her tongue, "NO!"

The pain was sharp, a ripping sensation, and she caught her breath at its intensity. As quickly as it came, it began to fade and she opened her eyes to look at the man above her.

He looked sick and her heart went out to him. The whispered words were so soft she barely heard them. "I'm sorry. I got carried away. It's too late now. Let me take away the hurt, Cathy. Let me pleasure you."

She could say nothing. The look on his face said much more than mere words could ever say. She lifted her arms encircling his neck and pulled him close. Somehow she knew she was giving him permission to continue. Slowly he moved back and then forward and he hesitated. She writhed under him, wanting to say without saying that it was all right. Their minds seemed to be able to communicate without words for he sighed and moved again. As if she had always known the rhythm, she moved against him and his breath caught. "Yes," he whispered as he lowered his head to take her lips.

With each stroke of his flesh, she moved up a staircase of rapture and suddenly, she felt as if she were going to explode. She sought the experience, begged for it, threw herself at him, pleading, "Oh, please, please."

Then it came, a thread of ecstasy that pulled away from the whole and then another and another, until she was pulsing with it. Somewhere above her, she heard a moan of pleasure and she knew that Drew felt what she had.

121

She drifted off into a soft warm place.

For how long she drifted, she wasn't sure, but she felt warm arms surrounding her. She turned slightly and opened her eyes. Drew was looking down at her, his thoughts and fears written into every wrinkle in his frown. "Are you all right?" he said. "I didn't mean to hurt you. You got ahead of me."

For a second she couldn't imagine what he was referring to and then she remembered the prick of pain and her reaction to it. "You didn't hurt me much, but—"

Drew kissed her lips to silence her. "This changes things. We'll get married in Philadelphia and—"

She gasped. "No!" Her mind was rolling in turmoil, almost as much as the ship under her. "We can't marry. My father . . . my family . . ." She remembered her role. "I don't know who I am."

Drew growled at her, "I know who you are and you are mine."

"No, you don't understand," she tried to explain, but Drew was not going to listen. He threw himself from the bed and drew himself up to his full naked height, and Cathy shuddered. This man was not going to listen to a thing she had to say. She watched as he jerked on his breeches and jammed his arms into his shirt.

He started for the door. "Get dressed. I'm sending James down to stay with you. I don't want to hear anything more about it. We will be married when we get to the United States."

As he slammed out the door, Cathy yelled, "I won't marry you. You can't make me." She sat and twisted her hands.

Suddenly, she remembered that Drew said James was

coming and she jumped down from the bunk and grabbed at her clothes. In seconds she was dressed. She reached for the woolen blanket that Drew had wrapped around her and her eyes flew to the dark stain in the middle. She felt a sudden heat and knew that her face was as stained as the blanket. With more energy than she thought she could muster, she grabbed the blanket and twisted it into a ball and threw it into the corner.

All at once, she realized she was no longer a maiden. She had just given herself to a man who was almost a stranger. She gave him the one thing that she herself could give a husband. She started to shake. What had she done? She sank down on the bunk to await James Rupert. Would it show, the behavior she had allowed? Would he know by just looking at her that she was a . . . a . . . a soiled dove?

She waited for the better part of an hour, aware that the intensity of the storm was gone. The ship still rose and dove back into the sea, but most of the side movement had disappeared. A sharp rap on the door drew a quick, "Come in," from Cathy and she braced herself for James's condemnation. Instead, he looked embarrassed.

"Cathy, I . . ." James stood at the door.

Cathy was almost as embarrassed. "James, come in."

James strode into the room and looked around for some place to sit. The only spot in the room was the bunk. He looked at Cathy, his uncertainty clear in his eyes.

She patted the mattress and hoisted herself up to the bunk. "Here, join me on the bunk. Drew said you were going to keep me company."

"I have another assignment as well. Cathy, please

don't feel embarrassed, but Drew told me. . . . That is, he . . . Oh, hell!''

Cathy blushed a deep scarlet. "He didn't!" she gasped.

James nodded his head, his own discomfort plain. "He told me that you won't marry him."

Cathy tried to speak her piece, but at the moment her voice would not cooperate.

James frowned. "Cathy, please, I'm not going to judge either one of you. The sparks between you two I saw days ago. I knew this was coming. I feel partly responsible. After all, I know Drew and I also know what a storm of this intensity can do to a man, even a good man, and Cathy, Drew is a good man. You'll have to let me shoulder a large part of the blame. I should have insisted that I stay with you for the worst part of the storm. Then you wouldn't have been so frightened and succumbed so easily."

Cathy looked at the man sitting next to her and her anger at him and the man who served as captain became a tangible thing. She snarled, "He told you the whole of it, didn't he? Didn't spare a single detail, did he?"

"Cathy, his words were that he seduced you and he wants to marry you."

"No! I have no intention of marrying Captain Sloan, or anyone else for that matter." She glared at James.

James frowned. "I know. Drew says that I'm to tell you that we know who you are. You don't have to worry about that, but, somehow, I think that you're not worried about that at all. Are you? In any case, Drew will be sending word to your father when we dock."

Cathy turned ashen. "Oh, no, James, he can't. I can't let him send word to my father. Please, you must help

124

me." Cathy wondered if she could think fast enough to come up with a plausible tale. No. She wanted James for her friend. She had to be honest with him at least. She sighed. Well, she would try to be honest. Slowly, Cathy told James about the consequences of the betrothal ball, her arrival in Barbados, and Nelson Goodspeed. She turned back to the subject at hand. "I can't marry Drew. I shouldn't have let him seduce me, but I still can't marry him."

"My God, girl, why not?" James scratched his head.

"It's not Drew, but the country he's from," Cathy stated quietly.

James felt a rip in the general area of his heart. "What do you mean, it's the country he's from?"

Cathy hesitated, then whispered, "My father had a younger brother. Charles and my father were very close. And, yes, my brother is named for him. But my father's brother was a second son so he had to make his own way. Charles bought a commission and became a captain in the British Navy. My father said that he liked the navy. My mother talked about him and how proud he was of his ship. Charles sailed away to America in 1812. He was in the battle of Erie. He didn't come back.

"My father never got over it. I think somehow he blamed himself. If he had shared the estate, then Charles wouldn't have gone to the United States and he would still be alive today. Because of his brother, my father doesn't like what he calls 'barbarians.' In fact, he comes close to hating Americans."

James groaned. "Cathy, there's something you don't know. Amelia, your cousin, your companion, whatever you call her, well, she and I are very close. Closer than friends. I've asked her to be my wife."

Cathy patted his hand. "Poor James. What did Amelia say? Was she for your suit?" Cathy mumbled to herself, "How could she be when she knows how Father feels?"

"Cathy, she didn't discourage me. In fact, she didn't mention your Uncle Charles. Does she know how deeply your father's feelings run?"

Cathy nodded and James scratched his head. "Then Amelia must love me, because she didn't say no!"

"James, you'll have to talk Andrew out of trying to marry me. My father will never let me wed an American. And, please, you can't tell him I've regained my memory. He'll send me back to Nelson." James agreed only to see what he could do with Andrew, and five days after they sailed through the storm, he took Cathy back to her cabin, to check her head he told Drew.

"Cathy," James whispered once they were in the cabin, "Drew has agreed to wait until Savannah before the wedding. That's the best I can do. He knows that things are coming back to you, and I told him that you remembered being a stowaway because you were being forced to marry, but that's all. I'm going to try to get him to wait until he's received word from your father, but I can't promise."

Cathy nodded her head solemnly. "Will you be taking me to the doctor in Philadelphia?"

James laughed. "I don't see how we can get out of it. If we're lucky, Drew will be involved with the cargo, and he'll be stuck here on the ship."

"And if we're not lucky?" Cathy raised her gray eyes and grinned at her friend. James gave her no answer. She followed him back up to the forward deck, her mind busy with the red-haired man before her. James Rupert was a marvelous man. He would make Amelia a wonderful husband. Cathy wondered what she could do to get her father to change his mind about Americans, for Amelia's sake, of course. Philadelphia, Cathy thought, here we come.

Chapter Nine

Cathy stood at the railing of the ship and gazed out over the city of Philadelphia. She felt as if she were returning home. For the last five days James had been describing the city to her in every detail during their long morning walks on the deck of the ship. She knew about the buildings and the way the city was laid out, where the homes were in relation to the Delaware River, and the trouble that'd been wrought along the Schuylkill River banks when the dam was built eight years before. He even gave her history lessons on the city and told her about the government that began there.

Because the subject of America and her cities were forbidden to her at home, she found everything he told her fascinating. However, she was not prepared for the vitality that the city presented. The buildings were almost new and the whole city seemed much cleaner than London, but the biggest difference was the rushing population and the satisfaction they seemed to have in moving in their chosen direction.

As she waited for the gangplank to be lowered and

James to escort her from the ship, she thought about the freedom these people claimed. That in itself must be the reason for the vitality she saw. She brought her thoughts back to the problem at hand. The doctor! James was taking her to the Penn House on Walnut Street, a block from St. Joseph's Church. He would obtain rooms for Drew and Cathy and himself and the very next day Drew requested that he take her to the doctor who had offices on 7th Street. Drew excused himself from accompanying them saying that he was much too busy with the unloading and reloading of the ship to take the time to see to Cathy. James and Cathy smiled at each other in conspiracy. They would see a doctor, but Cathy would not be the patient.

"I'll join you for dinner tomorrow evening, if everything goes well," Drew said as he passed Cathy into James's care. Cathy, her arm resting on the doctor's forearm, started down the street. She didn't look back to see the dark scowl on the face of the man she left behind.

The next afternoon, James and Cathy left the inn to pay a courtesy visit on his former teacher. Cathy remembered her delight when James explained that Philadelphia was where he attended school. The professor was more than cordial and his servant came offering tea as Cathy made herself comfortable on a dusty sofa. In a matter of minutes, the conversation turned to medicine. Cathy listened to the two educated men talking about gory details and she was fascinated. "You have more than adequate help, I see," Dr. Hoover smiled, inclining his head in Cathy's direction. James returned his smile. "I think she will make an admirable assistant."

After tea they took their leave, and Cathy confronted James. "I found the discussion intriguing. I think I'd like to help you."

James looked a little startled. "Well, if I ever need help . . ." His voice faded as they walked.

Cathy pressed her point. "James, I want you to promise me that the first chance you get, I get to help. I think medicine is—is, well, stimulating."

He jerked his head. "Until someone bleeds on you, or worse."

"Just wait and see. But you have to promise!"

James laughed at her enthusiasm. "All right, I promise."

Drew was waiting for them at the inn and James went into a long dissertation about the doctor's findings, and finally Drew cut him short. "Tell me the whole of it in a few words, Doctor."

"Time. What she needs is time. No permanent damage, nothing except time. This kind of thing happens once in a while. She should recover."

Drew looked puzzled. "Her family?"

"The doctor says to wait a bit more." James threw Cathy a look. He didn't like hoodwinking his friend, but he agreed with Cathy. There was a strong chance that William Pentworth would come with sword drawn for Drew, and James as well. Until Cathy figured out how to approach her father at least about Amelia, then James was for leaving well enough alone. They had only been gone from Barbados for three and a half weeks. Word that Cathy was missing from her brothers' homes probably wouldn't reach William Pentworth in England for another three weeks at best and James doubted that anything could be done for at least four months. They were safe for a time.

He thought about his conversations with Drew over

the last several days. Just trying to deal with the man about Cathy had not been easy. James still wasn't certain why Drew changed his mind, but he had agreed to wait to speak the vows until they got to Savannah. James counted on Cathy to come up with something before they arrived in that fair city. She'd have a week, perhaps as much as ten days before they sailed up the Savannah River and by then . . .

After Drew left to go back to the ship and Cathy stomped off to bed at the inn, James drew up a comfortable chair before a small fire and enjoyed a cup of Irish coffee. The October night held a chill and he gathered warmth from his drink. He let his thoughts drift to his best friend and what the man was going through with the beautiful woman with the complexion like sweet cream. Poor Drew! He chuckled to himself. Drew would be livid if he knew how James pitied him.

The day after the seduction, James explained part of his conversation with Cathy, the part Cathy and James agreed on, to Drew. The tall bear of a man looked at his red-haired friend in confusion. "I thought all women wanted to marry," he said.

"She may want to marry, but not until she knows who she is," James offered quietly.

Drew had been confused for two days and then he got angry. James could see it coming and whenever he or Cathy got too close to the man in question, Drew lashed out with venom. In fact, in the one and twenty years that James had known Andrew Sloan, he had never seen him so nasty. Drew was fun-loving, easy-going, always quick to laugh at himself and others. The one thing that Catherine Elizabeth Pentworth had done was rob him of his sense of humor. James straightened in his chair and finished the coffee. If Drew couldn't laugh, the trip from Philadelphia to Savannah was going to be decidedly boring.

On Friday, the trip from Philadelphia to Savannah began, and Drew was in no better humor than he had been while they were in port. When James saw the hot, anxious looks that Drew gave Cathy when he thought no one was watching, he finally understood. "Poor devil," James said into the wind. Andrew Sloan was in love and lusting after the girl standing on the bridge, and there was nothing the captain could do about it. "This voyage may be damned uncomfortable," James muttered.

James's words were nearly prophetic. They headed south, on open sea, with a brisk wind from the northwest. James thought that they were making good time. The seas were a bit rough, but certainly nothing compared with the storm outside of Jamaica.

That afternoon, while Drew was in his cabin working on his charts, a sharp, cracking noise pulled the attention of those on deck to the masts of the ship. Cathy had been sitting on a coil of rope at the bow of the ship, James sitting not five feet from her reading a medical journal. Above the wind a splintering sound was followed by a thud and the scream of some poor devil trapped under the wood and sail.

Cathy moved first, but James's legs were longer and he reached the tangle of oak and poplin before her. The anguished cries of the two men under the wood were awful to the ears and he pushed her back toward the stairs. "You promised," she screamed over the noise of the men. "I can help, I know I can. You promised!"

"All right," he snapped, not taking the time to argue. If she wanted to lose her lunch that was her problem.

133

"But understand this. These men are my first priority. If you faint, I'll leave you where you fall. Now, if you want to help, get below and tell the cook we need scalding hot water and lye soap! Wash your hands with the soap and have it ready for me."

Cathy swallowed the lump in her throat and ran for the back stairs. As she disappeared below the main deck, Drew was coming up the forward hatch. "Dear God," he whispered. He looked around for his second in command. "What's going on?"

Samuel rushed forward. "My guess is that the storm weakened one of the spars and the damage didn't show. I sent Wilson and Ivers up to tie the sail. Ivers is in that mess. Johanson's missin' and Wilson is still up there." Drew leaned back to look up at the man hanging from the rigging on the third spar. Samuel continued, "Ain't gonna come down. He's froze. I better go get him."

Drew put his hand on the man's arm. "I'll go."

Samuel looked up at his captain. "No tellin' if the other spars is bad. I'll get him."

Drew shook his head and answered, his tone firm, "It's the captain's job." It took almost an hour before Drew led the frightened man to the deck. By that time James and Cathy were finished with the two men who had been injured. It wasn't until dinner that evening that Drew found out that while he was in the rigging helping Wilson, Cathy was getting her first taste of surgery.

James smiled across at his brand new, slightly nauseated nurse. She had done a remarkable job and James was proud of her. Ivers had fallen with the rigging and some of the sail had cushioned his fall. He had a broken arm and lots of scrapes and bruises, but he wasn't hurt badly.

It was Johanson who was the worry. The tall, thin boy from the frontier didn't want to be a farmer. He'd become a sailor, and now he'd gotten caught by the falling wood. James wasn't sure how much internal damage there was. Cathy and the lad had spent several afternoons talking about the frontiers of America and James knew how hard it was to treat a friend. She had done a wonderful job.

"Cathy, would you want to lie down a bit before supper?" James asked softly.

She shook her head, not sure she could speak yet. Setting Ivers's broken arm wasn't too bad, but helping bind Johanson's ribs and wiping the bloody spittle from his lips had been harder than she thought. James was optimistic about the boy's chances, but Johanson wasn't through the woods by a long way. She looked at the two groaning men wrapped in fresh sheets. "I think I'll stay here for a bit, in case they need something," she said.

James chuckled. "No, I'll stay. You go topside and take some air. I promise I'll call you if there's a change. And Cathy," James smiled encouragingly, "you did a fine job. I couldn't have handled them both as easily without you. If you want, I'll let you help with some of the work in Savannah."

She flushed under the compliment and ducked her head in embarrassment. She did find medicine fascinating, and although the blood bothered her a bit, she wanted to assist. "If I can help . . ."

"You can," James assured her.

By dinner, Cathy's flawless complexion was once again a soft ivory. Now, even to the casual eye, there was a touch of bronze to her skin that came from her insisting that her hair was covering enough when she was on deck. She had been to sick bay and James told her that both

135

men were doing well. In fact, he felt certain that young Johanson would come out of it fine.

Dinner was quiet, but not unpleasant, until Drew asked James about his patients. Cathy scowled at him. "They're not James's patients. They're our patients."

Drew raised his eyebrows in shock. "Our patients? James?"

"Well, Drew, it's a long story. Perhaps it should wait until after supper."

Cathy bristled. "It's not that complicated, James. I made the doctor promise that when he had a medical emergency I be allowed to help. I assisted him today and he said I did fine."

"James!" Drew's deep voice vibrated through the room. "She's a woman."

"And a damn fine example," James added. Instinctively, he knew he'd said the wrong thing.

"Escort her to her cabin and then come back here. My God, she's a woman. Women don't do doctoring."

Cathy stood up, her fists clenched at her sides. "In England, the lady of the manor saw to all of the serfs' ailments."

"How would you know?" Drew snapped. James tried to conceal his smile, but before he could get himself under control, Cathy jumped up from the table, exited the room, and slammed the door shut with enough force to rattle the instruments on the wall of Drew's cabin.

"Damn," Drew muttered and dropped his head into his hands.

James scurried after Cathy to make certain she went to her cabin. By the time he made it to her side, she was opening her cabin door. He whispered, the laughter almost making gibberish out of his words, "You're a liar,

Catherine Pentworth, and one of these days you're going to get caught."

Cathy insisted that she work in sick bay. The louder Drew protested, the more Cathy insisted. She spent long hours with the two sick men for the next two days. On the third day, Drew nearly put his foot through the deck. "I don't care what she wants. Ladies, at least ladies on my ships, don't tend to injured sailors. It isn't seemly. If I find her down in sick bay again, I'll lock her and you in your cabins. Then what will the men do? Answer me that!"

So, Cathy was banished from the sick bay and she pouted and paced the bow of the ship. Drew grew angrier and more sullen by the minute as he paced the deck, the wheelhouse, or nearly any place but the bow. His men moved about the ship on tiptoes and James refused to come out of sick bay at all. The doctor thought about his comments at the beginning of the trip. Unfortunately, he'd been correct in his assumption that this voyage would be troublesome. But even he hadn't expected this much trouble.

To make matters worse, most of the coast was experiencing a mild, pleasant Indian summer and the winds were so faint they could hardly be called breezes. It was going to take all of ten days to get to Savannah. By the sixth day at sea, James refused to eat any meals with Drew. On the eighth day, Drew sent a tersely worded invitation to Cathy. James got the same invitation, but refused to acknowledge it. Cathy, however, read it carefully and decided that she had no choice. The master of the ship was demanding that she come for the evening meal. And, to be perfectly honest about it, she was tired of eating alone.

She dressed carefully in her only good dress. She tried to fashion her tresses into coils above her ears, but she wasn't terribly successful. When she decided that she was presentable, she started for Drew's cabin.

The cabin boy seated her at a lavish place setting, explaining that the captain was seeing to his other dinner guests. Cathy looked at the four place settings and relaxed. At least she wasn't going to be alone with the monster man, a name she gave him four days ago when he was berating the cook for his pancakes. Cathy thought about the incident and the pancakes. She thought the cook had done very well, considering that the man had no milk to use in the batter.

She thought of other occasions where Drew had allowed his anger to flare, as she waited for him. Several minutes later, he came through the door, his expression glum. The cabin boy stood at attention and Drew pulled at his chair and nodded to the boy. In seconds the lad closed the door behind him.

Hesitantly, Cathy looked at the table and then at Drew. "Sir, where are your other guests?"

"They're not coming," he said softly, "but, please, don't go. I don't think I could stand to eat alone tonight."

Drew wasn't eating alone but he might as well have been, for Cathy said nothing through the first three courses. The only sound in the quiet cabin was the tinkle of cutlery against china.

After the main course was finished, Drew pulled his chair away from the table and looked at the young woman across from him. "I owe you an apology. I owe James an apology. In fact, I owe the whole damn crew an apology."

Cathy stared at him, afraid to comment. What on earth was he going to apologize for?

Drew tried to clear his throat. In an arrogant tone, he said, "I'll start with you. I apologize!"

"For what exactly, sir, are you apologizing?" Cathy was incensed with his tone and attitude.

For a second he looked befuddled, then as Cathy watched, his hazel eyes grew dark and she read his anger. "I have behaved like an idiot, but it's all your fault."

"My fault?! Why you overgrown boy! I did not make you behave like an ass. That was your idea." She stood. "You've made my life hell, you have destroyed any prospect for a decent offer of marriage, and y—you . . ." She brushed at the tears that appeared out of nowhere and whispered, "Your behavior is not my fault."

Drew was at her side. "Ah, but you are at fault. Cathy, don't you know anything about men? I want you so badly, I ache with it. That's what has ruined me. Besides, I *have* made a decent offer of marriage. We will be married when we get to Savannah."

"No, we can't." She longed to tell him that she could never marry him, even if she wanted to. She froze next to the dining table. Did she want to marry him? "Yes, yes," her brain screamed. "He is the kind of man you have been looking for. You love him just the way your mother loved your father." She shook her head, denying the thoughts. No, she couldn't love him. She didn't know anything about him and he was a monster of a man, tender one moment and cruel the next. She couldn't love him.

She gave him another quick glance and leaped toward the door. As Drew grabbed for her, the door opened and the cabin boy stood in the opening, his tray in his hand.

Drew reached over Cathy's head and pushed the door shut. "See to it in the morning," he said to the boy.

He grabbed Cathy's arm and dragged her around the small table, and when he could get both his hands around her arms, he pulled her against him. In slow motion, he lowered his head until his soft breath caressed her lips. "We'll have a good marriage, Cathy. I'm a man of substance. You'll want for nothing."

She tried to shake her head, but his hand moved up to cradle the back of her neck and his lips moved the fraction of an inch necessary to touch her lips. It was a soft brush, a touch of longing, and Cathy's sob caught in her throat. Without a thought, her arms slid up the front of his shirt, across his shoulders, and around his neck. Unconsciously, her fingers twirled through curls that hung below his collar. As his lips brushed hers once more, she yielded, melting against him. She could feel his heart throbbing against her breast. The beat echoed through her head. Admit it, she told herself and she gave in sighing against his lips. Oh, how she loved this man.

Drew sensed her surrender and with a brain fogged with desire, he lifted her into his arms and cradled her gently. Carefully, he moved to his feather bed, and laid her down. "I want you," he whispered against her lips. As he nibbled with his teeth and stroked with his tongue, his fingers were busy with the tiny pearl buttons that closed the front of her gown. His fingers worked against her flesh and he kneaded and petted the fabric covering her breast. He gloried in the full swell that heaved with each breath. While he plied her lips, his fingers maneuvered under her chemise to one of her tiny nubbins.

Gently, he teased it, felt it peak, and suddenly nothing

140

else would do. He raised her and stripped the chemise away from her nipple. As he eased her back to the bed, he found his way to the hill of flesh. Before she was flat against the feathers, his tongue was working the nipple into an engorged mass of nerves, and enjoying the writhing of the woman under him.

Cathy was on fire. Never had anything felt so good. Pleasure encircled her breast and ran in spirals down her arms, across her chest, into her stomach. She heard moaning, never recognizing the sounds as her own.

Drew heard and rejoiced. She was his. He released one breast, only to pay the same homage to the other breast and nipple, using his hands to free her from the rest of her dress, petticoats, and her pantalets. With dexterity born of necessity, Drew was out of his clothes only seconds after hers had been discarded. He drew her under him, holding his weight above her.

He turned his attention to her face, her lips, her cheeks. He followed the line of her jaw to her ear, and nibbled on her sensitive lobe, chanting words of want, desire, and emotion. Gently, he separated her knees and sank into the feathers letting her feel the weight of his desire as it throbbed against her thigh. "Now, sweetheart. I want you now," he whispered, his voice so husky with desire that Cathy sensed rather than understood what he was telling her.

Drew prayed for control as he slowly slipped into the moist tunnel of love that awaited his quivering strokes. Advance, retreat, advance, retreat, and his world was ecstasy. He opened his eyes to stare into Cathy's. "I . . . I . . . can't . . . stop," he shuddered and closed his eyes.

Her hands crept around his neck and she held on to him as the only source of reality in her universe. Every

141

part of her was tingling and she remembered the exquisite pleasure that had occurred only once before. Could it happen to her a second time? She never expected to feel such a thing again, but it was happening. It was happening now. She pulled him tight against her as the bundle of stars deep in her was set free to guide her up into the sphere above the world.

Some instinct told him that she was with him and he felt her breath hissing against his shoulder. He held her and felt the tremors course through her body. How he loved her! Slowly, his world righted itself, and the thought registered. He tensed, wanting to deny the idea. He groaned and rolled away from her, his arm across his forehead. He did love her, and that was what the last two weeks had been about. Somewhere deep in his conscience he was fighting the knowledge, knowing somehow that he was caught up in something strange and new.

He pulled Cathy into his arms and opened his eyes. His husky voice whispered in the darkness, "What we have together is enough. We'll be married by Friday."

She could not deny him. What they had was incredible. She wondered if other couples experienced such total consumption with their lovemaking. Somehow, she couldn't picture Phillip and Martha enjoying this kind of excitement, but her father and his two wives, oh, yes. This had to be what they had and why her father was more than willing to make no more attempts to find it again. If she could talk to her father, she could convince him that she and Drew shared the same feelings that he had shared with his wives. In Andrew's arms, she dozed off wondering what the man beside her would say when she told him that she was in love with him.

Andrew snuggled up to Cathy and smiled against her

hair. She was a feisty thing, and his life would never be boring with her. In time, she would grow to love him, of that he was sure. He wondered what she would say when he told her that he was in love with her. He squeezed his eyes shut and enfolded her a little more tightly in his grasp. Oh, God, how he loved her.

Chapter Ten

Ever so slowly, Cathy felt the pull of reality invade the dark, pleasant world of her dreams. She stretched, raising her arms above her head. The events of the night before played back in her mind. She wiggled into the mattress in contentment and in that instant she knew she slept on her own uncomfortable, thin straw mattress, not Drew's feather bed.

She glanced around her room and noticed her clothing folded and placed on the trunk in the corner. Under the scratchy blanket tucked around her she was naked. Sometime during the night, Drew must have carried her and her clothing into the cabin. Shaking her head, she decided that she must have slept very soundly.

The memory of what happened before she fell asleep teased at her conscience and she blushed from her head to her toes. What must he think of her, to allow such liberties? The first time could be excused because she was terrified and an innocent, but this time she had not been afraid and knew exactly what was to happen. He said they would wed by Friday! Now, how on earth could she get away from him so that occurrence not take place? She sobered—did she want to get away from him? With that thought, a tiny part of her heart twisted and she slumped into the bunk. She admitted it, she really did want to marry Drew Sloan. She was in love with him! Her love was no guarantee, though, that a wedding was possible, given her father's feelings toward Americans.

She tensed. There had to be something she could do to make her father change his mind. After all, he wanted her married. He had been trying to get her married for several years. If she refused to marry unless he allowed her to marry Drew, then what? No, that wouldn't work; her father was as stubborn as Cathy. He must agree to the wedding before it occurred. She had one course of action. She threw off the blanket. She would have a conference with James. Whether he wanted to or not, he was going to help her. Somehow Drew must be dissuaded from his planned course of action, and James was the only one on the ship who could dissuade him.

When she climbed the last few steps and glanced around the deck, she spotted Drew in the wheelhouse. Her cheeks flushed pink and she turned toward the railing in embarrassment. Instantly, she noticed the telling position of the sun and she flushed more deeply. Drew didn't have any decency at all, letting her sleep until after ten!

The object of her thoughts stood behind her and his warm breath on the back of her neck produced a vague chill. She remembered his words of the night before and her problems with her father. Before he had a chance to say a word she whispered, "I will not marry you on Friday."

She heard him say, "We'll see." Then he was gone.

She moved away from the railing and toward James and the stairs back to her cabin. As she passed James, she hissed, "Help me. I am NOT marrying him on Friday."

James glanced over at the jealous face of Drew Sloan. The girl asked the impossible, James thought, and turned back to the sea. Well, he'd give it one more try, but with what excuse?

After lunch, James followed Cathy back to the deck. "I need to know one thing. How old are you?"

Cathy frowned. What did her age have to do with Drew's proposal? There was no reason not to answer the question, however. "I'll be one and twenty on January eighteenth."

James smiled slightly. "You have just 'remembered' your birthday." He noticed her glare. "That's the only thing, your birthday. I have an idea."

Cathy shrugged and went to sit on her coil of rope in the bow. Whatever his plan, it was better than the blank she drew about her situation. Besides, she told herself, James had at least as much to lose as she did.

Her father, Amelia, Drew, and James floated through Cathy's head that afternoon. In agony, her head pounding from her worries, she dragged herself back to her cabin. Strange, she thought as she neared her door, neither Drew nor James were on deck.

The reason the men were missing became clear as soon as she lay on her bunk. She could hear them shouting at each other from Drew's cabin across from hers. James must be trying to change Drew's mind, she thought, and she tiptoed to her door. Unashamed, she listened to the argument.

James was speaking. "I tell you, she won't marry without her father's permission."

147

Drew snapped back, "I don't care."

James sounded as if he was trying to be more reasonable. "Have you given thought to an annulment? Drew, she's remembering things. She's sure she's not yet of age, and she's positive that January is her birth month. She thinks her birthday is the eighteenth."

"Yah, like Victoria sounds right."

There was a pause, then James continued, "You don't make any sense."

Drew mumbled something that sounded like "Forget it."

James continued. "If she's not twenty-one yet, her father could have the marriage annulled. I think you better wait. Take the time to court the girl properly."

"It's a little late for that."

Cathy wanted to burst into the room and hit the man. James's comment stopped her. "I know."

Cathy flushed scarlet once again. James had more to say. "That's why I've decided to take you up on your offer. I'll open up my office on your plantation. I have no intention of allowing you to pull Cathy into your bed whenever the mood strikes."

Cathy could imagine Drew's face as soon as she heard his voice. "I made that offer before all of this happened. I should withdraw it."

James laughed. "No, you won't. You're too much of a gentleman. You know I'm right."

Drew laughed also. "Well, I'm not happy about the situation, but I'll wait until January."

Cathy stumbled back to her bunk. Well, that was settled. She wondered if James was correct about her father giving permission for the wedding. It really didn't matter, because with James at the plantation, she'd never have time alone with Drew. She rolled over against the wall, tears gathering in her eyes. A small section of her heart cried, "No!"

The warm lazy days of the Barbados summer faded into the busy days of fall. The stalks of sugar cane waved in the soft breezes as the island began to think of the harvest only three months away. Roselle sat quietly on the veranda of the big house and shared a cup of tea with Martha. The small ball that was Charles's child tightened and rippled as it tried for a comfortable position.

Martha saw the frown of discomfort. "Does the babe bother you overmuch?"

Roselle smiled. "He is very active." At the look of disbelief on Martha's face, she grinned. "Charles says that as much as this babe moves, it must be a boy. I agree. I wish . . ." Her voice trailed off to a whisper.

Martha looked uneasy. "I know. We are all worried about Catherine. If she had only taken the time to talk to us. . . ." Martha's voice died in the breeze. In the quiet that arose, male voices from the study filtered out to the porch, drawing the attention of both women.

Roselle glanced at Martha, her look of disgust as full of censure as her voice. "Those two are so busy blaming Phillip and Charles, they don't realize they are the ones responsible." Martha nodded. For the last four weeks, Charles and Phillip had borne the complaints of both Nelson and Bart. Both men were sure that they could have contained Catherine's wild spirit if either one of them had been given the chance. Martha was ready to scream.

Martha thought back to the morning they discovered

149

that Cathy had fled from Charles's plantation. The frantic scene left Martha so angry at Cathy, that if the girl had shown her face in the week that followed, Martha would probably have spanked her like a child.

At first everyone thought she had gone out for a ride. All but one of the riding horses were munching away at their feed. The missing horse, a small mare that Cathy frequently rode with an escort, had wandered back onto the plantation late that morning, following one of the plantation mules. Charles organized search parties, but when the men returned with no information, fear replaced anger. The girl had disappeared. Phillip suggested violence, but there was no sign. No, for some reason, Cathy had taken off, but where? Over and over the whispered question passed from slave to slave until Bart and Nelson heard. It became their song.

Bart insisted to Charles that by suggesting marriage to Nelson, the brothers forced Cathy to run. He made it clear to Charles and Roselle that he knew the poor girl wasn't interested in Nelson. He was, Bart pointed out softly, too old for her. He, Bart, was the better choice and Cathy knew it. She just didn't want to disappoint her older brother.

Nelson said almost the same thing to Phillip, contending that Bart's personality made him unacceptable, but Cathy obviously didn't want to hurt Charles's feelings.

Nelson didn't stop with telling Phillip, he told Charles, Martha, and even Bart. Phillip admitted that Nelson might have touched on the truth. Martha was more adamant. Cathy had to be found and married off to a man who could control her. Nelson won her vote and she pressured Phillip. He finally agreed, reluctantly, that if

Nelson could find her, he could wed Cathy. Nelson grinned in satisfaction and prepared his ship. However, they still didn't know where to look for the missing girl.

That was at the end of September. Now, with October growing old, Phillip and Charles had just left to travel to another island. Martha and Roselle asked where they were going and what was so very important, but neither man would tell his wife a thing. Bart and Nelson were not made privy to the reason behind the trip, either. Roselle found out that it had something to do with one of Martha's slaves. The woman disappeared the same night as Cathy, but nothing had been done about it, not with everyone so worried about Cathy.

Charles told his wife only that they would be gone for six to eight days. This was the seventh day. Martha turned back to her sister-in-law. "I hope and pray they come home today. I don't believe I can take much more of those two." She pointed her finger at the open window and the room where the two men were arguing. Roselle nodded in perfect accord.

Roselle had moved into Martha's home when Charles left with Phillip and now she needed her afternoon nap. She stretched out on the soft bed, consigning Cathy to a corner of her mind and fell asleep. Her husband's smiling face kissed her awake an hour later. "You're back," Roselle whispered and sighed with pleasure.

Charles nodded. "And with good news. We know that Cathy, under her own power, boarded a ship bound for the United States."

Roselle wiped tears of joy from her eyes. "Thank God. But where did you get the information? Was it the slave you went to see, the one who got away the night Cathy ran? Was she the one who told you? Did you bring her back for punishment?"

Charles grinned. "You're full of questions, aren't you? The *former* slave, Phillip freed her for the information about Cathy, and her man took Cathy out to a ship the night the two of them disappeared. The man and woman sat in the boat and watched until Cathy was safely aboard."

"Safely aboard? Charles, how can you think that Cathy would be safe on board a ship? How can you think such a thing?" Roselle whispered.

"We spent some time in Bridgetown before coming back here," Charles said quietly. "The man who commands the ship Cathy sailed is well thought of. I'm about as certain as I can be that nothing happened to our sister on board that ship. And, thanks to the information we got in Bridgetown, we even know the ship's destination. Nelson is making preparations to sail by this time tomorrow."

Roselle sat up and looked at her husband in surprise. "Nelson is going for her? What about you and Phillip?"

Charles looked a bit embarrassed, Roselle thought, as she swung her feet from the bed. There was more he wasn't telling her. He took her arm, but Roselle tensed. "Tell me all of it."

Charles cleared his throat. "Martha and Phillip told Nelson that he had their support in seeking Cathy's hand. Nelson will bring her back and they will be married before Lent."

Roselle bristled. "What was wrong with Bart? And, pray tell, what will happen if Cathy doesn't want to marry Nelson Goodspeed?"

Charles actually looked surprised. "Why wouldn't she want to marry him? He's quite a catch."

"She probably ran away from both men."

Charles shook his head. "Phillip and I talked about that on the trip home. Phillip thinks, and I agree, that we confused the girl. We're certain that she bolted because she couldn't decide and she knew she would have to pick one of the men. She's a tender-hearted little thing and she didn't want to hurt either man. Phillip and Martha have made the decision for her. Now she can come back and settle into the life of a married woman."

Roselle sat on the edge of the bed, stunned at the masculine logic and the arrogant manner in which Phillip and Charles had arranged Cathy's life. Feminine intuition told Roselle that her husband and his brother had just made the biggest mistake of their lives.

Dinner was quiet that night and after dinner Bart Waverly thanked Martha and Roselle for putting up with him. "I will be leaving tomorrow myself. Nelson will be setting sail for Philadelphia in the afternoon, and my ship will leave tomorrow evening."

Martha looked surprised. "Your ship? Why, I thought you would sail with Nelson. His ship is certainly large enough for the two of you."

Bart chuckled. "Nelson is sailing for Philadelphia. My home is in Georgia, ma'am. I have a plantation outside Savannah, Georgia. However, I'm not going home until I've visited several other islands. Nelson wants to go to Philadelphia and with luck, he'll bring Cathy right back. I'd be an inconvenience to Mr. Goodspeed."

Charles stood. "Roselle needs her sleep, so we'll say good night. I want to go with you to your ship tomorrow, Bart. I'm sure Phillip wants to see Nelson off." Good-nights were hurried and before long the big house was quiet.

153

The four men left at dawn the next morning and it was almost noon before they arrived in Bridgetown. After Charles said good-bye to Nelson, he drew Bart aside and the two of them agreed to lunch together. Charles opened the conversation. "Did Phillip say anything to you about your suit for Cathy?"

Bart's thin face looked stark for a moment. "Both Nelson and Phillip mentioned Cathy. It seems that your brother felt that she needed someone older. That, of course, was not the reason Nelson gave me. He graciously stated that Cathy and he had more in common than Cathy and me. Charles, are you sure Cathy will marry that bastard?"

Charles hesitated. "Roselle says the girl won't marry either one of you. Ye gads, I hope we can get her married to someone, and soon."

"You'll have to get her back before she can be married to anyone and I have my doubts that she'll return with Nelson," Bart announced prophetically.

By sunset, both men were on their way, Nelson to Philadelphia and Bart to another island. Far away, sailing up the Savannah River, Cathy stood next to the railing watching as the city came into view. She looked out over the crowd that was beginning to gather at the dock. The ship, she decided, was expected. In the crowd she saw sailors, businessmen, fancy women parading their wares, and what had to be the wives of some of the men on board. In a large landau, off to one side, Cathy caught a glimpse of a regal beauty and she wondered why that kind of woman was meeting this ship. There were no other passengers on board. It could only mean that she'd come

154

to welcome one of the . . . Cathy glanced at James and watched as he glimpsed the carriage, then looked away with no outward sign of recognition. She turned around to watch Drew. When he glanced out at the swelling throng, Cathy watched his eyes slowly survey the scene and fix on the carriage. His eyes turned hard and his face radiated disgust.

Well, Cathy pondered, what do we have here? There was no question the sophisticated lady in the carriage knew Drew, but she was not welcome, and Cathy wondered why. "This," she muttered under her breath, "may be interesting." She leaned against the rail and watched the crowd once more. Then and there she decided that she was going to be at the side of Drew Sloan as soon as the ship docked, come what may. As the sailors prepared the *Savannah Lady*, she marched to Drew's side, a possessive gleam in her eye.

Chapter Eleven

The lines were secured, the sails tied, and the gangplank lowered. Cathy stood so close to Drew that every time he moved she almost collided with him. Twice during the docking procedure, he bodily picked her up and moved her several feet in a different direction. Not once, though, did he tell her to go below, or go back to stand with James.

Even before the lines were tied, the woman left her landau and came to stand next to the pylons and Cathy watched with some satisfaction at the puzzled expression on her face.

Another half-hour passed before Drew announced with satisfaction that they had docked. He gave the order to leave the ship. He huddled with James for several minutes and when James rushed from the ship, he turned back to Cathy. "I've sent James ahead to an inn not far from here. He'll be back with confirmation. The two of us will escort you to the inn and to dinner. I imagine you are hungry."

Cathy's eyes drifted over the beautiful blonde who

now stood on the deck several feet from Drew and her. She must have come aboard after James left the ship. Drew, she noticed, ignored the woman. Curiosity grew in Cathy by the yard. Who was this woman and why was Drew pretending that she wasn't there? It got to be too much for Cathy. "You have a visitor," she said.

The expression on Drew's face turned from intent interest to a look of scorn. He pivoted to face the blonde, then reached for Cathy. "My dear," he wrapped his arm around Cathy's waist and forced her forward by several steps, "I think you'll have one thing in common with this lovely lady."

Cathy glanced up at him, for the tone of his voice when he said "lovely lady" named her as anything but. She tried for a calmness she didn't feel. "What will we have in common?" she asked, her husky voice barely above a whisper.

Drew pointed in the direction of the blonde. "She thinks I'm a savage, and the last time she saw me, she told me that I didn't know how to treat a lady. However, the differences between you begin with the fact that she's no lady and you are."

He turned away from them and Cathy felt the skin of her face color with embarrassment. Did he feel something for the woman? Was he saying those things because the lady had hurt him? Was he, she asked herself, her heart twisting into a little ball, in love with the blond goddess? A part of her wanted to scream at them both. He had no right putting her through something like this.

She gazed at the woman for another moment and then stumbled to the stairs and fled to her cabin. She opened the door, and threw herself on her bunk, tears cooling her burning cheeks. What was that woman to Drew and what was she doing on this ship?

Before she had time to form another question, her cabin door opened slowly and Drew slid inside. He stood behind her and she chose to ignore the man who brought tears to her eyes. The tension in the cabin built until Drew whispered softly, "Please forgive me for that. I had no desire to see that woman and she brought out the worst in me. I didn't realize how it must have hurt until you fled from the deck."

Cathy sat up in the bunk and brushed at her tears. "It makes no difference to me," she began, but he sat down beside her on the bunk and pulled her into his arms.

"Little liar," he whispered against her hair. He lifted her chin with his thumb and lowered his mouth. "Forgive me," he murmured against her lips. The kiss that followed reaffirmed the heat each felt for the other. "That," Drew said, before she could ask the question, "was Patricia Gamble."

Cathy looked at him. "Who is Patricia Gamble?"

He grinned at her. "She is one of the women in my past."

"Not far enough in your past," Cathy exclaimed as he chuckled.

"My distant past," Drew refuted her. "Patricia would like it to be in the present, but since I found you I have no desire for any of my past women."

"Just how many women are in your past?" she asked innocently.

Drew laughed. "That is not a question a lady asks of a gentleman and it certainly is not a question that a gentleman would answer. The only thing that should concern you is that however many there were they are all in the past now. There is only you, Cathy. You are

159

the only woman I want."

Cathy stared at him, stunned. He loved her, in other words.

He continued. "James has persuaded me to wait until the third week of January to marry you, due to your birthday. Before that, I have to go north to see my mother and my sister. I'll leave next week, and I'll be back by the end of December. Then, three weeks later, we'll be married."

Cathy grinned up at him. At least her father could not dissolve the marriage, if James was right about reaching her majority. She brushed the dampness from her face. "I am getting very hungry. Could we go to that inn now?"

Drew brushed her lips with a kiss. "Get a change of clothes together. I'm going to have to see about a decent wardrobe for you. We'll visit a dressmaker tomorrow. I'll be back in a minute."

He was gone longer than a minute, but Cathy had just stuffed her clothes and her mother's jewels into her valise when he was back at the door, a carpetbag in his hands. Together they started up the stairs. Twice Drew pulled her against him, so that he could taste her lips. They cleared the stairs and Drew looked at her with such longing. "Three months. Ugh! I don't think I can wait."

"Drew?" a shrill feminine voice questioned from the shadows. Cathy felt the man next to her tense. She tucked her arm in his and said softly, "Introduce the lady, so we can go."

Drew looked down at Cathy and suddenly he understood what she had in mind. He turned to the shadows. "Patty, I'm sorry that you've wasted your time, but I want you to meet Cathy. Cathy and I are going to be married in three months." He moved toward the gangplank.

As if in a nightmare, the blonde was between them, shoving Cathy away from Drew and against the railing of the ship. "No! No, she is not marrying you. I won't allow it. You don't love her. You're only using her, just like you used me. You are not going to marry her. You will marry me, not her, not—"

Suddenly, Patricia was jerked away from Drew. Cathy looked over at the couple now struggling against the rail. James's warm voice reached into the icy blood that flowed through Cathy's veins. "Drew, take Cathy to the inn. I'll hold this creature until she calms down, or until you and your bride-to-be are settled at the inn."

At James's words, Patricia screamed "No!" and melted against her captor. James's voice overrode the sobs. "Go!"

Drew took Cathy from the ship and as they began the quick trip to the inn, Drew was silent. Once they sat down at the table, Drew's troubled gaze looked deep into Cathy's blue-gray eyes. Softly, he apologized. "Cathy, I swear to you, I had no idea she would wait, or that she would attack us like that. When I left for England, she told me we were finished and I never guessed that she felt that I belonged to her. I never even hinted to her that I was interested in marriage. In fact, I didn't love her. I never mentioned love."

Cathy interrupted. "Could we talk about something else? If you want to tell me about her, do it tomorrow. I don't think I can take anymore tonight."

Drew smiled at her and nodded his head. "A quick meal, a hot bath, and a good night's sleep." Cathy tentatively smiled back.

Drew saw her to her room and then he disappeared. Cathy wondered if he worried about her reputation or if he had other women to see, and that's why she slept alone. The thought twisted at her insides. Still, she told herself, she wasn't married to him yet and besides, from what she learned from some of her friends in England, who had already married, men were not very faithful creatures.

Cathy crawled into bed, her thoughts bringing a sheen of moisture to her eyes. She was not going to cry, not over an idea, for goodness sake. She was just tired, that's what was wrong with her. After all, it had been weeks since she'd gotten a decent night's sleep. She closed her eyes and willed herself to relax.

At dawn, miles away, Nelson Goodspeed guided his fishing schooner away from anchorage in Oistins Bay, out into the waters of the Caribbean Sea. His course was already plotted and although the trip would probably take him longer than the American ship, he would make Philadelphia in four or five weeks, to his way of reckoning.

Despite the time of year, the first half of the trip was almost pleasant. The thought of returning to the United States, though, after five long years away from her shores disturbed Nelson. When he left, he swore never to return and yet, here he was, chasing his future bride to the country he had disowned. Well, he'd find her and start back to Barbados as quickly as possible.

Nelson arrived in Philadelphia the first week of

December, dispatching his first mate to ask along the docks after the *Savannah Lady* and her owner or captain. If the ship had arrived, Nelson planned to begin his inquiries about Cathy that very afternoon. The news, however, that the first mate brought back in only an hour's time had him white with rage. Oh, the *Savannah Lady* had indeed made port. She'd given up her cargo and taken on another, one that would continue to make the owner richer than he already was.

Nelson could hardly contain his fury when he found out that none other than Andrew Sloan was the captain and the owner of the vessel Catherine had boarded in Barbados. Rich, good-looking, he was everything a girl could want in a husband. He bristled. Well, Sloan was not going to have the girl. Not if he, Nelson Goodspeed, had anything to say about the matter. He pulled himself up to his considerable height. Catherine Pentworth was his. Andrew Sloan was only an inconvenience.

Inconvenience or not, after two weeks, Nelson had to admit that Captain Sloan must have taken the chit with him when he left the celebrated city of freedom. Nelson spent another two days trying to decide how best to proceed. He couldn't travel south, but he had every intention of hiring someone to follow Sloan and discover at the very least the location of his ships. The trouble was that Nelson knew few people in Philadelphia and he didn't want to stir anyone's curiosity. Also, if something just outside the law was needed, he wanted someone on whom he could count.

He walked along the docks, sizing up the men who worked around the ships. It took several days of intense study, but he thought he found two men he could approach. They worked together, one of the men seeming a little brighter than the other. Nelson didn't know what made him so sure that they would be willing to consider something a bit illegal if need be, but he was willing to bet his personal freedom on the matter.

His first mate arranged for the men to board his schooner and after an hour's conversation, Nelson sent them on their way. Nelson gritted his teeth in frustration —there was no guarantee the two men would learn something about Catherine Pentworth or Andrew Sloan, but it was a beginning. He smiled at the situation. If nothing else, he'd been right about their characters.

Until the men returned, however, he had time on his hands. His crew and ship were idle in a place he really didn't want to be. On the spur of the moment, he made arrangement to take a small cargo over to the islands. That, he decided, would keep his crew out of trouble and give him a bit of money as he waited. He loaded his cargo and set sail, smiling grimly. Once he had Catherine under his control he would make her pay for all of this inconvenience. Oh, and how she would pay.

Morning came in Savannah and Cathy crawled out of her bed. Last night had been no more relaxing than the nights on Drew's ship, she thought with disgust. Perhaps she should just quit the company of the man who had her life in shambles and find her way back to Philadelphia. She would go if she thought that her father would take her back without insisting upon a wedding with some other man.

A quick glance out the window confirmed that the day

was no better than her emotions, gray and blustery. Cathy washed herself, then donned the tired gray dress that formed one half of her wardrobe. She thought of her fancy day dresses and morning gowns in London. Her lips curled. Here she was restricted to two dresses, one blue and one gray. She smiled when she remembered that Drew mentioned a trip to the dressmaker.

She flopped down on the bed, her cheeks red with humiliation. Why, no lady of substance would ever accept such a personal article as a dress or gown, and here she was desiring a whole wardrobe. Damn that man, she wanted to shout.

Finally, there was a knock at her door and James leaned against the frame. "I'm ready to escort you to the dining room for a quick breakfast."

Cathy tried to hide her surprise at seeing James, and she gallantly suppressed the desire to quiz the good doctor about where Drew Sloan spent the night. "What are your plans now that we have arrived in Savannah?" she asked.

James chuckled, sensing that Cathy wanted to know about Drew. "Drew's busy with his cargo and I'm to see you to the dressmaker. He'll join us once he has the hold emptied. And after we get to the plantation, I'm setting up my office in one of Drew's farm buildings. It seems that I get to play at being your chaperone."

Cathy stared at her friend. She remembered the conversation she overheard. Surely he wasn't really going to try to keep her and Drew apart for three months. Even James could not be that unfeeling. She gasped at her thoughts. What had Drew Sloan done to her morals and why did she allow such thoughts to surface? Her face turned a warm red in her confusion. "Did you keep him busy last night?"

James was laughing as he held her chair. He nodded and said over her shoulder, "And every night so far. He's got it bad."

"What's the matter with him, what does he have?"

James clamped his mouth shut, and glared at the figure coming through the door. Drew Sloan wasn't even going to let her out of his sight for breakfast. Maybe a January wedding wasn't soon enough. He stuck his face into his coffee cup, hating the fact that Drew would have his lady love at his side long before James could entertain his heart's desire.

Drew laid two ivory parchment envelopes at the edge of James's plate. "I brought these as soon as Smythe brought them to me. One came several weeks ago and one arrived the first of the week."

Cathy and James both recognized the striking feminine flourishes. James stood stiffly and bowed his head to Cathy. "I beg you hold me excused. These are important."

Cathy wondered if Amelia would mention her disappearance, or if the Pentworth family even knew yet. She finally responded, "Oh, yes. Please. You're excused." The both looked at Drew and a suggestion of suspicion was marked clearly on his brow.

James made a mental note to tell Cathy that she would have to admit that she remembered who she was, or she was going to incur Drew's anger. An angry Drew was something even James didn't want to see.

After Drew and Cathy finished breakfast, James returned to the table and Drew got up to leave. "I must go back to my ship and the cargo. See to the dressmaker and we'll leave for the plantation right after lunch."

James nodded, held the chair for Cathy, and the two of them watched as Drew's long strides covered the distance from the table to the door in seconds. "Well, ma'am," James drawled, "let's go see the dressmaker."

James sat and waited patiently while Cathy and the woman called Widow Benson argued over the fabric and the quantity of clothes that Cathy needed. Finally, Cathy won the argument and she allowed the wiry little woman to measure her.

In the end, Cathy counted herself lucky. If Drew was purchasing a wardrobe for her, it was going to be serviceable, plain, and very limited. She ordered two blue dresses, one dark green gown, and several petticoats. She did order a cloak since she was certain that the weather would turn cold. She smiled pleasantly as James escorted her back to the inn. "Pack what you have and I'll order some lunch. Drew wants to be on our way before much longer," James told her as he followed her into the inn.

She turned around and asked, her face a studious puzzle. "Is the farm that far? From the way the two of you talked, it was just outside of this town."

James grinned. "It's outside of town, yes, and it's the closest plantation to town, but it's still a good ten miles journey to the property line."

James paused. "The plantation is enormous and the man has money, Cathy. You'd better get used to it. When he hears what you ordered from Widow Benson, there'll be hell to pay. He expected to buy a wardrobe, not a dress or two."

After lunch, James helped Cathy up into the wagon,

167

with Drew on one side and the doctor on the other. They traveled through the flat countryside for almost an hour before Cathy noticed a gradual change in the landscape. At one point, Drew smiled and said, "Heart's Haven begins here."

Cathy looked puzzled. "Hart's Haven. Is this another town?"

Drew chuckled. "Cathy, my mother named her home Heart's Haven. It's spelled H-e-a-r-t. My mother insisted that I claim it when my father died. It's almost six miles square. We have close to five thousand acres."

They rode for another half hour and trees draped in moss came into view. She could see what appeared to be a roof in the distance. The closer they got, the more Cathy's breath caught in her throat. When they finally pulled up in front of the house, Cathy's mouth hung open in shock. She never, not in England, not in Barbados, had seen such elegance.

The house was rectangular, and on all sides of the white building tall Roman columns held up the hip roof of cedar shingles. The huge front door was flanked by four floor-to-ceiling windows. A veranda at least as wide as her father's foyer circled the entire lower floor. The second-story veranda mirrored the downstairs one. Cathy gaped at the opulence.

The massive door swung open and a large black woman stepped out to greet Drew. "Why, Mistah Drew, suh, what took you so long? We been 'spectin' you for days now."

Drew grinned at the huge woman. "I brought the cause of my delay with me, Bessy. This is Cathy and in several months she'll be Mrs. Andrew Sloan."

A smile as big as the woman played across her face.

"Well, ah do declare. Why, Mistah Drew, you gonna take a wife? Well, ah do declare."

James glanced at Cathy and noticed how uncomfortable she appeared. Obviously, she wasn't used to sharing this kind of news with servants. He came to her rescue. "What, Bessy, no greeting for me?" said the redhead, taking a step forward.

Bessy laughed. "Now, Mistah James, you can't compare with my boy takin' a wife, but I'm glad you be back."

The small group was bustled inside the house and Cathy found the inside of the house every bit as elegant as the outside. Crystal globes and full-length mirrors lined the walls of the hall. The drawing room and formal dining room on either side of the hall glistened with dark paneling and enormous crystal prisms hung from expansive chandeliers. The curving staircase on the far end of the hall led upstairs and Cathy wondered how many servants it took to polish the glistening mahogany railing. Drew leaned over and whispered, "It takes a bit of getting used to."

Cathy nodded and for the first time wondered if she was good enough for Drew Sloan. Her father, after all, was only a lord of the realm. Thoughts of her father made her more uncomfortable. What would he say if he saw all of the wealth, and from an American at that. She closed her mouth and followed Bessy up the stairs.

The next week was a flurry of activity as James set up his office in one of Drew's outbuildings. Cathy was very much aware that Drew would have preferred James's office in the city, but he had offered. Cathy remembered the second day at Heart's Haven. She overheard them arguing. She truly wished that she had not been privy to their discussion. James told Drew that until Cathy and Drew were married, Drew could accept James in his home or let James take Cathy home to his sister.

"Of course," James had taunted Drew, "you can always bring one of your own sisters home to act as a chaperone."

There was a pause in the conversation and Cathy wondered if Drew had taken a drink or lit a cigar, then his words came, tense but hard as well, "Well, it's too late for a chaperone now."

Cathy's cheeks warmed in embarrassment. She knew James understood but to hear Drew mention it so casually was something else. She strained to hear James's words. "Well, I'm better than no chaperone."

Drew snarled back, his words cutting, "If you were any kind of chaperone, I wouldn't have had the opportunity to bed the girl and there would be no need for this wedding."

James's tone was almost too soft to hear. "You don't mean that."

Cathy never heard Drew's response and she didn't want to hear anything more from either man. The exchange already had moisture finding a path down her cheeks. Her tears sent her running silently for the steps to the second floor. It would not do, she told herself, to have to explain to either man why she was crying. No, she didn't want them to see her misery.

As she crept up the stairs, she thought of her verbal commitment to Drew. She gave her word that she would marry Drew. And, in truth, she wanted to marry him, but now everything was changed. Somehow, she would find a way to get out of the agreement. From what he just said, she knew he was marrying her out of a sense of duty. She wouldn't bring that kind of shame on herself or her family. She'd just have to tell him that this promise, like all of the other promises of marriage she'd made, must be broken.

Once she got to her room, she sat on the bed, shivering. Her thoughts turned back to the suitors that she had shamed with her broken pledges. Some of those men had even professed that they loved her. Had those men felt as she felt now: devastated, torn apart, and afraid to go on? It was a chilly thought.

Chapter Twelve

The next twenty-four hours were torture for Cathy. She stayed as far away from Drew as she could, certain that her heart was irreparably damaged. Once she got over the hurt, her anger grew until it threatened to consume her. Into this explosive atmosphere, Widow Benson arrived, prepared to finish Cathy's dresses. Bessy, at Drew's instruction, took Cathy and Mrs. Benson upstairs to the sitting room next to Cathy's bedroom. Cathy offered tea and while they waited, Mrs. Benson laid out the package she brought into the house. Lacy lingerie and billowy petticoats covered the sofa. For every one Cathy ordered from the woman, the seamstress had taken it upon herself to make six more.

While they waited for their tea, Mrs. Benson gave instructions to the three young servants Drew sent to help. "There are two small trunks, one with a bronze catch and the black trunk with the black leather grips. I'll need my sewing basket. Oh, and on the floor are two hatboxes. Those must come as well."

Cathy's eyes opened wide. Surely, two dresses, a cloak,

and one gown wouldn't take up two trunks. She found out soon enough. The dresses she ordered were finished, along with three more day dresses and a riding outfit. Four evening gowns and one ball dress needed finishing touches. Cathy glared at the woman. "I ordered only these three dresses. Who told you to make the rest of these things?"

The dressmaker looked surprised. "Master Sloan said that you and he were being married in January. These are to replace your trousseau that was lost in the storm. I thought he'd already told you. If I've spoiled his surprise . . ." The woman looked pained.

Cathy frowned. It wasn't Mrs. Benson's fault that Andrew Sloan fabricated a story to fit his own purposes. And, Cathy reasoned, Widow Benson shouldn't have to pay for Andrew Sloan's lies. Cathy smiled sweetly. "It is a surprise, but I'm sure that if you were not to have said anything, Andrew would have mentioned it to you. No, this is his way to take me unawares. I'll thank him later." She almost choked on the word "thank" and turned from the older woman. Cathy's mind began to churn with ideas of revenge. She'd think of something.

After the tea, Cathy stood for hours as Mrs. Benson checked the fit of each dress. All of them were beautiful and Cathy fought hard to remember that she hadn't asked for any of them. Bessy came in to check on the progress of the women and Cathy endured Bessy's clucking about the dresses Andrew ordered. When Bessy turned to leave, Cathy hit upon her revenge. As the dressmaker checked each seam of every gown, Cathy worked out the details in her mind. Before Mrs. Benson left, Cathy's spirits were high again and she could hardly wait for the next afternoon.

Cathy went to supper the next evening in the plain gray dress that she had Mrs. Benson stitch. Before the meal began, Drew was called to his office. He was in the office for almost fifteen minutes when Bessy came bustling into the house. James and Cathy, her eyes wide with innocence, waited for the master of Heart's Haven to finish his business and sit down for dinner.

Before Drew came to the table, half of the black female servants on the plantation came to the office. By the time Drew came out of the office, dinner had been delayed forty minutes. He glared at Cathy, said not a word, and sank into his chair. The meal that night was decidedly tense.

Cathy retired to the parlor and James spent a few minutes with Drew. He strolled in the parlor looking nonplussed. "Do you have any idea what's wrong with Drew? He won't tell me a thing, but he says you know."

Cathy giggled, and in a voice husky with satisfaction, she answered, "I know what he's angry about. He ordered a very extensive wardrobe for me. I didn't want it and I didn't ask for it. Since he'd already paid for it, I couldn't force the woman to take back the clothes. It wasn't her fault I didn't want the clothes. After she left, however, I went around to the servants and matched as many of them up with the clothes as I could."

James stared at her in astonishment. "You gave your clothes to the servants, the slaves?"

Cathy nodded, her smile of satisfaction not unlike the grin of a cat after a bowl of heavy cream. "The dresses, the gowns, the petticoats, even the nightgowns. I gave away everything except for the dresses, the nightwear, and the lingerie I ordered."

Drew said nothing to Cathy about the clothes and for a

week she basked in the elation she felt about the whole matter. Eventually it wore off and once again she remembered the conversation she overheard between Drew and James.

Several more days dragged by. Cathy tried hard to forget the overheard conversation, but at times she could close her eyes and hear Drew's scathing comment. She stayed out of his way but as the hours ticked off, she felt a cloud of despair slowly descend lower. For the first time in her life, she felt useless and used, wasted and old. The thought came to her that she was nothing but a spoiled child, a selfish creature.

No matter how she tried to avoid any contact with her host and his guest, she was forced to endure their company for at least the evening meal. By the beginning of the third week at Heart's Haven, she felt Drew trying to pull her out of herself. When her moodiness continued, James turned to her and said, "Well, Cathy, Drew suggested we talk. Tomorrow I open up the large room in the outbuilding for patients. I am going to need your help."

She looked at him, startled. "My help? Surely you're not serious?"

He smiled gently. "I thought you knew. Drew and I talked about it days ago. You need something to occupy your time and I desperately need an assistant. You are very good help, too. And you expressed a keen interest in medicine. I planned on using your services at the office."

"Oh, I couldn't. I'm not trained and . . ."

Drew cut her short. "You have nothing better to do. Why can't you help James? He wants you to help. I don't approve, but what I want doesn't seem to count for much."

Cathy blushed and remembered the dresses she passed around to the servants. She didn't give him a chance to add anything else to his remarks, but glanced over at James. "If you think I can help, I'll be there. What time do we start?"

Cathy missed Drew's pleased expression as she talked to James. He grinned back. "Doctors don't start early, but they end up going out at all hours. We'll start seeing patients at about one in the afternoon. Perhaps we should go over some of the supplies and surgical procedures. Why don't I take you over after breakfast, then by one you'll be comfortable in the building."

Cathy nodded and rose from the table. "If I'm to be your assistant tomorrow, I need my sleep tonight."

Drew reached for her arm and almost pulled himself out of his chair. "Cathy, wait. I want to talk to you."

"No, not tonight," she whispered, her face pale, her lips thin with concern.

Drew stood and then grabbed her other arm. "I have to leave tomorrow to visit my sister. We need to talk tonight."

She raised her chin and her blue-gray eyes glinted with pain. "We haven't anything to talk about."

Drew was not to be put off. "I think we do." He turned back to James. "You'll excuse us," and he pushed Cathy toward the hall and his office. Even with only James in the room, she had no desire to create a scene and she went quietly with Drew.

The office door closed softly and Drew pushed her toward a chair. "Before I leave to see to my sister, I want you to know that I know that your memory has returned. I know about England. I've already talked to James."

Cathy looked at him as if he had announced that the

world would end in an hour. She sputtered for a fraction of a second and then she hissed, "He had no right to tell you anything."

Drew smiled grimly. "At first he denied everything, but after we talked for a while, I came to realize that the only reason you kept the information to yourself was that you're afraid of hurting your father. I plan to write to him and explain everything."

Cathy bristled. "No. I can write to my own father. It's not your concern. Besides, I'm not sure that I want to marry you. After all, you really don't—"

Drew ignored her remarks. "I have two sisters, Jane and Paula. Jane lives in Richmond and I'll spend a week or two with her, then I'll come back before I travel to Philadelphia. Paula lives outside of Philadelphia and I'll see her and Mother, then I'll return. I'm inviting them all to the wedding and yes, there will be a wedding."

Cathy shook her head, a large lump forming in her throat. It made speech difficult, almost impossible, but she persevered. "You don't have to marry me. I'll ask my father to take me back."

Drew stared at her, his eyes registered confusion, pain, and finally anger. Cathy saw the pain and wondered what he had to be pained about. She was the one being forced. Drew snarled at her, "You agreed to marry me and I damn well intend that you will do so."

Her husky voice choked with emotion. "Yes, I agreed but that was before I found out you don't want to marry me. You don't have to worry, I'm not going to announce to anyone that we've shared the same bed. I have no intention of letting you marry me to satisfy an honor code. We can just forget the whole thing."

Drew grabbed her arm and jerked her into a standing

position, then he pulled her up against his chest. "I heard all about the dozens of broken betrothals in London and you are not breaking your word to me. *We will be married when I return.*" He practically threw her at the couch. "Now sit down until I have my say."

Cathy slowly sat on the brocade-covered couch. Drew was angry—no, he was furious and at the moment she figured she had taunted him enough. She sat quietly and concentrated on her fingers, twisting and twirling them in her lap. What did he want from her? she asked herself. Why was he so adamant about marriage when over a week ago he told the doctor that it was James's fault that there was going to be a wedding in the first place? Drew's words rang in her head and she brushed at tears that she would not allow to fall. Damn this man, she thought, and she took a deep breath. "Say what you must," she told him as she settled back a bit to listen to what she was sure would be a tirade.

Drew stood looking down at her for several heartbeats. Was marriage to him so distasteful? He sat down on the couch next to her and without looking at her face, he took her small hand in his much larger one and unconsciously rubbed his thumb across the surface. Drew took a heavy gulp of air and concentrated on his words. "Cathy, despite what you might think, we suit each other very well. Most marriages don't begin with as much as we already have. I know from James that your father doesn't like Americans, but when he sees that you have married well, he may change his mind. I have no idea of restricting you to the plantation and we'll travel back to England possibly as early as next fall.

"James seems to think that you make an outstanding assistant and I have no objections to you helping him

179

while I'm gone. Still, there's much for you to do here. The staff will help you in any way, all you have to do is ask. I only ask that you don't take it into your head to run off."

Cathy looked over at the man who was almost whispering, and in an equally quiet tone, she inquired, "What if I don't want to marry you? Will you send me back to my father?"

Drew shook his head. "No, I can't do that. I . . . I have dishonored you. I'm in a position to rectify my mistake and we do suit."

"But we don't suit," Cathy whispered, her husky voice choked with alarm. "I want to marry a man who loves me. I want a marriage like my father had with my mother."

Drew stood up and gazed over her head to stare out the windows of his office. "Love will come." He walked to the door not ready to admit to the woman in his office that what he felt for her was love. After all, she had no love for him. No, it was only her selfish concern that she be loved. At that thought, he wondered if he'd made a monumental mistake. It wasn't the first time he tried to dodge the thought. No, even if it was a mistake, there was nothing he could do. He must pay the price for taking her maidenhead, and if his life was less than happy it was his own fault. He whispered, "I'll be back," and strode from the room.

The next morning, Cathy came down to breakfast and James was finishing a cup of coffee. "Have you eaten already?"

James grinned at her. "I ate with Drew. He's gone, by the way, and he won't be back for two weeks. We have much to do, so don't dawdle. I'll get my things together while you have your breakfast and then we'll go over to my offices."

Cathy ate quickly and was waiting for James at the rear door when he came from his room. They walked to the outbuilding that had been turned into a medical facility. For the next two hours James showed Cathy where everything was and what her tasks would be. James chuckled. "Cathy, when I said I needed help, I was certain that I had more than enough to keep me busy. You're going to do all the little things I won't have time for."

By four o'clock that afternoon, James saw thirteen patients who had come because they'd heard he'd opened his offices. Runners from the plantations north of Heart's Haven sent word that their people would call during the next several days, and between making those appointments and trying to keep up with James, Cathy was exhausted.

On their way back to the house, Cathy looked over at the young doctor and said quietly, "I learned one thing today. I don't want to be a doctor's wife."

James laughed. "But you won't tell Amelia, will you?" Cathy shook her head.

After a quiet meal, Cathy retired to her room for a hot bath and a long sleep. She was so tired that she was sure when her head hit her pillow she would be sound asleep. She chuckled at herself the next morning. She didn't remember her head touching her pillow at all.

The next four days rushed by and Cathy wondered out loud where all the sick people were coming from. The afternoons were packed full of people and there was not a moment to waste. Twice James was in the middle of seeing one patient, when word was received that he was needed by another. He gave Cathy instructions and took

181

off in the buggy Drew assigned to him. Cathy ended up dismissing the waiting patients, changing bandages on two others, and attempting to rearrange appointments for those who insisted they still needed to see the doctor.

By the end of the second week, Cathy lived through a hundred experiences, some not so pleasant. The days flew by and she grew to understand and appreciate what a good doctor James Rupert really was. Amelia was getting the best of husbands.

While the days sped by, the nights crawled, and more than once Cathy was unable to sleep at all. It wasn't that she didn't try to get a good night's sleep. Several times, she fixed herself warm milk and tried reading some of James's medical books, hoping those would put her to sleep, but that elusive state skirted her.

Oh, she knew why sleep didn't come and in the knowing she realized just how much Drew had destroyed her peace. Each night, after she curled up in her bed and forced her eyes tightly closed, Drew's smiling face appeared in her mind. She could not shake him from her thoughts. Often, she saw him at the helm of his ship, directing the vessel through stormy waves. He was so real she wanted to reach out and touch him.

Sometimes, she could almost feel his breath, as his square, handsome face dropped toward hers. She wanted the dream to be real, for the kiss she strained to receive to be just as real. She would turn over in her lonely bed and curse her imagination for creating the scene.

Every day, before she left to help James in his office, Cathy closed herself off in the study and drew out parchment paper, quill, and ink. Each session began and ended the same way. She scrawled a greeting across the top of the paper with ease. "Dear Father," she started.

Her good intentions evaporated then and she found herself sitting at the desk, staring at the empty page.

At first, she chastised herself, mumbling, "You have to write and at least tell the man that you are safe. He probably thinks you are lying at the bottom of the sea." But her words did little good and she always left the room an hour later, the unfinished letter still on the desk.

Late one afternoon, Bessy found her busy at the desk in the doctor's office. "Mistah Drew back, missy," Bessy drawled softly. "He wants ya at the house."

Cathy stood for a second and tried to decide if the black woman would carry the kind of message she wanted to send to the man who was trying to control her life. It didn't matter that she had missed him, or that she had spent a dozen sleepless nights because of him. At the moment all she could think about was that as soon as he arrived he started telling her what to do. Well, she squared her shoulders, that was about to end. She would make certain that he understood he could not boss her around.

Chapter Thirteen

Cathy stalked out of James's office and stormed to the main house. Her patients needed her in the hospital. Andrew had arrived at a very bad time. A broken leg occupied James, and a small child, weak and listless, waited in the other examining room. She raged at herself as well. Even though the man had no thought for anyone other than himself, when he sent for her, her soul pulsed with pleasure. "You're a fool," she scolded herself as she slammed into the kitchen.

Cathy followed Bessy toward the study, her knees shaking. She tried to explain away Drew's effect on her, but she felt her heart leap to her throat when she saw him standing in the doorway waiting for her. Despite all of her denunciations, Drew Sloan turned her world upside down with his mere presence. I cannot let him have this kind of an effect on me, she told herself as she squared her shoulders.

Tense seconds passed as they gazed at each other, their thoughts unreadable. Drew stepped back into the study. "Come in, please. We need to talk."

Cathy needed more time to pull her burgeoning emotions together and lowering her eyes, she smoothed the cotton cord of the slate gray dress she wore with patients. When Drew reached to pull her into the room, she took the first step. "What is it that we need to discuss? I left several patients who need immediate care."

Drew only stared at her, not quite sure what she did in the good doctor's rooms. He spoke again, his deep voice rolling over her as the surf rolled over the sands in Barbados. "I have nothing urgent. It can wait. I didn't know that you were helping with the care of James's patients. In fact, I do believe it would be better if we waited until tonight. After dinner," he added.

What he wanted to tell her was not nearly as important as seeing her after the two long weeks he had been gone. Now, by telling her that they would talk after dinner, he was assured of seeing her after the meal. Unconsciously, he realized he wanted, needed, had to have her again. Desire consumed him. Yes, after dinner, they would *talk*. He grinned at the idea and felt like patting himself on the back.

Cathy contained her anger until she hit the kitchen door. There she gave in to a childish tantrum, hitting the door with her closed fists. When she was outside the panel, she stamped first one and then the other foot in a show of temper. Why, that man had nothing important to say to her at all. Here he had called her away from something worthwhile and then said it could wait. Well, he could wait, she thought. Of a sudden it was imperative that she eat in her room and go to bed after the meal. She smiled in satisfaction. She would *not* be entertaining Drew tonight.

Drew and James sat across from each other and ate without much in the way of conversation. Cathy had sent regrets. She had a splitting headache and she needed to stay in her dark, quiet room until it was gone. Her note had a ring of finality about it and both men had no doubt that Cathy would be in her room until morning.

Early in the meal, James had tried to tell Drew about some of his more interesting cases, but when Drew turned a shade of green, James changed the subject. When Drew offered nothing by way of comment, James stopped talking all together. Drew didn't want a quick-witted discourse tonight. James laid the blame on exhaustion.

Drew was exhausted, but not from travel. His sister fed him well and provided a marvelous corner room with a large feather bed for his use. He enjoyed his time with her and with her family. It was not the external surroundings, but the internal confusion that destroyed his sleep. Drew hadn't had a decent night's rest for weeks, not since the last time he held Cathy in his arms. He glared at James sitting across from him, knowing he couldn't go to Cathy tonight. James played his role of chaperone to the hilt.

Drew thought back to their discourse of only an hour before. James came in from his office and Drew dragged him into the study for a drink before dinner. James opened the conversation. "Does Cathy know you're back?"

Drew smiled, thinking about the pleasure he planned for himself after dinner. "Yes. I plan to speak to her about wedding plans after dinner."

James looked thoughtful. "I have nothing planned for tonight. However, if I get a call, then Cathy will have to retire." He glanced at Drew and added, "Alone."

Drew sat stunned. He'd given no thought to James joining the couple for their discussion. In fact, he didn't need or want James's presence. He said as much. "I don't think you need to worry about our discussion. I plan to talk to Cathy about the wedding. You don't need to sit in on that, for God's sake."

James smiled. "You protest too much. I definitely *will* sit in on your discussion."

Clearly, there was no need for James to play chaperone now, for the discussion had been cancelled. It crossed Drew's mind that perhaps Cathy and James conspired together to keep Drew from Cathy. Then, he thought the idea adolescent and dismissed it. The evening spread out before them, and Drew gave some serious thought to retiring. He could toss and turn in his bed as easily as he could pace the study floor, and at least in his room he wouldn't have James glaring at his every step.

Drew raised his glass and drained the amber liquid. He set his glass on the table and opened his mouth to excuse himself for the night when a frantic knock sounded at the front door. James bounded out of his chair and jerked his arms into his coat before Bessy bolted into the room. "Mrs. Parmaley, Dr. James. It's her boy."

James smiled. "Tell the boy to wait for me and send Bud to hitch the carriage." He turned to Drew. "Looks like you'll have to entertain yourself. I've a baby to deliver. This one may take all night. She hasn't delivered for twelve years. She's scared to death." He walked toward the door, Bessy handing him his black bag. To no one in particular, James commented as he went out the door, "I always thought women remembered what birthing was all about."

Cathy read in her room, her mysterious headache gone before she had closed her door. She heard the horse, the voices at the door, and the carriage that signaled yet another patient demanding to see the good doctor. It struck her that when Bessy left for her own small cottage behind the big house, she would be alone with Drew. She tried to shake off the feelings of alarm.

Even though she offered the excuse of a headache before dinner, she wondered if he would insist that he see her tonight. Part of her wanted the big man to slam his way through her door, pull her into his arms, and kiss her senseless. The more rational part of her was horrified. Her thoughts tumbled one over another and she sank into the mattress, afraid for a time to draw a deep breath. She tried to calm herself and ignore the hammering of her heart. The sensible part of her brain listened for footsteps on the stairs. She left the bed and paced back and forth until she realized what she was doing. Finally, she sat down in the small chair next to the window.

She let her mind drift back several hours to when Bessy announced Drew's return. Something, she didn't know what, pulled her to the man downstairs, something so strong that she could not control it. Lust, desire, or love, she couldn't even give it a name. Honest with herself, she knew she wanted nothing more than to become the wife of Andrew Sloan. And, here she stood, waiting breathlessly in her room for a late night visit. She leaned back against the chair and wondered when she had fallen for the man. Of course, he didn't return her feelings, and that was tragic. His need to be honorable tied him to her out of duty.

She stirred uncomfortably in her chair. She definitely

did not want to think about that. No longer willing to think about anything to do with Drew Sloan, she strained to turn her thoughts to home. She heard Bessy yelling out her good-nights. Slowly, as if she were dreaming the sound, a heavy thud followed the banging of a door. Again, a thud, and another. She could see Andrew climbing the stairs. She stiffened and held her breath. Would he come to her? Would he go directly to bed?

Inside, a virtual war waged fiercely. She wanted him to open the door. She needed a reaffirmation of his desire. Another part of her condemned her own desires, calling her wanton. As each second passed she heard him coming closer.

She glanced around her room and realized that several candles bathed her room in soft light, light that would show under her door. He would know that she had not retired! For a second the thought thrilled her then panic seized her and she jerked from the chair, her heart in her throat.

The heavy thuds against the floor ceased as Drew touched the carpet runner in the hall. Cathy stretched her neck in the direction of the door, praying that she could hear in which direction he moved. She stared at the door, wishing above everything that she could see through the thick oak. The doorknob turned and she knew! He was coming to her, now, this minute. She wasn't ready!

In that instant, her war ended. From her distant past she gathered courage. She would not allow him to touch her. She would fight him off. Pulling her dressing gown more tightly around her, she drew herself up to her full height and said, "What do you want?"

Drew swung the door open and gazed at the woman

that had pulled him from the study below. He couldn't tell her that he had to see her before he retired, that without a glimpse of her he could never have faced his cold, lonely bed. Instead, he said quietly, "I saw the glow under your door." With his arrogance as a cover, he grinned. "Besides, you should have known I would come. I told you we had to talk."

Cathy peered at the man in the doorway and the thought passed through her mind that she couldn't possibly feel anything for this lout. Everything in him she despised. He was arrogant, rude, selfish. If she wanted, she told herself, she could continue that litany for hours. She glanced away. "Surely, you could wait until morning, until a more decent hour."

Drew stared at her. Several hours before, when she came rushing into the study, she'd been delighted to see him, he was sure of it. It'd been written all over her face and her eyes had glistened with her pleasure. But now, cold and unfeeling, she stood in front of him. Her eyes glittered with ice and he shook his head, wondering at the difference. Right now, she stared at him as if she hated him. That could not be allowed and he took a step toward her, then another.

Cathy moved back against the chair and whispered, "Please, just leave."

Drew advanced another step and shook his head. No, he wasn't leaving, not until he proved to her and to himself as well that she didn't really mean the hate that radiated from her eyes. He took another step and another. Close enough to her now to touch her, he reached out his hand to her arm, his eyes searching hers for some sign of acceptance.

Cathy gazed into his eyes, eyes that looked brown in

the flickering glow of the candles. What she saw in those eyes firmed her resolve and she lowered her lashes. She must get him out of this room before her behavior gave her away. She moved away from him. At that moment she admitted, at least to herself, that when he came near she lost all control. She repeated herself, "Please leave."

"No, I don't think so. We have some things to settle and tonight is as good as any other. I still have to travel north to see my sister Paula and my mother. We need to get things settled between us now."

She frowned. "It can wait until tomorrow."

"No, it can't. James feels that he owes it to you to sit in on our conversations and I don't particularly want him involved. It's tonight!"

She had to agree. James would only complicate things. "All right. Say what you have to say and leave."

"Oh, it's not that simple. I wanted us to spend a little time together." He glanced over at her. "Would you be more comfortable if we went down to the study or the parlor?"

Cathy shook her head. She didn't want to leave the safety of her room. He couldn't stay here long and then she would be safe, safe from warring with her own conflicting emotions. She tried to move around him, into the center of the room, close to the door.

He seemed to understand the reason for her movement and grabbed her arm. "Cathy, we are about to be married. You have to get used to me."

She shook her head. "We aren't going to marry. I'm going to go home to my father where I belong. No man is going to marry me because he feels he has to," she said, glaring at him.

Drew licked his lips. That sounded suspiciously like

something he'd said to James. Using the hand at his side, he grabbed her chin and kept her turned toward him. "Has James said something to you about my duty?"

"He didn't have to. I heard you myself. I told you before, that when I marry, it will be because of love, not duty." She brought her hands up and dug her nails into his hand which held her chin.

He sneered at her. "You, my independent little cat, can sheath your claws."

He dropped his hand from her chin and wrapped it around her waist. With a swift yank, he pulled her to him. "Duty or not, we will be married in January."

She opened her mouth to negate his word, and he dropped his head. He didn't want to hear her denial. He hadn't planned to kiss her—well, not consciously, he decided, as her warm lips parted slightly and he felt her sweet breath against his cheek. His loins tightened instantly and a tiny voice whispered at the back of his mind. "Leave, leave now, you fool, or you'll have her in her bed in minutes. Then what will James say?"

Temptation sat on his shoulder and swept his conscience away. He gave in to desire and used the tip of his tongue to moisten the fullness of her lips, stroking them from corner to corner. "James be damned," he said to himself as he wrapped his arms around her and lifted her against his hard body. For days he'd thought of nothing but her, of her soft flesh, her sweet lips, her subtle fragrance. He wanted her, wanted her in a way he never had wanted a woman before. Thank God, he thought, that they were marrying. He stroked the moist cavern behind her teeth and caught the husky sigh that slipped from her lips.

Cathy leaned into Drew, and time ceased for her as his

tongue tasted her lips and then her mouth. Where the touch of sanity came from she didn't question, but suddenly she knew this could not happen. She must not let him do this to her. She tried to pull away, but he held her too tightly. She raised her arms and tried to shove at him. When that seemed to have no effect, she tried to turn her head.

Finally, he pulled away. "What—what's wrong?"

"No," her husky voice whispered. "No, you can't do this. I won't let you. You are not going to use me."

He smiled at her, a leer really, and she tried to pull out of his arms. "Yes," he said. "I'm going to use you, use you thoroughly and well. Now, relax and enjoy it."

Cathy was stunned. He didn't care how she felt. Numbness spread through her and she didn't even offer a token protest as he pulled her back into his arms. Again, he kissed her and the kiss caused a burning, a sizzling that reached into her soul. How could he do this to her, she asked herself, before the sensations he created consumed her. He'd admitted to her that duty demanded he marry her and he declared that he didn't mind using her at all. In spite of it all, her body responded; she loved what he did to her. She wanted more, yearned for more, coveted the ultimate. Tears formed behind her eyes and she struggled to prevent them from falling.

She told herself she didn't want to respond. She had to hold back, keep herself from him somehow. The pleasures that curled up from her toes and through her limbs must be denied at all cost. And yet, as much as she lectured herself, she knew the battle was lost. Her ragged breath kept time with her pounding heart in a cadence of criticism: let go, give in, just feel.

Drew felt the tension in her and gentled his kiss. He

194

ran his tongue down the edge of her jaw, over the corded muscles of her neck, across the pulse point that beat frantically against the base of her neck. He brought his hands up to her head, and with infinite care he ran his fingers through her layers of silken hair, toying with each series of ringlets. He pulled away from her and murmured in her ear, "You smell so good, like spring flowers."

Cathy tried again to pull away from him, but her traitorous body would not let her move and she sagged in defeat. Whatever he wanted would happen and her own frail form could not prevent it.

Drew felt her surrender and he kissed her again. This time, she kissed him back. Easily he swung her up into his arms and stepped back to the bed. He pulled the quilts back, laid her down against the sheets, and in the same motion, pulled her gown from around her. She made no attempt to stop him. What was the point? Her body wanted him as much as he wanted her. She closed her eyes and gave in to her feelings.

For a moment he left her, then she heard the rustle of his clothing and the clop of his boots. Once again she felt him next to her, pulling her toward his warm body. His lips descended. She moved her arms up to tighten around his neck. He pulled up and away from her and she waited. She opened her eyes and gazed up at him. Naked desire was etched on his face, but his lips curved into a soft smile, not a leer, but a genuine, happy smile. "You are so beautiful," he said.

Cathy couldn't help herself, she returned his smile. Obviously, the man couldn't see properly when he made love. Beautiful? Certainly not. Pretty perhaps, but not beautiful. She started to tell him that, but her open mouth only served to offer herself up to another devastating kiss. Her eyes drifted closed and she felt him move over her, nudging her knees apart. He lay atop her, his manhood resting against her thigh, hard, heavy, pulsing with desire. Another sigh slipped past her lips. Now. She wanted him now.

She wiggled her hips against his groin and he chuckled. He answered against her mouth, "Not yet. I want you panting with desire, the way I've been for the last two weeks." Cathy ran her hands up and down his back, over his buttocks, confirming her need.

He rolled away from her and she opened her eyes. She watched as his head descended to her breast and a gasp escaped as he grabbed her nipple between his teeth and gently chewed against the pulsing nerves that gathered there. She felt his long, warm fingers press across her ribs, her waist, her belly, leaving her skin tingling as if she were the wax from a candle and he was a ray from the sun.

His fingers moved down farther into the curls between her legs and she fought to prevent a scream of pleasure as he smoothed his fingers over her and into her. She squirmed, powerless to prevent the inferno from penetrating her soul. Consumed by the warmth of his desire, she raised her hips against his stroking fingers, unaware that she had gasped out her need.

Drew fled from her breast to her mouth as he positioned himself above her. His lips touched hers as his throbbing spear brushed against the sweet warmth it sought. Slowly, he let his tongue touch her lips, and retreat as his burgeoning member touched the edges of her feminine core. He felt her hands rush to his buttocks and as he rocked forward to tease again, she took matters into her own hands. He thrust his tongue into her mouth as she impaled herself on his manhood.

Drew fought for control, but it was far too late. He'd wanted her too badly for too long. He thrust into her once, twice, and he felt the seed of life pour from him in incredible pulses of pleasure. As he fought to prevent his weight from crushing the girl under him, he realized that she was pulsing against him and he moved against her again. He waited for her ragged breathing to return to normal and he smiled down at her. "I was afraid I'd left you behind."

She opened her eyes to stare up at him. Her wonder at what they'd shared was evident on her face. He pulled her against him, and as he held her, he gave in to his greatest fear. But, no, surely in time she would learn to love him. He held her as she drifted off to sleep. When he moved away from her, she whimpered against him. He tucked the covers over her and smiled. She thought duty forced his pledge. He wondered what she would say if he told her how necessary she had become for him. He frowned at the thought. He couldn't tell her that just yet, not when she fought him as she did tonight.

With soft steps, he traveled around the room gathering his clothes and extinguishing the candles. Back beside the bed, he brushed her forehead with his lips and headed to the door. He would forever be grateful to Mrs. Parmaley and the child that would be born tonight. A thought caused his brow to crease. They hadn't settled a thing between them. Well, it was just as well. With James present, they would finish the discussion tomorrow.

Chapter Fourteen

The conversation between Drew and Cathy took place in the study at ten o'clock the next morning. James, in his own bed by four, watched the two combatants and wondered if something had occurred after he left to help Mrs. Parmaley. Drew was tense, but Cathy was withdrawn, almost frightened, as she sat opposite the man who claimed that he would become her bridegroom in six weeks.

Drew discussed the wedding list and insisted that Cathy send for Widow Benson. James got the task of delivering the wedding invitations when Cathy had them finished. "The trip from here to Philadelphia will take a week, and I'll spend about two weeks with my mother and sister, then another week to get home. I should be back by the tenth of January if there's no problem with travel. I'm sending word to Jane and I'll tell Mother and Paula about the wedding, but don't count on my family."

Cathy said next to nothing and when Drew stood, she stood as well. "Cathy, this is a wedding not a funeral," he remarked as he left the room.

Cathy turned to James. "I feel like it's my wake."

James smiled a little too tightly. "I suspect you are suffering from the normal bridal nerves. Drew's a good man. He'll make you a good husband."

Cathy looked ready to cry. "But I don't want a husband, good or not."

Drew spent the rest of the day attending to plantation business before he left on his journey. He visited the church where they would be married and made arrangements for the banns to be read. By late afternoon he stood in the foyer, ready to take his leave. Cathy expressed her surprise when he left just before sunset. "How will he travel in the dark?" she asked James after he sent Drew on his way.

"I thought you knew. He's sailing."

Cathy's mouth formed a silent "Oh" and she left without another word. Her whole body ached with fatigue and she had no intention of giving James the opportunity to ask her about the night before. She ambled up the stairs toward her own room.

As she tossed and turned in her bed later that night, she reminded herself that she had to sleep, but every time she closed her eyes she could smell the manly scent that was Drew Sloan. She rose from the bed, lit her candles, and changed the bed linens. It didn't help. She wondered if his fragrance had been absorbed into her own skin. Ready to try almost anything, she perfumed herself. His scent finally faded.

Once more she stretched out on the sheet and closed her eyes. Now she felt his fingers touching her and she could see his smile as it played across his face. The tears gathered in her eyes and she got out of bed. Obviously, sleep was not for her this night, at least not until exhaustion claimed all thought.

James made no comment the next morning when Cathy came downstairs to have her breakfast. After she wrote the message to Widow Benson, he commented, "Why don't you rest a bit this morning, while I make my calls. I'll be gone for most of the day seeing patients. Don't even bother opening the surgery. I'll have Bessy tell anyone really in trouble what they should do and you can rest."

Cathy smiled apologetically. The last two times James traveled to see patients Cathy had gone with him. It made the trip more enjoyable for the doctor and with Cathy along to help with bandaging and his records, he finished in half the time. She also learned quite a bit. However, today she knew she couldn't concentrate. "You are sure you don't mind?"

James smiled. "You need some rest. And, Cathy," he said over his shoulder as he started for the door, "you rest!"

Cathy explained to Bessy that she didn't want lunch and she snuggled under the quilt. Her eyes drifted shut and she abandoned the conscious state. Somewhere in the distance, Cathy heard a noise and she struggled to open her eyes. Bessy was yelling and someone was pounding on the door. Cathy swung her feet over the edge of the bed and struggled to wipe the sleep from her eyes. The low murmur of voices drew her through the door and down the steps.

Bessy stood at the bottom of the stairs, a frown crossing her brow. "Oh, missy. I's so sorry." Her lilting voice had an edge of concern. "This here man says there's been an accident up on the road. He says them in the carriage need doctoring bad."

Cathy smiled at the anxious housekeeper. "Have one of the boys throw a saddle on Prince or Boston's Girl." Cathy had ridden both horses, handling them easily. "Let me get a case from surgery and my cloak and I'll go see what's wrong. I'll send word if I need help."

In a matter of minutes Cathy mounted Prince and started toward the scene of the accident. Halfway to the site Cathy heard the screams of a child. She turned to her companion and asked, "Why didn't you tell me there were children?" She spurred the horse forward with a kick from her booted heel. In the December light, she could see the outline of the toppled carriage and hear the whinnying and stamping of the carriage horses.

She slid from her mount and yanked the reins around a shrub with an economy of motion. In three strides she stood peering into the dark box through the window. She paid little attention to the luggage scattered out and in back of the vehicle. The screams of the child demanded attention. She also heard the sobs of a woman. The mother? Cathy wondered. The driver sat off to one side, his back against a large old oak, his right leg resting at a precarious angle. He'd have to wait, Cathy thought, as she studied the immediate problem of extracting the wounded from the carriage without doing more damage. In the distance she could hear a group of horses coming. She prayed that more neighbors were arriving to help.

A tall black man and two boys rode up on work horses. "Missy, we from the next farm. We come to help."

Cathy smiled and quickly thanked them. She began planning out loud. "I'll have to get into that carriage and

202

lift out the child. If the woman can be moved, I'll need assistance. I'm going to need a wagon, too. Could someone go for a wagon?" The smaller of the two boys looked at his companions and then pulled his horse up to stand in front of Cathy.

Cathy ordered, "Ask for Bessy. Tell her Cathy needs the wagon and blankets. Get two of the stable boys to help with the wagon. Heart's Haven." She pointed in the direction from which she had come. The lad nodded his head and started off in the direction of the plantation.

Cathy explained how she wanted to attack the situation. The man and the boy nodded slowly. Carefully, the tall man lifted Cathy up until she could get through the window of the carriage. She let herself down into the carriage and leaned against the seat. On one side lay a woman and a child with blond curls. The small child had been crushed between her mother and a large valise. Cautiously, Cathy reached down to pull the bag away from the child. The mother's gentle gray eyes watched her every move and Cathy talked softly to her. Once Cathy had the bag pulled away, she ran her hands as carefully as she could over the child. Several small bones were twisted into grotesque shapes and the child whimpered in agony.

"I have no choice. I must move her," Cathy told the mother. Gently, she picked the child up and handed her out to the black man who stood next to the window. Cathy gave instructions about the child and turned back to the mother. Another child was screaming in pain and Cathy glanced at the pile of skirts and petticoats on the ground and wondered where the second child was.

The woman answered the question. "I'm lying on

my son."

Together, her helpers followed her every word and with Cathy they eased the woman out through the window and then over the side of the carriage. Underneath his mother, with the blood running from a leg wound, a boy about seven or eight cried. Cathy looked at him closely and gritted her teeth. She could see the bone pushing through the skin. She needed James Rupert, and fast.

The woman lay on the ground, her small daughter in her arms when Cathy gave the order. She sent the second black boy on his way with James's schedule of visits. It might take the boy an hour to find him, but James had to come back to the surgery. That still left Cathy with making a difficult decision about the boy. Blood trickled from his leg and Cathy looked at him. "We have to move you. I know it's going to hurt, but I can't help until we get you out of here."

In the distance Cathy could hear the rumble of the wagon. Thank God, she thought to herself. She leaned out the window of the carriage and gave more instructions and the big man stepped close once again to follow Cathy's softly couched words of caution. Slowly, the man lifted the injured child and the boy's screams faded as he lost consciousness. Cathy smiled grimly, at least now they could get him out of the carriage.

By the time they had the child extracted from the vehicle, the wagon from Heart's Haven stood nearby. Cathy bundled up the boy and gathered his mother and the toddler into the wagon. She climbed up into the wagon bed with the boy and gave the signal. Slowly, and as carefully as they could, they crawled back to the plantation. The tall black man rode along, trailing Cathy's horse behind.

The household waited until the wagon pulled to a stop in the yard. Bessy had mobilized several of the household staff and they stood ready to run errands and help with the wounded. When one of the younger girls looked a little green to Cathy, she suggested that the girl give the man from the next plantation something to eat or drink. Bessy smiled up at the big man. "How you doin', Willy? This here's Mr. B.'s overseer." She turned to the girl. "Come on, Maebelle, we give Willy something to eat." Bessy turned away and Cathy opened the surgery.

Minutes ticked by and Cathy carefully cleaned up the boy. The baby whimpered in the arms of her mother, but Cathy feared her limited knowledge would hurt the child more, so she worked on the boy. "Please, James, come quickly," she prayed as she worked.

She had finished as much as she could do for the boy when she heard the crunch of a horse on the gravel path to the surgery. "Let it be the doctor," she said to herself.

James swung into the surgery. "Cathy, this lad said you sent for me."

Cathy pointed at the boy on the cot and his mother, still clutching the child. "Carriage accident."

He looked at them and sighed. "We'll try to set this, but . . ." His voice trailed off. Cathy could feel the futility. He'd told her once before that breaks that pierced the skin were very serious. He stepped over to the whimpering toddler and lifted her gently from the mother's arms. Softly, to distract the mother, he started asking questions.

"Me name's Bridget, Bridget Purdy," she answered,

her voice tight with fear. "We was traveling to my new place of employment. They ain't too bad, are they? We'll have to get there by next day, or I'll lose my position."

James shook his head. "We'll have to wait and see. I need to examine the little one and then you before I can give you a time." He lifted the baby to the small table he used and Cathy watched as his stubby fingers glided over the little girl. He looked up at Cathy and the expression in his eyes sealed the child's fate. Gently, he turned back to the mother. "She's hurt inside. I don't know if she'll make it. I don't think it will make much difference if you want to hold her."

Bridget Purdy looked stunned. "Her name's Prudence. She's only three years old."

James watched the woman for shock. "Bridget, why don't we put you to bed and get you warmed up. Cathy can hold the baby while I take care of the boy. What's his name? How old is he?"

The color of Bridget's face was fading from pink to a dull gray. "His name is William, after his father. He's seven."

James pointed to the chair next to the baby for Cathy. He picked up a blanket and spread it in Cathy's arms, then placed the twisted little body on the blanket. "Croon to her," he said as he reached for Bridget. "Come," he said to the dark-haired woman, and gently guided her to the open doorway. "There's a bed in this room and I want you to have a swallow of something that will warm you."

Two minutes passed and Cathy wondered as she held Prudence if she should call out for James. The baby struggled to breathe. Just as he walked through the door the child choked and bright red foam bubbled from her

206

mouth. James stepped up next to her. "Cathy," he said softly, his voice husky with pain, "she's not going to make it. Do you still want to hold her?"

The tears streamed down Cathy's face. She nodded her head. She'd already made her decision. She would hold her until the child passed on. While James worked on the boy William, Cathy crooned to little Prudence, her voice punctuated with her soft sobs. Minutes crept by before Cathy realized that the child had stopped breathing. Cathy, her eyes flooding with tears, whispered, "She's gone."

James glanced up and then said quietly, "Cathy, lay her down on the table and come here. I need you now, much more than Prudence does."

Cathy wanted to scream at him, but she gritted her teeth, laid the body of the toddler down and stepped up to the table where James worked on William. Cathy wiped while James stitched up the leg and when they finished James patted her shoulders. "Children are always so much harder to take than adults."

He washed his hands and turned toward the open door. "This is the part I hate. Dealing with the death of a child is so hard. I don't think our Bridget has had an easy life." He moved resolutely through the door. Cathy sat beside William and listened to the low voices from the other room. She heard the soft sobs and James's quiet words, but it seemed like a dream, and she pinched herself to make herself believe.

Cathy had no idea how long James stayed with Bridget, but eventually he came into the examining room. "Go tell Bessy that Bridget and I need something to eat, and then you go to bed."

"You can't stay here by yourself, not all night," she commented. "I'll send Bessy to stay while I rest. Then, I'll come relieve you." James stared at her for several minutes, his eyes dark and cloudy with thought.

"I think I'll agree, but only because I haven't recovered from my night with the Parmaleys. Oh, Cathy, send Big Jake from the farm." He nodded toward the small child still wrapped in a blanket. Cathy caught her own sob and ran for the door. Life was such a fragile thing.

After her nap and Bessy's meal of chicken and dumplings, Cathy headed back to the surgery. James sat propped up in one of the chairs, his eyes closed, and at first Cathy thought he'd dozed off. She tiptoed into the room and stood next to William before James opened one eye, and ran his hand through his red curls. "The boy is running a fever. I think I'll lie down on the cot in the other room. If you need me I'll be close."

With apparent stiffness, he dragged himself from the chair and started for the door. "If there are any changes, any at all, call me." Cathy nodded and watched him stretch and move into the other room. She glanced around the room. The body of the little girl had disappeared and the blanket which had covered her lay folded up and on the table next to the wall.

Cathy sank down into the chair next to the cot. James had splinted his leg and wrapped the boy up securely so that he couldn't toss and throw himself from the bed. Cathy brushed his hair from his face and wondered if the boy had ever regained consciousness. Where was the mother? she wondered. She didn't think that Bridget had suffered much in the way of physical injury. Oh, but the

208

emotional pain that woman had to endure! Her children torn from her side, one dead already and the fate of another hanging in the balance. Cathy turned her thoughts to her father. A sob caught in her throat. What had she done to her own father?

For the next two days Cathy sat beside William Purdy and thought about her father, her brothers, all of the people in her life. How unfair she had been, how utterly selfish. Her father and her brothers had no idea what had happened to her. She had been exceedingly cruel to all of them with her behavior. As soon as the child recovered, she would confront her spoiled nature and finally write a proper apology to her long-suffering papa.

Her decision made, Cathy turned her attentions to the boy and the terrible fever that left him delirious. "Is there nothing you can do?" she asked James for the tenth or eleventh time in an hour.

James frowned and Cathy watched as he clenched his fists. "Cathy, his leg needs to come off. His mother refuses. Says without a leg he's as good as dead anyway. She can't care for him and work."

Cathy looked disgusted. "Well, surely you can contact the child's father. He can—"

James interrupted. "Bridget might not want this bandied about, but William Purdy, it seems, didn't take well to parenthood. He left Bridget several months before the little girl arrived. She has no idea where he might be, or so she says."

"Well, can't you ignore her?"

"Now, Cathy. She is the boy's mother. I can't take off his leg unless she tells me I can. And I'm not all that sure he won't die if I do. Amputation is a shock and many

209

adults don't live through it. Too, I don't know how much of the poison is already in his system. What we have to do now is do a lot of praying so that this boy will recover on his own." Cathy smiled weakly. Once before James had insisted that she pray. Oh, she had prayed, prayed so hard and what had happened? Drew Sloan seduced her and in weeks he'd claim her as his wife. Of course, she remembered, they had survived the storm, they hadn't died. She began reciting the verses she learned as a child.

All the prayers she said, though, seemed to make little difference. William grew weaker; his cries turned to moans. Cathy turned worried eyes to James, but the doctor offered no words of encouragement. "There's nothing else I can do."

On the morning of the fifth day after the carriage accident, Cathy held the shoulders of the little boy, wetting his lips with a wet rag. "Come on, William, you can make it," she whispered before she eased him back on the cot.

The boy reached out for her hand and when Cathy grasped the cold, fragile fingers, he opened his eyes and smiled. Bridget sat in the chair nearby and she sensed his passing before Cathy. She stood. "He's gone," she whispered, her voice breaking.

Cathy looked down at the little boy. His eyes were blank and he seemed to be holding his breath. Cathy called out, "James!" The doctor appeared and strode to the small cot. He put his head to the small chest, listening intently, and then reached up to close William's eyes. He looked up and shook his head. His apparent pronouncement freed Bridget from her shock. She fell into Cathy's outstretched arms.

For ten minutes Bridget's wailing sobs rent the tense space of the surgery and Cathy held the shaking woman as tears streamed down her own cheeks. Then Bridget seemed to have spent her grief and she wiped her nose on the sleeve of her gown and straightened her shoulders.

She pulled away from Cathy and in a hoarse voice expressed her thanks. Cathy led her from the room and together they sat in the stiff caned chair in the hall of the surgery. Bridget's glance told Cathy the woman still had things to say.

Bridget cleared her throat and tried for a smile. She'd suffered through a hard life, Cathy thought as she looked at the small woman with dull brown hair and white streaks. Her gray eyes were underscored with black circles from her sleepless nights. The dark lashes wet with tears made the pain in her eyes a wrenching thing. Cathy reached out and held her hand.

That sharing started the words for Bridget. "I ain't two and thirty yet, did y'know that?" She didn't wait for a response from Cathy. "I met William Purdy in Erie right before the battle of Lake Erie. He said he was on some special mission for the States, but I think his special mission was his own. He wanted to shoot British officers. He told me once he lost all his money to one of them officers, but he didn't always tell the truth. Something musta happened to him when he was a child, 'cause he sure hated them men.

"Well, he married me. I was only fifteen at the time, but I thought I loved him." Bridget started to sniff.

Cathy stopped her. "Bridget, you don't have to tell me this."

Bridget tried to smile. "I want to tell you, if you want

211

to listen." Cathy nodded her head. Obviously, the woman needed to talk. Bridget took a breath and whispered, "I shoulda known what a blighter he'd be. Married two weeks and he took off. Left me with child, he did. 'Course, I had to work and I lost that child. Five years later, he came back. You think I was smart enough by then? Hell, no! I took him back.

"We traveled south then, to his farm. That were the excuse he gave for leaving me, that he had to build this here farm, right outside of Charleston. Said as young as he was, he was seventeen when we wed, he had a hard time getting the land. Didn't make no sense then, still don't make no sense.

"Well, for five years it were kinda nice. Oh, we didn't have much, but we worked hard and we had some good times. I lost two children and he seemed as sorry as I was. William . . ." Her voice choked up a bit. She wiped at her eyes and went on. "He was born in the spring and that summer we had a bad drought. The next summer was near as bad and we lost the farm. We moved into Charleston and I got a job as charwoman while Will went to work at a tavern. It weren't so bad until I got pregnant with Prudence. I was six months along and that bastard up and left."

Cathy stared at the bitter face of the woman next to her. She looked at least ten years older than her two and thirty. Bridget stood and offered one more thought. "I think the good Lord was watching out for my younguns. He knew that life with me weren't gonna be no good. I couldn't give 'em much and my boy had started to want. When a kid's got nothing and he wants bad enough, he can get mixed up with the wrong kind. That woulda killed me. No, the good Lord knowed what he was doing when he called my little ones home."

She started to move out the door and then she turned back. If Cathy had not been sitting, the look of pure hatred that radiated from Bridget would have driven Cathy to the chair. Her voice turned crisp, hard. "If I ever see that man again, I'll be hanged fer murder." The faces of the two little children that had left this earth jumped to Cathy's thoughts. She could almost agree.

Chapter Fifteen

The next morning, at the edge of the small family cemetery, William Purdy's small wooden casket joined his sister's smaller box. Several of the slaves, Cathy, James, Bessy, and Bridget stood quietly while Father Worthington of Christ Church read the rites of burial for the two children.

After a quiet meal, Bridget turned to James and Cathy. "I ain't got words enough to say thanks. I got a job waiting for me in Charleston with a good family. I don't want you to worry about me. I knew 'em before . . ." Bridget's voice trailed off and she wiped a tear from her eye.

Cathy seized the opportunity to press the offer she made the day before. "Bridget, please stay here. We can use you here at the surgery. James needs more help than he has. You don't have to leave."

"Yes, I do, miss," Bridget said firmly. "Here I'd always remember my little ones on that hill out there and I would grieve to death. In Charleston, I can make a new life for myself. I'll be better off there."

James laid his hand on Cathy's arm and smiled at her sadly. "Let her go. She's probably right, you know. She will get over it more quickly away from here."

Bridget left and Cathy turned herself back to the preparations for a wedding she kept telling herself she didn't want. Widow Benson came with ivory satin and a half-dozen fashion plates. They selected a design and the seamstress traveled back to town to begin the project. Cathy penned the invitations on parchment and James decided to wait until after Christmas to deliver them.

Early one morning, five days before Christmas, Samuel arrived at Heart's Haven, a square of parchment in his hand. For a tense moment, Cathy worried that something had happened to Drew. "Samuel, why are you here? Where is Drew? Has something happened to his ship?"

Samuel chuckled. "Ain't nothing wrong with the captain. He took the *Georgia Girl* north two weeks ago. I captained the *Savannah Lady*. In fact, I came back expressly for you. Miss Jane, Drew's sister, sent this." He handed her the note.

Cathy flushed with her mistake. Her reaction annoyed her. She scolded herself for feeling so relieved when she heard no harm had come to Drew Sloan. After all, she didn't want to marry the man, did she?

She considered the note in her hand, broke the seal, and read the letter. The flowing script asked politely if Cathy would consider coming to Richmond for the holidays. A room waited for her and Cathy could meet some of Drew's family. They wanted anxiously to meet her.

She raised her eyes and looked at Samuel. She glanced around and blushed again. The two of them stood just inside the door, in the foyer. She'd been so worried about Drew that she'd stood in the hall and read the letter, besides keeping Samuel standing in the hall as well. She clenched her jaw, disgusted with herself. "Samuel, please come in. I will ask Dr. Rupert what he thinks and while I'm doing that, can I get you something?"

James marched out of the dining room, a biscuit in his hand. "Ask Dr. Rupert what?" He greeted Samuel. "Come have a bite to eat. Cathy, what did you want to ask me?"

Cathy shoved the invitation at him and James chuckled. "Oh, go, by all means. In fact, I might go with you for a couple of days. Jane and Nathan Darrow are wonderful folks. She's not like Drew at all."

Cathy looked at James, her expression serious. She turned to Samuel. "When should I be ready to leave?" She missed the concerned frown that marked James's brow.

"Let's eat first," James insisted, "and then we'll talk about leaving."

Over breakfast they decided that they ought to begin the trip the next morning. It would take several days in a carriage to get to Richmond.

James told Cathy and Samuel, "I'll send my patients to one of the doctors in Savannah for the ten days and go along. I don't want to be alone on Christmas."

The trip went well, even though Cathy told James, "I never dreamed it would be so cold. This country does everything in extremes and that includes the weather."

James laughed. "Cathy, where Bridget comes from, Lake Erie, I hear they have snow two feet deep." She

217

made a face. She plainly did not believe that.

By the time they reached Virginia, a cold rain fell on the travelers. Jane Darrow, her husband, Nathan, and their two children, a girl, Joanna, after Jane's mother and a boy, Julius, after his father's father, waited in the dark red brick home just outside the town of Richmond. Jane bustled them into the large kitchen, a part of the house, and settled them at a large oak table. Soon, the family and guests sat consuming hot steamy mugs of cider, fragrant with the scent of cinnamon, and warm raisin buns glistening with a dark sugar glaze.

As they sat at the table, Cathy took the opportunity to study Jane and Nathan. She smiled at her hostess, the grin expanding when she remembered James's words. Jane Darrow didn't look or sound anything like Andrew Sloan.

Round, not as tall as Cathy, her bright blue eyes winked with pleasure under a head of curly auburn hair. Even her voice sounded nothing like her brother. Jane Darrow squeaked when she talked and her words came rushing out at a speed which left Cathy dizzy. Her movements were almost as quick. She had a vitality about her and Cathy liked her immediately.

Cathy turned to observe Nathan who leaned forward pondering the state of local finances with James and Samuel. Jane's husband was roly-poly too, with a round face and a double chin. She watched the little man smile and chuckle at James's words. What a perfect match, Cathy thought as she watched Nathan Darrow wave his hands in the air to make a point. While Jane Darrow left the table to worry over her guests, her husband checked his vest pocket and the timepiece that rested there. Cathy wanted to giggle with happiness. Something told her that she would have a marvelous time.

Cathy met the children and spent time with them in their nursery. Joanna, who was three years old, and Julius, who was four years old, were very nearly miniatures of their parents. Both children gazed at their visitor with bright blue eyes and tossed small heads ringed with a hundred red-brown curls with each answer they gave Cathy. As animated as their mother and father, Cathy lost her heart to them in her first two minutes in the nursery.

The Christmas celebration began the next evening as the children waited for Santa Claus. The Yule log was lit, the wassail bowl filled, and the pungent odor of cinnamon and cloves drifted through the house. With a twinkle in her eye, Jane brought forth a tray of delicate Christmas cakes decorated with the first name of each person in the family. Before the stars came out to dance with the billowing snow clouds, neighbors trudged through the snow to join in the festivities and the hours passed quickly.

Cathy crawled into her warm bed, tired but happy. A touch of homesickness pricked at her, but another part loved the fun she and James had had with the children. She brushed at a wayward curl. Christmas was truly for children.

The next morning, more delicious smells drifted into Cathy's room, along with two small bodies. She opened her heavy eyelids and gazed at the two round faces watching her anxiously. "Mother said we could see if you were awake," Julius said softly.

Joanna peered over the edge of the bed. "Are you awake?"

Cathy sat up in the bed. "Yes, I'm awake, and a Happy

Christmas to you. Has your Santa Claus come yet?"
Joanna nodded her head.

"He left something for you, too," Julius said with
some amazement in his voice. "How did he know you
were here?"

Cathy giggled. "Oh, he keeps track of all the little girls
and boys."

Joanna looked more than a little concerned. "But
you're not little, not like me." Cathy reached down and
tugged the plump child into her arms. Suddenly, having a
little one of her own was something that she wanted,
wanted in an almost bittersweet way. At that same
instant, it occurred to Cathy that she and Drew could
have started a little girl, just like his niece. Her face
turned a bright red.

Both children noticed and Julius commented, "Don't
you feel all right, Aunt Catherine? Your face is a funny
color."

Cathy cleared her throat and set Joanna down on her
chunky little legs. "I'm excited about Christmas, that's
all. Now, you run off and tell the cook I'll be down for a
cup of tea in a few minutes. I'll get dressed and be there as
quick as a mouse."

Julius looked at her, his bright blue eyes, so like his
mother, twinkling in humor. "The cat's faster."

"Oh, all right, as quick as a cat."

The children ran from the room and Cathy dressed as
fast as a cat, she thought to herself, as she shoved her feet
into her slippers. "Of course," she murmured, "this
freezing cold room has nothing to do with how fast I'm
ready."

Soon she was accepting a cup of steaming tea from the
cook and wishing the people of the household a Happy

Christmas. Joanna and Julius led her to the pile of gifts in the parlor and Cathy sat on the gold and green brocade sofa while Julius searched among the brightly wrapped gifts. Jane and Nathan came into the room and James stood leaning against the doorjamb. They all watched as Julius finally came up with a small box. Joanna squealed in delight, "'At's it."

Jane said quietly over the children's happy chatter, "Drew sent it a week ago. He said you couldn't have it until Christmas morning."

Cathy stared at the box of velvet. Embarrassment flooded through her. She came to enjoy Christmas with the children—she never expected anything from Andrew. That he should remember her when she had nothing for him was pure agony. She sat very still for a full minute. Never before had she thought about what she gave others. She had always been more concerned with what she got. At the age of twenty years, she was truly a spoiled brat. Wiping at a tear, she muttered, "He shouldn't have."

James strode to the sofa and sat down next to her. "You don't have to open it now."

"The children want to see what Santa Claus brought me," she said, a tremor in her voice.

With care, she pulled the small silver tab to open the box. She lifted the contents for all to see. Through the tears that formed, she smiled at the disgust on Joanna's and Julius's faces. The brilliant ruby surrounded with tiny diamonds made a beautiful ring and Cathy glanced at James. "I didn't expect this."

James chuckled. "We know, and that's what makes it fun. Drew didn't want you to forget him."

The rest of the day passed in a mist for Cathy. Jane

insisted that Cathy wear the ring. It wasn't a surprise to any of them that the ring fit the fourth finger of her left hand perfectly. Cathy asked James after she placed the ring on the appropriate finger, "How did he know what size?"

James laughed out loud. "He must have measured. I can't imagine when!"

Cathy blushed a deep scarlet and Julius stared at her, true concern outlining his cherub face. "She did that this morning. Aunt Cathy, are you all right?" Cathy turned a deeper red and the adults joined in the laughter.

A Christmas dinner as traditional as any Christmas Cathy could remember graced the table. A Christmas goose, all golden goodness, glistened before the master's plate. Turnips and carrots, potatoes and bread, and several minced pies with their fragrant spices blended with the scent of the succulent goose. When they had eaten all Cathy thought she could hold for a fortnight, Jane came into the dining room, a blue flame blazing from the plum pudding in her hands. The oh's and ah's came from the adults and the children alike. The groans from the men as they left the table brought a customary "Oh, dear. Are you all right?" from Jane.

Nathan leaned over and gave her a familiar peck on the cheek. "Never better, my dear, never better." Jane smiled in pleasure. In that instant, Cathy saw herself with Andrew, ten or fifteen years from that moment. Would he be so loving? She doubted it. Nathan obviously had married Jane because he wanted to. Andrew was marrying her because he had to. There would be no love, only mistrust, perhaps hatred. Cathy sighed in dejection.

Jane reached over and patted her arm. "Oh, my dear,

don't be sad. You'll be married soon and then Andrew can take you home. I just know how homesick you must be."

Cathy winced. Thank God, Cathy thought, her sister-in-law to be was not adept at reading her thoughts.

The next two days passed pleasantly. Samuel returned from a visit to a cousin north of Richmond and it was time to go. Cathy hugged the little ones, thanked Jane and Nathan for their hospitality, invited them once more to the wedding, and climbed into the rented carriage. James climbed into the box beside Samuel. The carriage pulled away from the waving relatives.

They stopped for lunch and after the meal, Samuel decided to ride up front with the driver and James straddled the horse Samuel had ridden from Richmond. They traveled for several more hours before they stopped once more to rest the horses. Cathy noticed James and Samuel huddled together, discussing something and from all of the frowning and the gestures, Cathy guessed that they were both angry about something. Just like men, she thought. They probably both wanted to ride the horse, instead of sitting with the driver or with her.

They stopped at an inn for the night when darkness closed around them, making travel difficult. Weary to the point of a headache, Cathy did little more than stir her stew. When neither James nor Samuel had much to say, she excused herself, thinking gratefully about the bed awaiting her upstairs. When she rose from the table, James stood as well and followed her up the stairs. "I want you to lock your door. Don't open up for anyone but Sam or me. Sam and I are in the next room, so yell if anything bothers you."

Cathy felt a chill race down her spine. Was something

wrong? What was he talking about? She was perfectly safe in her room. She nodded. "If you want, but I'll be fine."

"Just do as I say," he admonished.

Cathy locked her door, tore off her dress and petticoats, then crawled into the bed. She was too tired to worry about James or even Samuel tonight. Sleep came quickly and Cathy slept deeply, with no remembered dreams and no restlessness even though she slept in a strange bed. The sky held an edge of gold when she rolled over and looked out the half-curtained window. She stretched and smiled. Whatever James and Samuel thought might take place had not taken place. She was safe in her bed at the inn.

She asked the two men what they'd been afraid of when she got to the large room on the main floor. She looked at them carefully when they chose to ignore her. They both, she decided, must have slept very little, and she giggled at their groans. "Well, whatever you imagined never came to pass. In fact, if truth be known, you are both as suspicious as two old hens. I'm fine and I do believe the two of you lost a good night's sleep for nothing."

After breakfast, they traveled on, with a short stop for lunch. Twice, Samuel and James traded places with each other, but today Cathy had one of the two men in the carriage with her all the time. Neither one of them talked much—no company for her at all. Cathy held their previous night of sleeplessness to blame. They stopped for the night and after a somber meal, James escorted Cathy up to her room, advising again that she lock the door immediately and yell for help if anything disturbed her.

Once more, she greeted a golden sunrise, and after a hearty breakfast, she sat in the carriage traveling south. They traveled a good dozen miles before the carriage pulled to a stop alongside a disabled wagon. Cathy stuck her head out the carriage window to see why they'd stopped and James, who was in the coach with her, descended from the conveyance. Plainly in distress, the wagon needed help. The right front wheel bowed under the weight of the wagon and two of the spokes were missing. Massive grays stood pawing the ground and two sweaty men wrestled with the breaking wheel. James, Samuel, and the driver all volunteered their help and soon all the men worked in shirt sleeves despite the cold temperatures, straining and heaving against the wagon.

In time, Cathy noticed that the two men who belonged with the wagon eased away from the task and let her escorts handle the wheel. She thought it peculiar but never got a chance to call attention to the fact for chaos reigned in seconds. The world around her erupted.

The grays started the mayhem. The one farthest from the carriage snorted in pain and then thundered away, pulling the wagon and the wheel out of James's and Samuel's hands. A moment later, the motion of the grays affected the horses pulling Cathy's carriage. A sharp whinny preceded a lurch and the carriage moved. In seconds, the carriage swung back and forth and Cathy jostled from left to right, then was thrown against the forward seat. She pulled herself back up as the speed of the vehicle increased frighteningly. A sixth sense told Cathy that she must brace herself for the crash she knew would come.

She had time to wonder only if she had been saved from a watery grave to die in a carriage accident when her peripheral vision recognized a blur of a horse and man. Thank God, she sighed. Someone was coming to save her.

Now that salvation was possible, she looked at her hands, which were clutching the window frame, the knuckles white. The carriage still careened wildly from side to side, but they were slowing—weren't they? At first she couldn't be certain, but then another horse and rider flew by and the carriage slowed noticeably and then stopped. Cathy threw open the door and climbed down on shaky legs. Not since the storm at sea had she come so close to disaster.

Samuel stepped from around the front of the team and Cathy looked back in the direction from where they had come. James, bareback on one of the grays, galloped up with the small man who drove their carriage clinging to his waist. Cathy glanced around. The first horse and rider had disappeared and the wagon and the other gray was gone as well. Strange, Cathy thought as she walked toward James.

The men stood around talking in low tones. Cathy walked behind the carriage, grateful to be on firm ground and infinitely glad that the men didn't seem in any hurry to get started again.

Cathy selected a spot under one of the enormous pine trees and sat watching as the three men unharnessed the carriage, examined the horses, the tongue of the vehicle, and the harnesses. By the time everything seemed to satisfy all three another hour had passed. At Samuel's signal, Cathy and James piled back into the carriage, Samuel took his place with the driver, and they were once again on their way. Cathy dismissed the episode as nothing but an unfortunate accident. She gave thanks that her escorts came away unhurt. By the end of the fourth day of travel, they arrived back at Heart's Haven and Cathy was too tired to join in the celebration on the eve of the new year. She climbed the stairs and sank into the warmed sheets of her bed. Another week or two and Drew would be back, ready to say his vows, if her ring was any indication.

Cathy tried to sleep but despite her exhaustion, the wedding and Drew occupied all of her thoughts. In the dark and silent room she laid bare her feelings, prepared to examine them. Once she knew what she felt for Drew Sloan then she could make a decision.

Carefully, as if dusting off a fine piece of porcelain, Cathy allowed the sensations of Drew, the man, to surface. He excited her, made her feel things that she had never felt before, no question about that. But what about him, what did he feel? And, in spite of the sensations that plagued her, how did she truly feel, deep down, about the man?

She pulled herself up in bed, fluffed the pillows up, then piled them in back of her and leaned back. Drew said what they felt for each other was enough to begin a marriage, but for all she knew he only felt he had to marry her because he seduced her. Could there be more? Did she really love him as she thought at one time? What about her father and his dislike for Americans?

Her father might never come around if she married Drew. And for the first time in a very long time, Cathy thought about her father's feelings. She didn't want to hurt the man who sired her, not when he gave so much to his children. Even if he couldn't give his love, he cared for her, saw that she had the best always. What about Amelia and James? If she married without her father's sanction, would William Pentworth let James Rupert, an

227

American, near his ward?

Cathy shook her head and tears rolled down her cheeks. She answered one of her questions; she did love Drew. A thrill ran from her head to her feet whenever he came close to her. She could remember, as if she felt it yesterday, the sense of security when he held her. He seemed like a good man, James liked him, and she liked his family.

She could be happy as the wife of Drew Sloan if he had any feelings for her at all. If she gave in to her own desires, though, other people would be affected. Never could she remember being concerned for how someone else felt. In its newness, it felt dreadful. She slid down into the bed. Her happiness would have to be sacrificed for her family and her friends. There could be no wedding. She cried herself to sleep.

Chapter Sixteen

Drew returned to Heart's Haven on the fourteenth of January. The week before, Cathy spent frantic hours wondering if something had happened to him. After all, she told herself, she didn't want to see anyone she knew hurt or in trouble. Her feelings, she told herself, had nothing to do with the fact that when he returned she must confront him. Only a few days remained to retract the invitations James delivered against her wishes. Poor Mrs. Benson had finished the dress and it hung in Cathy's closet. Despite her pleadings, Bessy had the kitchen staff cooking as if they had an army to feed.

Cathy stood on one foot and then another as the household army gathered to greet the master. James and Samuel accosted him before Cathy got a chance to indicate that she wanted time with him. Before she did more than give him a welcome peck on the cheek, Samuel dragged him off to the office. The door closed with a resounding bang and Cathy wandered up to her room. Tonight, she told herself, or at least first thing in the morning, she'd have her say. She squared her shoulders and tried to convince herself that she would be able to reason with him. The wedding had to be cancelled.

In the office, on the other side of the house, Samuel and James waited for Drew to shrug off his coat and pour himself a drop of whiskey. "Damn cold for January," Drew muttered. He turned toward the two men. "All right. What is so damned important that I can't greet my bride appropriately?"

Samuel looked annoyed. "She went to Jane's."

"Damn it, man. I asked Jane to invite her. Did she like the ring?"

Samuel wasn't about to be sidetracked. "There was trouble on the way home."

Drew looked at the serious expression on Samuel's face and he gave James a quick glance. "Trouble?"

"We was followed from Richmond, two blokes," Samuel said. "Not members of your better society, dockhands, probably." Samuel stopped and waited for James to add anything.

Drew wasn't interested in waiting. "What did they want? Did you talk to either one of them?"

James answered, "We ran into them about seventy miles from here. They arranged an accident with their wagon. Rather, it looked like an accident. It wasn't."

Samuel took over. "They sent the carriage flying down the road after we stopped to help. When one of the gents took off after the carriage, I figured something was up and followed. James and the driver followed me. When I got close enough to the carriage, the fellow I was following took off and left me to slow the damned thing. The other man took off with the wagon and the other horse."

"Now, wait a minute. Are you sure you're not reading

something into the situation? How do you know that the men were after Cathy?"

James and Samuel both glared at Drew. Samuel offered his opinion. "I ain't that dumb. Our carriage horses took off because one of them jackasses stuck something into the horse's flank, something sharp. A nail or the point of a knife, probably. There was blood all over the flank."

James added his thoughts. "The horse bled enough for it to be serious, very serious. The only good thing was that the fellow jabbed instead of tearing or cutting the muscle. I got the poor animal patched up and we continued home. One other thing, we said nothing to Cathy. Sam and I decided that you can tell her. She thinks something spooked the horses."

Drew paled. "Was Cathy hurt? Did she see either of the men? Did she know them?"

Once again, James answered Drew's questions. "She saw the men that first night we stopped, and if she recognized them, I missed it completely. She still thinks the horses ran, and no, she wasn't hurt."

Samuel answered the next question before Drew could ask. "We don't know who they are and we are guessing that they want Cathy. Maybe they're after you. We never caught up with them to ask."

James told Drew about the two new graves in the family plot and Samuel brought the captain of the Sloan fleet up to date with information on sailings and cargoes. Before the facts and figures were all discussed it was time for dinner.

Cathy moved about her room, rearranging small items on her dressing table, waiting for the master of the house to finish his celebration with his friends. The minutes crept by and Cathy gave up trying to name a reason why the man that insisted they marry was loath to approach her. By late afternoon, Cathy knew that despite her feelings for Drew, a marriage between them would spell disaster, even if her father gave his consent. She wanted no part of a union where the other partner had no feelings for her. No, a marriage with a one-sided love would be a tragedy. After all, she had no guarantee that Drew felt anything but lust for her. She couldn't build a relationship with that, not a lasting one.

She gave some serious thought to leaving the house and seeking transportation north. She even considered sending word to Jane Darrow that she called off the wedding and that she wanted to stay in Richmond until she got word from her father. She shook her head. No, she couldn't involve Jane. She had to do this alone.

She sat on the edge of the bed, twisting her hands in nervousness. She wanted to stay to marry the man, but she could not. Every instinct in her screamed to be heard and she shook her head in frustration. By the time dinner was announced, Cathy had a frightful headache. Bessy's cold cloths eased some of the pain and she gratefully pulled off her clothes. She ordered the thoughts to stop and climbed into her bed. Perhaps it was just as well that Drew hadn't tried to talk to her yet. She was so confused that any attempts to explain how she felt would have made her seem foolish. No, she could talk to him in the morning.

She slept poorly and by the time she dressed and made her way down the stairs for something to eat, the sun was well up in the sky. The men, Drew included, had left hours before. She tracked Samuel down in the stable. "Where is Andrew?" she said. "I haven't talked to him since he returned and we have much to say to each other."

"Cathy," Sam said quietly, "he ain't gonna let you cancel or even postpone the wedding. He said last night when you didn't come down for dinner that you weren't gonna change his plans." Sam winced. Drew said that and a whole lot more. In fact, he and James spent the morning after Drew left for the ships discussing his attitude.

Cathy was no better. She sneered at Drew's first mate. "I don't have to say the words, you know. If I don't want to go through with this, I won't. Now, where is this bridegroom who's so anxious for a wedding, but can't seem to stomach the bride?"

Sam looked embarrassed. Drew shouldn't have put him in this position, not that there was anything he could do about it. Damn it all! He'd been in the middle of this pair since he found her in the hold of the ship. "He had some things to check at the shipyards," he offered.

"A likely story," Cathy muttered as she turned and headed for the back of the house. There were no patients scheduled for Saturday. James had left to make his rounds without her and Cathy had little to do. She visited the kitchen and when the cook politely told her she was in the way, she wandered into the parlor. She sat on the sofa and stared out the curtained window. She was sick to death of analyzing her thoughts. For the first time in a long time, she wanted nothing more than to sit on the lap of her father and talk out her innermost feelings.

The thought of her father reminded her of the numerous sheets of paper in the desk in the study with only her salutation on each sheet. Now! This was the time to write and tell her father what she'd done and where it had landed her. Maybe, if she got it all down on paper, she might see the answer to her problem. She hurried to the study.

Drew found her there an hour later, several sheets of paper crumpled about the room. She had the feather of the quill pen pressed against her lips and she appeared to be deep in thought. For the space of a second he wondered if he should bother her. His brow wrinkled in disgust. For over twenty-four hours he'd been home and she hadn't thought enough of him to try and see him. Once again he wondered if this union was a tragic mistake.

Cathy felt eyes on her and she turned from the desk to look in the direction of the door. Guilt, anger, and surprise warred for expression on her face and in a husky voice she blurted out, "What do you want?"

Cathy watched as Drew strolled into the room and sank into one of the leather chairs opposite the desk without a word. He tented his fingers and Cathy grew tense waiting for him to answer her rude query. "I wanted," Drew said, his deep voice sending a thrill through her, "to talk to my bride."

She looked down at the paper on the desk. In the hour she'd struggled with this missive, she managed only five sentences. She glanced back at him and then out the window to stare at a day turned gray and cold. Without turning her head, she said, her voice quiet in the large room, "I want to talk about . . . about the wedding. I don't want to be your bride."

Drew sat up in the chair. "Now, see here!"

Cathy looked at him then, and placed the pen down. "Please, hear me out, then you can have your say."

Drew settled back in the chair and Cathy stood up, pushed in the desk chair, and stalked around the desk toward the windows, trying to organize the turmoil of thought. When she stood before the window, she turned around. "There are some things that you don't know that may change your mind about this marriage. I've thought of little else in the time you've been gone. You also never heard my full story. After I've explained things, I imagine you'll agree with me that this wedding must be called off." Drew started to comment with a shake of his head and she silenced him. "Please. Wait until I've explained."

She told of her father's feelings about Americans and how upset he was to discover that he had invited the two of them to the ball. She tried to explain what she thought her father felt for her and she told him about her father's edict after that ill-fated ball, the journey to Barbados, and her brothers. "They picked out two men for me to meet and when I cared not for either one of them, Phillip and his wife decided that I would marry the one that was their friend, a gentleman by the name of Nelson Goodspeed." Drew gave a start, but Cathy went on. "I'm not going to marry Nelson, or for that matter, anyone, unless there's love. Nelson Goodspeed's only interest is my estates; he doesn't love me. I doubt he could ever love anyone. I took a trip into town and found out about your ship. One of the slaves helped me board. I fell trying to hide. The rest you know."

For several minutes, Cathy stood in place, waiting for Drew to ask questions or comment. Her cheeks were pink with her embarrassment. This marked another first, for she couldn't remember explaining herself to anyone, not even Amelia.

Drew rose in his chair and walked to her side. "Love can come," he said softly as he placed his hands on her shoulders. "And, Cathy, even if your father despises me for the man I am, he'd still insist that I marry you. He is a gentleman and he would expect me to act the gentleman as well."

She shook her head, tears finding a path down her warm cheeks. He brushed at the tears with his thumbs. "We'll marry Friday. On Saturday James is leaving for London. He'll deliver a letter from me, and if questions are raised, he will personally explain my actions to your father." Drew pulled her against his tall frame. "Besides, James is nearly sick with love for Amelia. If he doesn't get a chance to see her, I'm sure his mind will suffer." He pushed Cathy away enough so that he could look at her face. His eyes crinkled with laughter. "You wouldn't want to be responsible for James's deteriorating mental state, now would you? See, you have to marry me." He chuckled at his joke.

Cathy stiffened and pulled herself out of his arms. "I don't think it's funny."

Drew let her go. "No, to James it isn't funny either." He moved to the door. "We'll be married Friday. Everything will be all right."

As he moved down the hall, he frowned at his thoughts. James had tried to warn him. He said she had changed a bit. Like hell she had changed a bit, she'd changed a lot.

The week passed with the waking hours a tide of activity. The nights crawled by and Cathy found herself pacing the room that would be hers only for a few more days. No answers emerged to the myriad questions that floated through her head, and she gave up asking Drew for more time. Friday she would wed. No matter what her father eventually thought or said, she was about to become the wife of one of the savage Americans. What could the future hold for her, married to a man who felt obliged to elevate his seduction to an honorable state?

Tuesday night, she actuallly packed a bag and prepared to march out of the house. She thought back on her previous escape from an attempted marriage and the devastating turn of events. She quietly unpacked the valise and returned to her bed.

Friday came and she stood looking out her bedroom window at the gray winter morning. Several hours later, a cold wet snow arrived and with it came the servants to help outfit her in her wedding dress. Bessy situated the ivory satin bodice with its cameo neckline over Cathy's head. The sleeves, tapered from the elbow to the wrist were pulled into place and the puffs that formed the upper arm were adjusted over their wicker frames. Over a stiffly starched petticoat, Bessy smoothed the skirt with its embroidered flounces into place. She guided Cathy to a long mirror to see for herself the effect the gown had on her figure.

Cathy stared back at her pale face. Long coils of curls had been secured over each ear. The woman who stared back radiated perfection in the ivory satin gown. Mrs. Benson had embroidered tiny white satin rosebuds around the neckline, the edge of the tight sleeves, and across the waist. Strings of roses ran from the waistline to the scalloped edge of the first flounce. A veil of fine tulle fashioned with matching silk rosebuds crowned her head. She looked at the white Bible and the cascade of white roses that Drew gave her to carry. A single thought stopped her inspection. Wherever had Drew gotten white roses in January?

Sam waited at the bottom of the stairs to take her to church. He would deliver her into the hands of the

Darrows, and Nathan would escort her down the aisle. Jane insisted that she serve as Cathy's maid. James would serve as the best man for Drew. As Drew suspected, his mother and his sister Paula didn't come because of the weather.

Well-wishers nearly filled the church. Cathy recognized a number of the sailors from the *Savannah Lady*, and Samuel sat in the front row, grinning at her as she came down the aisle on Nathan's arm. She chanced a glimpse of the man who would be her husband in a matter of minutes. His size was formidable, intimidating, but his countenance was so easy to look upon. No wonder Patricia Gamble threw herself at Andrew, Cathy admitted. The man was handsome beyond words. The word *bonny* came to mind and Cathy stumbled for a fraction of a second, breathless with her discovery. She chided herself; she'd forgotten how attractive this man truly was.

Nathan slipped her hand to Drew and together they faced Father Worthington. The rest of the service was a fog in Cathy's mind, but she remembered the brush of Drew's warm lips against hers and the words he whispered into her veil above her ear, "It's done now." His words registered and she pulled away to gaze up into his piercing eyes. Afraid to ask what he meant, she meekly followed at his side as he led her from the church.

They left the church to travel back to the plantation and the site of the reception. Cathy didn't want to think about Drew's words, let alone figure out what he meant by them. She turned her attention to Jane and Nathan who sat with them in the carriage. Conversation whirled around her and twice Drew turned to ask her opinion, but Cathy had little to say as the carriage bounced down the streets of Savannah. She let her mind drift. As Drew and Nathan began a dialogue about trade in the area, she thought there was something to be said for Savannah. She truly liked the vital city, from the block-long squares filled with paths and stately trees, to the crisp, clean homes of its citizens. She closed her eyes imagining how the paths would appear in the spring and summer when brilliant blossoms edged the dirt.

Drew squeezed her hand and brought her back to the group. His face was full of concern and he asked softly, "Are you all right?"

She nodded and glanced at the faces of her new brother and sister-in-law. Some comment was needed. "Just tired," she said.

By the time their carriage pulled up to Heart's Haven, guests already milled about the foyer. Drew welcomed them and led the way to the ballroom in the back of the house, Cathy's hand tucked tightly in the crook of his arm. The room was brightly lit. Servants, dressed in black, carried silver trays filled with full champagne glasses. A glass of champagne managed to find its way to her hands, but she got to take only a sip as Drew dragged her from one inquisitive group to another. He introduced her to more than a hundred people.

The afternoon was a daze for Cathy. She couldn't begin to remember the names of the people she met and Drew never gave her a chance to talk to anyone long enough to associate the name with the person. Instead, he kept pushing her forward to another group. Occasionally, he pulled her into one of the darkened doorways and nibbled at her neck or brushed his lips against hers. Once she was positive that he intentionally cupped her breast and brushed his thumb against its taut peak. Her groan sounded more like a plea to continue than an entreaty to stop, even to her ears.

When dinner was announced, Drew led her into the dining room. She counted dozens of individual tables set up around the room with some tables spilling over into the parlor and even the ballroom. Drew led Cathy to one of the smallest tables in the dining room. Festive with candles and flowers, the table was only set for two. Once the bride and groom were seated, their guests sought a place to eat and as if on signal, servants flooded the room.

When everyone was seated, Cathy scooted her chair around next to Drew's so that they could sit side by side and at least look at the crowd. Drew objected. "I want you to sit opposite me so I can see you." He stood and pulled her chair back around so that they were once again across from each other. He sat back down and signaled for the serving to begin.

First there were steaming cups of julienne soup, with strips of turnips, carrots, and onions coloring the dark beef broth. Cathy wasn't hungry, but for appearance's sake she tasted the broth then laid her spoon aside. She raised her eyes to the intense stare of her husband. Her husband! Something in her trembled and she looked back at her place setting as a cut of delicate red salmon mousse was placed before her. She glanced up and watched a small portion of pink fluff slide into her husband's mouth. A tingle ran from her fingers, through her trunk, to someplace deep in her belly. She looked in fascination at his lips. Quickly, she lowered her eyes to her own plate.

All around her she recognized the sounds of people laughing and the tinkle of silverware against china. Then, for some reason, the sounds began to fade as if their guests were floating away from them. Once more, she was brought rudely back to the present as Bessy herself removed the plate of mousse and slid another plate, this time a golden brown strip of fish covered with almonds, before her. The tantalizing smell of fried trout tickled her nose and she maneuvered a bite up to her own mouth. Her mistake was looking at her husband.

He speared a strip of fish and held it to his lips. Ever so slowly, his tongue slipped from between his lips and licked the flakes of trout. Her eyes snapped down and she took a deep breath to calm her thudding heart. She raised her eyes to determine if the man was doing this on purpose. She shuddered. It certainly looked as if he knew exactly what he was doing.

Her throat drew tight and her mouth went dry. Her hand closed around the goblet of golden wine above her plate. She tasted it and placed the crystal back on the table. Her fingers rested against the stem and she felt the urge to slide them against the smooth, cool glass, up and down, up and down. The motion stirred her memory and suddenly she was warm, much too warm. Good Lord, what was happening to her?

She kept her eyes on the next course, roast turkey with oyster sauce and baked orange squash dripping with butter and brown sugar. She glanced up at her husband and her eyes locked with his. A drop of butter and sugar glistened in the corner of his mouth. She watched as he lifted his hand and wiped the sweetness back into his mouth, then licked the glaze from his finger. Cathy sat transfixed, unable to tear her eyes away from the man she had just married. His smug expression left no doubts. He knew precisely what he was doing.

The fragrant smell of roasted meat greeted her as the

next course came to the table. Cathy lowered her eyes in embarrassment. She was not breathing properly and her heart was beating in the most ridiculous manner. Sometime between the trout and the turkey, Cathy forgot there were other people in the room. She didn't even realize that Bessy placed a small crown roast of lamb stuffed with small potatoes and bright green peas before them.

Drew pulled off a rib and handed it to her and then he pulled off a piece for himself. Once again Cathy was tortured as he licked the dripping juices from the bone and from his fingers. His pearl white teeth opened to close on the meat, pulling a chunk of lamb into his mouth. After the meat disappeared, he placed the bone into his mouth and gnawed at it. The lusty sounds stopped her breathing. Hypnotized, she watched as his lips pursed and the muscles of his throat moved up and down. Never once did his eyes leave hers.

She wiggled in the chair, the moisture accumulating between her thighs. If he didn't stop, she would be panting all over him. Suddenly, she realized where she was. The bone Drew gave her when the roast was served fell from her numb fingers and clattered onto her plate. Just as swiftly, Drew had his napkin in his hands and the juice and meat were gone from his fingers. In one swift movement, he stood, pulling Cathy's chair away from the table. Without a word of warning to her or to the guests, he swung his wife up into his arms. In seconds, they were out of the dining room with Drew's family and friends laughing and calling out to them.

Cathy glared up into the face of her husband. "How dare you embarrass me like this!"

Drew chuckled. "My dear wife, when you see the

242

condition I'm in, you'll be more than grateful that I swept you from the room."

Two bright peach spots colored her pale cheeks and her mouth formed a silent "oh." She looked up into the face of her husband and the tension in his face told her exactly where they were going and for what reason. A flush spread over her face and a desire for the passion he could stir in her blossomed deep inside. She snuggled into his arms, no longer concerned with the dozens of guests that were dining only a few feet from the stairs.

Chapter Seventeen

A fire blazed in the hearth of the master bedroom. Drew released Cathy, letting her slide down the front of him. He held her close, absorbing her fragrance, feeling her draw gulps of air, hearing the gasps of anticipation as he trailed his fingers up and down her spine.

Cathy leaned into Drew, aware of the frantic beating of her heart and the answering cadence of his. She could feel his arousal, hot and hard against her belly. Drew lowered his lips to taste her sweetness, sending tingles of pleasure through the rest of her body. She took a ragged breath and rested against his encircling arms, knowing that she could not sustain herself without his support. Drew seemed to understand and drew her closer yet.

One kiss ended and another began and without thought, Cathy reached up to loosen the frill from around his neck. Her fumbling fingers struggled with the buttons of his waistcoat and his shirt. She felt his fingers working against the buttons down the back of her dress. He pulled back and studied her veil. "This must go," he muttered and Cathy nodded her head in agreement.

Suddenly, nothing seemed as important as being able to touch his naked body.

With that goal planted in her feverish brain, she began with a vengeance to loosen, to pull, and to discard his waistcoat and vest. She yanked his shirt from his pants and pulled it from his shoulders. Cathy never gave a thought to the clothing that she threw to the floor. Her thoughts demanded that she remove anything that would separate her flesh from her husband's.

She was unconcerned about the beautiful dress that Drew tugged from her, or the fragile veil that he dragged from her hair. Hairpins, tulle, satin, silk—all fell onto an ever-expanding pile on the floor. In no time, Drew knelt at her feet, rolling down her stockings, pitching those and her slippers off to one side. He even allowed her to remove his socks and shoes. Once the clothing disappeared, he pulled her into his arms and growled into her curls, "I'm not letting you out of my arms. Not tonight, and probably not tomorrow, either."

She turned toward him, glorying in his nakedness, satisfied for a short time at least to enjoy the warmth of his body. A tiny voice nagged at her. "He doesn't love you. You're only an object that he can enjoy for the moment." She commanded the voice to silence, telling herself that he had to have some affection for her, given the glances he settled on her. Perhaps, as he said, love would come.

Drew cradled her in his arms and approached the bed. It had been weeks since he held her like this and he wondered if he would be able to control himself. She was passionate, but he was hungry, nearly starved for the warmth she possessed. He would like nothing better than to throw her onto the bed and plunge into her moist heat. Although she didn't love him, he loved her and he could not treat her so. No, tonight he would show her without words how he felt, even if in the process he lost his sanity.

Cathy stretched out on the fresh linens, unconcerned about her state of nakedness. She wanted to be held by the man who claimed her as his bride. As if the thought was a command, Drew pulled her into his arms and lowered his head to her exposed throat.

Cathy sighed in pleasure as Drew nibbled his way from the base of her neck up to her ear. His warm lips brushed her closed lids, her cheeks, even her nose, as he headed for her lips. She couldn't abide his tantalizing touches and she grabbed his head, meeting his mouth. When he started to protest, she let her tongue caress the large pearly teeth, the full, hot lips. He tasted of wine and beef and man, and she thrilled to his essence. She cupped his cheeks with her palms, holding him still so that she could continue her kiss. It occurred to her that her behavior marked her as brazen, a hussy, a wanton, but still she could not drag her lips from his.

He broke the kiss and her groan was mournful. He chuckled. "We have all night, wife. If I let you kiss me like that for very long, this night would soon be over for me and I'm sure you wouldn't like that. No, you wouldn't like that at all."

Cathy opened her eyes and gazed into Drew's hazel stare, eyes full of passion and something Cathy'd never seen before. She almost asked him what he was thinking. Then his hand snaked up her ribs and cupped her breast. Anticipation rippled through her, sweet pleasure sang through her soul. She instantly forgot everything. In fact, she wasn't sure of her name. Her breath dragged through her lungs at a painfully slow pace and her body arched against the bed. "Please," she cried, not able to tell him what she wanted.

He lowered his lips to the tiny pink crest that seemed to beg for attention. He intended to pull the nipple into his mouth, but a thought struck and he blew gently on the nub. Cathy responded immediately, pulling his head to her breast. Drew laughed and attacked the rose-colored nipple, already hard with desire. He licked and suckled at her breast as she writhed on the sheets, her soft moans proclaiming her pleasure even though words could not be formed. Drew switched his attentions to the other breast, then lifted himself above her. Nudging her knees apart, he fitted himself over her. There was no question, he had to take her soon, or embarrass himself.

Cathy accepted his weight and whispered into his ear, "Kiss me."

Drew released her breast and raised himself above her. His lips touched her as his manhood sought entrance. His tongue slid into her mouth as his hardness slid into the warm moistness waiting for him. He continued the kiss but he held himself tense, knowing that the slightest motion would inspire the end. Gradually the pressure lessened and Drew eased himself back, then forward, then back again.

A need past anything Cathy had ever known consumed her and she pulled away from him, then arched against him in a rhythm as old as the tide. She needed the release he could bring and she needed it at that exact moment. Pleasure pulled at her, warm, hot searing. She held her breath and it began. Pinpricks of pleasure where they joined spread out like the ripples of a lake, washing over her with exquisite rapture.

When she could breathe again, she opened her eyes to stare into the astonished gaze of her husband. The other times he'd pleasured her, it had never been so intense or come so fast. She swallowed with difficulty and asked softly, "Was it all right?"

Drew rolled to his side, taking her with him. He sighed into her hair, trying hard to regain his own ability to speak. She asked if it was all right! "Dear wife, I have never experienced anything quite like that. It was . . . it was . . ." He realized that there was no way to adequately describe what had just happened. "Let's just say," he whispered in her ear, "it will be hard to match such perfection, ever . . ." Drew looked at the soft features of Cathy's face. She was already asleep. He sighed, pulled the covers up over them, tightened his hold on her, and closed his own eyes. She was his wife, she was his. . . . He drifted off to sleep.

How long he slept, Drew wasn't certain, but the stub of the candle sputtered against the darkness. He looked down at Cathy and wondered if he should wake her and show her again how he felt about her. In the flickering light, he studied her oval face and the long lashes that fanned out against her cheeks. Even in her sleep she looked troubled. Had he done the right thing by marrying her? he wondered. In her sleep she turned toward him and Drew bent down to brush his lips against the brown mole by her right ear. Tomorrow was soon enough to express his love again. He blew out the candle, laid his head on the pillow, and pulled her into his arms.

*　　　*　　　*

The sun had greeted a new day several hours before Cathy awoke in the big bed in Drew's room. She reached out to touch his side of the bed. It was cold! He'd been up for some time. Blushing at her nakedness, she reached for her robe which was lying conspicuously across the foot of the bed. Drew or Bessy? Cathy was afraid to speculate. She splashed some warm water from the pitcher on the washstand over her face and smiled. Someone knew she would soon be stirring, she decided.

Her expression turned from pleasure to concern as she wondered how she would dress. Her clothes were in the room down the hall and all she had in this room was her robe and the wedding gown. She glanced around the room for the dress. Some tidy soul had removed that as well. She slumped into the chair before the fire. Now what?

Before she grew more concerned, Drew stuck his head in the door. He grinned at her. "I have breakfast, but you'll have to get back in bed."

Cathy smiled in pleasure. "I don't remember when I ever had breakfast in bed. I don't mind getting back in bed for breakfast."

Drew looked hurt. "You're not going to stay in bed today? What a shame. Well, after we have breakfast, you can pack."

"Now wait." Cathy stopped on her way to the bed. Was he going to disrobe and climb back in bed with her to share breakfast? The tray was full of covered dishes, so a shared breakfast was very possible. What about packing? "Where am I going that I need to pack?"

"We," he said, setting the tray down on a small table by the chair she vacated, "are taking a wedding trip. We

250

need to get to know each other and I don't want any lost souls arriving for medical help. Especially since James will leave with the tide this evening."

She crawled back in bed. "Where are we going? And are you coming back to bed?" She looked a bit hesitant.

Drew chuckled and pulled the chair then the table up to the bed. "I'll eat here; you get breakfast in bed. We are going to Charleston. If you're ready, we'll leave tomorrow."

Cathy gazed at him, her face a study of confusion and surprise. "But Charleston is far away. I just came back from Richmond."

Drew laughed out loud, then took his seat. "Carriage travel is still a poor way to travel. The *Savannah Lady* is at our disposal. Samuel will captain it to Charleston, then go north to Baltimore for cargo and return to Charleston. We should be ready to come back here by that time."

For a second, Cathy was touched with anger. He never asked her about a wedding trip. Then she remembered the days before the wedding and how she had deliberately avoided him. He couldn't have discussed a trip even if he had wanted to. She picked up her fork and attacked the food on her plate.

Drew watched her expression. "Cathy, we don't have to take a wedding trip. I thought it would be a good idea to leave the plantation so that we could spend some time together without fear of interruption. If you would rather not travel to Charleston, we can go someplace else, or we can stay here, although I'd rather not."

Her lips curved slightly. "A trip to Charleston sounds fine. I agree we should get away. I'm surprised, that's all.

We never talked about it and I didn't even think you wanted a trip. We have done so much traveling in the last several months."

Drew lifted her hand and stroked her fingers with his thumb. "Cathy, here in the United States, we travel all the time. It's nothing to go from here to Philadelphia or Baltimore. Trails are being carved from here to the interior. There's a huge territory being opened up in the middle of the country and we have a good many states west and north of the mountains. It's a big country and if you want to do and see anything you must travel."

His eyes glistened with excitement. "There's even a turnpike under construction from Philadelphia through the middle states to the river and there's a special kind of ship, shallow with a steam engine, that's being used on the Mississippi. In fact, the cargo Samuel is picking up in Baltimore must go to New Orleans, then by steamboat up the river. I planned to tell you later about that trip, but when we return from Charleston, I'll have to take the *Savannah Lady* to New Orleans. I'll be gone for two months."

Cathy lifted her eyes from her plate. "Will I be traveling with you?"

Drew shook his head. "No, it can be rough this time of year. I thought you would rather stay here and handle some of the minor medical emergencies that come up. We don't want James to lose all of his practice while he's in England."

"When did you say you wanted to leave for Charleston?"

Drew looked pleased. "I'd like to leave tomorrow afternoon. You can have the servants help with the packing today, after Mrs. Benson arrives with your clothes."

"Clothes?"

Drew grinned. "I ordered another wardrobe. Now that you are my wife, and we'll be traveling to a big city, I thought you needed some more things. She'll be here in about an hour."

Cathy placed her fork on her plate. "How am I to dress now? My clothes—"

Drew interrupted her. "Are in the wardrobe. Bessy moved everything to this room yesterday before dinner. After all, this is your room too."

Cathy looked embarrassed. "I'm to share your room?"

Drew stood and started for the door. He nodded and glanced at his wife, his face solemn. "This is where you belong."

Cathy sat quietly for several minutes before the table. She had considered that their marriage might be a marriage in name only. After all, he felt a duty to marry her. It appeared that he had nothing like that in mind for them. They were to have a real marriage. A lance of pleasure stabbed at Cathy's heart. Perhaps a life of happiness and contentment was possible.

And, she thought as she stood, her bridegroom wanted to show her Charleston. She hurried to the wardrobe. She must pack, see to Mrs. Benson, and write a letter for James to take to her father. She had no time to waste. She pulled a day dress from the wardrobe. Before she left the room she glanced at the big bed, the matching wardrobes along the wall, and the hearth with its matching chairs. This great room, this very comfortable room now was hers.

In a happy frame of mind, she tackled the first task, the letter to her father. No easier to write than the previous letters, she ended up with only three sentences: *Dear Father, Please forgive me for worrying you. I am safe and happy. I am also married.*

She stared at the note for a long time, but she had nothing more to write. If she could sit down with her father and talk to him, she might find a thousand things to say, but the white paper and the black ink looked so cold and impersonal.

Cathy finished her letter just as Mrs. Benson arrived with a new trunk, a dozen dresses, and several boxes of lingerie. There was a fur-lined cloak, shoes, boots, and several bonnets. Cathy stopped her husband in his path down the hall and whispered in a stricken tone, "This must have cost a fortune. I don't need all of this."

Drew smiled at her concern. "I want you to have it. Humor me, all right?"

Hesitantly she nodded and made her way to Mrs. Benson in her old room where the gowns would be tried on. In less than an hour, Widow Benson was on her way back to town and Cathy stood amid a pile of finery, stunned to silence by the tale Mrs. Benson told and the amount of garments spread before her. Everything fit to perfection and the seamstress interspersed her exclamations of pleasure and pride over the garments with how they came into being.

Drew, it seemed, ordered every single item before he went to Philadelphia. He selected, according to Mrs. Wilson, every bit of trim, the bonnets, the slippers, the fabric for the gown, even the fur for the cloak. The wardrobe was complete; he missed nothing, from the ribbons for her hair, to the garters for her silk stockings.

Cathy glanced at the box of lingerie and blushed scarlet. Drew chose the finest, sheerest cotton for chemises and pantaloons, trimmed with the most scandalous amounts of lace. Obviously, they were not only to be worn, but also to be seen. She blushed furiously, knowing who would see them.

Cathy quickly packed them up so that the servants wouldn't see them. She was going to have a difficult time trying to wear them, without having the servants laughing and giggling over her undergarments. She finished just as Bessy bustled into the room, several of the younger girls behind her. "Time to pack you up, missy. The Mistah wants you in the office." She pushed Cathy toward the door. "Tell that boy his dinner's ready."

When she got to the door, Cathy turned around. "Bessy, I didn't thank you for yesterday. The food was beautiful and the house looked so nice. I know Drew was pleased, as I was. Thank you."

Bessy waved her hands at her young mistress. "Don't you think a thing 'bout it. It were mah pleasure. I done waited a long time to see that boy married an' to a gal that makes him happy. You go on and have yer lunch with that boy. We'll get you packed up, so's you can go to Charleston. Now, you go on."

Cathy smiled. Servants all over the world were the same. They knew exactly what went on in their households, from England to America.

They hurried through lunch which was food left from the wedding dinner. Over a cup of tea, Drew asked if she would like to accompany him to Savannah to see James

255

away. She declined, offering the excuse that she had too much to do. Cathy spent the afternoon in her room trying to fit her new finery into the trunk Mrs. Benson brought. Cathy felt the afternoon had just begun when she heard the carriage return and she groaned in frustration. It was entirely possible that she would never be ready to go to Charleston the next day. She chewed at her bottom lip and looked at Bessy doubled up with her head in the trunk. "We are not going to be ready, Bessy. I won't be able to leave for another day at least."

From the doorway, a husky male voice chuckled and asked, "Why not? You don't have to take much more than your nightgowns and your dressing robes."

Cathy whirled around, her face flaming. "I . . . You should not say . . . Bessy . . ." She was completely flustered.

Drew walked into the room and put his arms around her. "I'm sorry. I didn't mean to tease, but you sounded so undone. Cathy, I'm sorry!" She looked ready to cry. He kissed her forehead and whispered in her ear, "Bessy knows how I feel, but I didn't mean to embarrass you." He said out loud, "Take five day dresses, one evening gown, and one or two riding suits. Oh, and take that gray traveling suit. I got these to go with it." He pulled a nosegay of pink roses from a box he held.

"Oh, Drew. They're beautiful. Wherever did you get them? That reminds me, where did you get the white roses I carried yesterday?"

He looked pleased. "One of my college friends has a glass house and he is constantly experimenting with flowers. He's had some success with roses. The white roses were his idea. He'll be delighted that you liked them." He stepped away from Cathy. "Now, let's have something to eat and let Bessy finish here. She'll have everything you'll need packed and ready. She's very good at that."

The large black woman flushed with pleasure. "Ah, now, Mistah Drew. You tryin' to turn an ole woman's head? You go have yer vittles and I do things up here. Now, go on with you!"

True to Drew's word, Bessy packed everything and they were ready to leave Heart's Haven the next afternoon.

After a simple evening meal, Cathy and Drew walked around the deck of the *Savannah Lady*, watching the lights of Savannah fade as they sailed down the river toward the Atlantic. Soon they snuggled together, kissing and caressing each other under the light of the moon.

Late the next day they arrived in Charleston. The wide harbor bustled with ships and Cathy looked over the expanse of water between the ocean and the city. "Why," she said, turning to Drew, her expression one of shock, "this is an enormous harbor. You could put a whole fleet of ships here and there would still be plenty of room." Drew smiled at her exuberance. This trip would be exciting for both of them.

For eight days, they strolled the streets of the city, sat together watching the ships from White Point, and talked. Drew told her about growing up around ships and his desire to take his own cotton across the ocean to sell. He described his days in school, and his friendship with James Rupert. She told him about her brothers and her mother. She passed quickly over the thought that William Pentworth had no love left for her and described instead the education she had shared with Charles. She told him in detail why her father hated Americans.

They ate at several taverns and enjoyed two meals at the homes of two of Drew's college friends. Each evening they retired to their bedroom and shared a growing recognition of their exploding passions. Drew began to hate the thought that he had cargo to take to New Orleans. One evening after an especially passionate loving, Drew rested with his head on Cathy's breast and she admitted, "This trip is wonderful. I never knew wedding trips could be such fun. I'll think twice before I tell you I don't want to go someplace again."

Drew picked his head up and looked at her. "Good! I'll come back from New Orleans, spend two days in bed with you, and then we'll go north to meet Paula and my mother. They expressed their disappointment that I wanted to have you all to myself for this week. We won't stay more than a month, but I want you to meet them, and I want them to tell me what a wonderful choice I've made."

Cathy laughed. "Not a bit arrogant, not at all."

Two days later, they sailed back to Savannah. Drew escorted Cathy back to the plantation and he left the next morning to load another cargo into the hold of the *Savannah Lady*. Cathy took the carriage into Savannah and watched with tears in her eyes as Drew ordered the sails unfurled. He was leaving her for two months. She made her way back to the plantation, her heart heavy. The two weeks since her wedding had done one thing to Cathy. She was now so in love with Andrew Sloan that she wondered if she could go on with her life if his was to end. Her heart told her no. She offered a litany of prayers that she would not have to try to answer that question for years to come.

In the weeks that followed, Cathy threw herself into the management of the plantation. One former patient of James came by with a minor emergency and Cathy splinted and bandaged the broken finger. One of the slaves came back from the trip to Savannah and Cathy overheard him tell Bessy that two men were looking for a girl that fit Missy Sloan's description. A cold chill ran down Cathy's back. Had William Pentworth or Phillip and Charles sent someone to bring her back?

Chapter Eighteen

By the end of the second day aboard the *Savannah Lady*, Drew knew a loneliness he never imagined. The winds moved the ship through the spring waves, and he recorded knot after knot in the log. Drew paced the deck, the wheelhouse, and his cabin, missing his young wife with each step. By the end of the fourth day, his crew swore he wore a path through his ship. But all his pacing didn't shorten an hour of the trip.

Shortening this voyage, he reasoned, pulling himself back to the task at hand, meant shaving days off their sailing time. And that meant study and daring, but having Cathy back in his arms was worth the effort. With the decision made he studied the charts, took his readings, and plotted his position, daily calculating his speed. He made a mental note that never again would he sail without the brown-haired beauty at his side.

In his off moments Drew scratched his head, wondering what had happened to him. Him! Fun-loving Andrew Sloan, apple of his mother's eye, successful sailor and captain, a man that women flocked to with little regard to consequences, was dull, full of pain, and interested in only one thing, getting back to his wife.

At the thought of his lady, Drew smiled. He really should have confessed to her long ago how he felt. His love for the woman at his plantation consumed him. He closed his eyes and pictured her face, her neat, trim body, her full breasts. He felt a tightening in his groin and groaned with displeasure. If a man could be driven to insanity by celibacy, by the end of this cruise he might be a candidate. He willed her to the fringes of his mind.

Still in the late hours of the day, when Drew sought his bed, her perfection came back to him out of the darkness to taunt and tease. He saw her long silken legs, her tightly rounded buttocks, and he could almost feel her satin smooth skin. Her own special fragrance, heightened by a touch of soft rose scent invaded his memory and he crawled from his large bed to pace the corners of the cabin. Yes, he could well be insane by the end of this trip. He gave little thought to James and the task he set his friend.

A cold north wind sent the square-rigged merchantman, the *Carolina*, across the ocean at record speed. James pulled his greatcoat around his bulk and set his chin against the gusts. He strolled the deck, wiping the freezing mist from his bright hair with fingers nearly stiff with the cold. He reminded himself that Amelia waited at the end of this journey. For her he could survive.

When the slick planks made a stroll impossible, James spent the hours in his cabin, rereading all of the correspondence he received from Amelia. To date he had twenty-three letters. With every ship that came from

England, he had received at least another two and sometimes three letters. He consoled himself that she missed him as much as he missed her. And now, after seven long months, he was returning. He vowed he would not leave England without her.

Several minor weather skirmishes tossed the *Carolina* about, but with little damage done. They were never far off their course. Six weeks and three days after he left the Savannah River, James Rupert looked out over the land mass once called the mother country. They had arrived.

Many hours later, James left the ship with the packet of information Drew had pressed into his hands. Reluctantly, James turned his attention to the matters at hand and the small, tidy office close to the docks. Drew's first request concerned business and James saw the agent, then made his way into Londontown to find the hotel Drew suggested. It took almost no time before James found the place and he felt the city turn into a lady well known, if not loved. He ordered a bath, a meal, and put himself to rights. With his jacket and trousers pressed, his shirt fresh, and his skin feeling almost free of salt, he left his lodgings. He patted his jacket pocket. The letters were safe. He whistled at a cabby; Amelia waited.

The streets were crowded and James watched the milling throng heave, first in one direction, then another, as his carriage wandered toward the homes of wealthy citizens. He straightened his frill and creased his trousers with his fingers. Houses that held some recognition went by and James pulled on his gray suede gloves. The cabbie stopped and James swung down from the cab. "Wait for me," he ordered and strode toward the house.

In seconds, a very correct butler answered his sharp

rap. James drew himself up to his five feet and eight inches and presented his card to the butler. "I would like to see Mr. William Pentworth, if he is at home."

The butler held the door. "I'll see if he is receiving." The servant moved from the opening.

"Tell him," James raised his voice, "I've come about Catherine, his daughter." The butler didn't seem all that impressed and James was left standing in a small corner of the foyer. He stayed right there. He couldn't afford to antagonize William Pentworth.

The minutes drifted by and James wondered where Amelia was and if by some chance he might catch a glimpse of her, however brief. He looked around hoping that she would appear because he willed it so. With the arrival of the butler his attention returned to the first task at hand.

The tall, thin servant pointed at a door off the foyer. "In the study, sir."

James offered his thanks and headed toward the room the servant indicated. The door closed softly and James looked around the spotless office. A large desk of glistening ebony wood stood in the center of the room. In front of the desk and at strategic points in the room, high-backed leather chairs stood ready to receive guests. The rich, dark leather was well used and James wondered again about the father of Catherine.

He withdrew the letters and stood facing the door. It would not do to let William Pentworth catch him off guard. Minutes passed and finally when James began to think that he had been forgotten, William Pentworth came through the door.

William was just as James remembered, a little thinner perhaps, and definitely not pleased with the unannounced arrival of an American visitor. His bushy, gray brows were drawn into a straight line and his blue-gray eyes had the look of cold steel about them. His weathered olive face crinkled with concern and his pointed chin trembled. He raised his hand to stroke his chin. "You brought a letter from Catherine? How do you know my daughter, sir?"

"Mr. Pentworth, my name is James Rupert. I thought you might remember. I attended a ball here last June. I met Catherine for the first time then. Your niece Amelia and I have been writing." James took in the look of distress that crossed William's face. It appeared that Amelia had said nothing to her uncle about the American doctor to whom she corresponded. "These will explain more." He handed the two envelopes to the older man.

William took both crisp coverings and stared at the bold scrawl of one and the wispy feminine script of the other. "This looks like Catherine's hand," William said softly.

"Sir!" James was startled. It never occurred to him or to Drew that William would raise a question about the authenticity of the notes. "I can assure you that Catherine wrote the one and—"

William cut him off. "We'll see." He strode to his desk, yanked out the chair, and slumped into the leather. He offered no chair to James and as James stood watching the man behind the desk, he wondered if William Pentworth believed a word he said or Drew wrote. James carefully considered William as the man read and then reread Catherine's short note. Finally, with concern and disbelief scoring his features, William raised his eyes. "Do you know what's written here?"

Alarm settled over James and he cleared his throat in

pain. He had no idea what Catherine had written to her father. His pale complexion lightened a bit more, and he shook his head. "No, I have no idea what she wrote. I hope she told you that she is all right and that she is married. She is married!" James added, hoping to explain his presence if Cathy's note did not mention that all-important fact.

James struggled to stand still and confident in the face of William's chagrin. "She is married, sir. To my best friend. Please, would you consider the other letter?"

William glanced at the other letter and at the man before him. The letter in his hand, the one that appeared to have been written by Catherine, was as this young red-haired man said. She was in good health and she was married. William frowned. What sort of charade was this man orchestrating? Why, only two weeks before, Phillip wrote that Catherine had been pledged to a Nelson Goodspeed and wedding plans were proceeding. He raised his eyes to his visitor. "I'll read both of these letters several times over, I imagine. If I have questions, where may I reach you?"

James stared at the man, stunned. William Pentworth did not believe any part of what had transpired. He searched his mind for some tidbit of information from Catherine that would force the man to believe her note. He remembered! "Catherine would be here herself to tell you about the wedding, but you, sir, insisted that she wait until she was large with child."

James watched as the color slowly ebbed from William Pentworth's face. At least, James's remark gave the man something to think about. James named his hotel. "I'm sure you will see me several times over the course of the next several days." James turned on his heel and strode from the room. He and Drew made no plans for such a problem. Now what did he do? And this was certainly not the time to ask to court Amelia. He strode from the house and climbed into the waiting cabbie.

James spent the next twenty-four hours trying hard to think up something that would convince Cathy's parent that she was well and truly married. Nothing came to mind. For the present, he decided, he would concentrate on reaching Amelia. That might be as difficult as persuading William Pentworth to accept the truth about Catherine.

James found a young lad anxious to make a shilling or two, who claimed to know several of the families around the Pentworths' home. The boy was about ten, tall for his age, but clean. "I ain't been on the street very long," he confessed. "Me mother and me baby sister caught the pox. They died a month ago. I was with my uncle, but I ran away. He didn't want me, not with his own brood." James offered him a hot meal and the task. By the end of the day, the lad secured the names of Amelia's maid and two of the Pentworth stable boys. The lad, Griffin, Grif for short, moved into James's rooms, accepted the position James offered, and started carrying notes.

Grif hurried back to the hotel. "The lady sure was happy," he told James. "She was crying and laughing and she must have asked me six times if I wanted ter eat. I told her I supped with you." He handed James a small piece of parchment. "I'm to take yer answer yet tonight."

James broke the seal. She agreed to meet him at one of the teahouses close to his rooms the day after tomorrow at two in the afternoon. James grinned with pleasure. Quickly he sat and replied, "Take this to the lady and then we'd best get you some clothes and I think we better start with some education." He handed the correspondence to Grif. "Young man, would you be interested in a life in the United States?"

Grif stared at James, his big brown eyes wide and warm. His mother talked often about the land across the sea. Grif brushed a tear from his eye. "Me mother told me all about that place. She has three sisters over there. Ya, I'll go with ya to this here United States."

James looked at the boy. "It'll be awhile before I can leave, but when I go, you'll travel with me. However, in the next several weeks, I want you to learn to read and to write some."

Grif tucked the note in his pocket, and started out the door, a large smile plastered over his large front teeth.

With Grif to feed and clothe, and with a need to begin his education, James kept busy for the next day. As the time drew close to meet Amelia, though, he had trouble keeping his mind on much of anything. He succeeded in getting Grif to stay at the hotel and study his letters while James made his way to the teahouse an hour before Amelia was expected.

He laughed with delight when he saw her carriage draw up before the shop forty minutes early. James dashed to the carriage and it was all he could do to keep from swinging the brown-haired girl into his arms and planting a most embarrassing kiss on her lips. James stared into her brilliant green eyes as he handed her down to the cobblestone walk. "I've missed you."

Amelia smiled up at him, her place on the walkway forgotten. "I've missed you, too."

James drew her arm through his and escorted her into the teahouse. He settled Amelia's maid at a nearby table and seated Amelia at a table for two. He dragged his chair next to hers, grinned down at her, and kissed her hand. "I came to the house three days ago, but I didn't see you. Did William say anything? Did he tell you about Catherine?"

Amelia's dark lashes fluttered. "You came to the house? He didn't say a thing."

James took a deep breath. This was going to take more time than he wanted to give to it. He didn't want to talk about Drew and Cathy, he wanted to talk about Amelia and himself. "Amelia, Cathy married Drew Sloan in January." For the next half-hour, James told Amelia all he knew, what Cathy told him, and how William acted when James brought word.

James answered all of Amelia's questions and before he had a chance to comment to her about his plans, it was past time for Amelia to leave. "I don't think that you should come to the house to call just yet," Amelia said quietly. "If Uncle William hasn't accepted the truth of the letters, he won't let me see you. Shall we meet in the park where we met before?"

A blush stained her cheek and James grinned. "I remember every place we met, especially the park. Come tomorrow. Come early, about one. I'll be waiting."

He hired a carriage and helped Amelia up into the vehicle. Her maid followed and James lifted her fingers to his lips. "Until tomorrow!"

The next afternoon, Grif and James waited by a cluster of oaks in the park. Amelia was only a minute late but James died several deaths before he spotted her carriage. He introduced Grif formally and left Grif with Amelia's maid. He and Amelia began to walk. "I asked Uncle William if he had heard from Catherine lately. I told him I hadn't had a letter for months. He looked surprised, but he didn't say anything. He doesn't believe what you say."

James shook his head in confusion. "Has he heard from Catherine? He must have the impression that she is tucked safely away in Barbados. Would Phillip let his father think that things were well when they were not? I certainly can't see Charles letting something like that happen. Amelia, you have to find out what's going on. Cathy and Drew won't be coming here until your uncle asks them to. I know my friend! And your cousin is much too terrified of her father to try to talk Drew into coming. No, your uncle has to ask them to come."

Amelia sighed in disgust. "This is a tangled mess. I can't shake off the feeling that if Uncle William knew about you, I'd be forbidden to see you."

James frowned. "I didn't know that you hadn't told him about our letters. I mentioned it that first visit."

Amelia laughed. "I know. He asked me about it. I told him that we had corresponded several times. He seemed satisfied for the moment. I would have wondered more about it, I suppose, but I didn't get your note telling me you were here until the next morning."

James squeezed her fingers gently. "I'm not leaving without you this time. I'll wait until William will let me talk to you, then I'll ask for your hand. You won't mind a simple, quick wedding will you?"

Amelia's soft giggle teased at a warm spot in James's stomach. "No, not at all. In fact, the sooner the better. Let me find out what I can about Barbados and perhaps I can draw Uncle William out."

James escorted her back to the carriage and her maid and they agreed to meet in two days. James watched her go. "It'll be the damnedest, longest two days in the world," he grumbled.

Even Grif complained about James's solemn attitude, but the two days finally passed and James waited for the carriage that would bring Amelia to his side. She stepped from the coach, her eyes wide with pain, and James hugged her close. "I can tell from your dark green eyes that you have news."

They walked together without conversation for several minutes, then Amelia put out her hand to stop him. "Uncle William does not believe you. He showed me Phillip's last three letters. Phillip has chosen a husband for Cathy and although there is no mention of Cathy's reaction, or what she's doing, I can't believe that Phillip would lie to his father. Are you sure that Catherine Pentworth married your friend?"

"Amelia! I know Cathy. I met her here! We talked about Charles and you. The woman who married Drew Sloan is Catherine Pentworth. I don't know who Phillip has in Barbados, but Cathy is in Savannah."

Amelia frowned. "Something is not right and I'm afraid that Uncle William is getting suspicious of me. Perhaps we should not see each other for a time."

"Not a chance!" James swore. "I think it's about time that I talked to your uncle. I brought a few references with me this time. I'll make an appointment and talk to him."

"He may not see you."

"He'll see me!" James said with conviction. They walked on for several minutes. They passed a huge weeping willow tree, the thick leaves dripping to the warm earth. James glanced around. They were alone in this part of the park. He took her arm and quickly guided her under the branches. "My dear girl, I can't walk with you another minute without tasting your sweet lips."

271

James gazed into her deep green eyes, almost afraid that she would be fearful or angry or shocked.

Her eyes brightened with anticipation and James took her into his arms. Their lips touched for the first time and James knew a moment of bliss. He brushed a number of soft kisses against her mouth and once again pressed his lips against hers. He touched her pink petals with the tip of his tongue and she opened for him. Tracing her moist fullness, he ventured into her mouth, inviting her to taste of him. The kiss deepened and James knew a second of fear. Could he stop? He didn't want to let her go, not ever. He pulled away and smiled at her clouded gaze. "We better stop or, sweetheart, I won't be able to. I'll see William tomorrow. We better wed soon or I'll end up ravaging you."

Amelia looked at him shyly. "Can you ravage me if I'm willing?"

James groaned. "I'm not going to answer that. I'll see William tomorrow." He brushed her kiss-bruised lips again and resolutely led her from under the willow tree. "Tomorrow," he murmured as he guided her back the way they came.

It took several days to make an appointment with William Pentworth and then he saw James only because the father of one of Charles's close friends insisted. James presented himself for the morning appointment fashionably dressed and nervous as a child caught with a handful of stolen teacakes. The interview began poorly.

"I don't usually admit liars to my home," William Pentworth said crisply. "I don't like being pressured either. Now, are you here to apprise me of the next development in your charade?"

James stood his ground. "Mr. Pentworth, despite your

272

information, Catherine is married to Andrew Sloan of Savannah, Georgia. I am not here to discuss Andrew or Catherine. Today I have come about Amelia."

William looked annoyed. "What about Amelia?"

"I would like, sir, your permission to court Amelia Pentworth. My intentions are honorable. I am a doctor, I have a growing practice, and I want Amelia for my wife."

The annoyed look left William's face. For a second, James saw amazement, then anger. "You want what?" William thundered.

James answered quietly, "I want to court Amelia. I want her for my wife."

"No," William answered. He waved his arm. "Peterson will show you out."

James was not ready to leave. "I ask that you think about it, sir. I have letters of reference with me from your friends. I could make Amelia happy. We are in love."

William's smile was a sneer. "She'll get over you and the answer is still no. I don't care if William IV himself thinks the world of you, Amelia will not marry the likes of you. Is this what this ridiculous tale is all about?"

James remained stoic. He had no intention of letting William have the final word. "Sir, Catherine is in Savannah. I suggest you write to your source of information and ask where Catherine is. I do intend to marry Amelia. She is of her majority and she does not need your permission to wed. I am asking out of consideration, but if you refuse us, then I'll simply take the woman I know I can make happy and we'll leave."

William's smirk was growing. "You don't know Amelia well, do you? She'll never leave with you, I won't permit it. She is a good niece and she knows that I have provided for her all of these years. She'll do nothing that will make me unhappy or worse, angry. No, my proud, lying American, whatever ploy you're trying, Amelia is not part of the package."

William left the study and James stood alone for several minutes. A timid knock on the door announced Amelia. The edges of her bright green eyes were red with tears, her nose was red, and she looked as if she had not slept for a week.

"My God, what has he done to you?" James rushed to her side.

"He called me into his office last night. He knew, James, somehow, he knew." Her sobs began again. James held her close and waited for her to stop crying. She took a deep breath. "He does not want me to see you again. He doesn't believe you, and he says he'll never let me wed a liar. What are we going to do?"

James tightened his hold on her. It was almost as if he could see William Pentworth pulling her from his arms. "You go upstairs and get what you must for several days and we'll leave now. I'll take you to a church, just as soon as I get a special license, and we'll be married. Then, you can come home with me."

Amelia shook her head as he talked. She started sobbing once more when he finished. "No, I cannot. I cannot. He took me in when there was no one. He raised me, gave me clothes, an education, food. I went to parties, I had Catherine—"

James stopped her. "All right. I understand. I will send word that Cathy and Drew must come to England. Once your uncle sees that I don't lie, that what I've said is true, he'll change his tune."

Amelia wiped at her tears. "I don't think so. He doesn't like Americans, not at all. If Cathy and Andrew come

274

here, William will separate them. No, you must not send word. I'll write to Charles. He'll tell my uncle that you are not lying, and perhaps when William realizes that Cathy has married a colonial, perhaps—"

James frowned down at the woman in his arms. "That could take some time."

Amelia straightened. "We will have to wait. I cannot go against him. I'm not like Catherine. I'm not brave or courageous."

James grinned at her. "I wouldn't want you if you were like Catherine. I couldn't handle Catherine." He leaned away from Amelia. "I can't sit and wait here, though. I have patients, I'm building a practice. I must get back."

Amelia sighed. She dropped her chin and leaned against his broad chest. "I can't ask you to wait here, I know that. I'll send word when William has changed his mind."

James seemed satisfied with that for a moment, then terror filled his eyes. "He wouldn't try to marry you off to someone else?"

Amelia frowned. "No, I won't let him. If he tries that, I really will run away. I'll tell him that, too. If I can remain a spinster then I'll stay in his home, but if he tries to pair me up with someone, I will leave. However, I won't tell him I'm waiting for you."

James smiled. "I think he'll guess. Amelia, I have friends here and I'm going to put some money in a special fund for you. If William forces another on you, please promise me that you will see Lord Peter Hampston. I'll give you his address and I may even have him check up on you. If there is any trouble, he'll see you out of the country safely. He'll send word to me and I will meet you. He is a good friend. Now, promise me."

275

The corners of Amelia's delicate mouth turned up a bit. "I promise." And I promise that I'll get word from Charles before July, Amelia thought as she released James.

He pulled her back into his arms. "I don't imagine that William Pentworth will let me see you again."

He lowered his head to brush her lips when a husky voice jarred the lovers apart. "No, he will not. And you are leaving, Mr. Rupert, now! Amelia, go to your room."

James turned and watched Amelia run from the room, her sobs cutting deep into his soul. He faced William Pentworth. "Have you never been in love, sir?"

The man held the door, nodding his head. "And the heart does mend, young man," he said, his voice a soft purr.

James was ready to sail the next morning. He left word for Amelia, through Peter Hampston. It was all he could do. Even the chatter of Grif did nothing to ease his soul.

Chapter Nineteen

It was the last day of March and Andrew Sloan was nearly home. A happy grin finally replaced the frown he'd worn for most of the trip. He sighed in pleasure—the last part of the voyage was about to begin. The markers for the Savannah River glistened in the sun directly in front of them. For an instant, his scowl returned when he remembered that he'd managed to save only one day from his previous schedules.

Swinging the *Lady* into the river, he thought back over February and March. They made good time until they got to New Orleans. It took forever to unload his cargo and Drew ended up handling the purchase of a return cargo when his agent fell ill. His frown disappeared and he smiled with anticipation. Today he wouldn't worry about cargo. He ordered Sam to stay in port when he returned with the *Georgia Girl*. Samuel would manage the holds, and tonight Drew would be at Heart's Haven.

The setting sun provided a brilliant display of magenta, coral, and plum stripes as Drew dashed the last mile to Heart's Haven. He slowed his horse and stopped before the plantation house he called his home. Home! Never before had the word held much meaning for him, but now Cathy was there. He swallowed over a tightening lump in his throat. What if she had not missed him, didn't want him to return? What if she wanted to return to her father in England? He slipped from his horse and cautiously walked up the dirt path to the front door.

Cathy stood at the upstairs veranda windows looking toward the road and Savannah. If nothing had gone wrong, Drew would be back tomorrow. Twice, she'd gone into the city to check with Samuel about the *Savannah Lady*'s return. The last time, two days ago, Samuel said that Cathy had no place in the city. He was firm but insistent.

Cathy frowned, watching a lone horseman race toward the plantation. Was there trouble at the docks? Had Samuel sent someone to fetch her? That could only mean that something had happened to the *Savannah Lady*! Cathy froze at the window. She watched as the rider slowed and walked the last fifty feet or so. As the man drew closer, Cathy recognized the shoulders, the set of the head, and the size of the man. Drew was home!

She left her perch at the window and ran for the stairs, his name on her tongue. She threw herself down the steps and through the hall, singing out to anyone in hearing distance, "Drew's home!"

Drew walked to the door and as he reached for the panel knob, the door was jerked out of his hand. Cathy stood at the door, her face wreathed in smiles. "Welcome home."

Her husky voice reverberated through him and Drew

smiled back at her. "I'm home," he said. He chuckled when he realized what he'd said. The chit had turned his mind into something resembling Bessy's oatmeal. He reached for his wife.

Out of the sensual fog of the kiss that he planted on Cathy's lips, a kiss of welcome that took everything he had, Bessy's booming voice slammed through. She clucked at them, scolding and pushing at the same time, "Now, Miss Cathy, Mistah Drew, what will yer slaves be athinkin'? Now, Mistah Drew, that ain't no way to carry on. Mistah Drew! You gonna shame yer wife!"

Bessy was right, Drew thought as he drew away from the warm, soft mouth of his wife. He smiled down at Cathy's closed eyes. She was as hungry for him as he was for her. "Cathy, Cathy," he said softly, "should I apologize?"

Cathy opened her eyes to stare up at her husband. For an instant, she couldn't name her location. All she knew was that Drew was home and she was where she belonged. Of course, the fact that he was every bit as glad to see her as she was to see him explained a little of her exuberance. "Apologize?" She tried to bring her brain back to functioning capacity.

Drew chuckled. "Bessy thinks I'm shaming you. So, I apologized."

Cathy smiled through a brilliant red blush. "Then I guess I should apologize, too. I probably shamed you because I ran to you."

Drew leaned down and whispered in her ear, "Nothing you could do would shame me." Cathy smiled at him, her heart beating so proudly she missed the welcoming exclamations of the rest of the staff. An evening snack was warmed for the master of the house and Drew and

Cathy climbed the stairs to the master bedroom.

A small, cozy fire took the slight chill off the room and someone, Bessy probably, had removed Cathy's plain white cotton nightdress she'd been wearing and replaced it with a piece of green silk that Cathy had worn once in Charleston. Drew's thick emerald green velvet robe lay on a chair next to the bed and the crisp white linen sheets were turned back on both sides of the bed tonight.

Cathy blushed and giggled. "I think," she tried to control the husky quality of her voice, "that Bessy is a true romantic."

Drew took in the bedtime preparations and chuckled. "I do believe you're correct. I'll wager that your maid won't stick her face through that door. Tonight. Or tomorrow morning."

Cathy looked embarrassed. "Because of the welcome I gave you in the hall?"

Drew pulled her into his arms. "No, because of the welcome I gave you in the hall." He kissed her then, brushing her lips with featherlight kisses, holding her face in his large callused hands. He snuggled her close to his chest and whispered in her ear, "I missed you so damned much. I'm never going to sail without you. If you don't want to sail, I'll hire someone to sail in my place."

She pulled his head down to her lips, whispering against him, "I missed you just as much. I won't let you sail without me."

Drew clutched her tightly against him and as their clothed skin made contact, the months of privation ignited a flame that crackled and sparkled. Clothes became an intolerable obstruction and Drew pulled at Cathy's dress as he pulled at his own breeches. Cathy yanked at her skirt and his shirt, tearing buttons and fabric in her haste. Neither one of them could have named the articles of clothing that were being ripped and shredded from each other.

In seconds, bare flesh seared naked skin and Cathy sighed her contentment. Drew lifted her and rubbed her length against his body, tracing her hips and her legs as she used those same limbs to massage his flanks. He tightened his hold and carried her toward the bed, but before he released her, he raised her high enough so that he could consume her hard nipple. The moment Drew's warm mouth closed over the crest of her breast, Cathy groaned. She pulled his head tighter to her chest with one hand and breathed his name over and over in his ear. The other hand kneaded, stroked, even pinched the firm muscles of his back. She released his head to run her now free hand across his chest, over his ribs, her moans and sighs a litany punctuated with his name.

Starved passions created agony and Drew surfaced enough to know that he had to bury himself in her soon or he would embarrass them both. He practically threw her on the bed, but before he could follow her down, she knelt beside him, pulling at him, forcing him to his back, then straddling his hips. Her hands grabbed his hair and she threw herself against him, seeking his open mouth in her flight.

He kissed her hard. Before he released her lips, he lifted her hips and dropped her onto his swollen shaft. For one second he wondered if he had made a terrible mistake, for his control was gone, but it mattered not. Some primitive voice announced that Cathy floated off in ecstasy the minute he slammed into her. The pulsing muscles of her hot core registered her climax and Drew let himself fall with her into perfect pleasure. He

281

was home!

Hours, or perhaps minutes later, they stirred. Instantly, Drew thought about their joining and he felt a spark of fear. Had he hurt her? "Cathy, did I hurt you?"

She snuggled close. "No, but it was awfully fast, wasn't it?"

He glanced at the red flush coloring her cheeks and grinned. "Such a tigress," he whispered against her ear. He touched her warm cheeks. "When two people are right for each other and they are forced to deny their passions for a time, their first joining is often very fast. Now, I can make love to you all night and go as slowly as I want."

Cathy stretched out like the tigress he named her. "When will we sleep?"

Drew pulled her close. "Does it matter?" She shook her head as he cradled her against him. He proved that it did not matter, as he teased and caressed her for hours. Twice he sank into her hot moist core, drawing out the pleasure for both of them, until Cathy was whimpering like a child. Before dawn, they drifted off to sleep, content, sated, loved. His words, "When people are right for each other," played back and forth in Cathy's mind. He said they were right for each other. It no longer mattered that he didn't love her, that he originally married her because he felt responsible. They were right for each other, he said so. She didn't know when she had been so blissfully happy.

They slept in the next morning and when Cathy opened her eyes to smile up into the warm gaze of her husband, the rays of the sun were streaming into the master bedroom. "What time is it?" Cathy asked, her voice touched with concern.

"It doesn't matter what time it is, wife," Drew pulled her close. "Your husband has come home from the sea and you need to love him."

Cathy looked up at the classic lines of masculine beauty and blushed. She remembered all of the loving they had done only hours before and she remembered the wanton way she threw herself at her husband. She closed her eyes in embarrassment.

Drew seemed to know her thoughts. "Woman, passionate people love passionately."

Cathy opened her eyes with a snap. Was he saying he loved her or was he being poetic? She looked at his pleased expression and decided that he was being poetic. She wiggled out from under him and sat up, taking the sheet with her to hold against her bare body. "What are your plans, husband who is home from the sea?"

Drew swung his large frame over the opposite side, a bit annoyed that she had pulled away from him. "I did promise Mother and Paula that we would come for a visit. I have to see to my cargo, but by the end of the week I would like to leave."

Cathy was almost dressed. "How will we travel? I'm not fond of your carriages around here."

Drew nodded. "Neither am I. Some of the things I brought back with me from New Orleans will go to Philadelphia. We'll sail north and I'll arrange to buy cargo to bring back. The trip will cost us nothing."

Three days remained until the end of the week and in a short time, Cathy had everything ready. Friday afternoon trunks were taken to the *Savannah Lady* and Samuel was left with the task of overseeing the preparations for planting. When Cathy questioned her husband about the advisability of leaving during this important time of the year, Drew assured her, "Cathy, Samuel is a better planter than a sailor. He's really my second hand in shipping and in farming. He's also a good friend. Twice he saved my life. You should know that he is a partner in almost all of my projects, a full partner—we divide the profits. He works as hard at both sailing and farming as I do."

Cathy smiled apologetically. "I didn't mean to criticize. And you should have told me of Sam's importance before this. Why, I was only nice to the man."

Drew looked at her teasing eyes. "And you are the one project we *don't* share. Sam can get his own wife."

Sam moved into the room Cathy had used before she had married. Drew and he spent all of Friday, long into the night, in the study. It was almost dawn before Drew crawled into bed beside his wife. "You should be asleep," Drew reprimanded.

"I was," Cathy replied. "But I don't sleep well unless I can snuggle with you."

"Well, tomorrow night we'll be on the *Savannah Lady*, and, Cathy, you may have to learn to sleep well without me. I have to captain the ship this time."

The confusion that reigned the next day before the carriage left the house sent Cathy into tears. When they finally pulled away from the drive, Cathy turned to Drew and said, "Next year, we will not travel right before planting."

Drew grinned at her. "I can't agree with you more, madam. Next year at this time, I plan to have a son, if not present, then at least started."

Cathy paled and stared at her husband. A child! Quickly she counted and breathed a sigh of relief. Well, not this month, she told herself. She glanced at Drew and he was watching her, concern in his eyes. "Don't you want children, Cathy?"

She lowered her eyes. "Yes, but I haven't given them much thought." And children die, she remembered, thinking of Bridget.

They traveled quietly to Savannah. Drew wondered if somehow he had misjudged his wife. He wanted a large family, but Cathy seemed hesitant. He remembered that her mother had died in childbirth. Maybe that was it, maybe she was afraid. He tried to push the thoughts away, but his fears hovered at the edge of his mind.

Cathy thought about her life and what children would mean to her. Until she met Bridget, she always thought that children bound a marriage together. She glanced at her husband. A son with his hair, his features, to raise in his father's image would be marvelous. Perhaps with grandsons, her father would forgive her and learn to love her a little. She smiled a bit.

The trip to Philadelphia took no time at all. They reached the city in six days. Cathy stayed in the captain's cabin while Drew made arrangements for his cargo. Then he hustled her off to Germantown to meet his sister and his mother.

Paula Smithson was an older copy of Jane Darrow, short, plump, a winning smile. Joanna Sloan was a surprise. She was a tall woman, several inches above Cathy, with graying hair and warm brown eyes. She had high cheekbones, a broad face, and Cathy thought the word *security* fit her perfectly. Joanna Sloan was the picture of security. Cathy looked from her husband to his mother and smiled. Andrew Sloan bore a strong resemblance to his mother.

That evening, in the guest bedroom Paula had assigned them, Cathy asked her husband, "Do the girls look like your father?"

Drew grinned at her. "Yep! And so did Nathan." At her puzzled expression Drew explained, "Nathan was my older brother. He was the firstborn. He was the first to die as well. He was fifteen years older than me. He would have been forty-five next spring. When he reached the ripe old age of twenty-seven, the war broke out and he left to serve up North. He was killed before things got heated up. I didn't know him too well; he was an adventurer, but he looked like Pa."

Cathy looked at him. "Was your mother taller than your father?"

"Not that it matters, but, yes, she was a good four inches taller than Pa. Cathy, they loved each other to distraction. You said your father loved his wives. Well, my parents were also in love. Pa used to tell about the men that stood in awe of Mother. Nobody ever got close because she was so tall. Pa said he took one look and decided that he would never have to worry about another man. They were married three weeks after they met. When he died three years ago, they had been married for forty-nine years."

Cathy sighed and turned to look at her husband. "That's such a beautiful story."

Drew grinned. "I think so too."

The delightful weeks sped by. Paula was every bit as friendly as Jane. Roy Smithson, Paula's husband and a sea captain, was not home during their visit. Paula explained, "He's trying the China trade. Roy says it's very profitable, but he's gone almost a year at a time."

Cathy told Drew that night, "I don't think I want you

to think about the China trade."

Drew held her in his arms. "I've already told you that I take you with me or I don't sail. China is too far away for me. Roy can have all of that trade he wants."

Cathy learned quickly that Drew inherited his sense of humor from his mother and Joanna Sloan still liked to tease. Her hearing was failing and her eyes were not as good as she wanted, but she kept herself busy. She accepted Cathy's invitation to visit Heart's Haven. "If the good Lord doesn't call me home first," she said reflectively.

Drew wanted to start for home on the second of May, but between Cathy and his mother the trip was delayed for two more days. Joanna had not completed the stack of recipes she promised Cathy and Cathy hadn't finished the lace collar and cuffs she started as a gift for her mother-in-law. Drew gritted his teeth and told himself he should be thankful that the Sloan women got along beautifully.

The voyage back to Savannah was not as pleasant and it took eight days instead of six. Two storms ripped and tore at the sails and tossed the ship about like a cork in a glass jar. But, the *Savannah Lady* was sturdy and the only real problem Cathy had was that the storms kept Drew from their big bed.

They sailed up the Savannah River late on the afternoon of the thirteenth. Once they were tied up, Drew turned to his wife. "Would you like me to send for a carriage?"

Cathy looked up in surprise. "Why ever would I want a carriage?"

Drew grinned. "Well, wife, I thought you might want to go home. I'll have to stay on board and see to the cargo,

287

but, if you want, I'll see you back to the plantation."

Cathy threaded her fingers together and studied the dock before her. "If I go home, I'll have to sleep in a bed alone, and if I go home, you'll have to sleep in a bed alone. Those two storms kept us apart for five nights, and now that we're safe, all tied up tight, you want me to go home? No, husband, I think I'd like to stay right here."

Drew chuckled. "Right here, or in that bed downstairs?"

Cathy blushed and refused to look at her teasing husband, but they did share the big bed in the captain's cabin that night. Once, long after the sun had set, Drew whispered in her ear, "I'm glad you don't like to sleep alone."

The next morning, Drew saw to the cargo and Cathy spent the morning packing the trunks of clothing. In the afternoon, Cathy cleaned the cabin and Drew took Cathy to an inn close by for dinner and they had their fill of steamed cod cakes and corn bread. Then they started for Heart's Haven.

A strange carriage stood in the drive at the plantation and Drew turned to Cathy. "Looks like we have visitors. Perhaps Samuel is entertaining a new lady love." Drew helped Cathy from their rented vehicle and arm in arm they went through the front door.

They were through the door before they realized that not a soul had come to greet them. Cathy turned to her husband. "Drew, something is wrong, terribly wrong. I can feel it."

Cathy shivered and Drew placed an arm around her waist and pulled her close. "Anybody here?" he yelled.

Instantly Bessy came from the back of the house. "Oh, Mistah Drew, thank God you here. Oh, thank God."

Cathy looked at the tall dark woman. Her brown eyes were rimmed with red and her nose was swollen. Cathy stepped up to her and laid a hand on her arm. "Bessy, what happened?"

Bessy pulled a bright red square from her pocket and swiped at her eyes and then her nose. "It's Mistah Samuel, Mistah Drew. Somebody came in last night an' hurt him bad. The doctor's here right now. Oh, Mistah Drew, they busted the window and the bed, and Mistah Samuel, he sez, before he passed out, he sez, they was after Missy Sloan."

Drew left Cathy standing next to Bessy and he took off up the stairs, two steps at a time. Cathy could only stare at their housekeeper. Surely Samuel was mistaken. Who would want to hurt her?

Cathy didn't want to think and work kept thoughts at bay. She turned to the housekeeper. "Bessy, could you help me with the trunks? A couple of the boys can help carry and we'll send for one of the boys from the stable. Our horse and the rented carriage must be cared for." Quietly, she directed the household, keeping one eye on the door to her old room.

Night fell, the doctor pulled away from the drive, and the household settled into a kind of tense anticipation while Cathy kept her vigil in the master bedroom. Finally, when she was about to seek him out, Drew came into the room. "I'll tell you what I know, then we're going to get some sleep. Sam may need some care tonight and I told Bessy and one of the other servants I'd spell them in several hours."

Drew sat down on the bed, his face strained with worry. Cathy sat down next to him. "I want to help with Sam, too."

"We'll see." Drew patted her hand. He took a deep breath. "Sam was still conscious when we got home. He refused any medicine until he got a chance to talk to me. It seems that two men sneaked into the house by way of the upstairs veranda, prying open the windows to your old room. They were waiting when Sam came to bed. It was dark, Sam doesn't use a candle, and one of the son of a bitches hit him over the head. Didn't knock him out, though. One of the two grabbed at Sam and when they found out they had a man instead of a woman, they roughed him up good. They lit a couple of candles and started grilling him. They wanted to know where you were. They knew I sailed north.

"Sam wouldn't tell them a thing, so one of the bastards broke his arm. They probably would have killed him, except one of the stable boys saw the light and knew that Sam didn't use a candle. The lad rounded up two other boys and they crept into the house. I guess they weren't as quiet as they thought, because Sam vaguely remembered one of the men saying someone was coming. They took off, leaving Sam battered, cut up, and with a broken arm, but alive and very angry."

Cathy interrupted. "He's going to be all right?"

"If his blood isn't poisoned, but that's not what worries me. Tomorrow, I'm sending for some of my crew, and Cathy, you can't leave the house until I find out what's going on. I want to talk about your father and your brothers, but it will have to wait until tomorrow."

Cathy's expression told Drew that she didn't believe her relatives could have had anything to do with this. He reached over and patted her hand. "Come, my dear, let's get some sleep."

In no time they were in bed, but Cathy lay perfectly

still for a long time, her mind in a turmoil. Surely her brothers or her father would not have sent two crude men to snatch her from Andrew. She told her father she was happy and had come to no harm. Could he hate Americans so much that he would send someone after her? Goosebumps covered her as she shuddered with the thought.

Chapter Twenty

Early the next morning, Cathy accompanied Drew into her old room, their task to check the bandages on Sam's cuts. Cathy gagged when she saw the extent of the damage done to Andrew's partner. His black and blue eyes were swollen shut; his left arm was splinted and bandaged; and he had patches all over his face and his right shoulder. Drew glanced her way. "The doctor gave him a healthy dose of laudanum. I doubt that he even knows you're here."

After Drew checked on Samuel, he led Cathy down the stairs and into the study. He looked long and hard at the calendar on his desk. No doubt James reached London by the end of February or at least by the middle of March. If he notified Cathy's father immediately, and William Pentworth was angered enough, the man would have time to round up help and send them to Savannah on the next ship leaving London. The villains could have arrived soon enough to observe, ask questions, make plans, and strike. Drew shook his head in disgust. William Pentworth could have been behind this attack to force

293

his daughter home.

One thought bothered him. Samuel insisted that the two men spoke with no English accent. "More like some of Philadelphia's waterfront scum," Sam told him the night before.

While Drew considered Pentworth's involvement possible, Cathy maintained that her father would never send the kind of men Sam described to carry her home. "Drew, my father would have come himself. He's afraid of no man. Why, he's part Spanish. If he wanted me home, he would have come here and demanded that I leave with him. He doesn't hire others to do his dirty work." She tried to make her voice believable, and she wondered if she succeeded in convincing her husband. From his intense frown, she didn't think so.

"We'll watch and ask a few questions. I want someone to accompany you everywhere you go. When Sam recovers, he'll start looking for those two and when he finds them, *I'll* find out who hired them."

Cathy gazed up at his determined expression. Yes, he would do exactly that.

A week passed and Samuel slowly regained his strength. He stayed in bed, more to please Cathy, than because he needed to rest. Cathy kept him company, brought his meals and changed his bandages. She even talked the doctor into shortening the splint so that he could rest more comfortably. More than once she told him, "You were injured because of me. The very least I can do is make you comfortable."

On the twenty-third of May, nine days after Sam's attack, James returned to Heart's Haven. He introduced the small boy he had in tow, then spent an hour with

294

Sam, checking his arm and his healing cuts and bruises. While Cathy took care of establishing Grif in the hospital, James and Drew went to the study. The hours passed slowly. Cathy tended to Sam, spent time getting to know Grif, and wondered what was transpiring in the study.

Drew summed it up as gently as he could. "Cathy, your father didn't believe us. He insists that you are still in Barbados and that you are soon to marry a man of your brother's choosing."

Cathy felt ambivalence. Her father was not behind the attack on Sam, but he didn't believe in her marriage. Maybe, she told herself, he refused to believe because Drew was an American, and he hated them. It was a puzzlement. Her thoughts turned to James.

The doctor had thrown himself into his practice, sending out word that he'd returned to Heart's Haven. Cathy watched him, but he kept his face remarkably expressionless. He and Drew often spent time together in the study. With James tending to him, in three days, Sam sat in the office with James and Drew. After she served the coffee or snacks, Cathy was excluded from the room. She attempted a tantrum, but Drew flew into a rage. It took a day or two, but Cathy realized they had no intention of letting her know anything about their discussions.

Cathy pretended concern over their conversation when what she really wanted was information on James and Amelia. She finally caught James alone in the hospital a week after he came home. She sneaked in on him early one morning, and the incredible pain that was etched on his face when he thought he was not being watched stunned Cathy. Here, the men worried about her and James was the one they should be concerned about. Well, Cathy was going to find out what happened. "She told you that she wasn't interested, didn't she?" Cathy asked from the doorway.

James looked up, his surprise rendering him speechless for a minute. When he finally found his voice he asked, "Who?"

Cathy reprimanded him. "James, don't play games with me. I have been standing here for several minutes watching you. Amelia hurt you very badly. I can see that."

James flinched. "You don't know the whole story."

Cathy smiled sympathetically. "Then tell me."

James told her all the details. Cathy's reaction was a soft chuckle. "Phillip was never one to admit to a mistake and he's worse now that he has Martha. I'll write to Charles and insist that he write father with the truth. It's entirely possible, though, that my father may never want to see me again. You better make plans to go back to England and get Amelia. Kidnap her if she refuses to come with you. She'll only be angry with you for a short time."

While Cathy and James discussed the events in England, Drew helped Sam dress for the day. Sam told him about the visit of one of their neighbors to the south. "I forgot to mention it," Sam said, struggling with the shirt buttons, "but Bart Waverly came home in April. He stopped by to offer his congratulations, he said. I guess he heard about the marriage from some of the people who came to his ball celebrating his return. He wanted to know if Cathy is a local girl or somebody your mother forced on you. I told him you met her in England. I didn't think you wanted anybody to know she stole on board the *Savannah Lady*."

Drew laughed. "I did meet her in England, so you told him the truth, even if you didn't know. By the way, where has Waverly been, back to old Mother England?"

"He said something about visiting the islands and spending time with an old friend of his. He said he almost tied the knot himself. Some kin of his friend. Didn't seem too pleased about her getting away from him."

Drew looked suspicious. "Which island?"

Sam laughed. "I thought the same thing. Waverly said this girl was promised to some other man and she was from the islands, I'm sure of that."

By the end of May, Sam had recovered enough to begin making plans for his search. Cathy overheard him tell James and Drew, "I'll find both those bastards and then I'll take them apart, piece by piece."

Drew's angry voice cut into the conversation. "Now you listen to me, you overgrown cabin boy. If you find them, and I'm not too sure you will, I want to talk to both of them before you take your revenge. I have to know who's after Cathy. I'll get that information before you do anything! Is that understood?"

Samuel nodded his head, sympathizing with the man who stood in front of him. "If I find 'em, I'll give you first chance at 'em. And it should be fairly soon, 'cause I intend to leave here the minute James says I can move around."

It was another two weeks before James pronounced Samuel healed enough to begin his travels. In those two weeks the household settled into a comfortable routine. Drew was busy with the plantation, Cathy and James worked side by side in the hospital, and Grif ran errands for James and Cathy. Sam, protesting his boredom, strolled between the hospital and the house looking for some meaningful occupation. Several times during those two weeks, James took Cathy and Samuel with him on his calls out in the countryside.

Finally, the day came and James removed Samuel's splint, the last of the bandages to be eliminated. It took another week before Samuel had partial use of his arm. As he exercised his arm, the men finished the plans. Drew insisted that Sam take another member of the crew along. Sam and Barry left on the *Savannah Lady* on June twentieth for parts north and west. Samuel assured Drew he would send word when he found some trace of the men he sought.

Sam and his companion went west and the *Georgia Girl* sailed east to the islands and then England carrying two important letters. Drew sent a detailed missive to his father-in-law, explaining again why Catherine Pentworth was now Mrs. Andrew Sloan. The second letter was from Cathy to Charles Pentworth. She pleaded with her brother to send word to her father that she was most definitely not on Barbados.

The summer seas, so often gentle, stirred up a hearty storm and the *Georgia Girl* missed the island of Barbados completely. She limped on toward England. She had been sorely tried in the storm and she was hurt. England was weeks away for her.

Drew and Cathy relaxed, both of them certain that the letters would arrive in short order. Despite the information James supplied, Drew still couldn't dismiss the thought that William Pentworth was at the bottom of their problems. Cathy wanted her father's blessing, or at least word that he never wanted to see her again. What she wanted now was an even closer relationship with her husband. She settled back to wait. All things in time, she told herself.

June in Georgia was delightful. The warm summer sun caressed the leaves of the growing cotton plants and traced shadows across the small vegetable tract at the side of the main house. Grif and Bessy worked in the garden, Cathy tended the flowers, and Drew worried over the fields.

On one particularly bright day, Drew pulled Cathy from the kitchen where she was planning the meals with Bessy. "Let's take a holiday," he said. He called out to Grif in the garden, "No work today! I'm calling it a holiday."

Grif was out of the garden like a pistol ball. "Can me and Billy go fishing?" Grif and Bessy's oldest grandson had quickly become good friends.

Drew laughed and turned to the large woman. "Can Billy go fishing?"

Bessy chuckled. "I 'member, Mistah Drew, when you was just that age. My Isaac and you used to go off and go fishin'." Grif shot out of the kitchen to find his friend before permission had truly been granted.

"Let them go," Drew instructed. "It's too nice to try and confine them. I remember, too, Bessy. And the missus and I are going on a picnic."

He reached over and patted Cathy on the bottom. "Now, run up to your room and get into something comfortable," he leaned over and whispered in her ear, "something that I can get you out of with little difficulty."

Cathy blushed and started for the stairs. She turned around once, opened her mouth, then closed it and ran up the stairs. Drew left his menu for their lunch with Bessy and disappeared to get the horses. In less than twenty minutes, Drew helped Cathy onto her horse and they started southwest.

They'd traveled about a half-hour, when Drew pulled up even with Cathy. "I'm taking you to my special place. I used to come to this place when I had some thinking to do, or when I didn't want anyone to disturb my rest." He chuckled at his memories. "I was a lazy child!"

Cathy glanced over at her husband. Drew Sloan didn't have a lazy bone in his body. They rode on for another half-hour and Drew reined up before a small wooded area, thick with undergrowth. Drew swung his leg over the saddle and dropped to the ground. "If I remember, there's a secret path." He strode over to a cluster of trees and pulled several branches away from a paticularly thick cluster.

Cathy sat her horse, watching. She giggled. "I think, Mr. Sloan, that you have visited most recently."

He looked up, grinning. "Would you believe this morning? That's why I decided it was a good day for a picnic. I stumbled on this place earlier today. I did come here as a boy and it's pretty much the way it used to be. Of course, the opening needed some help."

Once the cluster of branches were pulled apart, Drew came back to help Cathy from her horse. He tethered the horses, grabbed the blankets and the picnic basket Bessy prepared, and guided Cathy through the narrow opening.

On the other side of the bushes, Cathy's eyes opened wide with delight at the natural cove enclosed with trees, straggled pines, thick maples, and dogwood shrubs. Through the pines, thirty or forty feet beyond, a small stream splashed into a pool, crystal clear and shimmering in the sunlight. A pleased gasp slipped from her lips.

Drew chuckled at her delight. He spread the blanket. "First our meal, then a swim, and who knows?" He leered at her as he opened the basket. "Now, what would you like for lunch?" He pulled out two glasses and a bottle of wine.

Cathy looked shocked. "You plan for us to drink our lunch? I don't think I can survive on just wine."

Drew leaned down and playfully stuck his nose in the basket. "There are good smells in here. Come, seat yourself and we'll explore these smells." He pulled at her hand until she fell to the blanket beside him. "Now, what is milady's fancy? There's ham . . ." He lifted a cloth-wrapped parcel out of the hamper, handing it to her. "And chicken . . ." Another parcel ended up beside the first. Then, more and more wrapped packages appeared, and Drew shouted with exaggerated enthusiasm, "Hard boiled eggs! cheese! bread! Ah, ha! Cakes!"

She giggled at his antics. "I can't eat all of this," she gestured with a sweep.

"You're not expected to eat all of it," he said sternly. "Most of it"—he stressed "most"—"is for me. I must keep up my strength."

She swatted at him with the linen napkin he'd handed her first. His teasing fascinated her. He liked her, she could feel it. Soon, very soon, she told herself, he would

301

declare his love. Her heart beat with anticipation. Of course, she'd admitted to herself long ago that she loved him and more each day. His warm eyes, brown in the shadows of the sun, sparkled at her. She smiled at him.

While they ate, Drew told her about the times he remembered coming to this cove as a young boy and later as a man. After they ate their fill, Cathy repacked the hamper. Drew stretched out next to her, running his fingers over her ankles, the instep of her foot, across her toes. He looked up. "Has anyone ever lauded your pretty feet?"

She laughed and covered up the exposed appendages. "Not that I can remember."

Drew reached up and eased her down beside him. "Most of you is pretty."

"Most?" Cathy asked, trying for a voice that sounded insulted.

Drew rose up on his elbow and leaned down to brush her lips. "All of you is pretty, beautiful, gorgeous." He kissed her gently. "Now, my beautiful wife, let's take a nap."

Cathy stared up at him, surprise written on her face. Drew patted her thigh. "Later," he whispered. Cathy gave in to the feelings of contentment and let her mind drift. She didn't realize that she fell asleep until Drew woke her, holding her and whispering her name between little nipping kisses. She stretched in his arms. "About that swim . . ."

She sat up and started pulling at her clothes. Drew sat up with her. "Witch. Here I was just getting started. . . ."

"You did promise me a swim. Now, last one in is a rotten egg."

302

"Cathy," Drew shouted at her as she ran toward the trees, "you can swim, can't you? It's deep."

She stopped at the pool and watched as he strolled through the trees, his naked body resplendent in the shimmering afternoon sun. She gingerly tested the water with her toes. "Agh! It's cold."

Drew grinned. "And deep. It's fed from this stream but also from an underground stream. Come on." He pushed her into the water. She shivered and dived down into the center of the pool. It was freezing cold but after swimming back and forth for several minutes she lost some of her chill. Drew swam next to her. When she stopped to tread water, the cold seeped into her bones. "It's cold," she chattered, her teeth announcing the effect of the frigid conditions.

"I must not be as insensitive as I was when I was younger." Drew swore and turned around toward the edge of the pool. "Let's get warmed up."

When they were wrapped in one of the blankets, Cathy asked, "Why was it so cold?"

Drew shrugged his shoulders and hugged her naked body close to his, running his hands up and down her side briskly. "Must be the underground stream. Of course, I'm not sorry. I'm heating up enough under this blanket to turn to steam. I'd like to know how you learned to swim so well. Most women wouldn't go near a pond."

Cathy giggled. "Most women don't have two older half brothers that insisted she keep up with them." Cathy pushed the blanket down around her breast. "It is getting warm, isn't it?"

Drew eased her down onto the blanket, following her. "Never satisfied," he teased, his breath brushing her ear.

She tensed, looking up at him. "No one comes here, do they?"

He shook his head, afraid his words would not clear the lump in his throat. She was so damn beautiful lying on the blanket, her dark wet hair tangled around her. Her blue-gray eyes were wide with her desire and he lowered his head to take her lips. She was his wife, and soon she would love him. He could see her desire, the fondness for him in her eyes. Soon, she would tell him what he wanted to hear.

He lowered his head and whispered against her lips, "I'm going to kiss every inch of you."

She whispered back, "Every inch?"

He brushed her lips and, lifting his head, he stroked her forehead. "I'll kiss you here." He touched her nose, her eyes, her ears. "And here and here." He trailed his fingers down her throat. "Here and here." He touched her breast, then her nipple. His voice was growing deeper and more husky and Cathy luxuriated in the tones that flowed over her like honey. He ran his hand down the valley between her breasts, across her ribs, to the indentation of her waist. "And I'm going to kiss and lick these and this."

Cathy drew a ragged breath, wondering how far down his questing fingers would roam. She tried to ask, but the tingles of anticipation kept the muscles of her throat immovable. She dragged a deep breath of air into her lungs and arched against the blanket.

He leaned over her, watching her eyes turn almost slate gray in desire, and he smiled in satisfaction. He drew a breath himself, his words so soft, he whispered them in her ear. "After that, I'll kiss your navel and I'll use my tongue on your toes, your legs, your thighs."

He swallowed hard and ran his hands over her knees, up her thigh, to her woman's mound. "When you can't stand it anymore, I'll kiss you here."

Cathy tensed in shock. "No, not there," she squeaked, her voice too hushed to be convincing.

Drew smiled down at her and pulled her into his arms. She was made for loving. And he intended to show her just how much. He started at her forehead, just as he said he would. He kissed her eyelids and moved across her cheeks to her ears. He could hear and feel the ragged flow of air as she tried to breathe. She wanted his kisses. He smiled to himself; she was probably shocked at how much.

Cathy tried to breathe, but the air had to be dragged into her lungs. His whispered words sent tingles across her flesh, just as his lips sent flutters across her skin. Surely he didn't intend to kiss her all over?

She felt his tongue against her throat and across her shoulders, and she shuddered with desire. What was he doing to her? The part of her brain that still could function laughed at her. "Exactly," it answered, "what he said he would!" She lay on the blanket, pleasure coursing through her, cascading over her flesh, fanning out to leave her weak and wanting. Words stumbled over her lips. "Come to me."

His lips left her breast and he sighed, "Not yet." His head drifted back to her breast and she pleaded, "Please!"

His breath felt hot against her nipple as he answered her plea. "No!"

She raised her hands and ran her fingers through the

305

damp, brown silk of his head. The smell of wet hair, clean and male, teased at her nostrils and she closed her eyes to better appreciate the fragrance. She identified the scent of him, his wet body, even the pine trees. Deep inside, she knew that he had awakened every nerve in her body with just his words. She wasn't even aware that she held his head to her breast, arching against him, in response to all the encompassing thrills that bombarded her.

He knelt at her feet before he started working his way up her legs. Her breathing slowed, anticipation and fear warring through her. Then he stopped! Her eyes snapped open, her lips parted to cry out her loss, but he moved up between her legs, his eyes glazed with desire. He spoke. "I want you to want this." She couldn't speak, she only nodded her head. Yes, she wanted anything and everything he did to her.

His head dropped between her legs and his words, "You're mine," surged through her, touching her soul. His hot breath seared her woman's flesh and his tongue touched her, sending her thoughts spiraling out into a vast world of pleasure, until she thought she would never be again. A low keening cry vibrated through the trees and she did not recognize her voice.

The man over her heard and gloried in the sound. He tightened his hold on her buttocks and carried her over the threshold of pleasure. She was his, for now, next month, next year, for this life, and into eternity. She was his soul mate, his wife.

Before she could return from the place he sent her, he covered her and sent his manhood deep into her. Her pulsing flesh stroked him and teased him and he lost himself in her, spraying his hot seed against her. He sang her name in tribute. "Cathy, Cathy . . . Oh, God, Cathy."

He rolled to her side, pulling her against him. He had to rest, to recover, for his soul had been ripped from his body and given to the woman at his side. Together, they slept.

Chapter Twenty-One

The sun hung low in the sky when Cathy roused from her nap. A slight movement, a noise, disturbed her and she rolled away from Drew. Her movement awakened him and his eyes fluttered open. Cathy smiled. "I think we slept too long."

Drew sat up and looked at the sky. "I didn't mind, but it's time to go back. We should get back before dark, but . . ." He grinned at her, his unspoken words making her blush.

Cathy pulled at the clothes spread on the ground around them. A touch of apprehension filled her and she glanced at her husband. Did he feel it, too? she wondered. She hurried to dress, the darkness of the cove pressing against her nerves. In minutes, mounted on their horses, they trotted back to the plantation.

The warm summer sun faded fast as they approached the buildings. At the sight of the house they slowed the horses to a walk. The return to Heart's Haven took half as much time as the morning trip to the woods. At the stable, Drew smiled at her questioning glance. "We rode in a semicircle this morning. I wanted you to think we were farther away than we were."

"That wasn't honest," she responded as she watched him dismount.

"Maybe," he muttered. He seemed distracted and Cathy followed his gaze. A horse, still damp from a hard ride, lounged at the stable door. Grif came bounding out of the stable, and behind him, Samuel walked next to James.

Grif shouted, "We was coming after ya."

Drew helped Cathy from the saddle and together they strolled over to greet the traveler. Cathy asked the first question. "Did you find the men who beat you up?"

Drew glanced down at his wife. He didn't think it a good idea for her to hear what Sam found out until Drew and James got a chance to discuss it. "Cathy," Drew said, pulling her back from the group, "would you go tell Bessy that we're back." To the men he asked, "Have you had something to eat?" Sam shook his head. Drew turned back to Cathy. "Tell her to get something ready to eat, cold chicken or ham, something quick and easy."

Cathy nodded and started for the house. She turned around, amazed that she'd allowed her husband to exclude her from the conversation. How she had changed. She hurried to the kitchen. She'd convince him later to tell her what Samuel said.

After Bessy's sandwiches and hot coffee, they retired to the study to discuss the information Sam brought back. Now a little disgruntled at her exclusion, Cathy went up to bed. While she waited for her husband she dozed, but the minute he pushed the door closed, she was alert. It was late, very late, when Drew sank down into the feather mattress. "What did you find out? Did Sam find the men?" she whispered.

Drew chuckled. "I should have known you'd be wide awake the minute I got here. Do you know it's two o'clock in the morning? You should have been asleep hours ago."

She answered, "I had a long nap today, remember?"

He smiled at the memory and whispered, "Yes, I remember. Now," he reached over to snuff out the fluttering light of the candle, "let's get some sleep. I'm very tired." He lay down and reached for Cathy.

Instantly, she bolted into a sitting position. "You can't be serious. I want to know what Sam learned. What are you going to do? Where's Barry? Are you leaving with Sam?"

Drew sighed and sat up next to her. "All right. I won't get any sleep until I tell you, will I?"

Drew took a deep breath. "I guess the first thing I'd better tell you is that Sam, James, and I are leaving in the morning for Charleston. The two men that attacked Sam are there. He traced them to that city, but before he got a chance to talk to them himself, they got very drunk and went on a rampage. Barry is waiting in Charleston, just in case the sheriff decides they've learned their lesson and kicks them out of the jail before I get a chance to talk to the sheriff. Samuel talked to him, but Sam wasn't sure the man believed his tale. I have to leave as soon as I can. I don't want them getting away from Barry until I've had my chance."

Cathy felt a cold finger of apprehension track down her back. "Must you go? Can't Sam get the information from them?"

311

"Cathy, I have to go. They were after you. I have to find out who sent them."

"Let me come with you," she pleaded.

"Not a chance," Drew snapped. "There might be some fighting. Someone could get hurt."

The words were wrenched from her. "I know."

Drew realized her concern. "Cathy, I know you're worried about me, but please. There will be four of us to their two. Would you like to have James stay here with you?"

"No," she wailed. "I don't want a doctor, I want you."

Drew pulled her close. "I'll be back in three, maybe four days. It won't be much time at all."

Cathy lay next to her husband terrified. She couldn't explain why apprehension lay so heavily on her, why fear consumed her, but it did. She couldn't explain herself to Drew, as she thought back over what she had babbled at him. She forced her eyes closed; he would be gone a short time. Surely, she could manage for three or four days. James would be with him so that if he got hurt, James could care for him. It took another hour of introspection before she drifted off to sleep.

Morning came and the men prepared to leave. Before they started for the docks, Cathy got a chance to pull James off into a corner and entreat him to watch out for Drew. "Don't let him get hurt."

James grinned at her. This marriage had turned out much better than he thought possible. She loved Drew and he was obviously in love with her. William Pentworth, James thought, didn't have a chance. When Cathy's father discovered how much of a love match she'd made, he'd have to acquiesce. Amelia would be his before the end of the year.

Cathy watched them go. For the next day, Cathy wandered around at a loss. Drew's efficient servants left little for Cathy to do. Not that she could do most of the things needed to run the house. In fact, most of the things that kept other women busy were not things at which Cathy excelled. Her stitches were satisfactory, but she rarely had the patience for sewing. She couldn't keep her mind on reading. Without Drew, riding around the plantation had no appeal.

The second afternoon, Grif came to the rescue. He took her fishing. In minutes, she had a huge, slimy, gray fish with no scales, a flat head, and whiskers like a cat, dangling from her hook.

To Grif's disgust, Cathy gagged, and then retched. He dragged her back to the house under protest. To her embarrassment, she heard him describing her performance to Bessy. "How a lady can be so good in surgery and then vomit at a catfish . . . Boy, Bessy, she ain't no fun at all."

She listened to Bessy's soft words. "The missus is lonesome for her man."

Grif's response made Cathy smile. "I ain't never gonna get tied up in knots over some dumb woman, no I'm not."

Cathy trotted up the stairs to her room chuckling. She could imagine him shaking his head in disgust.

She sat on her bed, the events of the afternoon running through her mind. She amazed herself! Grif was right about her reaction to the fish. She never got sick. Why, the things she saw in surgery should have been responsible for the loss of many a meal, but only once or twice could she remember a problem. She tried to tell herself that worry over her husband had caused her upset. She stretched out on her bed and drifted off to sleep. She would have missed dinner if Bessy hadn't come trudging up the steps to wake her.

Bessy looked concerned. "You feel all right, missus? Grif said you got sick at the fish. Maybe you come down with something."

Cathy shook her head. "If the truth be known, it's probably because I haven't slept well, what with Drew and James in Charleston. I guess I'm just tired."

"You have a little something to eat and then I'll fix you a hot bath. You sleep." Bessy smiled and started for the stairs.

Dinner was a quiet affair and true to her word, Bessy fixed a hot herb bath for Cathy after the meal. Cathy relaxed in the steaming tub and after the bath she toweled herself off, donned a light nightgown and sprawled between the crisp sheets. She fell asleep before her head touched her pillow.

How long she slept she didn't know, but when she awoke darkness surrounded her. Something brought her out of her dreams and she rolled from the bed. She listened carefully. A rapping sounded, as if someone were tugging and rattling at the front door. She wrapped a heavy dressing robe around her, lit a candle, and started for the stairs. Holding the candle high, she ran down the steps. One of James's patients needed the doctor, she decided.

At the bottom of the steps, Cathy ran her hands through her hair and pulled the robe closer. She placed the candle on the corner table next to the door. Grif should have come to wake her, not some person banging

314

away at the door. Obviously, the person doing the pounding hadn't bothered to go to the hospital. She wondered why. She threw open the door and stared at a small boy clutching his cap in one hand. The other hand was raised to pound at the door.

"I got to see the doc. My pa's been hurt," the boy shouted at her when she asked if he wanted someone.

"The doctor's not here. How bad is your pa hurt? Dr. Preston in Savannah is seeing Dr. Rupert's patients until Dr. Rupert returns. I'll send someone to get the Savannah doctor, if you'll tell me where you live."

He stared at her in terror for a moment. Then he shook his head violently. "No! My pa can't see nobody but Doc Rupert." In the soft candlelight, big crystal tears glistened against the child's cheeks.

Cathy tried a smile of confidence. "Will I do?"

The child looked almost pleased. "Do you work with Doc Rupert?" Cathy nodded and he brightened considerably. "Ya'll do!"

Cathy told the boy to wait and she headed up the stairs to dress. She threw on her clothes, wondering again why he hadn't gone to the hospital. "I'll ask him when I'm dressed," she muttered as she stuffed her feet into her boots. She trudged down the stairs and faced the small lad. "Now, my young friend, if you'll tell me your name, we'll get the buggy. Come on."

He glared up at her. "Name's Jake and gotta horse."

Independent males, Cathy thought. Smiling, she said, "Jake, I need a carriage."

She started for the stable. "We'll bring your horse along and you can tie him to my buggy." She turned to look down at Jake. "Why didn't you go to the hospital?

Most of the patients go there first."

She couldn't read his face in the dark, but his voice answered her question. "I didn't know there was no hospital."

At the stable, she roused two of the stable boys from their sleep and at her direction, they harnessed James's mare to the chaise Drew bought for her when they came back from Philadelphia. One of the boys wanted to call Bessy. "You can't go off like this, mam, not without Bessy aknowin'. Why, it's gotta be after ten o'clock!"

Cathy smiled. "Jake's father is hurt. You tell Bessy that I've gone to . . ." She paused and turned to the boy. "What's your father's name and where are we going?"

Jake shuffled a moment and then whispered, "My pa's Ben Smythe and he's at Rosepoint. He's hurt bad. We gotta go."

Cathy instructed Jake to tie his work horse to the back of the chaise then she swung up onto the seat. To the stable boy who protested her departure, she said, "Now, you know where I'm going and I'll be back as soon as I can."

"But, mam! What about Grif?" The black boy grabbed at the reins, forgetting his place in his concern.

"I'll stop at the hospital and get the medical bag and Grif, don't worry." The relieved expression on the boy's face almost made Cathy laugh out loud. Why, he had to be at least two years older than Grif.

"We have to stop at the hospital," Cathy told her visitor.

Jake frowned. "Mam, we gotta hurry."

Cathy smiled in confidence. "I have to have the medical bag and I'll only take a minute." She pulled the

316

chaise—Drew called it a shay—to a stop and handed the reins to Jake. "I'll only be a minute." She slipped from the conveyance and started for the building.

Again, Jake muttered, "We gotta hurry, mam!"

"A minute," Cathy said as she opened the door. She grabbed the bag from the shelf in the office and slipped into the room where Grif slept. He slept soundly and although she called him and shook him, she couldn't rouse him completely. He lifted his head and looked at her with dull eyes. He seemed to hear her, but he didn't respond. She gritted her teeth; she didn't have time to wait. "Oh, Grif, a lot of help you are!" She smiled at the child. He played so hard and worked so hard that it was no wonder he didn't want to waken. She left him to sleep away the night.

She quit the hospital, James's bag in her hand. With an agile leap, she jumped back in the chaise and dropped the bag at her feet. She turned to the small child sitting stiff as a board on the upholstered bench. "Where are we going, Jake? You'll have to tell me just where your father is. North, I think you said, and then west. Or east?"

Jake gave directions and Cathy set the horse at a trot. The boy looked almost frightened, and Cathy decided that he was very worried. If the man was badly hurt, it might already be too late to help him. She glanced once again at the boy and at his tragic expression. Cathy said quietly, "Jake, everything is going to be all right, you'll see."

The late June night sky was dusted with clouds, some heavy at times, and the soft light of the quarter moon drifted in and out of the gray puffs like a child playing hide-and-seek. In the distance, Cathy saw the silver

317

ribbon of water that marked the Savannah River. She turned to the mute child. "Is Rosepoint on the other side of the river?"

Jake nodded, but not a sound slipped past his lips. For a moment, Cathy wondered at his preoccupation, then she shrugged at her concern. The boy's father was hurt and his thoughts dwelled on that circumstance. She headed for the ferry.

The soft glow of the lantern signaled that someone waited at the ferry and would see them across. She had traveled this way before with James, but never alone or this late at night. She shuddered at her actions and wondered if the operator of the ferry would remember her. Perhaps the man with the ropes would be a different person altogether. She pondered why Jake came for her and not one of the men in Savannah. She answered her own questions—it would have taken another hour to reach the city and she doubted that Jake knew his way around Savannah. Once more, she dismissed her concern.

Before she had a chance to worry more, a figure stepped away from the rope-covered piling. "You need the ferry, doc?"

Cathy called out, "I'm not the doctor, but I'm seeing to someone, in his place." She glanced around her at the dark night and the small boy in her carriage. She should have brought Grif and someone else with her, the sensible part of her brain lectured as she paused at the edge of the wooden barge. It was too late to turn around. She tried hard to swallow her fear. Something in her manner spoke eloquently of her fright and the boy jumped down from the carriage. "We gotta hurry," he

318

cried out and grabbed at the reins leading the horse onto the wooden planks.

On the opposite side of the river, Cathy swore she heard the thump of horses' hooves. Again she considered turning back. Jake looked up in her face, his anxiety plain. The silvered light shone against his tears. "I hope I ain't too late."

For one moment, Cathy scolded herself for her own suspicions, then the boy leaned away from her, mumbling, "I'm sure sorry, mam, but he said he was gonna hurt my pa bad if ya didn't come." Cathy stared at Jake. The words slowly sank into her brain. Something was wrong, very wrong.

She turned to the operator of the ferry, her voice deep with her fear. "Take me back to the south side of the river. Take me back now!"

The man at the pole refused to acknowledge her plea. She turned to the boy. "Tell him to go back, tell him!"

Against the backdrop of sand and clouds several horses moved to the edge of the river and across the water Cathy heard a voice harsh in its familiarity. "I don't think so, Catherine. Not tonight."

The *Savannah Lady* sailed up the river to her spot along the wharf and Drew stood at the bow, his face dark with anger. As far as he was concerned, they had wasted the last four days. After a long two hours with the sheriff, Drew and Sam spent some time with the two pieces of scum that Sam named responsible for his beating. Drew threatened, Sam got in several licks, but the thugs had no idea who hired them.

Both men shook and begged for a drink. After Sam planted a couple of good jabs into the belly of the larger of the two, the men tried to cooperate, but their descriptions were so vague that it could have been almost anyone. A man hired them from the docks of Philadelphia. That was the only sound piece of information they gave.

The sheriff took Drew's and Sam's statements and arraigned the men. They'd be in the Charleston jail for weeks, the lawman assured Drew. The lady they meant to kidnap was safe for a time. Drew agreed with the sheriff. Cathy was safe at least until the man with the funds discovered that his men failed. He hit the rail in his agony. Who wanted his wife? Until he knew, it wasn't safe for her to leave the house at Heart's Haven.

Drew looked over the crowd assembled at the Savannah dock. He waved to acquaintances and friends congregating on the wooden boards. Strange, he thought as he looked out over the faces. The sheriff and Father Worthington both stood at the back of the throng. "What the hell?" he muttered. He turned to James who stood at his side. "What are they doing here?" He pointed to their dour faces.

The gangplank was lowered into place and Drew jumped over the side, walking the board when Father Worthington met him. "Drew, lad, let's go back on board."

He nodded to James and the solemn procession moved up the plank. "In yer cabin, Captain," the sheriff added.

The door of the captain's cabin was barely closed when Drew rounded on the two older men. "What in the hell— pardon, Father. What's going on?"

320

Father Worthington frowned and folded his hands. "Drew, boy, I've bad news. Your lady left to help someone ill. We don't rightly know but there must've been some kind of an accident at the ferry. She was . . . She didn't . . . Drew, the Lord God has taken your lady home."

The closeness in the cabin was split by an anguished cry of disbelief. "No!"

Chapter Twenty-Two

A solemn procession left the ship and moved quietly over the dock. A buggy appeared out of nowhere and James pushed Drew into the vehicle. The crowd on the dock sensed the tragic mood of the group and pulled away from the raw pain that could not be hidden. Drew climbed into the carriage, sat with his eyes closed, and his forehead wrinkled in a frown. His huge frame was tense, as if he waited for James to tell him that it was a joke.

James gave the order. "Heart's Haven." The carriage moved off at little more than a walk. Not a word passed between the two men seated across from each other in the carriage. James's heart twisted, for he loved Cathy as a friend, a sister.

They were almost to Heart's Haven when Drew raised his pale face. "I don't believe it. It doesn't make sense. No, I can't believe. It's a mistake."

James gazed at his friend, not really surprised by Drew's reaction. Grief had stages and denial was the first. Drew would grieve for a long time, James knew. Perhaps the man beside him would never be able to love again.

James glanced out the window before he answered Drew. "We'll talk about it when we reach the plantation."

A morbid solemnity greeted them at the plantation and James wondered if the red eyes of the servants would bring reality crashing down on his companion. Even in the somber tension of the house Drew denied the fact. "She is not dead. I won't believe it. She is not gone!"

James led him into the study and poured a large brandy for both of them. He guided Drew to a leather chair and sat down opposite him. "Drew," he said softly, "listen to me."

As James's voice droned on and on, Drew thought back over the last two hours. Father Worthington's declaration had forced a cry of anguish from his throat, but then he'd disclaimed the news. The sheriff took over, explaining that two boys had found James's mare standing on the north side of the Savannah River that morning. One section of harness was broken. The body of the chaise, battered and partially crushed, was on its side lying in the mud of the bank where the horse had dragged it.

The boys raced for help and soon a dozen men scoured the area looking for the injured or dead body of James Rupert. It took a visit to Heart's Haven before the true occupant of the chaise was discovered. Cathy had gone, in James's stead, to help an injured man. With her she had taken a small boy she'd called Jake.

At the sheriff's insistence, two men volunteered to talk to Hurly Joe, the operator of the ferry, but the old man told them he went home about ten o'clock. "Most everybody who wants t' cross knows where I be. Nobody showed up last night." The sheriff explained to Drew that they suspected Cathy went to the ferry and, not knowing about Hurly Joe, she and her young escort attempted to ferry across the river alone.

Drew argued, but no one listened. He shook his head. He could not believe that the woman who gave his life meaning had lost her life trying to help someone else. He accused James. "If she's gone, and I still don't believe she is, then it's all your fault. You taught her about medicine, you encouraged her and insisted that she help you." Without warning, Drew hurled the glass of brandy against the hearth, splatttering liquid and glass in every direction.

For the next twenty-four hours, the banks of the river were searched above and below Savannah. Not a trace of Cathy's clothing or her body could be found. Drew spent hours with the searchers, but not James. He had his hands full trying to console Grif. The boy threw himself at James sobbing, "It's me fault. It's all me fault. I shoulda been with her." Even though he was only ten, and tiny for his age, he insisted, "I coulda saved her."

James, with Bessy's encouragement, planned a funeral service and Father Worthington came to the plantation to pray with the family and friends. Drew stood off to one side, listening to the words but hearing none of them. He was numb. Cathy's disappearance could not be explained and Drew lost hope. The one woman he loved had been taken from him and his heart was torn to bits. Cathy's death slowly became a reality. Drew didn't know if he could live with such a truth.

Days slipped by, one after another, and Drew sat in his study a full glass of brandy never far from his lips. Twice James tried to talk to him, but he paid little attention, shouting at his friend, "Just leave me alone."

Cathy'd been gone for ten days when James took things

into his own hands. He sent for help. Jane Darrow arrived and James met her at the door. "I wasn't sure you'd come when I sent that note."

Jane untied her bonnet. "How bad is he? I gathered from your note that he's seldom sober."

James shook his head. "Oh, he's sober enough. He hasn't been able to stop the pain with the brandy, but if he keeps consuming the amount he's drinking now, he'll lose touch with reality eventually and we may never get him back."

Jane started for the study, but she turned. "Would you see to my trunk? I'll talk to Drew now." James stood frozen in the foyer, afraid to leave. Perhaps Jane needed help. He heard her greeting. "Brother, I want you to give me that glass." He heard Drew's reply: "Go to hell."

He backed up when Jane and Drew started yelling at each other. Jane shouted cruel reprimands, telling Drew that he wasn't the only man to lose a wife, that he was an adult and not a child. Drew's comments were peppered with curses and pleas to be left alone, but Jane did not relent. After nearly an hour, the study grew quiet. James heard the hushed sobs of sister and brother. He slipped out of the house needing some time to grieve as well.

Jane stayed for four days. Cathy's clothes were given to the church and one of the other bedrooms was redecorated for Drew. Jane sat with him while he wrote a letter to William Pentworth, then she packed up and went home. James took the letter to England down to the docks. A mail packet was sailing to Baltimore and from there on to England. William Pentworth would learn of his daughter's death by the middle of August. James's future, he admitted, was as desolate as Drew's.

*   *   *

Cathy paced in her prison, fanning herself vigorously against the heat of the room. The top of the two windows in the room were open a slit, but not enough to allow for a decent breeze. She was hot, she was tired, and she was furious, a condition she'd been in for two weeks now. If that wasn't enough, almost every day when she first rose, her stomach rolled. She gritted her teeth in frustration and thought back to the last night of June and her kidnapping.

She'd frozen on the ferry when she heard the hateful voice from Barbados. Nelson Goodspeed jumped off his horse and waited for her at the bank as the ferry touched land. She struggled but it hadn't done a bit of good. The man was strong and he was determined. He dragged her to a waiting horse, lifted her into the saddle, tied her hands to the pommel and hooked the reins of her horse with his.

He gave a series of directives and the men with him scurried off to do his bidding. Two rather despicable creatures stayed with Nelson at his request. Once he seemed satisfied with the movement of his men, he ordered Cathy's horse forward and he whipped his own mount into motion.

For hours, Cathy's horse walked or trotted beside Nelson. A half-dozen times they stopped and Nelson allowed her a bit of privacy. However, the entire time she cared for her needs, Nelson insisted that she continue to talk to him. Her embarrassment nearly destroyed her, but it didn't matter to Nelson. As far as she could determine, Phillip's friend didn't have a sympathetic chord in his soul.

As night lightened and then changed to dawn, they finally stopped. Two tents appeared and Nelson handed Cathy some bread, cold meat, and fruit. He tied her right hand to his left and then forced her into the tent, pushing her down on a blanket. He lay down. "Now we are going to rest."

Cathy was incensed. "I'll not rest next to you, you animal. I want you to release me now! I want to return to my husband."

Nelson smiled indulgently. "Catherine, you will rest, and you will rest beside me. We will discuss your so-called marriage when we get to Barbados."

Cathy leaped to her feet, dragging Nelson into a sitting position. "I'm not going to Barbados with you or with anyone except Drew Sloan. You just wait. Andrew will come after me, and when he finds you—"

Nelson yanked her to her knees. "He will not come after you. His friends will tell him that you are dead!"

"No!" Cathy whispered and sank to the blanket laid on the ground as a pallet for her.

"It is the only way," Nelson said softly.

Cathy cried herself to sleep. It was afternoon before Nelson shook her arm. "We must move on, Catherine. Come on, wake up. We must go."

Cathy moved as if she were in a daze for the several days it took to travel to Charleston across the dirty rutted roads. Her mind a blank, she had trouble remembering where she was and why. She ate, slept, and took care of her own needs without a thought. In her mind she repeated, "Drew is not coming; he thinks I'm dead."

Late one afternoon, they stopped before a sprawling white clapboard building and Nelson announced, "We've arrived."

Cathy lost the haze that had surrounded her for four days. She grew alert. Immediately, she thought of escape or at least getting a message through to her husband. She was furious. Nelson caused her trouble for what? Cathy

328

gathered her travel-weary body and snarled, "I want to know why you have dragged me to Charleston?"

Nelson sneered back and helped her down from her horse. "I've taken rooms here at this inn. We will stay here until my ship anchors. In less than a week, we will be on our way to Barbados."

She cursed, threatened, tried to scream, but Nelson refused to tell her anything more, except that the people at the inn knew she was "affected." The week stretched out into two weeks, then eighteen days. Every morning he brought her breakfast. After she nibbled at the food, he escorted her around the property of the inn. She liked the view because the inn was set on a small rise outside of the city. She could see the harbor, but then so could Nelson.

The inn itself was pleasant enough—large, clean rooms, and good food, but Cathy never got to talk to the staff. The only person she saw was an old, sour-faced woman, who made frantic hand gestures whenever Cathy asked her anything. Nelson told her the day they arrived that he hired the woman especially to care for Cathy. "It seems," Nelson said later, expanding on the servant's background, "the old lady's husband took exception to the amount of nagging she did. He cut out her tongue, then beat her soundly. Now, she doesn't hear well and she can't carry tales."

Cathy wanted to ask if Nelson and the poor woman's husband were related, but she decided that her sarcasm wouldn't help her cause. After he brought her the evening meal that first day, she asked once again, "Why are you taking me back to Barbados?" He refused to answer.

Over the long days, she thought about her situation

and the more she considered what she knew the more confused she became. At first, she thought the order to bring her back came from the island itself, but, she reasoned, her gentlemen brothers wouldn't condone a kidnapping. After her brothers, there was her father, but that didn't make sense, either.

Her upset stomach plagued her. She blamed her inability to keep anything down a direct result of the trip and Nelson's treatment of her. However, Cathy's concern for herself grew when she realized that in spite of her illness she wasn't losing any weight. In fact, her own dress and the two dresses Nelson bought seemed a little tight. When they reached Barbados, she told herself, her brothers would take care of her. They would return her to her husband and everything would be all right.

At noon on the eighteenth day, when Nelson brought her lunch, he started spouting orders. "My ship weighed anchor this morning. The old lady will help you pack and then we'll go down to the bay. I intend to leave with first tide early tomorrow, so I want you on board." He glared at her. "And don't try anything. I won't mind locking you in a cabin for the whole trip."

Cathy's clenched fists rested on her hips. In another two weeks she would be in Barbados with her brothers. When they learned about her marriage, they would send her back to Drew. Until then, she could put up with this tall, unpleasant creature. Perhaps one of the cleaning maids would find the notes she left scrawled in soap and food in the closet and in the wardrobe. Someone would send word to Drew that she was alive.

"I'll go with you and I'll go quietly. I'm as anxious to get to Barbados and away from you as you are to leave Charleston. Just tell me when you want to leave this inn."

Intense anger flitted across Nelson's face and Cathy ducked, afraid that he would strike her. When she glanced up at him, he seemed to have some of his control back and he stomped from the room. At the door he shouted in her general direction, "Two hours!"

In less than two hours he stood in the doorway, but Cathy expected him. A half-hour before, she'd finished with her packing, freshened her hair, and sponged her face. He didn't appear to be happy with anything, much less her appearance. He scowled and held the door open. "I couldn't get a carriage. We'll have to ride to the dock in a cart."

Cathy smiled at his anger. "I don't mind. I would rather ride a horse but, if you want a conveyance, so be it."

He looked ready to strangle her. "Don't try anything!"

She refused to let the smile slip. "I told you I would go quietly. I intend to do just that, but I give you fair warning: when we get to the islands, Phillip and Charles are going to know, in detail, what you put me through."

She sauntered out to the cart and climbed up into the front seat. She kept her eyes straight ahead, willing her temper to stay below the boiling point.

Nelson climbed into the cart beside her. "Where's your bonnet?"

Cathy stared at him in confusion; she didn't have a bonnet. "I don't have a bonnet. I have this straw hat." She reached around and lifted a flat-brimmed straw hat with several ragged daisies twisted around the crown.

"Put it on," he snapped. Cathy stuck it on her head and glanced at the man next to her. He was still furious. Cathy sat very still, trying to understand his anger.

331

She glanced over at another couple stepping down from an arriving carriage. His reasoning became crystal clear. With the bonnet the woman wore, Cathy couldn't see her face. She smiled in pleasure. Without a bonnet, Cathy could be recognized and Nelson Goodspeed didn't want to take that chance.

He grumbled, "Well, can't do anything about it now. Let's get to the ship." They took off at a fast clip, but soon they caught up to town traffic and Nelson had to slow the horse and the cart. Cathy watched the activity and as they passed other travelers she smiled her brightest smile. Some of the people had to remember her, they just had to.

Finally, they arrived at water's edge and a waiting sailor lifted Cathy down from the cart and forced her into a dinghy. Nelson clambered aboard and gave the order. She chanced a look in his direction. The trip from the inn to the bay had done nothing to improve Nelson Goodspeed's disposition. The man was so angry that Cathy shivered in fright. She found herself wondering if he was a violent man.

Another face watched the disappearing boat and when Cathy's dinghy reached a small skiff in the harbor, the woman turned and traced her steps back to the market. A hundred questions ran through Bridget's mind and she stumbled through the streets, her emotions strung tight. She recognized the woman immediately, the man as well. What was Catherine Pentworth, a young woman who so tenderly cared for Bridget's dying children, doing with William Purdy, the man Bridget married in Erie?

By evening, Bridget had a headache three times worse than the ache she had the day she lost her children. Catherine hadn't looked unhappy, but William's expres-

332

sion was one of anger. The girl was in for trouble, that much Bridget knew. Perhaps if she could get word to Catherine that William was not a nice man... She crawled into her cot in the servants' quarters, trying to decide what she should do.

The next morning, after a word with her employer, Bridget trudged back to the bay. The ship that Cathy boarded the day before was gone. Bridget made a few inquiries. The sailors volunteered information slowly, but eventually she learned that the ship arrived from Philadelphia the day before and was now on its way to Barbados. One helpful soul mentioned that the captain owned the ship. She smiled when she heard the name. So, that piece of scum called himself by a different name. No wonder Catherine didn't know the man.

Bridget could do only one thing, she decided, as she trudged back to her house. She owed it to the girl and to the doctor that tried to help her. She sat with her employers, explaining what happened in Savannah and what she saw today. Taking her small purse, and coin from her mistress, she arranged for the coach to Savannah. James Rupert needed to know that Catherine Pentworth was in the hands of a man who was a cheat, a liar, a deserter, and already married—to her!

Chapter Twenty-Three

The coach hurled Bridget toward Savannah and with each mile, cruel memories haunted her. She kept repeating that she owed the girl. She helped her once. She drifted off to sleep, only to awake at the fringes of a nightmare. She wiped at her damp cheeks and glanced at the two other passengers in the coach. She breathed a sigh of relief when she noticed that they were still sleeping.

The coach moved along the rutted road, swaying and jumping as it ignored the pathetic excuse for a path. Inside, hot, tired, and full of recriminations, Bridget wondered yet again if she made the right choice coming south to tell the doctor about Catherine. People would call her a busybody. Some sixth sense, though, told Bridget that William was doing something that bordered on illegal and the thought occurred, could Catherine be there willingly?

She couldn't defend her compulsion to tell James Rupert what she had seen. For whatever reason, her need to tell was so strong that she was traveling to him.

Shaking her head in consternation, she wondered if she'd lost touch with reality.

For twenty-four hours, the coach shook her and the other passengers until she was numb. When the coach slowed for the tenth time, she raised the leather curtain and gazed out over familiar scenery. The large white house of Heart's Haven loomed in the distance. The driver stuck his head around the wooden frame of the coach and shouted at Bridget, "That it?"

Bridget nodded and then realized he could not hear her head move. "Ya," she shouted back.

At the entrance to the plantation the coach stopped and leaned as the driver swung down to help Bridget from the conveyance. He looked her over and then glanced at the dazzling house, sparkling in the morning sun. "You sure?"

Bridget tried to smile. "I'm sure." She took her small valise from the driver's hand and walked through the stone posts that marked the drive. She didn't bother looking back at the coach, but before she had covered a few feet, she heard the hooves of the horses crunch against the stones in the road. Well, she sighed to herself, she was committed now, and if these people didn't like her interference, she'd walk back to town. She'd hiked greater distances before.

She made her way to the hospital and knocked on the door, but the boy cleaning the main room didn't stop his chore. Without a glance in her direction, he announced, "Dr. Rupert's at the main house."

She stumbled across the lawn and mounted the steps to the front door. Bessy answered her knock, and Bridget noticed that she was wearing a black mourning band around her arm. For a fraction of a second Bridget's heart paused in its beating, but no, it couldn't be Dr. Rupert, the boy said he was at the house.

"Please, Bessy, can I see Dr. Rupert?" Bridget mumbled. The words were barely out of her mouth when Bessy ushered Bridget in. Before she entered, Bridget turned and looked back up the long road from where she had just come. In the distance, she saw a regal carriage driving up. Another patient for the doctor? Bridget wondered.

She didn't have long to wait before she heard James Rupert shout for her to come in. Bessy showed her to the parlor. James came through the doorway. "Bridget, what can I do for you?"

Bridget looked at the red-haired doctor and at his tense face. In that moment she heard voices and another door close. She couldn't lose the doctor to another patient, not yet. She blurted out her message. "The girl, Catherine! I saw her with my husband, the one I told you about, in Charleston."

James stared at her for a full minute, then he said softly, "Bridget, it couldn't have been Catherine. Catherine was swept out to sea three weeks ago after a ferry accident. You've mistaken someone else for her."

Bridget looked stunned and then she shook her head violently. "No, no! It was Catherine! I heard William call her Catherine. Of course, he's changed his name. He calls himself Nelson Goodspeed now and he was taking her to Barbados. I know. I followed him to his ship."

A tall man, immaculately groomed, stood inside the doorway, his dark eyes as stunned as James Rupert. His soft voice cut through the silence in the room. "I know Nelson Goodspeed. He lives in Barbados. He and I left the islands together. He came here, looking for

337

Catherine Pentworth."

Bridget's face crinkled into an I-told-you-so smile and she rested her fists on her hips. James sank down on a small damask sofa near the door as the truth of Bridget's words registered in his brain. "My God. She was kidnapped?"

Just then Bridget watched a third man stroll into the room. "Who was kidnapped? Hello, Bart. What brought you here?"

Bart turned wide eyes on Drew. "I came to extend my condolences, but they may not be necessary."

"What is he talking about?"

James shot up and grabbed at Drew. "I think you better come and sit down. Bart, you too, because I think we'll need your story as well." James paused until Drew was seated. "Now, Mistress Bridget, would you please tell my friend what you told me?"

Before the next hour drew to a close, the household at Heart's Haven became the scene of colossal chaos. Drew paced and shouted at everyone in the house. James sent messages as rapidly as he could write. Bart offered his own carriage and team to help with their delivery. Samuel rode out of the plantation twenty minutes after Bridget finished her tale, on his way to prepare the *Georgia Girl* for the trip. Bessy and three of the servants started throwing clothes into valises for James, Drew, and Grif. Even Bridget, after Bart told his tale, consented to travel with them to confront the man she called husband.

Bessy stopped her packing to serve a quick dinner of cold meats. Four hours after she arrived, Bridget sat back down in a carriage for the trip into Savannah. There, she and the men with her would board a ship. She shivered at

338

the speed with which the whole thing had transpired. William Purdy, she decided, was in for a very rude awakening. He had taken the wife of a determined man. She couldn't help the smile that teased at the corners of her mouth.

A soft evening breeze sent the sails of the *Georgia Girl* fluttering against the lines. Gentle waves escorted the lady away from land to a rendezvous in the islands. If the weather held, Drew announced only minutes before, after he checked the charts, they would make the island of Barbados by the twelfth or thirteenth of August.

Half an ocean away, William Pentworth paced the deck of the *Southern Song*, a merchantman bound for the island of Barbados. They had been at sea for two weeks and for the most part it had been a pleasant voyage. William thought of his niece resting in her cabin and the reason he had started this journey. It all began with a letter, one of several that William got in a week's time. This letter was written in a formal, feminine hand and the address was Philadelphia, Pennsylvania. It was signed by a Mistress Joanna Sloan.

That letter was simple and almost curt in its contents. Mistress Joanna Sloan wrote to tell William Pentworth that she had just finished entertaining his daughter, now her daughter-in-law. Mistress Sloan was enthusiastic in her acceptance of Catherine. "She is a daughter to do her father proud," the woman wrote. William was encouraged to visit Joanna, if ever he was in Philadelphia.

William remembered his two-day rage. As he looked back, he decided his sons made him much angrier than Catherine. They lied to him, Phillip particularly, and

339

William was determined to find out why. And, once he discovered why Phillip lied, then, William sighed, he had to do something about Amelia.

He shrugged his shoulders as if to make his burden lighter and ambled toward the bow of the ship. For nearly four months, ever since that young doctor left, Amelia had been a problem. She had lost weight, was probably still losing weight, and the dark rings under her eyes announced to the whole damned world that she wasn't sleeping.

At first, William thought that James Rupert had dishonored the girl. She wasn't pregnant, he was sure of that. So, what was wrong with her? The few times they entertained, he'd practically had to force her to dress and join in the festivities. She refused to see any young people her age. A nice young man, son of a business acquaintance, approached him about Amelia, but she begged off, pleading illness as an excuse. Well, she might be ill, but he was sick, sick and tired of the whole affair. If she wanted the damned doctor, then he would get her the doctor, colonial bastard or not. He wasn't going to watch one of his own nieces die of heartbreak and then blame it on him.

No, he banged his fist down against the rail, after he had words with Phillip and Charles, he would send Amelia to James Rupert, damned if he didn't. According to the captain of this vessel they should make the islands by the middle of August. And Catherine? What would he do with Catherine? Good riddance to her as well. If she wanted an American, then she could have him. He sighed his frustration. Where, as a father, had he gone wrong?

*   *   *

Cathy was miserable. She had never been more miserable in her whole life. She rolled over on the bunk and stared at the dark wood beams above her. Just the thought of the motion of the ship was enough to bring the retching back. She had contracted a dreadful illness. Any food she consumed came up in minutes. She knew that soon she would die.

Nelson assured her each morning when he brought her fresh water and tea that wouldn't stay down, that when they anchored in Barbados and moved onto land, she'd recover. He couldn't avoid a jab or two about her husband, though. Yes, he told her, Drew thought she had been swept away by the Savannah River. In his deep voice, Nelson told her, "He'll never come after you. He thinks you're dead. He'll marry someone else." She didn't feel well enough to argue with him, but his words contributed to her upset. Her retching often brought tears, tears for the love she'd never declared.

By the morning of the fifth day, Cathy insisted that if she were going to die, she wanted to die in fresh air. She ordered Nelson to help her out on the deck. He refused at first, but Cathy used what little of her strength she had left to scream at him. He relented and soon she rested against a coil of rope, and despite the July heat, she wrapped herself in a blanket.

The warm sun felt wonderful and by the time the brilliant ball began its western plunge, Cathy felt better. She muttered to one of the sailors near enough to hear her, "I'm hungry. Are there any biscuits or tea?"

The fellow left grumbling and Cathy grinned, wondering if Nelson had told the man to see to her. If that sailor was her nursemaid, Cathy guessed, it was certainly not to his liking.

341

A short time later, he returned with several biscuits, a pot of hot tea, and honey for the bread. She ate with relish and for the first time since she came aboard, the food she ate stayed in her stomach. She left the deck for a nap, but after the evening meal she returned to enjoy the late afternoon breeze. Shaking her head in amazement, she realized that on deck she felt fine.

Cathy's illness was a puzzlement to her. On the trip from England to Barbados, nearly everyone on the ship was seasick, but she had no trouble. She wondered if her system had changed dramatically. She thought back over the weeks just past and she went rigid. Her system had changed greatly for it had been over three months since her last flow.

She chastised herself for forgetting something so necessary for every female. Cathy sat very still. Could she be carrying Drew's child?

The thought was at once exciting and frightening. Now, Charles and Phillip would have to let her go back to Savannah. A thousand questions ran through her head, all of them alarming, and she desperately wanted someone to talk to. In the moments after she realized her condition, she thought about telling Nelson. Then, almost as soon as the thought became a reality, she dismissed it. Nelson must not know. For some reason, she didn't want to share the information with anyone but her husband.

The days slipped by and Cathy found that on deck she had no trouble with her stomach. If she spent much time below in her cabin awake, she became ill and ended up hanging over the chamber pot. On deck, somehow the fresh air cleared away the feelings of nausea and she even took to eating her meals seated against the ropes in the bow. She made friends with the cabin boy, but the rest of the crew, even the sailor who played nursemaid that first day, kept their distance. For the entire three weeks at sea, she never learned one of their names.

Finally, when her patience was wearing very thin, she spotted a green landmass. When the cry came, "Let go the anchor," Cathy almost cried out her happiness. Now, she would see her brothers. Now, she would go home to Drew.

Before she could savor the end of the trip, Nelson stood beside her. "Catherine, you are to go below until we are ready to disembark."

She looked at him in dismay, her mind covering a hundred reasons why he didn't want her on the deck. The cabin boy explained that they had no cargo to unload, so that offered no explanation. She tested her theory. "How soon will we be leaving the ship?"

"Not until later, much later."

Cathy frowned. "After dark?"

Nelson smiled, certain that she understood. "Yes," he responded as he nodded his head.

Cathy looked at the bow of the ship, at the sails thrown about. "I'll stay in the bow. I get sick below deck."

The look of disgust that crossed Nelson's face, Cathy decided, left no room for negotiations if her physical condition didn't change his mind. She waited impatiently for him to think the thing through. "All right. I don't want you sick again." He smirked at her, then his deep, crisp voice taunted, "This has been a calm trip. I can imagine what you're like in heavy seas."

Cathy wanted to say something, anything, in her defense, but almost despaired of calling attention to her condition. She said nothing.

343

Nelson made another disparaging sound and turned back toward the stern. "Stay in the bow and don't walk around. I don't want anyone from shore wondering what I brought back with me."

Cathy took her place against the coil of ropes and the pillows of gray sail. She shivered in the warm tropical breeze. The sooner she was off of this ship and back with Phillip or Charles, the safer she would feel. She had to endure another four or five hours of Nelson Goodspeed before they left the ship and then she would never have to see him again.

Cathy thought about their arrival in Barbados. She had mentioned Charles and Phillip, but Nelson had not. She told him that she was leaving him to go to her brothers, but he said nothing. He had said they would leave the ship after the sunset. She grew terrified as she realized that he just might not turn her over to her brothers. Dear God, no! She would escape.

She watched the sailors as they scurried around the deck, and she watched the waves bombard the beach. Even if she could somehow slip into the water undetected, swimming to shore was out of the question. The ocean was too rough and Nelson had anchored his sloop too far out for her abilities. Her fear grew as she leaned against her coil of rope and watched the sun sink into the horizon.

As she watched the sailors on deck, she knew that soon they would be leaving the vessel. A chill of apprehension flitted up her backbone. With a huge lump in her throat, she watched as Nelson strolled toward her. She was afraid of Nelson Goodspeed!

As Nelson ambled toward her, Cathy frowned at her thoughts. When had she begun to fear the man approaching? When he first pulled her onto the extra horse north of Savannah, she'd been angry, furious. She didn't remember the kind of fear that was trying to paralyze her now. It had to be his cold gray eyes, she decided. Up until the anchor was let go, his eyes were normal, but now they gleamed with a fanaticism she hadn't noticed before.

"Catherine," he said softly, "I want you to go below now and pack. I let you stay on deck as long as I could. Go and gather your things."

Cathy had no intention of doing anything until she knew what he planned. "Not until you tell me when you are taking me to my brothers."

"You will see your brothers soon enough."

"I want to know when, and I'm not leaving this ship until I know."

He grabbed at her arm. "You will pack NOW. We will talk later."

She drew herself up to her full height. "We will talk now. You are not my keeper. I am a married woman and—"

Nelson cut her off. "That marriage doesn't count. You have only been living with the man, and I might add, that sin will cost you."

"I am married!" Cathy shouted.

"No, you are not, not until you are married to me!"

Cathy gasped and slumped against the rail. "I am married," she whispered. "I can't marry anyone else. I promised, until death us do part."

Nelson's cruel laugh cut through her. "The wedding was not legal; you've only been Andrew Sloan's whore. You can't be his wife."

Cathy gathered her tattered courage. "The nuptials

345

were legal. I was of age, the proper papers were signed by both of us and by our witnesses. Besides, I don't want to marry you."

Nelson's chuckles destroyed her attempt to make him back down. When he quieted, he turned back to her. "Catherine, you could not marry without Phillip's permission. Any contract you might have entered into was null and void because Phillip had already said you were to marry ME. Now, I am taking you to my plantation. If you try to escape, I'll send my overseer after you with instructions to treat you like a runaway slave. We beat runaways at my plantation.

"Now, about your brothers . . . They will be informed that you are back in Barbados. They will be allowed to see you AFTER we have been married. We are leaving the ship now. I have much to do. Prepare yourself! You'll be my bride on Friday, the twelfth."

Cathy backed away. "Never," she muttered and wrenched her arm away from him. "I'll see you in hell," she hissed as he grabbed for her again.

His voice cut as much as the fingers that tightened into the soft flesh of her upper arm. "Forget Andrew Sloan. You are mine now, you and your money."

Chapter Twenty-Four

In the end, Cathy lost out to Nelson. She fought, but he was bigger and stronger than she. With surprising ease, he forced her to the cabin and made her pack. When her pathetic wardrobe lay packed in a carpetbag, he dragged her up the steps, and handed her over the rail to his waiting first mate. Her heart stuck in her throat as the first mate handed her to another sailor who sat her down in the rocking dinghy. Nelson followed and gave the order. "Row!" His sailors rowed them ashore, and he had a carriage waiting.

Cathy looked around the dull, dirty white room that had been her prison for the last day and a half. The brilliant sunlight shining through the open windows made the drab walls and dusty furniture look even more neglected. The events that took place after they left the ship haunted her. Twice, on the drive to the plantation, Cathy tried to leap from the carriage, but Nelson sat next to her, and he grabbed her and managed to stop her each time. When the carriage pulled up before the dark shape of a two-story house, Cathy guessed they had arrived, but she refused to question her captor.

That night, she'd been locked in the room with only an old woman of indeterminate age to see to her meals, water, and linens. The same slave appeared the next morning, more than willing to talk. At one point, Cathy wondered if Nelson gave orders that the woman talk to her.

The second morning, the old woman had even more tidbits to offer. "The banns, they be published. Yesterday, today, and tomorrow. The wedding gonna be Saturday, not Friday, on account of Father Churner ain't abide by a Friday weddin'. Yer brothers come, but Mistah Nelson say 'not yet.' They gotta wait until Saturday. And this afternoon, the lady come from town for to make a weddin' dress fer you. Mistah Nelson, he want pretty, and pretty he gonna get."

Cathy put her hands over her ears to shut out the servant. She didn't want to hear any of this. She thought of her brothers. The old woman said they'd come, but Nelson refused to let them see her. Had she been asleep? She didn't remember hearing a thing!

She thought of the wedding planned for Saturday. No! she silently screamed. If Nelson didn't release her by Saturday, then she'd disclaim him at the church. She wasn't going to be saddled with two husbands when she wanted only one. Nelson was not going to silence her then, if that was the only way she could get out of this coil of trouble.

She glanced at the slave. "I's called Harvest, 'cause I came at harvest time," she told Cathy.

"Harvest," Cathy asked, "this is Wednesday, isn't it?"

"Yes'm," Harvest smiled. "Today be the tenth day of August. Saturday be your weddin' day."

Cathy frowned and drew a deep breath. That woman insisted on mentioning the wedding every chance she got. "Harvest, I want you to deliver a message for me."

"Oh, mam, I can't do that."

Cathy continued on as if the old woman hadn't spoken. "I want out of this room. If Nelson doesn't let me out, there'll be no wedding Saturday." Cathy grimaced, there wasn't going to be one anyway. "You tell him, please."

Harvest left with the tray and the tin of wash water. "I's gonna tell him, but he ain't gonna like it."

Harvest brought her lunch and refused to talk to Cathy. The dressmaker came for a fitting, which Cathy refused until Harvest whined, "Girl, Mistah Nelson gonna beat me, iffin' ya don't cooperate." Cathy relented.

The sun was slipping over the hills and the trees when the lock to the door of Cathy's room rattled. The door swung open and Nelson stood in the doorway, smug and arrogant. "You want out of the room? I might consider it, if you . . ." his voice trailed off.

Cathy wondered what he felt she had to bargain, but she said nothing. Instead, she walked over to the window, and stared into the garden below. Perhaps it was just as well if she stayed in her room. She spun around and glared at him. "I've changed my mind. I don't want to walk after all, certainly not if I must abide you."

Nelson shouted, "Suit yourself," and slammed the door.

Cathy could have kicked herself. She should have kept her mouth shut until she managed at least to get out of the room. Now, she was stuck until Nelson decided to relent. He might not bother until time for the wedding. She sank down on the bed and brushed at her tears. At least on Saturday, she would see her brothers. They would send her back to Drew. They had to send her back to Drew. "Drew," she choked, and peeling off her dress, she crawled into bed. When Harvest came to bring her warm wash water, Cathy was sound asleep.

The next morning, Cathy woke before dawn. Harvest must have known that she would not sleep long, for breakfast arrived before the sun climbed above the horizon. After breakfast, Cathy scrubbed and dressed. Harvest came back for the breakfast tray, her face wreathed in smiles. "Mistah say you can go out in the garden this mornin'. Ya want to go now?"

Cathy started for the door, her face alive with her pleasure. She stopped and glanced at Harvest. "Is he joining me?"

Harvest frowned at her question. "It ain't good, girl, for ya to dislike yer intended, but no, he can't sit with ya this mornin'. I tole him I'd see to ya. Now, ya want to go?"

Cathy swept out of the door and down the stairs, before Harvest closed the door. The servant trailed behind giving her directions. Cathy laughed in delight. She was in the garden. It was as beautiful at eye level as it was from her second-story window. She spotted a stone table and bench. "Harvest, could I have a pot of tea out here?"

Harvest nodded and ambled back toward the house. Cathy looked around and wondered where Nelson's plantation was in reference to Phillip's and Charles's homes. "Must be farther south and closer to the western shore," she mused. Phillip and Charles lived in the center of the island. Cathy's curiosity grew.

When Harvest returned with the teapot, Cathy had her questions ready. "Harvest, which church will have the wedding?"

350

"Mistah Nelson, he's a member of St. George's Church, Mam," she said proudly.

"Where is St. George's?" Cathy was trying to place the church. Phillip and Charles both attended St. John's Church. An idea occurred to Cathy. "Which way is Bridgetown?"

"That way." Harvest pointed west. Cathy smiled and said nothing else. She had a very good idea where Nelson Goodspeed lived.

Harvest looked at her, her thoughts almost readable. "Now, missy, ya see here. Ya ain't leavin' this place. I ain't gonna let ya go, no sur, I ain't. Saturday, ya gonna be wed to Mistah Nelson, 'cause he says so."

Cathy sobered. Saturday was still three days away. Once she got to St. George's Church, she could have her say. Until then, she must not lose her temper or give away her plans. Cathy smiled at Harvest. "I only want to know where I am. I'm not going anyplace."

Harvest moved off, but Cathy watched as the old woman glanced in her direction often. Cathy relaxed and gazed at the sky. The huge, fluffy white clouds rolled across the blue sky like a pot of boiling laundry. She laughed as she played a child's game and picked out teapots and kittens in the mounds of white. Cathy stared at the wonder before her as the puffs gathered and grew like clumps of cotton from the pluckers. For nearly two hours, she sat entranced with nature's display. Finally, she gathered her things. The blue sky was fast becoming obliterated by the growing balls of white. This was all happening much too fast. The white faded into gray and for the first time Cathy heard a whine of wind. They were in for a fierce storm. With her teapot and cup, Cathy ran for the house.

Nelson's servants huddled in the corner of the conservatory. Cathy looked at their faces. They were terrified. Cathy turned to Harvest. "What are they afraid of? It's just a summer storm."

Harvest rolled her eyes skyward and shuddered. "Nah, chile. It ain't no reg'lar summer storm. This here kind comes once in a while. The wind blows so hard it takes whole buildings away. Some say the spirits are destroying the white lord's things, but it takes the servants' things, too. It's bad, real bad."

Out of nowhere, a tall man, older, with sagging jowls and snapping black eyes came into the room. Cathy recognized him from the swift introduction the evening the ship docked. Harry Jenkins was Nelson's overseer and he was angry. "Get these women outta here," he said, pointing to Harvest. "The men are coming to batten down the shutters."

He stared at Cathy, almost as if he saw her for the first time. "Miss, Mr. Goodspeed is in the south fields helping with the carts and things. I'm sure he'd want you to go into the cellar."

"What is it?" she asked, her voice a husky panic. "What kind of storm is this?"

"Could be a gale, mam, or it might be a hurricane. Time will tell. If it's a big blow, you won't be staying here. This house won't stand." Harry spun on his heels and raced out the door, shouting at the assembling men as he went.

The house would go? Cathy stood rigid with fright. What kind of a wind could blow so strongly that it would take the house? She looked around at the walls, the stairs, the ceilings. Slowly, the room grew dark as each window was partially covered by long weathered boards.

She heard the wooden mallets tapping at the shutters and each stroke matched the panic in her heart. If the house couldn't stand, then how could she survive?

She didn't have long to think about it, for someone tugged on her arm. "Missy, Missy. We got to go to the cellar. Missy? Missy? Y' alright?"

Cathy stared at the black woman for a fraction of a second, trying to remember where she was. Flashes of a storm at sea battered the edges of her memory and, suddenly, she wanted Drew, wanted him to hold her in his arms and whisper that this would go away, that she would live, she would be fine. She cried out, "Drew!"

The expression on Harvest's face read concern, and Cathy looked in the woman's eyes. I must control myself, Cathy scolded. Harvest pointed toward the door. "Out."

She grabbed Cathy's hand and dragged her through the door, toward another set of steps at the corner of the house. Once they were outside the house, Cathy stared at the violence nature forced on the land. Trees were nearly bent in two. Swirls of dust trailed up and down the garden paths, fighting for the right to move. The wind screamed at Cathy with a deafening roar, and in the distance she could see spikes of brilliance reach to touch the ground, but the wind was crying so loudly that she heard no thunder.

It wasn't dark. Cathy wondered why it wasn't dull and gray, as in most storms. Somehow the light made it worse. She felt the old woman tugging at her, but she couldn't move. The air was heavy, wet, and pressed against her skin, and she wondered if air could be so heavy that you could not breathe it. She took a step. Almost as if in passing condemnation for the movement, the rain came. Sheets of rain forced Cathy to bend and follow Harvest in the rush to shelter. This was no summer storm, Cathy chided herself, this was the end of the world.

They joined the other household staff in the cellar and before Cathy could make herself comfortable on the small cot in a corner, Harry Jenkins came through the door. "When it calms we'll go to Sunbury. We sure can't stay here."

Cathy turned to Harvest. "Why will we leave when it calms? That makes no sense at all."

Harvest turned her face toward Cathy and even in the uneven light of the cellar, Cathy was surprised at the lack of color in Harvest's face. "The man is saying that there be a calm during a hurricane. My man went through one once. It rained and blew and then it stopped. It stayed stopped for a while and then it came again, only worse than before."

Worse than before. The words rocked against Cathy's nerves and once again she wanted to scream for her husband. At the moment, Cathy would have given almost anything to get her hands around Nelson's neck for dragging her back to the island and making her endure this storm. Of course, she silently agreed, she could do the man little real harm, but, oh, how she would love to try.

For what seemed like hours, Cathy sat huddled with the others in the large room below the house. Crates of household goods, food stuff, and sundry other supplies for the plantation were pushed against the far wall and Cathy thought several times that sorting through those things might give her something to do, rather than listen to the soft sobs of some of the younger servants. Occasionally the foundation shook with the force of a

354

wind gust, and Cathy heard an almost human whistle through the roar. Every thought ended with a prayer as the wind rattled planks and limbs against their fortress.

Finally, the roar began to fade and the shaking stopped completely. Thank God, Cathy wanted to shout with delight. The calm. Harry was moving everyone out of the room. "Come on. We can't stay here. We gotta move. We ain't gonna have all day." He pushed and pulled until he had everyone outside. Cathy followed the servants.

Her first glance was at the sky. She could see tiny streaks of blue against the gray clouds. Surely, she thought, the storm must be finished. She watched as Harry wet his fingers and stuck one into the air above his head. "I figure we got about two hours at the most."

That seemed to tell everyone what they needed to know except Cathy. "Two hours for what?" she shouted. The surge of activity drowned out her words. From some corner a cart appeared, then another. A mule was dragged from the leaning planks of the barn. Cathy chanced to look around her.

God has stepped on the earth, Cathy thought as she viewed the destruction. Huge palm trees were lying on their sides. Branches of trees, torn from their parent, littered the ground. Water stood in pools everywhere. She glanced at the house and gasped at the starkness of disaster. Shutters were hanging. Sections of wall were strewn across the garden. Garden? There was no garden, only sticks. She stepped away from the corner by the cellar and looked at the house more closely. The roof or at least a good part of it was gone.

Harvest moved against her and Cathy glanced at the old woman. Tears were streaming out of her eyes. Cathy felt a twinge of guilt. After all, this was the woman's home. "Come, missy. We gotta go." Harvest pushed her toward the carts.

Cathy looked at Harry Jenkins and at Harvest. She was not going to ride in one of those carts. In fact, she wasn't going to the place they mentioned at all. This was her chance, perhaps the only one she'd get. She had to take it. "I'm not going to get in a cart." She refused to move. "I'll ride. Get me a mule or a horse."

"I don't know if we have any horses, mam. Come on, it ain't far. Mr. Goodspeed will be there waiting for ya, and I tole ya we only have about an hour, maybe a little more."

Cathy dug her heels into the wet ground. "I am NOT riding in a cart with servants." Cathy had a feeling that Mr. Jenkins was more than a little class conscious. If he was, she was going to use it.

"Now, miss. Ya can have a cart by yourself."

"NO," Cathy snapped. "The servants need the carts. I want a horse. I'm sure you can find one."

For a minute, Cathy thought that the man would pick her up and throw her into a cart. For some reason, though, he relented. "I'll drive a cart and ya can have my horse. Only, let's not waste any more time. We gotta go."

Cathy smiled. "Go! I'll follow you."

Harry turned to object and Cathy gave him a condescending grin. "I must follow you. I don't know the way."

Cathy took the reins from Harry's hand and started to mount the horse. Harry turned back to the mule he was harnessing and his voice was grim. "Don't try nothing foolish, miss. Hurricanes kill."

Cathy wasn't ready to abandon her plans. She maneuvered the gelding up to the cart that held Harvest. "Is this Sunbury far? Is it on the main road?" Cathy looked off toward the west. "Is it close to the church?" Her face filled with horror. "What if Sunbury and the church are both gone?"

Harvest reached out of the cart to pat the leg of the girl. "Don't you worry none," the servant purred. "Iffin this place be here, for sure Sunbury will stand. And the church stand up to bad storms before. Just you wait. When we get to that rise," she pointed to the north, "you'll see the top, astandin' tall and proud."

That was it! That isolated piece of information would make her escape possible. She would wait until she could see the steeple of the church and then she would have a direction. At the church, she would ask for protection until she could get to her brothers. They had to have survived this, they just had to. Suddenly she was anxious to begin the journey. "Are we ready to leave yet?"

There was a discussion about Cathy's place with the caravan. She insisted that she travel after the carts. "I can handle the horse much better if I am not surrounded by strange vehicles. Please, can we go? I want to be some place safe soon."

Harry finally agreed and they began to move. Cathy brought up the rear. With Harvest in the last cart, Cathy stayed close to the old woman for several hundred yards.

They came to the rise and Harvest pointed, calling out to the trailing girl, "See, there. See the steeple? The church still stands. There'll be a wedding on Saturday."

Cathy glanced around her at the destruction and wondered if she could even make it to the church. Huge trunks of trees lay on edge as if the hand of God had tired of the island and tried to sweep it clean. Chunks of wood that were probably part of someone's home lay strewn about as if dumped from the sky. Water puddled everywhere. The air was heavy with the dampness. Only a hint of a breeze touched her cheek. Cathy shook her head at the devastation. Harry was right, hurricanes did kill.

Cathy let the distance between her and the last cart lengthen slowly. By the time Harvest's cart passed over the next ridge, Cathy rode nearly a quarter of a mile behind. As the cart disappeared from her view, she lost no time in turning her horse and racing back the way she had come. Please God, she prayed, let me get to the church.

Cathy wondered if the rising wind was God's laugh at her request. Perhaps, she thought as she clung to her horse, she'd forfeited her life in her attempt to free herself from Nelson Goodspeed. She'd tried once before, and that attempt nearly killed her. Now there was not only herself but her unborn child. She laid her cheek against the damp neck of the horse and pleaded for speed.

Chapter Twenty-Five

"Land!" The call came from the crow's nest. Drew closed the Bible he used for the Sunday services and sighed in relief. Barbados at last. "Men," he addressed the crew, "I'm sorry about toiling today, but I want to be resting at anchor long before dusk." He ordered more canvas stretched against the winds and grabbed the glass. A silent prayer went soaring toward the heavens: "May she be well and waiting for me."

The distance to the island shrank, and Drew stood against the rail staring out at the mound that was the island. He lifted the glass to his eye often, the frown on his face growing longer with each glance. He turned to James who had joined him after the service. "There's something wrong here. I see what looks like piles of rubble and there's very little green for the number of trees I remember." He passed the glass to James and gave the order to reduce the sails. "I want to take a closer look. We'll sail close to the shore until we're south of Bridgetown. When we get to Carlisle Bay we'll drop anchor. It should be closer to Cathy's brothers, and we'll avoid the traffic around Bridgetown."

James handed the glass back to Drew. "Looks like the island suffered a storm. That might explain the heavy weather we had." They had sailed through two storms and James told Drew he was thinking seriously of giving up sailing. "After I bring Amelia back, I may never set foot on a ship again."

The closer they got to the shoreline the more devastation they noticed. Drew felt his heart sink as he began to make out trees ripped from the soil and small structures that must have been slaves' quarters scattered against the hills. The island had suffered a storm of unusual violence. Even the men on board quieted as they drifted closer to the island.

Bridget came up from her cabin and stood next to the men, watching the frantic activity near the bow. A half-dozen sailors stood at the railing, long poles in their hands, wrestling with enormous chunks of wood, tree stumps, and branches, trying to keep them away from the ship. "My God! What happened?" She looked out toward the island. "What kind of storm could cause this kind of destruction?"

James said the word that covered Drew's heart with ice. "Hurricane."

Drew lost some of his color. His voice was hoarse. "Cathy!"

James read his mind. "The inhabitants know what to do. This kind of storm is not a stranger to the islands. Why, we've had several, not as bad as this but . . ." his voice trailed off.

"Cathy doesn't like storms. She's not a native here, like her brothers," Drew pointed out.

"Her brothers live here, have lived here for several

years. I'm sure they knew what to do." James tried to console his friend.

Drew whispered, his voice strained, "God, I hope so."

With the debris in the water Drew ordered the sails trimmed. It slowed them to a crawl, but they made Carlisle Bay before three. The anchor was lowered and Drew had a landing party formed in ten minutes. Even Bridget insisted that she come along. "I can help with some of the wounded. There's gotta be a big number of people hurt. I can do my share."

Drew started to protest, but James silenced him. "I think that's a superior idea, Bridget. I may be needed as well." He disappeared down the stairs and returned a minute later with his black bag under his arm.

For a second, Drew looked upset. "We are looking for Cathy."

"And after we find her?"

Drew scowled at James, then ordered all of the participants in the search party over the railing and into the boat that would take them to shore.

Six miles down the coast in Oistin Bay, another landing party prepared to leave ship. Amelia clung to her uncle's arm. "I'm not staying on the ship by myself. I'm going with you. If things are as bad as you think, I want to go along. I can find something useful to do. I don't want to stay on the ship with only five or six sailors standing guard."

William Pentworth glared down at his niece. There was no point in trying to change her mind or argue with her. Two weeks ago he could have had his way, but not now. Two weeks ago something had happened to Amelia

Pentworth. William had no idea what thoughts passed through her mind to bring about the change, but for some reason, Amelia became a woman with a mind of her own. He couldn't remember the exact day of change but, all at once, she started to eat. The dark circles under her eyes dulled and finally disappeared. She told him one afternoon as she stood at the railing of the ship, "I intend to find James Rupert, Uncle. I intend to become his wife. I would prefer to do so with your blessing, but if you cannot give it, it doesn't matter."

She had turned and walked away from him, leaving him with his mouth hanging open. He didn't bother telling her that he had already decided that she might as well have the colonial bastard, if that's what she wanted. At that same moment, he made up his mind that he wasn't ever going to enlighten her. He was as stubborn as she. Now, two weeks later, her brilliant green eyes were slanted half-closed and the determination that blazed from them told William he lost the argument before he began one. Amelia was going with the landing party. There was nothing he could do, so he gritted his teeth and prepared to help her over the railing.

Once they were on the shore, the damage from the storm hindered every attempt at movement. William tried to hire two vehicles, only to be told that the roads were covered with debris. "I must get to the homes of my sons," he said to the man next to him.

The man, obviously a sea captain by his dress, glanced in his direction. "I've been told that most of the homes are gone. Four churches stand and those are full of the injured. Perhaps you should seek out your sons at one of the churches."

William shuddered with apprehension. "I'd hoped the

362

interior fared better."

The captain's look was full of concern. "Worse I hear. I hate to be the bearer of unfortunate news, but one of the plantation owners came by here only a short time ago. He's heading one of the many search parties that formed. You see, there are many people still missing. I would suggest that you talk to him or another with knowledge of the destruction before you attempt to track into the middle of the island."

"Where might I find this man?" William asked, looking at the frenzied activity around them.

"He moved off toward the north. He can't have gone very far. Here, let me send one of my sailors after him." He turned to a short, wiry man several feet behind them. "Jake, run ahead and tell Phillip Pentworth to return. There's a man here who needs some help."

William's face blanched. "Did you say Phillip Pentworth?"

The captain nodded, and William took a deep breath, regaining some of his composure. He forgot all about his anger with Phillip over relief that at least one of his sons was alive and well. Could it be that Phillip was looking for his brother. What about the wives, Roselle and Martha, and the grandsons? The minutes dragged by as William waited for the return of Phillip or at least the sailor.

Finally, above the crowd, William saw the head of his tall son. Phillip spotted his father a minute later. "Father! What are you doing here?"

"We can discuss that later. Is everyone all right?"

Phillip's mouth was a thin line of fear, and his eyes shifted away from his father's concerned gaze. "Charles, the women, and the children are fine." He glanced up. "We are looking for Catherine."

William stood stunned, and the reason for this trip to Barbados flooded his memory. His pointed chin rose and his eyes sparked with anger. "Don't you attempt to lie to me. I *know* Catherine is in the United States."

"She was in the United States, but she came back. After the storm struck, Catherine took off during the calm. We haven't found her yet. We may never find her."

William turned ashen. "Where is her husband? Is he looking as well?"

"Father, the marriage was planned for Saturday. This storm hit Thursday."

"A marriage for Saturday? What about her husband in the colonies? What about him?"

Phillip looked confused. "Catherine wasn't married. . . ."

William grabbed at the arm of his older son. He stared at Phillip, afraid for a moment that his mind was going. William said softly, "Catherine was married. Now what about this Saturday wedding? Who was she going to marry?"

"Father," Phillip began, "are we talking about my sister Catherine, the one you sent here so that Charles and I could find her a husband? Are you talking about that girl?"

"Phillip, I am not senile or insane." Quickly, William recounted the visits James Rupert made and the letter William received from Joanna Sloan. He gazed at his oldest child. "I think you better begin with Catherine's arrival here. Tell me everything. We are missing some pieces."

When Phillip finished, William was in a rage. "You mean to tell me that you haven't seen the lass? She could still be in America for all you know. This Nelson Goodspeed doesn't sound too trustworthy to me. I want to talk to the man. Where is he?"

Phillip looked contrite. "He went back to the east coast this morning. Charles went west and I went south. Charles and I are meeting north of here in a little over an hour. Nelson will be in Sunbury in the morning. You can talk to him then."

Charles waited close to the water's edge for a report from the men he sent to Bridgetown. Several new ships arrived, and he hoped that additional supplies and perhaps a doctor or two might make their way to the devastation. They were fortunate that they had ample warning at their plantation. However, according to Harry Jenkins at Nelson Goodspeed's farm, they had no warning. Or rather, no one recognized the storm for the terror it had become.

Charles wanted to strangle Phillip for not insisting that Catherine return to one of their homes, instead of leaving her at Nelson's place. When Nelson told them how exhausted she was, it seemed like a good idea to leave her where she was. And, of course, no one talked to Catherine about hurricanes and their destructive disposition. She must have been terrified out of her mind to run in the wrong direction, away from Sunbury. He glared down at the uprooted trees and the piles of rubbish thrown around the beach. Was any marriage so distasteful to her that she'd willingly run into the teeth of a storm? Could she have survived such a catastrophe?

He was so engrossed in his thoughts that the voice calling his name didn't register for several seconds. He picked up his head and shouted back, "Who needs me?"

James Rupert came striding up the beach. "I wasn't sure at first that it was you. God, it's been so long. I can't believe our good fortune. Where's Cathy? Let me introduce a man you'll want to know. Andrew Sloan, Charles Pentworth. Charles, this is Cathy's husband."

Charles stared at his friend and fellow student. "James? James Rupert? What in the hell are you doing here? And what husband? What are you talking about?"

Twenty minutes later Drew's agonized cry filled the air. "She can't be gone! I've traveled for two weeks to bring her home." His voice broke and everyone in the party tensed, afraid he was going to break down. Slowly, he regained his composure. Through tight lips, he said, "I'm gonna kill that man."

James spoke softly, "We don't know that she's gone. All we know is that she took off. Knowing Cathy, she could be almost anyplace."

The color had drained from Charles's face. "I have to meet my brother south of here in about an hour. You better come with us. We'll go back to Sunbury and you can have it out with Nelson in the morning."

For the moment, Drew had no better plan and he trudged behind Charles and James, his heart twisted into a painful lump of muscle. If he lost her, after all of this, he wasn't sure he could go on. Bridget stepped up next to him and patted his arm. "She'll be all right. That girl can survive."

They walked for over an hour before they stumbled onto another group clustered along a littered road. This time James cried out. When he spied his Amelia, he rushed forward to take her into his arms. Only the presence of her worried uncle and Drew with his tragic

366

air prevented James from pressing her for a more visible return of his affection.

With a heavy heart, Charles introduced Phillip and offered an abbreviated version of Andrew's story. Both brothers turned to their white-faced sire. "Father," Phillip said quietly, "Andrew Sloan sailed from Savannah to find Catherine. It would appear that Nelson Goodspeed kidnapped our sister. She may not have wanted to leave Mr. Sloan."

William glared at Andrew and then at Charles and Phillip. He sat down on a large upended log. "I have never seen anything so bungled in my life. If anything has happened to Catherine . . ." He chanced to gaze at Drew as the words left his mouth. The raw emotion of desperation and pure pain etched the young man's mouth. William was rudely reminded of the pain he felt when first Agnes and then Marie Ann were torn from his side. Andrew Sloan was a man in love, in love with his Catherine. Suddenly, he wondered how his daughter felt about this man before him.

Charles stepped to his father's side. "There's a church about four miles ahead. We'll have to stay the night there. It's going to be too dark to continue on. I hope we have enough light to get to the church."

James stood with his arm tight around Amelia. "I thought all of the churches were gone."

Phillip answered, "There are four still standing. Most are filled with the sick and injured, or the homeless. We'll have to find a corner, but we'll at least have cover. We're in luck that the one closest to us is still in one piece. We'll stop at St. George's for the night and begin our search in the morning."

Amelia, Bridget, and William were helped into the

mule-drawn cart Phillip had commandeered at Oistin. Slowly the group staggered over limbs and trunks, around mounds of slimy rubbish, over piles of garbage, inching their way west. Amelia and Bridget held handkerchiefs against their noses, but the nauseating smell of decaying vegetation caused more than one set of nostrils to flare in disgust. Hours dragged by and dusk was dancing red, mauve, and lavender ruffles through the sky as the roof of the church came into view. Everyone in the group heaved a sigh of relief.

Charles helped the women and his father from the cart and James pulled Amelia back to his side. He gazed into her sad, upturned face. "I'm going to stay here tomorrow and help with the wounded."

Amelia's lips curled slightly. "I'll stay with you. I can't participate in the search and I don't want to be in the way. If I work here with you, at least I'll feel like I'm doing something to help."

"I'll find someone in charge and offer our services." James started for the door of the church.

Amelia and Bridget stood inside the courtyard waiting for James while Andrew and the other men gathered to care for the two horses, the mule, and the cart. When James signaled for the women, they stepped forward and James pointed toward a tall man in a clerical robe. "Father Churner has the most critical cases in the sanctuary. I'll see what I can do to help him. You and Bridget," he directed his words to Amelia, "find out if anyone else needs immediate care."

Amelia looked surprised. "Don't they have doctors? You're not the only medical man they have, are you?"

James shook his head. "There are a number but they are north, east, and on the plantations. The doctor that was helping here was called away this morning. One knowledgeable woman has been helping with the more serious cases. She'll work with me. For now, check everyone to make sure they are all right." He started up the aisle toward the front of the church.

In the candlelight of the church, James knelt by the side of an older man. He had a broken arm, cuts, and bruises on his face and he was warm with fever. He called out, "Woman!"

A soft voice answered from a corner, "Yes?"

James wondered at the familiarity of the tone and dismissed it. "Could you help me here?"

James watched the man's chest rise and fall, waiting. He heard the woman approach and glanced up. His light blue eyes locked with blue-gray ones, and even with the rag tied around her head like the natives, there was no mistaking his helper. His voice was no more than a whisper as he murmured, "Cathy!"

She stared at the red hair and the round face of her mentor. "James? James Rupert? No, you can't be James! Are you?"

James didn't bother to answer her questions. He yelled for Amelia. She came running. She stumbled up the first altar step when she saw the woman next to James. "Cathy!"

James gave orders rapidly. "Go out to the courtyard and get Drew and your uncle. Better tell them both that Cathy is here helping. I don't want to have to treat heart palpitations or vapors." Without a word, Amelia disappeared down the aisle of the church.

Cathy continued to stare at James. Slowly his orders sank through her shock. Andrew! Amelia went to get Andrew. Andrew was here! She glanced around her, her hands going to the rag she'd wound around her hair that morning, to the blood-stained day dress that she'd donned four days before, now nearly in tatters. "I look terrible."

James grinned at her. "I have a feeling neither of the men are going to care a bit how you look."

The double doors of the church were flung open and against the brilliance of the setting sun, the silhouette of a large man paused. Above the noise of the homeless and against the moans and groans of the injured, the deep voice of the man permeated the gathering gloom in the bowels of the church. "Cathy!"

Her first two steps were hesitant, afraid that after the horror of the last four days, she had been reduced to dreams. The silhouette moved and Cathy whispered his name. She gathered her skirts in her hand and ran the next six steps.

They met in the center of the church and Drew had her in his arms before she could call his name. Tears ran down his cheeks and he didn't worry that someone might see and snicker. He held his wife, his beloved, in his arms. The Lord had not taken her away, and she had survived the storm. He clutched her to him, afraid that somehow she might yet be dragged from his arms. He kissed her forehead, her cheeks as wet as his own, and murmured soft senseless words against her skin.

Cathy clung, trying to burrow into the soul of the man who held her. He was her life, her reason for being. Without him, nothing would have meaning. She snuggled closer, her arms draped around his shoulders and her lips pressing kisses against his cheeks, his chin. Her mind tried to decipher his whispers.

A cough just behind Drew alerted them both that they

370

were far from alone. Beside the countless numbers of natives and farmers, Cathy raised her head and looked into the glistening eyes of her father. Behind him stood Charles and Phillip. Slowly, she let her arms slide down from Drew's shoulders. She struggled to find her voice. "Father?" She glanced back at her husband. It suddenly occurred to her that these two men shouldn't be together, yet they were. The thought tripped across her tongue. "When did you two meet?"

Drew answered, his deep voice thick with emotion, "About three hours ago. We both came to find you."

With her beloved holding her tightly, Cathy asked her father the one question that stood out in her mind, "Father, why?"

Even in the dull light of the church, William looked stooped, tired, and Cathy realized with a start, old. "Why? Dear God, girl. I've been worried sick. First I find out that you have run off to America and this numbskull doesn't tell me a thing." He pointed to Phillip. "Then, I get a letter from his mother," he pointed at Drew, "telling me what a lovely daughter I have and how she has been welcomed into another family." He glared at Drew, then his daughter. "It's time I turned over your care to a younger man, whether he's an American or not. I love you too much to go through anything more with you. Perhaps your Andrew will be able to control you better than I have."

Cathy listened to his words and stared at him as if he'd announced that she had two heads. "You love me? I . . . I didn't know. You never said you did."

Drew let Cathy step away from him and into the arms of her father. "You never told me," she whispered. William held her close, tears streaming from his eyes

371

now. He took Cathy's face in his hands and kissed her forehead, then released her back into Drew's waiting arms. William extended his hand. "Welcome into the family, son."

Drew grasped the hand held out to him. "Thank you, sir. And, rest assured, I will guard her with my life. I love your daughter more than I thought possible." Drew turned to face the woman at his side, puzzled at the soft gasp she uttered. "I do love you. I know you knew." It was almost a question.

She squeezed him. "I love you, too," she whispered, for his ears alone. Then she turned to greet her brothers and Amelia. James and Bridget, who were busy with the injured, would be seen later. There was much to be done, and after reminding them, Cathy turned to get back to work. Amelia stepped forward. "You rest, spend time with Andrew. I'll take over for you."

Father Churner approached Drew. "She hasn't stopped often to rest." He pointed to Cathy. "Why don't you take her out into the courtyard. We have a fire burning and there's some fish and perhaps some chicken left. And we always have a pot of tea brewing."

Drew led Cathy from the building, one hand around her waist. Together they walked out into the soft summer evening. Against the backdrop of destruction, Cathy saw nothing but the wide smile and deep, warm eyes of the man she loved. She leaned her head back against the hollow of his shoulder. She couldn't wait another moment to share her news. "Oh Drew. I've missed you so much. I have to tell you something."

When they were seated before the fire, Drew slipped both arms around her and pulled her close. He nuzzled her right ear, still too frightened that she would disappear to release his hold. "What do you have to tell me?"

"How do you feel about children?" her husky voice whispered.

Children. Drew pulled away from her and gazed into her face. Had she bargained to take some of the homeless children home with her? No, that couldn't be, for up until scarcely an hour ago, she didn't know he was there to take her home. He stared down at her, trying to read her mind so that he could give her the answer she wanted. "I like children," he answered honestly.

She leaned back against him once more, a sigh of happy contentment slipping past her lips. He gave her a little shake. "Why the question?"

She snuggled closer. "It would appear that you'll have a chance to prove how much you like children at the end of February next year."

He sat quietly, at first her words making no sense. Suddenly, he came out of his fog. "February? Cathy, are you—? You're not, not with this storm? Cathy, are you pregnant?" He looked stunned.

A touch of fear gripped her heart and she nodded her head carefully. Drew's roar of delight brought natives and relatives into the courtyard. By the time William got through the crowd, Drew stood with Cathy cradled in his arms, and addressed William, "Cathy's told me you wanted her married and with child. It appears, sir, that both your wishes have been granted."

Chapter Twenty-Six

Word of the arrival of Charles and Phillip's distinguished father spread rapidly along the coast. The next morning, before Charles and Phillip led their group of weary travelers toward Sunbury, the jangle of military tack announced a delegation of officers sent to issue a welcome to William Pentworth. The younger people stood aside as Phillip introduced his father to a man nearly his own age, the captain of the regiment. Capt. Bryon Kittlingham gave William a formal salute and wondered aloud, "Did you, sir, have a brother, or perhaps a cousin, in the navy?"

William's smile turned grim. "My younger brother, Charles, served in the navy. In fact he was killed during the last war."

The captain nodded. "I thought so. I was one of the young lieutenants who investigated his murder."

"Murder?" Phillip turned on his father. "You never said that Uncle Charles was murdered."

"The culprit has gone unpunished for many years now. When the army couldn't find William Nelson, nothing else was done about it. I didn't want to tell you or Charles, in case you felt you needed to do something to right the wrong. It was bad enough that my brother lost his life." William stepped toward the cluster of horses. "Come, I want to see my new grandson and his cousins."

The soldiers offered a more satisfactory conveyance than the cart from the day before. Bridget, Cathy, and William climbed into the carriage, with the rest of the men mounting the horses the military brought. James and Amelia insisted that they stay at St. George's for one more day to help with those still confined.

Drew announced bitingly that he'd take care of Nelson Goodspeed and then he wanted to take Cathy back to the ship where he knew she would be more comfortable. He wanted her back in his bed. With the conditions described at Sunbury, he was sure there would be no privacy for them. He extended an invitation to William as well, but at least for the next several days William claimed he wanted to see his sons' families. "I may travel to this city, Savannah, with you when you're ready to return. I would like to see where my daughter and my niece plan to make their homes." Drew smiled in anticipation. He was certain that William would be stunned with the elegance of Heart's Haven.

His smile turned into a deep scowl as he thought of the man he would soon meet. He remembered Nelson Goodspeed from the confrontation in England. Why had the man stolen his wife? Drew shook with anger. He could, if he didn't keep tight control on himself, kill Goodspeed on sight.

Drew turned toward the open carriage to watch his wife. She sat passing the time in a delightfully animated conversation with her father. A broad grin replaced Drew's frown. She was going to present a son or daughter to him before spring. He wondered if he looked as moonstruck as he felt. A quick glance and the all-knowing grin from his father-in-law answered the question without a word of conversation.

The caravan picked its way over and through the gouged and torn terrain. The devastation appeared as great east of the church as it was to the west. The island had very nearly been leveled by the storm. Drew wondered to himself how many lives had been lost and he thanked God that Cathy was not one of the casualties.

They traveled for almost two hours before the buildings of Sunbury came in view. Drew watched as the hostess came toward them, welcoming them without a concern as to whom they were or from where they came. The military escort stopped for refreshment before they began the trip back to Bridgetown and the devastation there. Cathy and Bridget followed the hostess to refresh themselves. Drew glanced around, intent on finding Nelson before the man found him.

Charles Pentworth approached him. "Andrew, may I call you Andrew?" Charles waited for his answer.

He gave it quickly. "Please, call me Drew."

"As you wish. Drew, I think we should conduct our business in private. Phillip has taken the initiative and is speaking to our host. William and Catherine, you, Phillip and I will meet with Nelson in the library, if that's all right with you."

Drew frowned. "Perhaps the captain should be invited as well. What the man has done is certainly not honorable and considering that his present wife is standing beside my wife, I suspect he is involved in something illegal."

Charles paled. "His present wife? My God, what kind of monster is Nelson Goodspeed?"

"That's why I think Captain Kittlingham should join us. Perhaps we should include Bridget as well."

Charles nodded anxiously and hurried off to detain Captain Kittlingham. In less than ten minutes, all of the interested parties were invited into the parlor. The library was much too small for the eight people involved. Phillip hurried off to find Nelson and insisted that he present himself immediately.

Drew studied the long thin face as Nelson approached the group. Drew chose to sit back away from the crowd. He wanted to observe and survey the man before Nelson got a chance to lie, if that was his intention. Drew watched as Nelson spotted Cathy. A satisfied leer curled Nelson's lips and Drew fought the urge to smash the man's face beyond recognition.

As Drew watched, Nelson spotted Bridget standing behind Cathy. The color slowly faded from his cheeks and then the whole of his face. Nelson Goodspeed knew Bridget Purdy! Drew was so busy reading Nelson's expressions that he missed the look on Captain Kittlingham's face.

William Pentworth glanced from Drew to the captain and he was stunned. Bryon Kittlingham's face was taut with hate. It seemed that the soldier knew the man well and didn't like him. William had no intention of letting his sons or his son-in-law conduct this meeting. He spoke to the captain. "Sir, do you know Nelson Goodspeed?"

The captain glanced at William and then at Nelson. "I do, sir. However, I would like to wait to press my charges until the others have had their say."

William grudgingly let Phillip take the floor. William listened as his son accused Nelson. "I want to know, Nelson, how you were going to marry Catherine when she was already married? When you were already married?" Phillip's voice was thin and brisk, his anger apparent. Catherine looked embarrassed.

Nelson sneered as if his answer would solve all his problems, "Catherine was promised to me. She could not marry without your consent, and the woman next to her was never truly my wife!"

Bridget's gasp said it all. She let loose with several curses that singed the ears of the men. "Damn you to hell, you bastard. I have the marriage certificate. It's in the cabin with my things. I brought it with me, knowin' what a whoreson you are. I kin prove you're my man in a day. I kin get it afore you leave this place."

Drew stood up and moved to Cathy's side. "That won't be necessary, madam. Mr. Goodspeed is not leaving."

Bridget muttered, "His name isn't Goodspeed, it's William Purdy."

The captain stepped up. "No, his name is William Nelson." William Pentworth gasped and sat down quickly. "Sorry, sir," Captain Kittlingham murmured. "He's not getting away from me this time." Cathy glanced at Drew's astonished face and moved next to her father. At the moment, William needed her comfort.

William Pentworth stared at the tall, aristocratic-looking man before him. "You killed my brother." William found his feet. "I demand satisfaction."

Drew moved to the side of William Pentworth. "He stole my wife and left me to mourn her death. I demand satisfaction."

Phillip glanced at the captain. "The choice is yours, Captain."

The captain never got a chance to state his preference, for at that moment Nelson took things into his own hands. He jerked Bridget to him and moved to the door. He issued his own demands as he went. "I'm leaving and I'm taking my wife with me. No one's going to stop me. She won't live long if you do." He dashed through the door and shoved his way past the crowd of homeless guests. At Cathy's gasp, the men in the parlor burst onto the porch.

A voice in the crowd stayed Nelson. Martha Pentworth grabbed at him and laced her arm through his. "Nelson, someone told me that Catherine's been found." Martha raised her voice, summoning her friends. "Listen, everyone. Catherine's here. We'll have the wedding tomorrow. Somebody can ride for Father Churner."

William stepped up next to Martha. "Hello, daughter. I'm afraid there's been a mistake. You see, the man you're hanging onto is already married. Captain Kittlingham, here, is taking him to Bridgetown. Mr. Nelson is wanted for murder." Kittlingham grabbed Nelson, William grabbed Bridget, and Martha fell to the ground in a dead faint.

Cathy stretched and snuggled down in the deep feather mattress of the big bed. Next to her lay her sleeping husband. After the night of love that Drew lavished on her, she should have been soundly asleep, but her mind was much too busy with the events of the last week. Slowly, the island was being cleaned up. Drew had brought her back to the ship the afternoon after the confrontation with Nelson.

She shuddered as she remembered that afternoon. Captain Kittlingham had taken charge of Nelson, or whatever his name was. The final surprise of the afternoon, though, came when another tall blond man stepped from the crowd, his face scarlet. Cathy gasped and a vision of claret wine dripping over those curls came to mind. She stepped back against Drew in alarm.

"Captain, please take your hand from Mr. Goodspeed. I'm sure this is all a mistake," the blond ordered.

The captain gave him a disgusted glance. "Just who are you, sir, and what do you know about Mr. Goodspeed?"

"My name is Guy Forsythe, and I've been with Nelson Goodspeed for months now. He and I are business partners."

Drew stepped forward. "Business partners? Why, sir, you have a poor choice of business partners. Did you know that Mr. Goodspeed has been accused of murder?"

If possible, Guy's face turned a deeper red and he snarled at Cathy and William Pentworth, "Are you accusing him? I certainly wouldn't abide by your say so."

Captain Kittlingham stepped forward. "*I* am accusing him, sir, and if you're his business partner, perhaps I should hold you as well."

Guy's face lost its color. "Why . . . no. I haven't done anything. I financed his expeditions, that's all. I haven't done anything, nothing illegal. I only gave him money."

Nelson snarled, "Oh, yeah? The plan to take Catherine was your idea, not mine. You came to me in England, I didn't search you out. You wanted part of her estates and you wanted her father humiliated. You're in this as deep as me." Drew pulled Cathy away from the argument. Together they returned to the *Georgia Girl*.

That night Cathy had been much too exhausted to do more than lie in Drew's arms. Come morning, though, they were reacquainted in the most pleasant manner. That same day, James came bearing news. William insisted that James and Amelia be married in as many days as it took to read the banns. James was beside himself. They would be married on Thursday. James wanted Drew as his witness and Amelia was coming to ask Cathy to stand with her.

Drew decided right then that he and Cathy should repeat their vows before her father, and he and James set off to talk to Father Churner about the legality of such a thing. Drew explained when he recounted the conversation several hours later that Father Churner was slightly perplexed. Drew grinned. "However, we will be renewing our vows with James and Amelia."

Cathy was delighted with the idea. On Thursday when James and Amelia spoke their vows, Andrew and Catherine promised to continue to love and honor each other. The party that followed lasted well into the morning. Drew gave James and Amelia the big soft bed for Thursday and Friday night, but she and Drew claimed it again. Samuel, with an enormous grin, saw that James and Amelia settled in the first mate's cabin.

In a few hours, William Pentworth would arrive and they would start for Savannah. Strange, once the idea of marriage held such terror for her, but now . . . She looked over at the man lying next to her. She was surprised by the warm gray-brown eyes staring back at her. "Oh, I didn't know you were awake," she said.

"What were you thinking about? You looked concerned."

"A lot of thoughts were running through my head. Oh,

Drew, I love you. I want to go home to Heart's Haven."

He pulled her into his arms. "I love you. I can't wait either, for a lot of things. Like a child, home, even your father's reaction to the United States."

Cathy smiled in amusement. "He really does love me, you know. I said that at a ball once."

Drew chuckled. "And I remember what followed. I remember the streaks of lightning when I swung you in my arms to dance. And that kiss . . ." Drew's voice grew husky with desire. "Come, love. Come, do the dance of love with me." He raised himself above her.

She smiled up at him and whispered back, her voice a thread of sound, "Forever."

HISTORICAL ROMANCES BY EMMA MERRITT

RESTLESS FLAMES (2203, $3.95)

Having lost her husband six months before, determined Brenna Allen couldn't afford to lose her freight company, too. Outfitted as wagon captain with revolver, knife and whip, the single minded beauty relentlessly drove her caravan, desperate to reach Santa Fe. Then she crossed paths with insolent Logan Mac Dougald. The taciturn Texas Ranger was as primitive as the surrounding Comanche Territory, and he didn't hesitate to let the tantalizing trail boss know what he wanted from her. Yet despite her outrage with his brazen ways, jet-haired Brenna couldn't suppress the scorching passions surging through her . . . and suddenly she never wanted this trip to end!

COMANCHE BRIDE (2549, $3.95)

When stunning Dr. Zoe Randolph headed to Mexico to halt a cholera epidemic, she didn't think twice about traversing Comanche territory . . . until a band of bloodthirsty savages attacked her caravan. The gorgeous physician was furious that her mission had been interrupted, but nothing compared to the rage she fell on meeting the barbaric warrior who made her his slave. Determined to return to civilization, the ivory-skinned blonde decided to make a woman's ultimate sacrifice to gain her freedom — and never admit that deep down inside she burned to be loved by the handsome brute!

SWEET, WILD LOVE (2834, $4.50)

It was hard enough for Eleanor Hunt to get men to take her seriously in sophisticated Chicago — it was going to be impossible in Blissful, Kansas! These cowboys couldn't believe she was a real attorney, here to try a cattle rustling case. They just looked her up and down and grinned. Especially that Bradley Smith. The man worked for her father and he still had the audacity to stare at her with those lust-filled green eyes. Every time she turned around, he was trying to trap her in his strong embrace.

Available wherever paperbacks are sold, or order direct from the Publisher. Send cover price plus 50¢ per copy for mailing and handling to Zebra Books, Dept. 3057, 475 Park Avenue South, New York, N.Y. 10016. Residents of New York, New Jersey and Pennsylvania must include sales tax. DO NOT SEND CASH.